STREET GAME

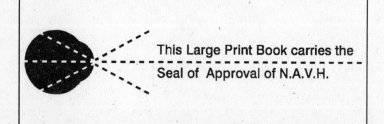

STREET GAME

CHRISTINE FEEHAN

THORNDIKE PRESS

A part of Gale, Cengage Learning

GALE
CENGAGE Learning

Detroit • New York • San Francisco • New Haven, Conn • Waterville, Maine • London

GALE
CENGAGE Learning™

LIBRARY OF CONGRESS CATALOGING-IN-PUBLICATION DATA

Feehan, Christine.
   Street game / by Christine Feehan.
     p. cm. — (Thorndike Press large print romance)
   ISBN-13: 978-1-4104-2702-1
   ISBN-10: 1-4104-2702-1
   1. Large type books. I. Title.
   PS3606.E36S77 2010
   813'.54—dc22
                               2010007661

Published in 2010 by arrangement with The Berkley Publishing Group, a member of Penguin Group (USA) Inc.

Printed in the United States of America
1 2 3 4 5 6 7 14 13 12 11 10

For Mary Scriven, a woman who brings joy into my life each time I see her. Always keep your childlike joy of living.

FOR MY READERS

Be sure to go to http://www.christinefeehan
.com/members/ to sign up for my PRIVATE
book announcement list and download the
FREE e-book of *Dark Desserts,* a book of
delicious desserts compiled by my wonderful readers. While at the website, join the
community and all the book discussions!
Please feel free to e-mail me at Christine
@christinefeehan.com. I would love to hear
from you.

ACKNOWLEDGMENTS

As with any book, many people helped to get it right. First and foremost, I have to thank Master Sergeant Retired Lloyd Stottsberry, a man who has dedicated his life to the service of his country. He would probably shoot me for calling him heroic, so I won't, but you get the picture. His help was invaluable. Any mistakes are entirely mine.

Many thanks to Brian Feehan, who has that mathematical and fiendish mind and always answers the call for murder-and-mayhem discussions. Domini, you know I'd never get a book out without you, and of course Kathi Firzlaff, who catches all the little things for me. Mason, thank you for the tips on skateboarding.

And of course the book would not be complete without a special thanks to Dr. Christopher Tong, coeditor of the "state of the art" series *Artificial Intelligence in Engi-*

neering Design (volumes I, II, and III). He is currently developing The World Meeting Place, a Web 3.0 AI–based site aimed at enabling the world's people to collaborate on solving the world's problems. He has been a manager, consultant, teacher, and researcher at many well-known institutions including Rutgers, MIT, the IBM Thomas J. Watson Research Center, the Xerox Palo Alto Research Center, and Siemens Research. He lent me his assistance in learning how artificial intelligence works, and also spent many hours figuring out an AI encryption program. His help on this book was absolutely invaluable to me.

The GhostWalker Symbol Details

SIGNIFIES
shadow

SIGNIFIES
protection against
evil forces

SIGNIFIES
the Greek letter *psi,* which
is used by parapsychology
researchers to signify ESP or
other psychic abilities

SIGNIFIES
qualities of a knight—
loyalty, generosity,
courage, and honor

SIGNIFIES
shadow knights who protect
against evil forces using
psychic powers, courage,
and honor

nox noctis est nostri

THE GHOSTWALKER CREED

We are the GhostWalkers, we live in the
  shadows
The sea, the earth, and the air are our
  domain
No fallen comrade will be left behind
We are loyalty and honor bound
We are invisible to our enemies
and we destroy them where we find them
We believe in justice and we protect our
  country
and those unable to protect themselves
What goes unseen, unheard, and unknown
are GhostWalkers
There is honor in the shadows and it is us
We move in complete silence whether
in jungle or desert
We walk among our enemy unseen and
  unheard
Striking without sound and scatter to the
  winds
before they have knowledge of our

15

existence
We gather information and wait with
    endless patience
for that perfect moment to deliver swift
    justice
We are both merciful and merciless
We are relentless and implacable in our
    resolve
We are the GhostWalkers and the night is
    ours

CHAPTER 1

Black night. No moon, no stars. Just the way he liked it. Master Gunnery Sergeant Mack McKinley crouched in the alley, close to the tall, dirty building, allowing his senses to become tuned to the familiar sounds. A cat raked through a garbage can, a drunk moaned and shivered in the cold. Waves pounded the beach and sloshed against the pier just behind the building. Three stories up, lights went out, leaving the long row of windows like giant, gaping black mouths. McKinley smiled at the image, smiled up at the windows. His smile was not pleasant.

This was the all-important tip. Tracking the explosives through Lebanon, Beirut, the South American freighter. And then to San Francisco. Always one step behind. He had moved fast to check out the information, praying it was correct. They had less than twenty-four hours to find the guns and the five-man unit of Doomsday. He sneered at the name of the terrorist unit, but he had to give them kudos for scaring the crap out of every country they had visited. They left behind wreckage and carnage and death. More — they left behind fear.

Urban warfare was an art any way one looked at it. His team had knowledge of the streets, were the best there was, but it was dangerous work, and required a cool head. Too many civilians, too many potential hostages, too damn many things to go wrong. But his men were good at it, more than good — he counted them among the best, and Sergeant Major Theodore Griffen wanted Doomsday taken out. And when the sergeant major gave an order, it was carried out immediately and to the letter.

The warehouse was wired. He knew it, could feel it. But something . . . His men were in position, waiting for him. As always, First Sergeant Kane Cannon was at his back. They'd started on the streets together, two kids trying to stay alive, eventually pulling in six other boys and two girls, all with different abilities to make up their ragtag family.

From the streets Kane and Mack and one of the girls — Mack didn't want to think about her — had gone on to college. The others had gone into the Marine Corps. All had a gift for languages as well as many other things, such as what he was doing now. They were recruited right out of school and trained as operatives until the psychic testing. That had been a huge mistake, and all of his family had followed him — as they always did.

Force Recon — Special Forces. Psychic testing where they'd all come back together, just like on the street. More specialized training. SEAL training. Urban war games. Even more specialized training until they were pretty much killing machines. They had stuck together and knew one another's every move. They trusted one another and no one else, not in the business they were in. Well . . . with the exception of the new kid, but that was a whole other story. It was no good thinking about that right now, not when he was surrounded with the ones he loved, leading them into a situation that was explosive at the very least.

Mack signaled for the others to pull down their night goggles, making it easy to see in the blackness of the night. He and Kane didn't need them. They could both see in the dark as easily as during the day. A result of the experiments they'd lent themselves to. Stupid, but they'd done it for the good of the country and their need for a home.

Yeah, he knew the psychological bullshit everyone spouted. It was probably all true too, but he didn't much care. It was also one hell of an adrenaline rush.

Still, he waited, hesitating before signaling his team forward. His men were coiled and ready. He had a bad feeling, deep in his gut, and he never discounted his instincts. Something wasn't quite right, but he couldn't put his finger on it.

What is it, Top? Kane questioned, using the telepathic communication they had perfected as children, and which the military had enhanced when they volunteered for the psychic GhostWalker program.

Something's wrong? Not wrong, maybe. Just not right. How the hell could he explain that strange kick in his belly?

I feel it too, but I'm not sure what's out of sync here. There was another long moment of silence. *Abort?* Kane asked.

Mack took a breath. Let it out. *No, but let's all be very cautious.*

Of the group of them, only the new kid the sergeant major had insisted they add to their team couldn't communicate telepathically. Telepathy had been the common denominator that had drawn them together on the streets. They were all different and they'd all recognized the psychic gift in one

20

another. Mack had been the acknowledged leader and Kane had always, *always* had his back.

He glanced at the man and saw that Kane was doing what he did best, searching the huge warehouse with his strange eyes. He could, if he wanted, see right through the wood and metal to the heat inside, a gift from Whitney and his experiments. Unfortunately, if he used that special gift, he paid for it with blindness for several minutes after, rendering it an extremely dangerous talent to use in the field. There were several new abilities in all of them. Animal DNA. A new genetic code. They hadn't signed on for that kind of experiment, but when they'd woken up, they had been changed for all time. Kane kept from trying to look through the walls and used his enhanced sight to detect movement only.

Mack signaled his men forward. It took minutes to bypass the alarm on the side entrance door, far longer than it should have. The alarm was too complicated for a wharf warehouse. Who put together a sophisticated triple-alarm system so complex it took Javier, his best tech, precious time to unravel it?

We've got ourselves a pro system, here, boss, Javier said. *One I've never seen before.*

21

Whoever put this mother together knew what they were doing. There was frank admiration in his tone.

No activity in the lower warehouse that I can spot, Mack, Kane said. *I can't detect heat on the second floor either, but someone's on the third floor.*

Just one person? That made no sense.

Just one.

Mack moved first, his brain more reluctant than his body. He rolled inside the door of the first floor, under a trip wire, and crawled military fashion beneath the maze of track beams. The entire room was empty, deserted, with the exception of scattered building materials here and there. The sophisticated alarm system seemed ridiculous. Something was nagging at the back of his mind, refusing to leave him alone.

Where are the sentries, Kane?

I don't know, bro, but this is all wrong.

The roof was clean, protected only by an alarm. His man, Gideon, was up there now, with a rifle and a radio. Gideon could see in the dark, hear like an owl, and shoot the wings off a fly in the middle of the night if necessary. Mack should have been feeling good, but that punch in his gut was getting stronger. And where the hell was the sentry on the ground level? Was this an elaborate trap? Had Doomsday been tipped off that they were coming?

The little band of terrorists had no cause, no politics, no religious war to fight. They were mercenaries, a brand-new type spawned by the times. They showed off their talents, sparing no country, no man, woman, or child, with one idea: working for the highest bidder. They sold their services to whoever paid, which made them difficult to track, as no one could ever figure out who they worked for and where they would be next. This was the GhostWalkers' one opportunity to get them, by following the weapons, yet Mack just couldn't shake it that something was wrong.

Even as his mind struggled desperately with the problem, he was aware of every detail around him, aware that the newbie, young Paul, was an inch too high, close beneath one of the beams. Mack hissed and all movement ceased. The warehouse was utterly still. His cold gaze pinned Paul. Mack signaled with a flat hand. The rookie's body hugged the cold cement. Despite the cover of darkness, Mack knew Paul flushed crimson.

The kid blushed a lot. What the hell he was doing with their team, Mack couldn't figure out. Basically, they were babysitting, and that could get them all killed. No one on the team wanted the kid with them, but Sergeant Major Griffen had been more than insistent. It wasn't that the kid wasn't highly intelligent — he was. He also was psychic, although none of them had gone through Dr. Whitney's program with him. All the GhostWalkers tended to know or at least recognize one another. Paul was an exception. Mack didn't like question marks, and the kid posed too many.

Mack rolled free of the interlocking track beams. The loudness of the freight lift was out of the question. It had to be the stairs, each one more perilous than the next. There would be two flights to get to that third floor.

Where the hell are the sentries? The question nagged at him, would not let him go.

Everyone was on high alert now, the question as disturbing to them as it was to him. He waited a heartbeat, but couldn't find a reason not to continue.

He moved cautiously. Four stairs . . . seven. He felt it on eight. The wire puzzled him. It was an alarm, not a mine. His mind seized on that, worried at it.

Mack had done this so many times that he knew exactly how each one of his men was feeling. Adrenaline pumping, heart racing, fear choking, guns rock steady. Something was off-kilter. Wrong. The word fluttered in his head, beat at him like tiny wings.

Definitely off.

Kane's anxiety heightened his own.

Mack gained the second floor. Where the first floor had been mostly empty space and building materials, this one was packed with electronic equipment. A bank of computers was built into the far wall, the only thing completed. Everything else was in boxes, all electronics equipment, high-end.

"Bingo," Paul's whisper came over the radio, trembling with excitement. "Moving day."

Check it, Kane. Maybe we're looking at how they transported the guns.

Inside electronic equipment? This is satellite tracking, cameras, stuff like that. Not guns. We've stumbled onto something, but I'm not certain it's what we're after.

Mack wasn't certain either. He shook his head, his mind screaming at him now. This was all wrong. No sentries. This type of equipment was far too advanced for the kind of terrorists that made up the Doomsday organization.

He moved up the staircase. Third stair this time. No explosives. Seventh stair. He rolled beneath the beam on the landing, came up

25

on one knee, breathing deeply. *Here! Here!* His men were spreading out, back-to-back, in a standard search pattern.

What is it? What's wrong? Find the answer! Find the answer! Mack moved carefully through the furniture.

The furniture, Mack. All wrong, Kane hissed in his mind.

A long plush couch, a hand-carved wooden coffee table, a priceless Persian rug. Beautiful, expensive. A small object on an end table. A dragon. Like in a living room. A home. Knowledge came a heartbeat too late.

Something stirred just feet from him, a weapon glinted.

"Break off! Break off!" He yelled it even as he launched himself toward the small figure crouched behind the recliner. His body, solid, heavily muscled, hit the smaller, softer one squarely, knocking the woman flat, pinning her to the floor.

She shocked him by fighting hard, going for pressure points, obviously having a working knowledge of hand-to-hand combat tactics. It took some strength and finesse to subdue her. He successfully blanketed her body with his, tensed for the bullets he was certain would tear into him. His team was well trained, superb even. Not a shot was

26

fired. Even so, as a precaution, Kane caught Paul's weapon, pushing it away so it wasn't pointed at McKinley's body.

There was a long, deadly silence. Mack could hear her breathing, her heart racing. There was no struggle once he'd pinned her; she lay perfectly still beneath him. For a moment he was afraid he had knocked her unconscious, but her breathing was too ragged.

"Is anyone else up here?" He whispered the words in her ear.

She shook her head.

Kane and the others began a standard search pattern. McKinley hoped she was telling the truth. She smelled fresh and faintly exotic, her skin satin smooth, petal soft. The scent, the feel of her, was oddly familiar. Too familiar. His body recognized her before his brain did, reacting with enough testosterone for his entire unit, mixed with more adrenaline than any of them could possibly handle.

McKinley slowly, carefully, eased his weight until he was certain he wasn't hurting her, yet still kept her pinned. As each member of the team barked, "Clear," he shifted enough to get a good look at her face. One leg remained firmly over her thighs, a warning not to move.

Behind them, a lamp was switched on. "All clear, sir." That was young Paul. His men were all staring, yet trying not to stare. The woman was in a long nightgown. See-through. One of those diaphanous, filmy things that clung to every curve and sent a jackhammer through the middle of a man's skull. Her gown had pulled up her thigh, revealing a more than generous expanse of gleaming skin.

She had tousled hair, a riot of curls, and large, haunting, sapphire-colored eyes. He would know her anywhere, anyplace.

Jaimie. He said her name, at least he thought he said it, but no sound emerged. Maybe he'd just breathed her name. He touched her thick mane of silky, midnight black hair, his fingers sliding into one of the curls and tugging, letting the strands slide through the pads of his fingers, trying to regain the breath she'd stolen.

"Get off me, McKinley." The fear was in her voice, but she was striving for control. "What are you doing here? Hi, boys. I missed — most of you," she greeted from the floor.

"Hey, Jaimie," Kane said.

"Man, Jaimie," Javier added. "Sweet damn security system. I should have recognized your work."

"Great to see you, Jaimie," Brian Hutton added with a little grin. "Although we're seeing more of you than brothers are comfortable with."

"What the fuck are you wearing?" Mack demanded. Lust punched hard and mean, his entire body tightening, his cock hard as a rock. He was furious with her, scared for her. Shocked at seeing her. What was going on? She had fucking left him. *Left* him. Disappeared without a trace.

His hand gripped her throat and he trapped her there on the floor, letting her feel the strength of his anger — of his need. He leaned close. "Did you find yourself, Jaimie? Did you find everything you were looking for?" *Did you miss me the way I missed you? Did you bring my heart back, because I have a damn big hole where it should be.*

He stared down into her eyes — eyes he'd always fall into, eyes he'd always drown in. *Damn you, Jaimie. Damn you to hell for this.* The attraction was worse than it had ever been, flooding him until his body was no longer his and discipline and control had gone out the window.

"Don't you dare look at me that way."

She swallowed hard. He felt the movement against the palm of his hand. "What way?"

"Like you're afraid of me. Like I'm going to hurt you." There was panic in her eyes, fear almost amounting to terror, and it sickened him.

"Mack." Kane's voice was very soft. "You've got your hand around her throat and you're sitting on her. That could be interpreted by some as an aggressive action."

Mack hissed, his head snapping around. "Anyone else have anything brilliant they want to contribute?"

No one else was that stupid — or brave.

He loosened his hold on her throat but retained possession, feeling the satisfyingly frantic beat of her pulse in the center of his palm. "What the hell are you wearing?" he demanded again. "You might as well be wearing nothing at all."

"It's called a nightgown," Jaimie replied, her voice sarcastic. "Mack, let me up. In case no one's ever told you, you're heavy."

He was solid muscle. And right now every single inch of him was as hard as a rock. Moving was going to be painful, one way or another.

Sighing, because everyone was going to know exactly what she did to him, he shifted very carefully. "Get some clothes on." Abruptly, Mack was on his feet, pulling her up with him. A quick flick of his eyes and his men found the ceiling interesting.

They were grinning like idiots. All of them. Even Kane. Mack resisted swearing at them.

"Have the decency to turn around," he ordered the others.

Morons. Every single one. He didn't turn around. He glared at her. Daggers. "That's a hell of a thing to wear unless you're entertaining, Jaimie. Are you entertaining?" His hand slid down to the satisfying hilt of his knife. He'd do some entertaining of his own if some son of a bitch was moving in on Jaimie. Not waiting for an answer, he tore off his jacket and threw it at her. "Cover up."

"Go to hell, Mack. This is my home. My bedroom, in case you haven't noticed."

Still, she slipped her arms into the jacket and inhaled, rubbing her cheek along the material without thinking, and then stalked across the room to yank open a drawer. "You're a long way from home." Jaimie made the observation as she donned a pair of charcoal sweatpants. "Not to mention you're a little overdressed for these parts."

He noticed her hands were trembling as she pulled the edges of his jacket together. Her voice was exactly as he remembered.

Soft, husky, beautiful. Like clear running water. It hurt him to look at her. Her chin was in the air — the same defiant Jaimie he'd known forever. But she wasn't looking at him, not directly, and that wasn't like Jaimie.

"The next time you want to drop in, local custom demands that you do me the courtesy of knocking." She paced away from him, back again, unable to rid her body of the adrenaline. "What are you doing here, Mack?"

"We followed a shipment of weapons."

Her eyebrows shot up. "To San Francisco? To my home?"

"Right to your front door, baby."

She winced. "I'm not your baby, Mack. That was a long time ago. What are you really doing here?"

"Our information . . ."

"Mack, come on." She crossed to the window and looked out over the pounding waves. "You and I both know this is too big of a coincidence. If you weren't the one to arrange it, then your informer wanted you here. Wanted us together."

He wanted them together, so whoever had done this, deliberately or not, Mack owed them. Jaimie had disappeared out of all of their lives some time ago. She'd been a big part of their street family and now here she was — practically in his lap.

He crossed to stand behind her, gently taking hold of her shoulders and moving her back away from the window.

Kane cleared his throat. "The information was, the shipment we're after was off-loaded and stored in this block of warehouses. Corner. High security. That's this warehouse, Jaimie."

Her sapphire gaze touched his face, jumped away. "Actually, it's not. You want the one at the end of this block. Mysterious trucks in the middle of the night. Hard cases, trying to look friendly. You want that warehouse, not mine." Her gaze swung back to Mack. There was something faintly accusing in the depths of her eyes, but then she glanced away from him — as if she couldn't bear to look at him.

Deep inside, there was a stirring, an answer. Mack could feel his body's reaction, taut, dangerous, a man's reaction. Jaimie Fielding. His fists curled. His Jaimie. Stubborn Jaimie, with her outrageous sense of humor, her computer brain, and her pure ethics. Her small teeth bit nervously at her lip, drawing Mack's immediate attention to the fullness of her soft mouth. He had always wanted to crush her lips beneath his when he saw that mouth — still did. She'd *left* him.

"I think my rights as a United States citizen have been severely violated," Jaimie pointed out. "You just invaded my home."

Mack swept a hand through charcoal hair. "Can it, Jaimie," he snapped. "This isn't funny." Seeing her threw him. Drawing her scent into his lungs sent his body into some kind of permanent overdrive. He was supposed to be disciplined, but somehow, with Jaimie around, his body went haywire, thinking with other portions of his anatomy rather than his brain.

"Do I look like I'm laughing?" Her eyebrows arched in inquiry. "I can assure you, I wasn't trying to be funny." At his look, her full, lush lips curled, pursed. "Well, so, all right," she conceded. "Maybe I was a bit. Your hotshot intelligence group made a big mistake. Left you with egg all over your face. Not to mention I was waiting for you."

Mack snatched up the frying pan lying beside the sofa. "I suppose you thought you were going to bean the entire team with this."

A low rumble of laughter swept through the room. Jaimie smirked at them. "Laugh all you want, hotshots. If I'd been your enemy, you would be dead or wounded right now."

"She has a point." Mack's glittering eyes swept the room. "We're lucky this isn't the place."

Kane watched Mack watching Jaimie. It looked like trouble to him, but then, it always had been trouble when the two of them had been in close proximity. Combustible. Like a match to dynamite. He found himself grinning. "Did you provide the anonymous information?"

"Not a chance," Jaimie denied staunchly. "I'm sort of doing my own thing here and wouldn't call attention to myself. Nor do I want an angry neighbor torching the place with me in it if I set the hounds on them."

"Why all the security?" Paul demanded, unconvinced. "And what's with all the electronic equipment?"

"I'm a spy for Russia," Jaimie snapped. "Where's your search warrant? This is still the United States, whether you have an invisible badge or not."

"He's new, Jaimie," Kane said softly. "Cut him some slack."

"He's a hothead." Her hands were still trembling. Jaimie felt her stomach lurch uncomfortably. "And he'll get one of you killed." She pressed one hand to her midsection hard.

"Take them out of here," Mack ordered Kane, frowning at her action.

"You can go down to the first floor. There's heat, but little else," Jaimie said.

"I wouldn't mind looking at your equipment on the second floor," Javier said. "Looks like a sweet setup."

"I'll just bet you'd like a look. It's my new business, Javier." She flashed him a smile. "And I'm not letting you anywhere near those computers. I don't need the competition."

"Maybe you don't want us to look at them for a reason," Paul said.

Jaimie shrugged, her gaze cool as she looked the man up and down. "Maybe."

"I'll take them to the first floor," Kane said. "And contact the sergeant major to see where our information went haywire."

Jaimie switched off her elaborate security alarm to speed things up. Mack waited until they were alone. He followed her into the kitchen area and watched as she reached for the teakettle. Tea. Of course. She always made tea when she was upset.

"Are you all right?" he asked gently.

"You took ten years off my life," she admitted.

He leaned one hip against the cupboards, drinking in the sight of her. "What are you doing here? What is with all the equipment?"

"Just something I'm working on."

She refused to look at him. Her shoulders were stiff. Her body posture screamed at him to go. "I've missed you, Jaimie." Stubborn, he wasn't about to back off from a confrontation. She'd taken his heart and soul when she'd left. He'd been a zombie, a machine without a direction. He couldn't take his eyes from her. He knew there was accusation in his voice, in his expression, but damn it all, she deserved it. "You disappeared without a trace."

"You had a choice, Mack," she reminded. "You made it very clear to me where your priorities were. They weren't with me. With us. It's called self-preservation."

"That's bullshit. You knew I had no idea you'd just disappear."

"As I recall, you said in no uncertain terms you weren't ready for any kind of commitment. I took you at your word. What did you think I'd do?"

Weep for him. Wait for him. Crawl back and beg his forgiveness. Not fucking disappear. Never that. She'd taken his life. She'd taken everything he was from him. "I expected you to realize I was busy."

She kept her back to him; her hands shook

37

as she lifted the whistling teakettle. "Busy? You mean your drive to make the world right? Your need to save everyone? You walked out on us, Mack. If you want to pretend you didn't, if that makes it all good for you, it's all right with me. I survived. You survived. You have the life you want. I'm good too. I moved on, so I'm guessing we're both good."

"Is that what you're guessing?" He waited until the kettle was safely back on the stove before gripping her arm and spinning her around to face him. "Guess again, Jaimie."

She didn't struggle as he'd expected her to. She simply went very still and looked down at the fingers circling her wrists like a steel vise. Her gaze flicked up to his face, lingered on his mouth for a heart-stopping moment before her eyes met his. He had the curious sensation of tumbling forward.

"Mack, let go of me."

He nearly didn't. He nearly jerked her against him and took possession of her mouth. That perfect mouth that could drive a man out of his mind, take him to paradise. He knew she'd melt into him. He knew she belonged to him — every last inch of her — but he wanted more than her body. He'd had something precious and didn't know it until he'd lost it. He dropped his hand and

38

was annoyed when she rubbed the mark of his fingers from her skin before turning back to her task.

He stared at her back for a long moment, trying to find a way to reach her. Anything. The rage and pain of his loss were too close to the surface, rendering his quick brain useless. This was his Jaimie, yet not.

"Jaimie," he said softly. "Talk to me."

She kept her back to him. McKinley. She'd never called him McKinley, even when they'd been best friends. Cannon, McKinley, and Fielding. Where one had been, there was the other, but he had been Mack, always Mack.

"Was this really an accident? A co-incidence?"

His fist tightened until his knuckles turned white. "Of course it was an accident. What else?"

She turned around then, her large eyes luminous, beautiful. Eyes a man could get lost in. "It's a bit far-fetched, don't you think? You just happen to get the wrong warehouse and find me in it."

"It's a small world."

"Don't give me clichés, Mack," she cautioned. "You scared me to death. I thought you were a burglar."

"And you were going to attack him with a

frying pan? What the hell's the matter with you?" He had to keep his hands in check when he wanted to step forward and hold her trembling body against the shelter of his. When he needed to touch the silk of her hair and smooth the frown lines from her face.

"I'm keeping a low profile. Shooting a burglar or beating the crap out of him is a good way to advertise my presence, isn't it?"

He drew in his breath. "You're working undercover."

She leaned against the sink and looked at him with her killer eyes. He felt the impact like a wicked punch to his gut and then lower, the pain reminding him he was more than alive.

"I'm starting a new business that requires a good reputation, privacy, and respectability."

"That's a load of bullshit. I'm family. If I'm nothing else to you, at least I'm that."

Her eyes flashed fire at him. Threw sparks. "You broke my heart, Mack. You threw me away for your adrenaline rush. Well, you've got the life you wanted. I learned my lesson, and believe me, it was a hard one. You wanted sex and I was handy. I'm attracted to you and was willing to give you just about everything. I didn't see for a long, long time that *that*" — she jerked her chin toward the thick, rock-hard bulge in the front of his jeans — "was all that mattered between us, all that you were ever going to give me. It isn't ever going to be enough for me. I've got a life now, Mack. I'm never going to feel like that again, the way you made me feel. I hated myself. I don't want to see you again. I'm asking you to just stay away from me."

"Like hell. Like hell I'll stay away from you." He stepped closer, his breath coming in ragged gasps. He burned for her. Every moment of every day. He couldn't think straight without her. She stilled his mind. Made him human. "I can't breathe without you, and damn you, you know it. You don't get over what we had. You can't. I can't. We belong together no matter what bullshit you're telling yourself."

She shocked him by standing her ground. Staring at him. Her body was still, coiled and ready. She was trembling and there was a slight quiver to her perfect mouth, but she didn't crumble under his demand as she always had.

"It was your choice to throw us away, Mack, not mine. I'm not going to argue with you about my feelings. You just aren't

41

entitled to know what I'm feeling anymore. You aren't entitled to anything of mine. Not my body and not my heart."

"Think again. If I kissed you, touched you, you'd still belong to me."

She gave him that casual shrug that ripped his heart out and made him madder than hell. "Probably, Mack. We always had that firestorm to fall back on, but I realized something when you walked away from me: That's all we had. You told me what to do and I did it, like a puppet. Your puppet. I was good in bed, but you didn't need me for anything else. There are millions of women who are great in bed. Find one of them, one that just wants sex. I want more and I deserve more. I *need* more. You can't give me what I need, Mack. I've accepted that."

He could hear the quiet acceptance in her voice and panic welled up. She wasn't stringing him along. She was serious. He risked a breath when his lungs burned for air. He took his gaze from her and looked around the huge warehouse. It was a home. Unique. Like Jaimie. She was far from Chicago where they'd grown up. As far as she could get. She really hadn't provided the information. This wasn't her plan; someone else had gotten them together. She had made a new life for herself . . . There were flowers in a vase on a table. Roses. Red and white. Jaimie's favorite.

Jealousy burst like a dam, flooding him with poisonous rage, a dark red stain that spread fast, gripping like a demon. She'd killed him when she disappeared, left him half a man and damn her, she'd just moved on as if he wasn't part of her heart and soul the way she was his.

"Is there a fucking man living here with you?" He bit out each word. Wrenched the sounds between gritted teeth.

"I'm not doing this with you. I told you I wanted a family, Mack."

"We were a family. We are a family. It's always been us." And what the hell did that mean exactly? He continued to look around the spacious floor for signs of another man.

"Do you remember what you said to me when I asked about getting pregnant?"

"I told you it was fine."

She shook her head. "That is not what you said, Mack. First you looked angry and you demanded to know if I was pregnant. When I didn't answer you, you said if I was pregnant, we'd handle it."

"Well, we would have."

"*Handle* it? That's not wanting a family, Mack. That's making the best of a bad situation; or worse, maybe your handling it was to suggest an abortion."

"Damn it, Jaimie, I would never suggest you get rid of our baby. Is that what you thought? You know me better than that."

"I thought I knew you. I thought we both wanted the same thing out of our relationship. It was a shock when I discovered I was wrong." She shrugged. "I handled it. But it's best if we don't see each other."

"Because we belong together." There was smug satisfaction in his voice.

"Because we aren't good for each other." There was finality in her tone.

"Jaimie, are you happy?" Everything in him stilled. Waited. Her answer would determine his fate. He wouldn't ruin what Jaimie had if it was really what she wanted. Jaimie would never lie. She might avoid the question, but it wasn't in her to lie. He knew her too well.

The tip of her tongue touched her lip. She blew on her tea, avoiding his eyes. "You didn't need a family, Mack. I was always surprised that so many didn't. I wanted desperately to belong. That was why I joined you in the first place and later did undercover work. I needed to belong somewhere, to feel I was part of something. I haven't found that yet, but I will. At least I know what's important to me and I'm going after it." She flashed him a small smile that didn't quite reach her eyes. "I'll be all right."

Everything in him settled again. If she wasn't happy, that meant he had a chance. It might be a slim one, but he was a Ghost-Walker and he thrived on slim chances.

"I'm coming back. I have to go to work, Jaimie, but I'm coming back. If you have another man in your life, get rid of him. He isn't making you happy."

Her eyes flashed again, tiny sparks. He felt the answer in his gut. He had never been able to stop his response to her, and since his psychic enhancement, the pull between them was electric. He remembered her as a teenager, a young girl, all eyes and hair and that awesome mouth. When she smiled she could make the sun rise. He'd never met anyone else as intelligent. She could keep up with him on any subject, her mind quick, like the computers she loved so much. He'd spent hours just talking to her back then, watching the animation on her face, knowing she was his — that she'd always been his.

Very carefully she set the teacup onto the sink, more to keep from throwing it at him than to prevent him from seeing her hands shake. "I'm not starting up with you again,

Mack. It took too much out of me. I loved seeing all of you. I've felt terribly alone these past couple of years, but I can't go there again. I'm asking you to please leave me alone."

He stepped close, crowding her body with his so she could feel the heat radiating from his body and the brush of hard muscles against her soft curves. "Honey." His voice was gentle, tender even, as it only managed to be with Jaimie. "You might as well ask me to stop breathing." He caught her chin in his hand and lifted her face to force her to meet his gaze. "You're home to me, Jaimie. I'm tired of being without you. I've never wanted anyone else. I'm not walking away from you. Not after finding you again. I don't care if someone threw us together on purpose. I don't care how it happened. And don't try disappearing. Don't do it, Jaimie. This time I'll come looking, and God help both of us if I have to kill a man over you."

She jerked her chin out of his hand. "I hate the way you have to be so alpha, beat your chest all the time. I'm not a bone to fight over."

"No, you're a woman worth everything on this earth to me."

"Well, that's a big change, isn't it?"

"I'm not fighting with you. God knows we did enough of that. I'm done fighting with you. I want to come home."

She pushed at the wall of his chest. The shove didn't even rock him. A flicker of anger crossed her face. "You haven't changed at all."

"You always loved me just the way I am, Jaimie, alpha or not."

"I was a kid and anything you did was incredible and cool. I'm all grown up now and I know the difference between physical attraction and love. I want love. I want a family. I won't settle for anything less and you don't have that kind of commitment in you. You aren't tearing out my heart, Mack. Go do your thing. Get your adrenaline rush, but when you come back all hot and bothered, find another woman to expend all that energy on, because I'm not available."

A muscle ticked in his jaw, always a bad sign. It took discipline to keep his hands off of her. "We'll see, Jaimie. I'm coming back and I'd better find you here, alone."

He turned on his heel and stalked out.

CHAPTER 2

Kane sank back on his heels. "I don't like this, Mack. We've got two guards sitting in the warehouse playing cards. Other than that, there's no one. I can't detect heat anyplace else. If the weapons are really there, why aren't they being heavily guarded? Are we really going to believe that we tracked these weapons through three countries and during all that time they were under heavy guard, and now they're just left unattended in a warehouse a block from Jaimie?"

"Yeah." Mack sighed. "Hard to swallow, all right. Madigan is a savvy arms dealer. He would never let the Doomsday group know where he had the weapons, and he sure as hell wouldn't leave them exposed where anyone could take them. Maybe we're too late."

"Only way to know is to go inside and check it out," Kane said, reluctance in his voice.

Brian slid forward on his belly, keeping his body low. "Gideon reported in. He's on the roof. No cameras, no guards. Something doesn't smell right. There're a few alarms Javier could easily bypass."

Mack looked at the faces around him. He'd known them all since they were boys. Knew each one, knew they'd follow him to hell and back. And the new kid. Paul. Just a young pup, his face showing fear, his eyes determined.

"No, it doesn't smell right, Brian," he agreed. "Jacob, you and Ethan work your way around to the other side of the building and take a look up and down those warehouses. Keep your ass low and tell me if we've got surprises waiting for us. This isn't Oz, boys, so no heroes. You might run into a few civilians here and there. Stay out of sight."

"Yes, Mama, we know the drill," Jacob said.

"I mean it, no heroics. We don't know what we're into here," Mack reiterated, pinning them both with a stern eye.

Jacob Princeton nodded and he and Ethan slithered down the steps like two fast-crawling snakes, rolled into the shadows, and disappeared. Mack scanned the warehouse once again. "Kane, check every warehouse. Look for a grouping or singles — sentries or a group bunched up ready to come at us. They have to be hidden somewhere. Marc, you and Lucas find us at least two clear routes out of here. Take us up and over the rooftops."

He wasn't taking his men into a trap. He was going to ram this right back down their throats. But . . . He glanced at Javier Enderman. Javier looked the least like a soldier of any of them, and yet was maybe the most lethal.

"Get back to Jaimie, Javier. You know what to do. She won't like it and she'll give you hell, but you kill anyone that comes near her. Don't let anyone in or out of her place. I don't have to tell you what Jaimie means to me . . ."

"To all of us," Javier corrected. "She's ours too, Mack. I won't let anyone get to her."

"I want to hear your voice in my ear every second, Javier. You suspect anything, I want you telling me. Don't wait to confirm. I want to know if her neighbor blinks or a rat makes its way in. You got me?" He wanted to go himself, but Javier would stick to Jaimie like glue and no one, *no one,* was better up close and personal than Javier.

"I'll keep her safe, Top."

"Don't trust anyone, not even those we know. We've got a rat problem ourselves."

Paul stirred, frowned, and then glared at Mack. "Are you accusing me of something?"

"You're just the new kid, Paul," Mack said. "Not necessarily the rat. And if we all get blown to hell, I'm guessing you're going to be right alongside us."

Javier winked at the boy. "That doesn't make a whole hell of a lot of sense, although if you were a dumbshit rat, maybe it would."

Paul stared at them for a long moment, obviously making up his mind whether or not to take offense. He seemed satisfied that they didn't consider him the rat and shrugged. "I'm no dumbshit rat."

"Glad to hear it, boy. Just the same, I'm keeping a close eye on you, so stick to me like glue," Mack said, and winked at him.

Javier slid back into the shadows and worked his way down the fire escape to the uneven sidewalk. He stayed low, sticking as close to the side of the building as he could, his gaze restless, moving along the buildings. There were too many windows and doorways. Tension wound him tight, coiling his gut tighter and tighter. Every entryway was a potential threat. Each boat tied up to the wharf. Every car. Everywhere he looked, above and around him, were places the enemy could easily be hiding.

Voices had him crouching low, a statue, not so much as breathing in the cool night air, not wanting the vapor trail to give him away. Nerves stretched taut. *Couple of civvies, Top.* The two men were older, grizzled. Unlikely terrorists, their heavy worn sweaters smelled of fish and age, yet their belts were heavy with tools. He could see a knife tucked down into a scabbard lying along each man's thighs.

That was the trouble with urban warfare. You had to have good instincts, nerves of steel, good eyesight, and fast processing to be able to move through a city where anyone — man, woman, or child — could be a potential enemy.

Don't go hero on me, Javier. We're all going home tonight.

Mack's determination flooded Javier with warmth. He didn't ever like to admit it, but even Mack's lectures could make him feel as though he belonged.

Javier waited in silence, unmoving, watching the two old men shuffle along the sidewalk until they came to a car. The vehicle seemed as beat-up as they were. He watched them drive down the street, the car hiccupping and puffing out gasps of black smoke.

We're good here. Just a couple of C.O.B.s. Javier reported the two civilians in the battle zone. He stayed in the shadows as he made his way down the blocks of warehouses back up toward Jaimie's place.

So far he'd had good cover, and there were few people out so late. The wharf was quiet, although music blared somewhere off to his right and Javier could smell the distinct odor of marijuana. Kids, he guessed, finding a place to hang out and stay warm when they had nowhere else to go. He remembered those days, when the wind blew cool and cruel and he would look up at the windows mocking him with warmth and laughter, the days when his world was so stark and hungry and he was utterly alone. He'd thrown a few rocks in those days, angry and starving for both food and affection, until Mack had found a couple of street bullies stalking him and intervened. He hadn't told Mack the toughs would have lost the battle. He didn't want to take chances that he wouldn't fit in and Mack would throw him back.

He'd stayed quiet and looked as young and as nerdy as he could. He had better than 20/20 vision, yet he often hid his dark eyes behind thick clear lenses. He had been smarter than just about anyone until he met

Mack. The man had changed his life. Brought him purpose and definitely saved him from a life of crime.

He felt a smile coming on. He got to do all the things he wanted to do, but now they were legal. Of course, Mack kept a close rein on him. Just as well. Sometimes he went totally berserk and didn't have a lick of sense. Mack was always the voice of reason and things like this — this assignment, being chosen to guard Jaimie — were signs of respect and just made him love Mack all the more.

He was coming up to the open area. Jaimie had picked her location carefully. Her warehouse could be approached from water on one side or by land on three sides. Two of the three sides were as open as they could get. Anyone coming at her would have to expose themselves. She could sit up in her tower and pick them off one at a time — if that was Jaimie's way, which they all knew it wasn't. She would have an escape route. More than one. Jaimie was the biggest pacifist he knew. What she saw — and loved — in all of them, he never knew. They were all fighters, but like Mack, Jaimie was family, and he'd go to hell and back for family.

He stayed very still, scanning the area, his gaze quartering from rooftops to windows and then sweeping along the open sidewalk. Two men rounded the corner and paused to light cigarettes, hands shielding the flames, hiding their faces in the brief flare of light, but not before he caught a glimpse of their eyes. They were dressed in casual fishermen gear, but two things caught his attention. Their boots and their eyes. They were doing the same thorough scanning of the area, and he saw them look upward several times, toward that third floor where Jaimie Fielding was probably dropping off to sleep.

Jaimie's about to get company, Mack, he reported.

Mack swore softly. *Can you get to her without exposing yourself?*

Javier looked at the wide-open space running along the front of Jaimie's building and the two men between him and his destination. *That's affirmative, boss.*

We'll be sweeping up behind you, Javier. Don't kill any of us.

Tell the boys to identify themselves before they set foot inside Jaimie's home.

You got it. Be damn careful until backup comes, Mack warned again.

Careful is my middle name, Top.

Grinning, with eyes on the two men studying Jaimie's building, Javier quickly turned his jacket inside out. The black combat jacket now looked like a kid's jacket, complete with hood. He dragged the thick black-rimmed glasses from his pocket and set them on his nose. He spun his MP7 with its silencer to lie under his arm where he had easy access, and drew a skateboard and ball cap from his small duffel bag. If someone stopped him, the bag wouldn't stand up to a thorough examination, but he wasn't taking prisoners.

Javier shoved the hat backward on his head, dropped the board to the walkway, and began to kick-push his skateboard down the sidewalk. Just before he emerged from the shadows he half turned toward the sound of music and raised one hand. "Later!" He shoved with one foot and took the board out into the open, directly in a path to intercept the two men.

He glanced up as if seeing them for the first time and deliberately did a perfect varial flip, turning the board 180 degrees, and then landed back on the board and kept going. It was a fairly easy trick, but showy. The men turned toward him, but he could see they were really watching Jaimie's building and looking up at the rooftops, buying his kid act.

As he approached the two men, they visibly went on alert, one sliding his hand inside his coat. "Get out of here, kid," the one with the gun growled. The other spat on the ground.

Javier did what any self-respecting teen would do. He flashed a cocky grin, pushed hard with his foot, sliding back in preparation for a back-side heel flip. He crouched down, popped the board up, kicking out his heel and starting a 180 turn, but he failed to land it, stumbling off the board and almost plowing right into the two men. He spread his arms for balance. The skateboard flew into the air, striking the first man right in the center of his chest, driving him backward. The second man cursed as Javier's body slammed into him. The tiny sliver of steel in the center of Javier's palm slammed deep into the jugular vein. The man coughed, reaching up toward his throat as Javier's tackle carried them both toward the ground.

Javier turned as he fell, flipping his knife underhanded at the second man as he half rose. The blade buried to the hilt in the man's throat. He moved fast, even as the first man choked and gagged, already dying. Dragging the two bodies back into the shadows, he moved quickly across the open space, using the skateboard for speed. Jamming his finger on the button that rang her doorbell, he prayed Jaimie would buzz him through without any questions.

"Come on, Jaimie, let me in," Javier demanded, trying not to feel the itch between his shoulder blades where a big bull's-eye seemed to be painted on his back.

The locks disengaged and he shoved the door open and all but fell inside, dragging his MP7 free as he crouched low and crawled his way to the windows to peer outside. She'd let him in too fast — she'd known he was coming. Jaimie always knew.

I'm in, Mack. We need a cleaner for the two pieces of garbage I left just inside the alley outside of Jaimie's door.

Jaimie has to be the target. Gideon, watch this rat trap, Mack instructed the others. *The rest of you, pull back and make your way through the streets in standard search. Find them. Take them out quietly.*

Javier wired the doors and windows as quickly as he could. *I've got this place rigged, Mack. Do not approach without one of us letting you in.*

Mack's breath of relief was audible and made Javier smile. *Keep her undercover,* he advised.

You got it, Top, Javier promised.

Yeah, Mack said. *Just like you were careful*

58

and avoided engagement. Cleaners, my ass. I told you to be careful.

I don't have a scratch on me. He lowered his voice even more. *Jaimie's coming down the stairs. I want to keep her on the third floor, boss.*

We're working our way to you, doing a thorough sweep.

Javier knew how nerve-wracking a thorough sweep was, moving through enemy territory with civilians in the battlefield. He gave a silent salute toward his team and hurried to intercept Jaimie. "I'm coming up to you, Jaimie. Give me a couple of minutes."

"Javier? What are you doing? Is Mack okay? Did things go wrong?" There was anxiety in her voice. The lights suddenly blazed through the room.

He realized immediately she thought he was coming to tell her Mack was hurt. "No, no, babe, Mack's fine. Everyone's good. Don't turn on the lights. Get them off."

There was a heartbeat of silence and the lights went off again, plunging the first story into darkness. He heard rustling as she sank down at the top of the stairs. "Javier?"

There was the smallest of quivers in her voice and he felt a reaction in the pit of his stomach. Either of the girls could do that to any of them. Jaimie and Rhianna. The family revolved around the two girls. He didn't want to think about Rhianna, off doing God knew what undercover in some foreign country.

"For a minute I thought . . ." She trailed off, sounding very vulnerable.

"I know. He's fine. Everyone is. Just checking on you. You know how Mack worries."

"Do I?" Jaimie sounded sad now. "I haven't heard from him for two years. I don't think he worries all that much, Javier. But then, I'm all grown up and maybe don't need it anymore."

Working fast in the dark, he strung more explosives along the windows, wrapping the warehouse so that anyone trying to get in was going to have a nasty surprise. "Go on upstairs and make us a cup of tea. I'll be right there," Javier suggested.

"It's three in the morning," she pointed out. "What are you really doing here?"

"I told you. Mack worries." He kept his eyes moving around the windows, checking constantly to make certain Jaimie couldn't be seen. The stairs were protected from sight, he noted with a sigh of relief.

"Things went to hell?"

That was Jaimie, straight to the point. "No, we've got it handled. Mack's working his way back here with the rest of the crew. You might want to put on the coffee as well."

She made a sound somewhere between annoyance and amusement. In the dark it made him smile. She had that effect on everyone but the boss. She had an entirely different effect on him. His smile stretched to a grin.

"I'm not letting everyone move in with me," she announced.

"You gotta take that up with Mack," Javier said. "I'm just the scout, testing the waters, clearing out the land mines, you know, leading the way."

"Couldn't you have led him off the end of the pier?"

Javier flashed her a grin. "Mack would retaliate, Jaimie. You're safe enough. We keep an eye on him."

"What does that mean?"

"It means go upstairs and make a pot a coffee. The boys are going to be cold."

She sat there watching him. "You're expecting company."

He gave a casual shrug. "I always expect company. I'm paranoid. I even sleep with my pretty little gun."

She laughed. "I believe that." She started back up the stairs, hesitated, and half turned back toward him. "Javier, you aren't going to blow up my house, are you? I don't have insurance for that."

"Don't insult me, Jaimie," he replied. "You know I'm a specialist. My charges go exactly where I want them to go. Your home will be perfectly safe."

She nodded, tried a smile, and went on up to the third floor.

Javier noted she was as quiet as ever. Jaimie had been recruited out of college and trained as an operative. She certainly hadn't lost any of her skills. She was amazing in knowing where her enemies were at all times, was maybe the best of them, but she couldn't kill. There was no pulling the trigger for Jaimie. Javier couldn't understand why Mack let that bother him. The woman was just wired differently. She always had been. He remembered her as a little girl, all eyes and wild hair and a brain that wouldn't quit. She'd started high school at eight years of age, Mack and Kane already fifteen and watching over her.

Javier? Mack whispered in his mind. *You where you can talk?*

That's affirmative.

We've removed the bodies. I ran into a couple of suspects, but they backed off her place. I think they're watching it, though. I've

*got them under surveillance. We're going to
set up shop in a couple of places.*

*There's no doubt they were making a grab
for her. Whose are they, Top?*

*Not the ones we were looking for. Someone
else is in this mix. Kane got the information
from Sergeant Major Griffen that Madigan had
a heart attack and is in the hospital. That
explains the low profile here. They don't want
to tip off Doomsday to where they're keeping
the guns or to the fact that Madigan is indis-
posed. He probably gave them some story
about a delay. We should have a little time to
set up here and watch the warehouse and
keep Jaimie safe as well.*

A heart attack? Javier asked.

Yeah, a little convenient.

It could happen, Javier pointed out.
Stranger things had.

*The problem with the address? Jaimie be-
ing here? Madigan having a heart attack
before he can get the guns into Doomsday's
hands? Those conveniences just keep piling
up,* Mack said. *Watch her and don't trust
anyone.*

I never do, Javier responded as he made
his way up to the second story.

If Mack thought they were all being
manipulated, the chances were great that
they had been. Mack rarely was wrong when

63

he got a strong enough hunch to say it out loud.

On the second story, two more boxes were opened that hadn't been earlier, which meant Jaimie had been upset after they left and had worked rather than gone to bed. He added a few charges to slow down any unwanted guests and made his way to Jaimie's living quarters. The aroma of coffee hit him immediately.

Javier grinned at her. "I forgot you make the best coffee on the planet."

The upper story had a few dim night-lights glowing; he didn't want shadows across the windows giving away their positions, but she hadn't turned on any bright lights. Jaimie turned around and leaned one hip against her counter. His stomach knotted. Here it came. Damn it. He had hoped Mack would get this, not him.

"I haven't seen any of you in two years and within minutes of seeing you, I've got trouble on my doorstep, haven't I, Javier?"

He tried an angelic grin. It worked on most women, but she knew him. She didn't smile back and her eyes flickered. Oh, yeah. She was upset. "I like to think we arrived just in the nick of time to save the damsel in distress."

She sat on the counter and swung her legs.

"Just how much danger is there, Javier?"

He winked. "None now that I'm here. We'll just stay away from the windows. You do have an escape route up here, right?" He couldn't imagine a planner like Jaimie not incorporating a secret escape or two.

She nodded curtly. "Don't be cute with me, Javier." She narrowed her eyes and looked at him closer. "Come here."

He took a step back, wary of that expression on her face. He'd seen it before on a woman and it never boded well. "I'm just hanging out with you, Jaimie."

"Really? Then why is there blood on your sleeve?" She wrinkled her nose. "I smell fresh blood."

The woman had always had sharp eyes. And an even keener sense of smell. Javier shrugged. "All in the line of duty. You had a couple of rats sniffing around your back door, babe. I just took care of them for you, is all."

She shook her head, jumped from the counter and turned her back on him to busy herself with the coffee. He noted her hands shook. "I'm not doing this again, Javier. You can't let Mack drag me back in." She didn't add cream or sugar, handing the aromatic liquid to him just the way he liked it. "I can't go back to that life. This is my home now. I've established myself in business here and I have a chance to succeed."

"Mack would want you to succeed," Javier pointed out, going straight to the heart of the matter. "He'd never do anything to jeopardize you."

She looked away from him again, her mouth trembling before she managed to bite down hard. He was good at details, better than most, and although Jaimie was adept at covering her emotions, he knew her too well. He took a sip of coffee and savored the great taste.

"Mack and I don't work together," she said. "You're my brother, Javier. It ought to matter that I don't want to see him."

"He's my brother too, and you're killing him with this separation, Jaimie."

"He walked out on us. None of you seem to understand that."

"I understand I haven't seen you in two years." He couldn't help the accusation in his voice. She'd been the closest thing he had to a sister.

Jaimie ducked her head. "I know. I'm sorry. That wasn't fair of me. I couldn't have broken away from him unless I made a clean break from all of you."

"We had to mean something to you."

She did look up at him then. Quick.

Startled. Shocked. "Of *course* you do. You're my family. I know I should have kept in touch with all of you. I missed you terribly, every single day. I had no one and I guess I consoled myself with the fact that you all had each other."

"I saw Mack after you disappeared. He was insane."

"He didn't come after me."

Javier took another swallow of coffee. No, Mack hadn't followed her and brought her back, and Javier couldn't explain that one. No one understood Mack, except maybe Kane, and he wasn't prone to talking much about Mack. They'd all tried to talk to him, but Jaimie became a taboo subject and they learned fast not to mention her.

"I'm not over him," Jaimie admitted. "I saw him and I just crumbled inside. I can't go through all that again, Javier."

"I don't know what's going on, Jaimie, but I'm not leaving here until I know you're safe. That warehouse may or may not be stocked with weapons. We'll get inside and find out. We're ghosts, that's what we do. But not now, not tonight. Tonight your safety is the priority. We'll have to figure out what's going on."

"He's going to stay, isn't he?"

Javier cursed inwardly. "Yeah, babe, he's

going to stay. He'd never take a chance with your life either."

She sighed and shook her head. "You hungry?" Her head came up suddenly and she half turned toward the stairway.

Javier followed her gaze, keeping his voice as casual as ever. "I'm always hungry. You know that."

You have a couple of rats poking around your back door, Mack's voice whispered in Javier's mind. *I'm working my way up behind them.*

Javier set down his coffee cup, caught Jaimie's arm, and tugged even as she was moving away from the refrigerator, her eyes wide in understanding. *Escape route?*

She didn't ask questions. Jaimie wouldn't. She was a professional all the way — there'd never been a doubt about that. And she had known about the same time as Mack had spotted them. She always knew. She led the way across to the corner on the water side. Moving a small table, he could see the door in the wall.

Down a chute. I have a boat waiting.

He gave her the signal to stay put right there and drew out a gun to hand her. Jaimie shook her head. He gave her his sternest scowl. It did no good.

Jaimie refuses a weapon, Mack.

68

and prevent the others — men like Javier who needed action — from doing anything that would land them in prison. Mack hadn't seen how aggressive all the men were becoming. He hadn't noticed a lot of things he should have noticed. He was swept up in the training and forgot the things Jaimie was good at.

She saw people differently. She felt things — knew things — and she knew they were being lied to. She saw through the patriotic talk and the propaganda, but Mack couldn't hear her. He'd already been so far into the experiments and training that there was no reasoning with him. He knew she didn't like urban warfare. She didn't ever want to have to make a judgment call and risk killing an innocent. All Mack saw was a chance to use his incredible psychic talents to save the world.

Because Jaimie was wired that way, and she never stopped digging, she managed to piece together a little information on the existing GhostWalker teams. There were four that she'd uncovered. The first and oldest was comprised mainly of men with army backgrounds, Rangers and Green Berets, although there was an FBI agent with extensive military training on it as well. The men had undergone a tremendous number of experiments as well as training. A few of them were anchors, men who would draw the overload of psychic energy from the others so they could function properly. They usually worked together as a team, the anchor staying close to those who couldn't work without one.

The newspapers had reported that Dr. Peter Whitney, the brains behind the Ghost-Walker experiments, had been murdered, yet she'd had contact with him after that time. Brian Hutton had worked in a unit that had guarded a facility where he'd been working, and several others, Kane among them, had done so as well. She had a high security clearance and had continued to help analyze information. During that time she'd kept tabs on her family to ensure they were all doing fine and no one was double-crossing them as she suspected had happened to Team One.

She rubbed her temples, trying to stop the headache already pounding there in spite of Javier's presence. Team Three — Mack's team — was comprised of all anchors, very rare in the world of GhostWalkers, and she knew they often had to work alone on their assignments, impossible for someone overcome by psychic overload. She had been the exception. She still wondered why they'd made the exception for her, as she wasn't an anchor and couldn't work alone. She believed Mack and Kane had something to do with the decision, but she couldn't be certain. She'd never been able to access her own records. For all her skills, she hadn't been able to get to her file — and that bothered her more than anything.

Something was going on and the men didn't seem to question it as she had. Team Two was comprised of mainly SEALs. There had been a few shady things happening within that team as well. Jaimie scrubbed her hand over her face. Two of those men had been lured into the Congo and tortured, barely escaping with their lives. Someone was trying to destroy the teams. To her mind, the third team, Mack's team, was the most vulnerable.

As urban warfare specialists, Team Three was sent over and over into situations that would fray the nerves of the most skilled combatants. Urban warfare was a danger-ous art, a unique combat that only the most gifted and steady men could really handle for long periods of time and, sadly, it was becoming a necessity. She feared for the team's vulnerability. If someone in their own government was working against them, it wouldn't be that difficult to put them in harm's way.

As for the fourth team, comprised of mainly the elite Air Force Pararescue Special Forces, they were ghosts in the wind, as was their commander. She had uncovered little about that team beyond their confirmed existence.

The tapping of a finger on the counter caught her attention. She looked up. *You all right?* Javier asked.

She nodded. But she wasn't. Her stomach was in knots and she wanted to throw up. This was not coincidence. She'd worked hard to get out of that life, to build a future, not only for herself but for the others. They would need it later, when all was said and done — if they survived. Psychics had a difficult time without a controlled environment. She meant to build up a surplus of money and a safe haven for her family. Instinctively, like she knew so many other things, she knew everything she'd worked for was being threatened.

Mack's voice whispered in Javier's ear this time, using the radio so Paul was a part of the orders. "Come up behind them, Kane."

Gideon's voice interrupted. "We've got a sleeper, boss. Third window, second story. I caught a flash."

"You certain?"

"Don't insult me. He had to have seen Javier take out his men."

There was a small silence as Mack examined the two dead men. "These men are military," Mack's voice nearly growled. "What the hell's going on?"

Javier's heart jumped. "You telling me I killed a couple of our own?"

"We're getting pictures and fingerprints. No IDs on them, but they're military. They came prepared to take her," Mack assured. "They have an injector that looks like a tranq, but we won't know until we test it. Ties. Firepower. They aren't innocent, so don't sweat it."

Easier said than done. Javier shook his head and tried a few deep breaths to settle his churning gut. His every instinct had told him they were the enemy, but military? The same side? "What the hell are we into here, boss?"

Jaimie shook her head. She couldn't hear what Javier was saying, but she could read lips. They were all questioning what they were involved in. She'd made a mistake thinking the government would let her go. Once a GhostWalker, always a Ghost-Walker. She thought working as an analyst would satisfy them, but obviously she'd been wrong. Whatever was happening, the power orchestrating behind the scenes was determined to draw her back in, and planned on using Mack and her family to do it.

A spurt of resentment had her kicking out at the wall in defiance. She'd told Mack. How like him to just go his own way with all of them following him, no one bothering to think about the how and why of anything. Now they were all in this mess. She'd done her best to convince them, but would any of them listen to her? She had a brain. A big brain. High school at eight. Graduating with honors from the University with a doctorate by the time she was twenty. Come on. Of course they wouldn't listen to her. Mack was so much smarter.

She kicked the wall a second time, wishing it was his shin. Mack. He was out there in the night, staring up at her window, gun slung around his neck, putting his men — no, not just his men; his *family* — in deadly peril, and loving every moment of it. Worse, even with all of her intellectual reasoning, she was just as bad as the others, following him anywhere he led, even when she knew it was down the wrong path.

Who could resist Mack? Not her. Certainly not her. And he was back. He'd looked at her so differently. Not even in the year they'd been lovers had he ever looked at her with that particular expression he'd worn tonight. Not even when passion had burned hot and out of control between them. Not ever.

She pressed a hand to her stomach. Did she never learn? He was poison to her. She forced herself to look at Javier, to concentrate on his lips.

"He's on the move," Mack's voice intoned in Javier's ear. "Don't let him get away."

"He's moving across the rooftops with incredible speed, boss," Gideon said. "I'm after him, but I don't have a prayer of catching this guy. He's souped-up with something."

"Who's on the move, boss?" Javier stirred, tried to peer out the window at the rooftop across from him. Something was moving fast, no more than a shadow. No more than a ghost. "The son of a bitch watching Jaimie?"

Jaimie's heart jumped. She always knew when she was being watched. Her internal alarm system never failed. How could it be possible that someone had set up to watch her and she hadn't known? Maybe Mack was wrong. Doubt ate at her. Mack was many things, but he was seldom wrong about this kind of thing.

"He's gone, boss," Gideon reported.

"We've got the bodies and we'll take them in. Gideon, you and Kane find out who's watching Jaimie. Go through that room with a fine-tooth comb. Get me something. Brian, you and Jacob follow the two creeping around Jaimie's warehouse and report back to me. I don't need to tell you that I don't want you seen and I don't want them dead." Mack paused. "Javier, get on Jaimie's computer and find everyone places to rent around Jaimie's warehouse. Scatter them so that we have every angle covered. House-boats, whatever. If you have to arrange to get someone thrown out so we get what we need, do it. But do it tonight. Kane and I will be staying with Jaimie."

Javier glanced at Jaimie, who scowled back at him. "Does Jaimie know she's going to be having permanent guests, boss?"

Jaimie's eyes widened as she heard what he was saying. Javier turned away, feeling slightly guilty; after all, Jaimie was a sister of the heart. "I don't think she's going to like that much."

"Well, that's just too damn bad, now, isn't it, Javier," Mack said.

CHAPTER 3

Mack and Kane and all the boys hadn't been near her in two peaceful years. Now, within two hours of their arrival, it had started all over again. Blood and death. Jaimie stared out the window, her gaze fixed on the ever-changing motion of the dark water below. Javier had spent the night and the next day with her. Now he was gone and Mack and Kane were on their way up, finished with all their paperwork and cleanup and coming back to — what? She couldn't go back to that life with them. She wouldn't go back.

Facing Mack again was going to be tough, but she had to find a way to be nonchalant around him. He was family, just like all of them were. She had to keep it that way and not let the secret, hidden excitement at the thought of him overtake her brain. Hormones could be controlled. She didn't have to give in to her feelings. She'd out-think him and stay out of trouble.

She gave a little sniff of self-contempt. Even she wasn't buying what her mind was selling. The freight elevator door opened on the far side of the room and she turned to see Kane and Mack emerge. They both looked exhausted, lines etched in their faces. They'd been up at least forty-eight hours before they'd even made it to San Francisco and they'd pulled another all-nighter cleaning up the mess Javier had made and then making their reports.

Her heart leapt with joy in spite of her determination to keep her perspective. She was in danger any way she looked at it. She padded across the floor on bare feet to stand in front of them, determined to start out in a position of power and authority; after all, this was her house and they weren't invited. "Just how long do you both think you're going to be staying here?" she demanded, pretending dismay at the pile of gear. With a bare toe, she touched a gun case. "It looks like a weapons dump in here. Is this really necessary?"

Kane moved around the heap of drab-colored duffel bags and gathered her into his arms. He wasn't tall but he was a bear of a man, dwarfing her instantly. "Don't you ever, ever pull something like this again,

Jaimie. You left us without a word. And you know damn well we couldn't follow you."

Kane wasn't a man to mince words, or to be afraid to face her wrath. The whole incident had been too damn traumatic for all of them and he didn't want it repeated. He hadn't said a word in front of the others, but she was going to hear him — especially after Mack had enlightened him about his conversation with her. She wasn't disappearing from their lives a second time.

Jaimie thought he was going to break every rib she had. He was squeezing the breath out of her as he emphasized his words.

It was Mack who came to her rescue, gently pulling her from Kane's grasp, a grin softening the hard edge of his mouth. "Don't kill her, Kane. I know we discussed it, but didn't we just decide on severe punishment?"

"Something like that. You look great, honey, too good to be out on your own without protection. What the hell was the frying pan for?"

Jaimie groaned in exasperation. "I've had the lecture, thank you very much." She threw a little glare toward Mack. "I was safer without a gun. And don't start in on my alarm system. I'm just testing various systems and I don't expect anyone but the average burglar to break in."

"Well, just look how wrong you can be." Kane's vivid green gaze was taking in the wide-open space. "Wow. Again I say wow."

"Admiration, I hope." Jaimie's hands went to her hips. "Respectful admiration. Mack didn't give me any."

"This place is out of sight."

Mack rolled his eyes. "I should have known you'd be as dippy as she is. It's a warehouse. Jaimie is living unprotected in a seamy part of town in a drafty old warehouse." Mack indicated the far corner. "Take a look at that pint-sized bed."

"Did you think you were going to take over my bed?" Jaimie demanded, her large eyes flashing a warning at him. He was *not* taking over her life or her bed.

"First order of business," Kane said. "Tomorrow, Jaimie, we get a couple of decent beds in here. You have any beer?" He was already striding toward the refrigerator.

"Of course she doesn't have any beer," Mack scoffed. "She doesn't drink. And where do you think you're going? You can't leave this stuff here."

Kane was peering in the brand-new, very modern refrigerator. "Uh-oh, little Jaimie has some explaining to do." He pulled out a bottle of Corona and popped off the top.

Mack's eyebrows shot up. "Didn't the doctors tell you not to drink alcohol, Jaimie?"

"Stop trying to sound like my father."

She attempted to shove him, her hand flat on his heavily muscled chest, but shoving Mack never worked. He simply brought up his hand to cover hers, pressing her palm over his heart.

"You don't have a father," Kane reminded, swallowing half the bottle of beer in one gulp. "That's our job."

Jaimie tugged to get her hand free. She never discussed her past if she could help it, not even with the ones who had seen her through it all.

"And we're good at it," Mack pointed out smugly. His hand kept hers trapped against his chest. "Why would you have beer in the fridge?"

"Entertainment purposes, and stop ruffling my hair." She ducked under Mack's hand.

"You cut it." Kane made it an accusation.

"It's just the right length for ruffling," Mack pointed out. "Entertaining who?"

"Whom," Kane corrected, his head back in the refrigerator. He came out with a handful of turkey slices. "Thank God you're over your vegetarian phase. I nearly starved."

Mack hefted two bags over his shoulder and followed Jaimie across the carpeted floor to the bedroom wall. "Who's she entertaining with beer?" he demanded. "Let's get some answers here."

"Stop harping." Jaimie curled up on the bed, watching him stow the gear in the corner.

"It isn't harping if I don't get an answer." Mack stood right in front of her, his dark, gleaming eyes on her face as he began to unbutton his shirt.

Jaimie couldn't tear her gaze away from his hair-roughened chest, the hard, defined muscles, his flat six-pack belly. She swallowed hard as his hands went to the waistband of his jeans. "Don't you dare take your clothes off in my bedroom, Mack."

He flashed a taunting grin. "You don't have an overabundance of walls, little darlin'. Where exactly am I supposed to get undressed?"

"Well, not right here, for heaven's sake." Her long lashes fluttered in shock. "The bathroom would be much more appropriate."

Kane found a deep, comfortable armchair

and sat down with a second beer and a sandwich. "Get away from that innocent little thing, you oversexed lout," he said mildly.

"Tell her to answer the question." Mack didn't take his glinting black gaze from her startling blue one as he dared her.

"I did answer your question. Go ahead and change in the bathroom." Jaimie's chin lifted belligerently.

"The other question, the important question. Who's the beer for, Jaimie?"

Her fist thumped the pillow. "You're going to make me crazy, Mack. All right. It's for my assistant, Joe Spagnola. Are you satisfied now?"

"Damn it, Jaimie," Mack snapped, his eyes blazing.

Kane sat up straighter, a dark frown on his face.

"Well, I couldn't do this alone," Jaimie hastily defended. "There's a lot of work and he's been invaluable."

Kane snorted derisively. "Invaluable."

"She gives him beer to drink," Mack muttered under his breath. "How old is your Joe Spagnola?"

Jaimie threw her hands in the air. "Look, he's thirty-two or so, I don't know. What difference does that make?"

"You got this guy up here drinking beer in your bedroom and you don't know what difference it makes?" Mack said, taking a step closer to the bed. His hands were at his sides, fingers opening and closing ominously. "Is he single?"

"Oh, for heaven's sake."

Kane hitched himself closer in the chair. "You bring that guy up here alone with you?"

Jaimie made a T out of her hands. "Whoa, there, guys. Stop right there. Time out. I'm not a teenager anymore and you are not my guardians." She glared up at Mack. "I'm not *yours*. You got that? I'm not yours. I know what you're thinking and you can just forget it. You aren't going to do one single thing to Joe. Not one. In fact, you will be polite to him."

Kane and Mack exchanged a long, wordless look. Mack turned away and stalked to the bathroom, every line in his body conveying pure outrage.

Jaimie threw her pillow after him. The pillow hit the bathroom door just as he closed it. "Don't egg him on, Kane," she ordered. "You know how impossible he is."

Mack called out to her from behind the bathroom door, his tone somewhere between a threat and suppressed rage. "Some-

85

how I don't think your Joe is going to get along too well with us. Drinking beer in your bedroom. What will you think of next?"

"He was not drinking beer in my bedroom," Jaimie denied hotly. "Where do you come up with this stuff? And it wouldn't be any of your business if he did," she added furiously.

The bathroom door flew open so hard it slammed against the wall. Mack swept up the pillow, hardly breaking stride. He was wearing dove gray sweat bottoms, obviously a concession to her modesty, and nothing else. His body rippled with muscle, with pure strength, as he moved toward her with all the stalking grace of a predator.

"It's my business, honey, anytime anyone is in your bedroom. Scoot over." He tossed the pillow on the bed behind her.

"I'm not going to scoot over," Jaimie argued. "Find your own bed."

Mack sank down on the edge of the mattress, suppressing a grin as Jaimie automatically retreated. "It's late, Kane. You aren't going to sit up all night eating, are you?"

"I was thinking about watching television. Do you realize how long it's been since we watched TV?" Kane pulled off his shoes. "You lack closets, Jaimie girl. We'll have to do something about that."

"It's not finished yet," Jaimie pointed out. "But it will be something when I'm all through. This floor will be my home, everything fairly open still, but with more cupboards and closets. The bathroom's great. We finished it last week. Admit it, Mack — the bathroom's a work of art with all that tile. It's a masterpiece."

Mack ruffled her hair again, deliberately easing his body farther onto the bed and stretching out his legs. "So, all right, that's true. The bathroom is a work of art. Even you, Kane, will appreciate it."

"Joe did it," she said smugly.

Mack swore under his breath and made a move toward her. She scrambled backward on the bed until her back was against the wall.

"What is all this, Jaimie?" Kane wasn't going to be polite and wait until she confided in them.

Jaimie drew up her knees, hugged them to her, rocking a little back and forth, her smile enough to blind a man. "The second floor is my lab, where I'll do all my planning and experimenting. The first floor will be an office, bathroom, and room for my models."

"Models?" Kane echoed.

"Of buildings. I own a security company. I've left Professor Chilton and branched out on my own. I started consulting work with him and now I'm swamped. I prove existing systems can be breached and design systems specifically for corporations. I have some government contracts, as I still do analytical work and retain my security clearance. That's where all my training comes in. I get to break into these places. It's very lucrative, not to mention fun."

"Does Spagnola do this work with you?" Mack's voice was very low.

"He's a builder, not an electronics expert," Jaimie answered. Out of long habit, she rubbed at his frowning mouth with her fingertip. "He's nice, Mack."

The trouble was, the feel of him was so achingly familiar. Mack's lips were velvet soft. He opened his mouth, his strong white teeth nipping her fingertip, sending unexpected liquid heat curling through her body. She snatched her hand away as if he had burned her, rubbing it on her thigh as if erasing his touch.

"It's dangerous work, honey. Security guards don't have all that much training. Or worse, if it's a government enterprise, you might run across an itchy trigger finger somewhere."

"Oh, please, Mack, let's not start discussing dangerous jobs." Jaimie swept her tousled hair from her forehead. The moment she released the silky strands, they settled right back in a soft, thick halo.

"You knew that was coming." Kane laughed, his head back, uninhibited, the way he always laughed. But his eyes weren't laughing, Jaimie noted. "And you deserved it."

"Get your gear out of the middle of the hallway," Mack said.

"He always resorts to dishing out orders when you get the best of him," Kane reminded Jaimie.

"Speaking of dishes, clean your mess up," Jaimie said primly.

"No one was speaking of dishes," Kane denied. "I said dishing, dishing, you know, like . . ." He trailed off with an exaggerated sigh. "Oh, all right, then, but this is under protest. You used to do our dishes."

"I was twelve and you blackmailed me," Jaimie said, scowling darkly at him. "If I didn't, you weren't going to let me go to any of the football games." She tilted her chin. "Now I call the shots."

"Says who?" Mack flipped her over so she landed on her stomach. Instantly his leg was across her thighs, his upper body pinning her down. He leaned wickedly close, his warm breath on the nape of her neck. "I just let you think you call the shots, honey. I draw the line at this Spagnola character."

"Mack, let me up." Jaimie tried not to laugh. She wasn't going to encourage him. He felt so familiar, so right, but she knew better, and playing around with him was like playing with fire. Sooner or later she was going to get burned. On the other hand, he was waiting for her to fight with him over sharing the bed and she wasn't going to do it. He would never touch her with Kane in the room. He might want to, but he was exhausted and Kane was a good chaperone. She was safe, and she could act like it meant nothing to her. Let him think it didn't matter to her at all.

"Will you two stop horsing around?" Kane yawned. "It's three o'clock in the morning. Let's turn in."

"The great TV watcher." Mack reluctantly shifted his weight from Jaimie. He took great care to retain his hard-won portion of the bed. "Pack it in, honey, hotshot has spoken."

"I'm not sharing my sheets," Jaimie announced with a fierce, meant-to-be-intimidating scowl. "You can sleep on top of the covers."

"I bought them," Mack pointed out, tracing the hand-embroidered dragon nearest him. "That should give me a few rights."

"I'll share my other pillow," Jaimie conceded, "but only because you sent me all those dragons." She *loved* the collection of dragons, mostly given to her by Kane and Mack over the years. She might forgive him a little just for that.

"Wait a minute, wait a minute," Kane protested. "You know that jeweled one from Egypt? I bought that one."

"Like hell you did. You were making goo-goo eyes at some belly dancer, as I recall," Mack lied, settling more comfortably onto the mattress, his thigh touching Jaimie's.

It had been so long and she felt like heaven, all soft skin and heat. She smelled a little like heaven too. It was only the fact that he was so exhausted that he dared take a chance sharing her bed again. Jumping her was not the way to win her back, but keeping the old familiar footing would go a long way toward smoothing his path.

Kane retrieved the rest of their luggage and dumped it unceremoniously in the corner of Jaimie's bedroom. "The man said you looked like an assassin; he wouldn't take your traveler's check. I paid, remember. Is the couch comfortable?"

"Aren't you two supposed to be used to roughing it?" Jaimie demanded, exasperated with both of them. "And Kane never makes goo-goo eyes at women. That's you."

"I paid you back, Kane," Mack insisted, ignoring Jaimie.

"When did you pay me back?" Kane asked suspiciously, as he headed for the bathroom.

"You're in a lady's house," Mack called out. "Don't forget the toilet seat. And it was in Milan."

"I can't believe you said that." Jaimie was horrified. "I'd forgotten what it was like sharing a house with men." She buried her face in the coolness of the pillow.

"He isn't very well trained," Mack explained loud enough for Kane to hear.

"Turn on the alarm, Kane," Jaimie reminded as the man emerged wearing a long-suffering expression and navy blue sweats. She smiled to herself. Sweats seemed to be quite the rage in nightwear when she'd bet her bottom dollar they never slept in clothes if they could help it.

Kane activated the alarm, rolled out his sleeping bag on the couch, and turned off the light. "It wasn't Milan."

"I paid your fine so you wouldn't go to jail. Hell, Kane, you tried to steal the cop's hat."

"You dared me to." There was a flurry of rustling sounds, a loud thump announcing

Kane hitting the floor. Fortunately, his censored comments were muffled by the carpet.

"Never try sharing a bed with him," Mack advised. "Jaimie?" Now his voice turned very casual. "Professor Chilton was one of your instructors at Stanford, wasn't he? How did he end up in London doing consulting work?"

"His brother-in-law worked in some capacity for a corporation. He recommended Professor Chilton after the company had a series of break-ins. It was lucky for me he checked into the same hotel I had gone to after I . . ." She broke off, grateful the lights were out. She didn't have anything to be ashamed of. She'd left because she had to go in order to survive. If Mack couldn't understand that, too bad.

A hint of defiance entered her voice. "I checked into a hotel after I left our apartment and the next morning I ran into him in the lobby. We had breakfast together; I really needed a friend. Naturally, we talked electronics. One thing led to another, and before I knew it, I was in business." She didn't add that running into the professor had given her the freedom to keep from running back to Mack, afraid and a failure. It had actually felt good to make her own decisions and be responsible for her own life, once she'd gotten past the pain of separation.

"So you think you're good enough to make it on your own?" Kane prompted. He took a few minutes to get settled again.

The room was pitch-black, Jaimie's eyes working to adjust as she stared up at the ceiling. "I was better than Chilton, Kane, right from the start. He knew it too. I used his name and he used my expertise. He's back teaching — that's what he loves — and I've got enough of a reputation now to hold my own. It worked out great."

"So you actually break into buildings?" Mack didn't sound happy about it.

"Sure, I study the security system and find a way to beat it. The theory being, of course, if I can do it, so can someone else. Then I try to design a system exclusive to the particular needs, setting, and personnel of the client. Sometimes it's a onetime shot; other times I'm on retainer as a full-time consultant. I'm also developing new software for a bomb detector. There's a lot of interest in that."

"I've got to hand it to you, Jaimie" — Kane's voice was frankly admiring — "you've done well for yourself."

Beside her, Mack stirred restlessly. Jaimie

ignored him. "Thank you," Jaimie said softly to Kane. She refused to care whether Mack approved of what she did or not. She thumped the pillow and snuggled deeper, trying to ignore his close proximity.

"I didn't spot your cameras." Kane was casual, his voice coming out of the darkness from the direction of the couch.

"My cameras?" Jaimie turned toward the wall, curling up, her voice drowsy, unconsciously sensual.

"None of our team triggered the alarm. I looked at the tapes myself yesterday during the report. You know we always record any action. We made it into the warehouse clean, yet you knew we were there. You even knew who we were. You grabbed the frying pan instead of the gun."

Mack could feel Jaimie go perfectly still. Her body trembled. She twisted the edge of the sheet between her fingers. Without conscious thought, Mack's hand went to the nape of her neck, easing the tension out of her.

Kane allowed the silence to stretch and lengthen. It was a full five minutes later before his soft, insistent voice disturbed the night. "The cameras, Jaimie, where are they?"

"I didn't bother with cameras on the

ground floor." Although she sounded sleepy, Mack was certain she was selecting her words carefully. "The cameras will be on the second floor."

Mack found himself smiling at the misleading nuggets of information. She hadn't changed much. She was less sure of herself with them when it came to work. She was picking and choosing what information she wanted to give them, but she had a difficult time not falling into the old pattern of camaraderie and friendship.

"And Kane," Jaimie added, "I don't use a gun."

Kane didn't buy any of it and was being unusually stubborn, not letting her off the hook. "So how did you know?" he persisted.

Jaimie curled up away from Mack, settling back into the pillow, snuggling beneath the covers. "I guess you must have been a little noisier than you thought." There was a lazy note of humor now.

"Damn it, Jaimie." Kane was frustrated. "That's not possible."

"No?" She was laughing openly at him now. "Then it had to be my acute sense of smell. Take your choice. What other explanation is there?"

Kane's curse was only partially muffled by his sleeping bag. Beneath his hand, Mack could feel Jaimie's shoulder shake slightly with laughter. She had managed to elude Kane's questions again, the same questions he and every instructor and field operative she had been pitted against had asked.

Mack lay still, savoring the feel and scent of Jaimie. His arm curved possessively around her waist. Her breathing stopped for a moment, her body tense. He smiled to himself as she fought with herself. Which was the lesser of the two evils? Let him have this one little thing? Or provoke him into something more dangerous by protesting? She left his arm in place with a soft little sigh.

Mack was fairly satisfied with the way things had gone. They had danced around each other, but Jaimie had missed him every bit as much as he had missed her. It was there in her eyes. She was determined to bring them to a brother/sister relationship, to treat him as she would Kane or Javier, but he was just as determined to get her back. And he never stopped when he wanted something, whether it was personal or work. He would find a way around every argument.

His grip on her tightened involuntarily. He had known, two years ago, he was falling deeper and deeper under her spell, but he hadn't known how much a part of him she really was. Until he woke up one morning to find her gone. Life went from laughter and adventure to a bleak, desolate kind of hell. Oh, he had functioned, like an automaton, but the best part of him was gone.

He knew the exact moment she let go and drifted off to sleep. She slept with all the trusting innocence of child, her body warm and pliant, her face so beautiful he ached inside. Everything masculine and protective welled up in him along with very primitive possessiveness. He eased his body beneath the covers, molding around her, a kind of heaven and hell. His arm clamped around her, his chin resting on her silky head.

Slow, smoldering desire flared into urgent demand. His body burned for her, an unmerciful, relentless, savage need. His skin crawled with it, his head pounded. The heat was a living flame until every inch of his skin was burning. Mack McKinley was a man who lived with the truth about himself. He recognized his strengths and weaknesses, he acknowledged the hidden demons he controlled with absolute discipline. He carried a kind of ice-cold rage in him, but still, this shook him. This felt out of control, beyond control even. He didn't need the complication of fierce, combustible chemistry raging between them. He wanted to court her slowly and carefully, seal her to him for eternity. This time she wasn't getting away from him.

Jaimie moved in her sleep, the curve of her bottom sliding invitingly, painfully, over his throbbing, aroused body. Mack nearly groaned out loud. So, okay, this wasn't working out the way he had planned. He rolled over, away from Jaimie, silently cursing his body's raging need. He had been with her hundreds of times, taking her each night, almost every morning they'd been together, but the hunger had never been so strong, so urgent. Just the scent of her filled him with such a powerful need he wasn't certain he had the strength to resist. The urge was almost animalistic. He shifted positions again, trying to ease the relentless aching.

A soft chuckle floated tauntingly from the center of the room. "Can't sleep?" Kane asked.

"Go to hell," Mack growled, resisting the urge to throw something.

"I think you're screwed, Mack. If it's as bad as I think, that bastard paired you two. You were already attached physically and emotionally. Good luck."

Mack knew Kane was referring to Dr.

Whitney's infamous breeding program. He had paired GhostWalker males with some of the females. Kane had served a short period of time at one of the breeding facilities — in fact, he'd aided some of the women in escaping. Brian had also served at one of Dr. Whitney's facilities. Few knew where the doctor was working; he moved in secret and was heavily guarded at all times. Mack and Kane had come to the conclusion that it was not in anyone's best interest to work with or near him.

Kane had testified in a closed hearing, as had Brian, turning over evidence of Whitney's breeding program to Sergeant Major Griffen, as per the chain of command, but the meeting had been top secret and no one knew the outcome. The men had rejoined Team Three under Colonel Wilford's command and had gone on several missions. Griffen worked directly under the colonel and presumably had turned all evidence and reports over to him. Kane didn't talk about his time with Whitney, but he hadn't slept much since and he'd definitely been searching for someone. Mack was fairly certain it was one of the women he'd helped escape the breeding compound. Mack still had trouble believing such a thing had existed.

"Tell me about pairing. What is that?"

Kane sighed. "Are you sure you want to know? Sometimes it's better to keep your head in the sand."

"Tell me about Whitney," Mack insisted.

Mack did his job and took his men where the sergeant major directed them. They had a damn good record when it came to rescuing hostages from cities where no one knew who was the enemy and who was innocent. He enjoyed being enhanced with all the added things it allowed him to accomplish, but the rumors he was hearing about some of the experiments Whitney had conducted along with the genetic enhancements made him realize they were dealing with someone who might be brilliant but as mad as a hatter.

"He's been allowed to do whatever he wanted without answering to anyone for so long that he believes himself above the law, above even the president. He considers himself a great patriot and defender of the country. He believes the end justifies the means."

"So basically you're telling me that everything Jaimie told me about him and his experiments is probably true and I should have listened to her."

"Yeah. That's what I'm saying. I said it

back then too. She's too damn smart to ignore."

"I hear a reprimand in there."

"I'm just saying, you hurt Jaimie again and I'm going to tear out your heart and feed it to you."

Kane sounded casual enough, but he wasn't kidding. Kane, like most of his team, was protective of women. Mack's mother had been the one stable influence most of them had. All of them had developed what the psychs referred to as being overprotective. And maybe they all were, but when it came to women, they didn't like anyone messing around with them.

Kane had risked his career, his life, everything he was, to do the honorable thing and help the women get out of the facility where they were being held. Orders or not, as far as Kane was concerned, what Whitney had demanded of them wasn't honorable. He had done everything in his power to take the evidence to the commanders to get it stopped. Now Kane had a deep distrust of Whitney and the chain of command, which meant Mack did also. Ever since Kane had returned from that assignment, Mack had watched his best friend's back even closer.

"I hear you."

"And the next time she tells you something is a red flag, put your damned ego aside and listen to the woman."

"I'm all about the listening." Mack sounded as pious as possible.

Kane rolled over and groaned. "I'm getting back on the couch. I swear, if we're staying here for any length of time, I'm buying a bed tomorrow."

"We're staying. And you're getting soft. You've slept on the ground more than you've slept in a bed over the last few years. You're also getting old."

"Says the boss from his superior position on a nice soft bed."

"It's a single bed, Kane. It may be soft, but there isn't much to it, and lying next to her is killing me."

"Then move, you stubborn bastard."

"Not a chance. I'm establishing my territory. She's not going to let me back into her life so easily. She's made up her mind to stay away from me."

Kane tried to make himself smaller on the couch. He had a thick, heavily muscled chest and big arms. One kept flopping off the couch uncomfortably.

"You know, Mack, things aren't always black and white. Sometimes, for whatever reasons, we have to do things that we can't live with. They just sit in the gut and keep

103

you up at night. We're all wired differently. You have a gift, something inside you that lets you make a decision and live with the consequences. The rest of us aren't so lucky. Jaimie had to do what she did to survive. After what I saw in that compound with Whitney, if I could get out, I would, but they aren't going to let any of us go. Not now. It isn't about the money and training anymore. We're too dangerous to them."

Mack was silent, turning the words over in his mind. Kane had come back troubled from his last assignment. Not only troubled, but suddenly very leery of every mission, questioning everything, as Jaimie had. Mack had known then that the questions in his mind, the doubt rising up with each new nugget of information about Whitney and his experiments, weren't just because Jaimie had planted the seed and suspicion was growing.

Kane and Brian had come to him, careful of what they said, fearful that they were on a death list and not wanting Mack to be there with them. He had gone up the chain of command and set into motion a hearing. He hadn't been allowed to go with his men.

"I'm sorry, Kane. You're right. I should have listened to her. I should have investigated what Whitney was doing before I took us all down this path. Once we were on it, I just wanted us all to survive." He had watched over them, trying to figure out what each of them had been gifted — or cursed — with and how best to cope with it.

"We're all responsible, Mack. We all listened to the propaganda, took the tests, and thought we were lucky when we passed. I can't even say I don't like my abilities. We were all lucky in that we can work alone. Most of the others can't exactly survive on their own in the world. But something's not right about any of this, and they know I went after Whitney and I'm not going to stop until he's brought down. I think Jaimie knew it all along. She never trusted him. She kept asking us to slow down."

"I thought it was the violence. She's always been squeamish about violence." Mack inhaled her feminine scent and nuzzled the soft mass of curls. He'd even loved that about her. The trait seemed soft like Jaimie and made him feel all the more protective of her. He'd been in that position since they were children and it seemed natural and right. He led. She followed. Except she hadn't followed him this time; she'd run. Fast. Far.

He'd kept track of her. He'd used his connections and he'd known her last residence before she'd moved here, to San Francisco. He would have found her here as well. Because Jaimie Fielding wasn't going to get away from him any more than the Ghost-Walkers were going to get away from the government. They'd known going in: once a GhostWalker, always a GhostWalker. Kane was right. They were just too damn dangerous to lose track of.

"You all right, Kane?" He asked in the darkness the words he could never seem to ask in the light of day. Kane wasn't always a sharing man.

There was a long silence and then a sigh. "I don't know. I did some things — bad things. Things I'm ashamed of and I can't take back."

Mack held his breath. Kane never talked about those weeks in Whitney's facility and what he'd had to do to survive. Mack waited. Hoped. Sent up a silent prayer that Kane would keep talking.

"I hurt a woman, Mack. I did my best to help her, but still, she suffered because of me. I have to live with that. I don't know where she is, but she's carrying my child."

Mack's heart nearly stopped beating. "Are you certain, Kane?"

"Yeah. I'm certain. She's out there somewhere, unprotected. On the run. Hiding from Whitney. Probably hiding from me."

"And you want to find her?" Mack asked cautiously. The news was more disturbing than he could almost believe. Kane. A woman. A child. Kane saying a woman suffered on his account. He wanted more of an explanation, but with Kane, one waited until he volunteered the information.

"I *have* to find her. She's carrying my child." There was a pause. A heartbeat. "I can't let her go, Mack."

"Then we'll find her, bro. We'll find her."

CHAPTER 4

Jaimie woke with a start, her heart pounding, her mouth dry. Another nightmare. Wouldn't they ever go away and leave her in peace? She moved and immediately came into contact with Mack's muscular thigh. He was asleep, his breathing even. From across the room, Kane snored gently. Very carefully, knowing what a light sleeper Mack was, Jaimie turned over, propping herself up on one elbow so she could look down into his face. She wanted to touch him, reassure herself he was really there, right beside her. Reality, not a dream. He looked younger in his sleep, ridiculously long lashes guarding his cold, black eyes. His thick, dark hair spilled over his forehead. There was a blue black shadow along his jaw.

It was frightening how it made her feel having Mack there with her. Confused. Elated. Scared. Safe. Mack had always made her feel safe, even though she was grown up now and he led them all into dangerous situations. Mack made them feel safe and somewhat immortal. He made them believe that if they were together, they could do anything.

Beside her, Mack stirred, murmured her name softly, his breath warm on her neck as he turned, fitting his body around hers, his hand sliding to her hip. The edge of her shirt had ridden up and Mack's fingertips pressed into the bare skin at her waist. It felt as if four red-hot brands were touching her. The fire spread through her body like a storm she couldn't control. Her breasts ached, there was an answering rush of liquid heat just as there always had been. As if two years hadn't gone by. Just like that, it started all over again.

Jaimie tried to ease away from him, but there wasn't much room, she was already on the edge of the bed, up against the wall. As she moved, Mack made a small protest in his throat, his body following hers possessively, one leg sliding over her thigh to trap her against him. His hand slid over the curve of her hip to move along her flat stomach, fingers splayed wide as if taking in as much of her bare skin as possible.

Jaimie rubbed her hot cheek into the coolness of the pillow. If she squirmed around, heaven only knew what Mack might do in his sleep. Suddenly, she was scowling darkly. Obviously, he must be used to sleeping with a woman. While she'd been alone for two years, he had found others to replace her. The thought infuriated her.

"Move over, you jerk!" Jaimie shoved at his shoulder, hissing the words in a low, furious voice.

His mocking laughter was soft in her ear, alerting her to the fact that he had been awake all along. Jaimie turned toward him in a little fit of temper, shoving at the heavy wall of his chest.

"Settle down, honey. I was only teasing you." Both of his hands covered hers, clamped her palms to his heavily muscled chest. His thumbs moved over her knuckles, the small, intimate gesture disturbingly sensuous.

"This bed isn't big enough for the two of us," Jaimie said, alarmed at the breathless catch in her voice and the way her body just wanted to melt into his.

"This bed is ridiculous," Mack agreed, "but it's all we have."

"It's my bed, McKinley. It's perfectly adequate without you in it." Jaimie tugged at her hands to free them from his grasp.

Mack tightened his grip, black eyes glinting with humor. "Where do you expect me to sleep? Kane took the couch."

"He fell off it, remember? Let go. You weren't supposed to get under the covers." She was whispering to keep from waking up Kane.

"I was cold. Honestly, Jaimie, don't be so hard-hearted. You wouldn't want me to catch pneumonia."

A faint derisive snicker came from across the room.

"My sentiments exactly," Jaimie concurred. She was wearing herself out with the ridiculous tug-of-war over who had possession of her hands. She knew Mack in this mood. He would go on for hours; worse, she was beginning to have trouble containing her own sense of humor.

"Stay out of this, Cannon," Mack ordered. "I have enough trouble with Jaimie here. You know how out of sorts she gets when she hasn't had enough sleep." Deliberately, he tugged her body onto its side, his arms firmly around her again.

"I'm never out of sorts," Jaimie protested.

Kane cleared his throat. "Actually, honey, that's a bald-faced lie. If you don't get eight hours of sleep, you're vicious."

"No one asked you," Jaimie groused.

"You woke me up," he grumbled. "What

do you expect? Oh, all right, I'll help you out. If she's going to be so damned contrary, Mack, I'll take the bed and you can have the couch," Kane suggested slyly.

"It's my bed," Jaimie pointed out belligerently. "I didn't offer to share with either of you."

Mack nuzzled her silky hair, inhaled her fresh, clean scent. Like hell Kane was going to switch places. Kane knew it too. "I can't believe your manners have disintegrated in such a short time."

"We worked hard to teach you," Kane added sorrowfully.

"It was the other way around. Without me, you two wouldn't even know what civilization was all about," Jaimie argued indignantly.

Mack took several silky strands of her hair in his mouth, tugged gently as he allowed them to slide off his tongue through his lips. He laughed softly when Jaimie took a poorly aimed swipe at him, missing by several inches. "This woman has such a temper, Kane." Mack surrounded her arms with his own, crowding even closer, dwarfing her with his size. "So contrary."

"I don't think so," Jaimie protested. She pressed her smiling mouth into the pillow. They'd always been like this. Talking back and forth and making her laugh when she didn't want to.

"Fortunately we'll have plenty of time to work on these little imperfections," Kane said.

"I've got a great idea," Jaimie ventured. "I'll take the couch and you two jokers can share the bed."

Mac's arm muscles tightened perceptibly as he clamped her to him. "I'm not about to share this dinky little bed with that shaggy bear," Mack objected. "He kicks like a mule."

"He wakes up throwing punches." Kane imparted the information with relish. "I refuse to be anywhere near him."

"The arrangements are just fine." Mack was emphatic.

His fingers brushed her breast and she wasn't smiling anymore. Just like that her body flooded with heat. She was certain it was an accident, but it didn't matter. She couldn't do this, slip back into the old patterns so easily, teasing each other and feeling the fire sweeping through her body, hot and wild and so tempting. She felt alive again and that scared her so much that for a terrible moment she couldn't think or breathe. Her heart slamming hard in her chest, she leapt from the bed, right over the top of Mack, landing like a cat, crouched on the floor, and then scrambling backward, away from him.

"Jaimie?" Mack sounded troubled. "Are you all right? We were just teasing, honey."

She forced words past the sudden lump clogging her throat. "I'm okay. I still get claustrophobia at times." She was hyperventilating, just as she had all those nights for months when she woke up alone without Mack beside her. She could feel sweat beading on her forehead, dangerous now, because both Mack and Kane could smell fear. Cursing under her breath, she moved to the window, staring out over the water.

The sea always calmed her. That was a good part of the reason for her chosen location. She wasn't an anchor and the chaos of people could cause severe damage. The sea helped block the waves of energy coming at her, or maybe it just drowned out the worst of it. Whatever. She didn't want to think about what Whitney had done and what she'd become thanks to him. She couldn't lose herself, not when it had taken her so long to build her self-esteem and courage. Mack couldn't just come back and steal it all away. She wasn't that same innocent girl.

When she was with Mack, he overshadowed her. She knew she was intelligent, more so than both Mack and Kane, yet she never felt strong around them. They had a different kind of strength and for some reason, she could never quite feel equal to them. She couldn't blame Mack for treating her as someone he had to take care of when she didn't act like a partner, but she had stood on her own and she liked herself. She didn't want to go back.

A tingling awareness crept down the back of her neck and she took a breath. "Who do you have watching me, Mack?" There was accusation in her voice.

Mack glanced at his watch. "It's Gideon's shift. In another hour Jacob will take over on the roof. We've got a ship coming in around eleven and the boys will be coming off that and securing residences around the neighborhood. We made certain the rooms we wanted were open. You've got someone watching you across the way. He's got to be a GhostWalker, or he's a damn good terrorist. We didn't even get close to him. He won't go back to his room, so we've got people going through it. If he left anything behind, we'll find it."

"If he's that good, there won't be anything," she said with a sigh as she swung around and leaned one hip against the windowsill. If Mack was right, her warning system had definitely failed. She shook her head. Everything had been right. Good. And now, in one moment, she was back into something she couldn't handle. Mack and Kane had turned her life upside down just like they always did.

Jaimie turned back to the window and stared down at the water, her fingers twisting together, betraying her agitation. "Maybe you'd answer a question for me, Kane."

"Does it have to be tonight?" Kane asked easily. "Or rather this morning?"

Mack sat up, swinging his legs over the side of the bed. Both Jaimie and Kane sounded tense in spite of their deliberately casual tones. He knew them both too well. The muscles in his belly knotted uncomfortably.

Jaimie didn't turn, but stood unnaturally stiff, hands linked behind her back like a soldier — waiting for bad news. "Now would be a good time."

"So shoot."

"What do you think the odds are on you and Mack chasing a shipment of explosives halfway around the world and ending up in San Francisco at the wrong warehouse?"

"Jaimie, I told you." Mack stood up and padded across the room on silent feet to stand behind her. "Do you think I would lie about this? Lie to you?"

"Let Kane answer me," Jaimie suggested quietly. "I think it's a legitimate question, don't you, Kane?"

Mack shook his head. "I took the order from Sergeant Major, not Kane. I made the mistake, didn't adequately check things out." Mack hastened to defend Kane. "We were so close to catching them after following the shipment and I didn't want to delay even a few minutes."

"I want Kane to answer my question, Mack," Jaimie insisted, her voice very low.

Kane's sigh was audible. "No, you don't, honey, you already have your answers and a closed mind."

"That isn't an answer."

"What are you accusing Kane of, Jaimie?" Mack demanded.

Kane ignored Mack and posed his own question. "What are the odds on you training nearly three years, topping everyone in every drill, and freaking out on the first mission?"

Mack stiffened, instant rage coiling in his gut. "Damn you, Kane, you're going too far." He looked from one to the other. "I don't know what's going on here, but stop."

Jaimie's fingers curled around Mack's

forearm, silencing him. "No, Mack. I want him to continue." There was no mistaking the accusation in her voice.

Mack turned to look at his oldest and closest friend, the man he considered a brother. Kane remained lying on the couch, his legs stretched out, his fingers linked behind his neck, his eyes staring up at the ceiling as he spoke.

"What are the odds you would have a terrible fight with Mack and me, when we never had a fight before?" Kane's voice was very even, almost unconcerned. "And what do you think the odds would be, Jaimie, on you taking off, checking into a hotel you picked at random in a city you picked at random, and running into your old college professor?"

Jaimie's nails dug into Mack's skin. He didn't think she was aware of it. "That isn't an answer, Kane. It's like you to try to throw me off the track, but I'm not going to let it happen."

"What good is this?" Kane demanded, the coolness abruptly evaporating. "We're here with you. Does it matter what brought us here? You had all the time in the world to figure things out. You didn't want to know. Why the hell do it now that we're here with you? Why care now how it all came about?"

118

"Maybe I can accept manipulation better than I can accept betrayal."

Mack swore and yanked her around. "What the hell does that mean, Jaimie?"

She blinked back tears and met his furious gaze. "Kane knows what it means. Am I being set up, Kane?"

"Well, damn it, Jaimie." Kane sounded astonished. "You're my family. You're Mack's woman. Why the hell would you get it in your head that I'd do anything but protect you?"

"This doesn't feel like protection to me." Jaimie moved away from Mack with a small, defensive gesture.

Mack's stomach knotted. "Jaimie." He didn't know what to say.

"I have a life now." She motioned toward the window. "And now I'm right back in the middle of something I don't want. I'm not an anchor the way all of you are. I barely get by. It's a struggle every single day. Most nights I lie in bed with a killer headache wondering if I'm going to make it through the night. I'm not going back, not for either of you."

Mack ignored her small retreat and followed her, wrapping his arms around her. "You never get headaches if I'm with you."

Not headaches. But heartaches, and that

was worse. She wasn't going to let him comfort her, or change the subject. Deliberately, Jaimie stepped away from him.

"What are you really doing here?" Jaimie walked to the sink and poured herself a glass of water to gain her equilibrium. Mack looked hurt. He *felt* hurt. That was the last thing she wanted, but their coming was no coincidence.

Mack raked both hands through his hair in agitation. "I told you it was a mistake."

Jaimie wandered across the room to the street side, staring moodily down at the tendrils of fog reaching in off the bay.

"Come on, Jaimie," Kane said, his voice utterly calm. "We didn't bring this down on you and you know it. We're the convenient whipping boys. You were manipulated and you let yourself be. You wanted out and you jumped at the easy way out. It came with strings. As for who is watching you, they were here before we got here. You're safer with us close than not." He yawned. "I'm not getting up at five A.M. to hash this out. If you two are going to keep talking, do it in sign language."

Get her away from the window. Get her back! Gideon's voice burst into Mack's head.

Without hesitation, Mack leapt forward

and tackled Jaimie, bringing her to the ground. Kane rolled off the couch, hitting the floor and fighting his way out of his sleeping bag, gun already in his hand, indicating Gideon had called the warning to both men telepathically. Kane crawled to the window, where Mack's body covered Jaimie's. She didn't protest or ask questions, but lay quietly beneath both men.

What do you have, Gideon? Is Superman back?

I wish. I think these two came looking for their buddies. They're loaded for bear.

Can you get a shot at them?

Yes. I can take both out, but it won't be quiet, boss.

"Tell me," Jaimie said.

There was no panic in her voice, but there was suppressed rage. Mack's gaze met Kane's above her head. "Who are they, Jaimie?" Mack asked.

"You tell me, Mack," she shot back and for the first time, struggled to get out from under him.

"You little liar." Mack hissed the words in her ear, bending close, trapping her beneath him. "You know who they are. They aren't terrorists coming to get you, are they? Not the ones we've been following."

"They aren't any friends of mine." She

turned her head to glare at Kane. "I'm not going back. Not *ever.* I don't care how many you send after me. I will never go back to work for Whitney. I've hacked into enough files to know what he's doing and he isn't alone in it. He experimented on *children.* And he's got a breeding program. The women are forced to pair with a man of Whitney's choosing. It's barbaric and illegal and the women are held prisoners with no one to help them."

Mack saw Kane wince and covered for him automatically, catching Jaimie's chin and forcing her to look at him. "Does he know you've been collecting evidence against him?"

"Get off me, Mack." She bit out each word between her teeth. "Right now."

He stayed where he was for a full minute, looking into her eyes. With a sinking heart he realized the truth. "You don't trust me."

He had lost something beyond measure if she didn't trust him. Jaimie had believed the sun rose and set with him. She had believed in everything he did and said. He'd been her hero. He waited but he saw it on her face, in the way she schooled her expression. She wasn't going to tell him anything about her current life. Not one thing. And that just might get her killed.

"Damn it, Jaimie. This is Mack. You know me. You know Kane. We're your family."

The voice in his head whispered again. *One is a sniffer, like Jacob. He's running his hand along the doors and windows and he knows they're wired to blow them to kingdom come. I could take them out.*

We don't know enough yet, Mack objected reluctantly. He wanted Jaimie safe and the temptation to kill the two men was strong. But if they were GhostWalkers under legitimate orders, Mack's team had already made one serious mistake when Javier killed the two men earlier. They were trying to identify the bodies fast. They didn't need to add two more.

He eased his body away from Jaimie. She sat up, her back to the wall, drawing her knees up, staying below the window. They stared at each other.

"We're family, Jaimie."

She shook her head and there was a flash of pain in her eyes. "I don't know what we are anymore, Mack, but we aren't family. You chose them over me. The GhostWalkers. And they're evil. I can't trust anyone who is part of it."

He swore and turned away from her, his hands itching to shake her. This was his fault. He knew it was. She'd lost faith in him and no longer looked to him or the others to help her. But whatever she was into was definitely trouble.

"We have the same code of honor we've always had," Kane said, his voice calm, much calmer than Mack could have managed. "That's ridiculous for you to think just because an evil man started the program that it makes us all tainted. Our commanding officers run legitimate missions and we save lives. We specialize in hostage rescue and put our lives on the line all the time."

"So why are you here, Kane?" she demanded again.

Mack frowned. Jaimie was being very persistent and Jaimie was extremely intelligent. He looked at his best friend. "Do you know something I don't, Kane?"

Kane sighed. "Do you really think this is the best time to go into it? Of course I knew they'd watch Jaimie; you knew it too. She's a multimillion-dollar weapon and she's smart as a whip. Not to mention she can do things no one else can do and no one, not even Whitney, can figure out how the hell she does it. I have no idea what she's into or why these men are sniffing around her home now."

Gideon's voice whispered in Mack's head

again. *Superman has joined the party. He's good, Mack. His camouflage is every bit as good as or better than mine. He's like a damned ghost. I barely caught sight of him. He moved to get a better angle on the two moving around Jaimie's house. He's got the mean end of a rifle on them and looks like he knows how to use it.*

Mack looked at Kane over the top of Jaimie's head, knowing Gideon had sent the information to Kane as well. They had another player in the mix, with no way of knowing if he was a friend or enemy.

Has he spotted you? Kane asked.

I don't think so, but I'm pinned down. If I move to check out the two below, he's got a clear shot at me.

Mack turned the information over in his mind. *Stay where you are. Javier wouldn't have left an opening for visitors to come in, and Jaimie's got this place fully secure. If they break in, we'll know about it, most likely with a big boom. Keep your eye on Superman. Try to get a good look at him through the scope, but don't expose yourself. Just watch him.*

"Are you going to let me in on what's going on?" Jaimie asked.

"Like you share information with me?" Mack asked and instantly regretted it. "We're trying to sort it all out. Gideon spot-

125

ted the two men moving around the first floor, looking for a way in. They were obviously looking for their friends, the ones Javier took out."

"I see. Did you tell Gideon not to include me in the broadcast, or did he make that decision all on his own?" She knew Gideon had to be following orders.

Mack ignored her question. "And then someone else showed up on one of the rooftops and he's watching them too. We're fairly certain he isn't with the others. I think we've got two factions here."

"Great. You show up, Mack, and my life is instantly turned upside down." Jaimie swept both hands through her hair, struggling not to cry.

The insanity had started all over again. And the hurt. As much as she hated it all, she should have been included. She fought to make a life for herself, but now . . . She shook her head. She couldn't entirely blame Mack, although she wanted to. It would be so much easier to drive a wedge deeper between them, but that was a coward's way out. She didn't want to love him. To feel weak inside when he was close. Her body felt out of control, alert and alive around him. Almost desperate, and she wasn't a desperate woman.

She was blaming him unfairly for the firestorm she'd brought down on herself. She'd been gathering information against Whitney, but more important, she'd been trying to find out who was supporting him, who was sanctioning his criminal experiments. Hacking into a government site was risky business. She had a high security clearance, but not high enough, not when they were protecting their connections with Whitney. Someone had buried him deep and there were so many layers and red flags, she may have tripped one without knowing it. She hadn't thought so, but she had no doubt in her mind that if she was found out, they would erase her. She'd gone after them anyway.

Whitney had taken all their lives. He'd promised to enhance them psychically. He already had conducted experiments on children, which none of them had known. He knew the effects it would have on them, but he'd done it anyway. Worse, he'd altered them genetically as well. And he'd paired them using pheromones, with the idea of breeding the perfect soldier. The man was a maniac and someone had to stop him. Unfortunately he still had powerful friends in high places and he had access to all the money in the world. He could move around from one facility to another and often had military protection where he went.

She couldn't blame Mack, as much as she'd like to, and it made her ashamed of herself that she'd let him think she believed he'd brought trouble with him. As much as she didn't want to admit it, he probably had saved her a lot of trouble. She had two escape routes, and may have gotten away, but she had sunk most of her money into her current project, looking to build a future not only for herself but for the others should there be need.

"I'm sorry, Mack. I shouldn't have said that. This isn't your fault and I know it isn't." Jaimie sighed and leaned back against the wall. "I had a couple of years to pretend my life was my own. I don't know who these men are. As far as I know, I haven't had anyone watching me until Gideon discovered the room across the way. And I have to tell you, no one has ever managed to surprise me, so either he just set up there, or I'm losing my abilities."

"The room had been lived in for a time, Jaimie."

She bit her lower lip and looked away from him, for the first time very shaken. If her radar system was faulty, she was in real trouble. She'd always been able to detect danger. She knew where the enemy was and became aware of anyone stalking them. Even snipers would have a difficult time targeting her. If that was no longer true, there was no place she was safe.

"What does Gideon say?" She knew Gideon was always their eyes. The man was an eagle, a ghost, and a phenomenal shot all rolled into one.

"He calls the man Superman. Says this Superman has the same attributes as he does. Do you have trouble detecting Gideon? Maybe it's something in his makeup."

She frowned. "I don't know. Gideon's never hunted me. At least not to my knowledge. He's always been with the rest of you."

"Do your thing, Jaimie," Kane suggested. "Tell us where they all are. Everyone you can detect."

Her brows drew together. It was a gift they all wished they had, to be able to detect the enemy's exact position. She was never certain exactly how she did it, her mind just expanded and she felt the energy, dark, sometimes malevolent, but always strong. They all wanted to know how she did it, but there was no real explanation. They thought she was stubborn, and maybe she'd become stubborn, sick of what they wanted from her.

She closed her eyes, inhaled to clear her mind and let go, seeking outside of herself to find those hunting her. She felt the ocean first, the surge of power that connected with her almost immediately, heightening her senses and expanding her range. She felt the two men moving around the corner of her warehouse, staying low as they carefully examined the building for weaknesses in security.

She felt their heartbeats, the adrenaline in their systems. She felt the breath moving through their bodies. Anger. Fear. Puzzlement. She could almost read their thoughts, but the body chemistry was enough to know they were enemies. She forced herself past them to encompass the street and buildings running alongside her warehouse.

A man huddled on the steps of the building to the right of her. His mind was a haze, a blur of no thinking, just shivering. He was cold and wanted more alcohol, but was oblivious to anyone else. Up the street a group of a four partied together. Drugs raced through their systems, not adrenaline. She examined the rooftops. She knew Gideon was up there somewhere along with the one they called Superman, yet she couldn't find either of them.

She opened her eyes and looked at Mack.

"I don't know how long I've been under surveillance. He has to be a GhostWalker. I can't detect Gideon either."

"But you can detect both of us?" Mack asked.

She nodded. "And the two outside moving around the first floor, looking for a way in."

"But not Gideon or the other man?"

She shook her head. "That's never happened before, Mack. Not once. Not in all the times I trained. What's different about Gideon?"

"I don't know, but I don't want you saying anything. We'll need to protect that information. Don't document it," Mack cautioned.

She crawled away from the window to the center of the room where her furniture was. "Because you know they'd dissect him to see if they could make you all that way."

"The mysterious 'they' again," Mack said. "You use 'they' and 'you' a lot. You're a GhostWalker too, Jaimie. You gave your consent just like the rest of us. And not everyone in the program is corrupt."

She sank into a chair across from Kane. "I know that, Mack. I just despise the entire mess. Whitney's given some people cancer. He's hurt them in order to see if he could

131

speed the healing process. He's so far out of control and someone knows it. More than one someone, yet they protect him. They want his research and we're all expendable to protect it. And we have foreign governments wanting one of us to dissect so they can build the same kind of soldier. Do you think any of us are going to have a life if we don't get out now?"

Kane slipped his gun back beneath his sleeping bag, knowing Jaimie hated the weapon. "We're going to be fine as long as we stick together, Jaimie."

Her eyes met his. There was despair there. She was too intelligent to be reassured like a child and they both knew it. She had logged in hundreds of hours going over Whitney's experiment. It read like a horror story. Her temples throbbed with pain, an aftermath of using psychic ability. It helped with Mack and Kane in the room, but still, the pain made her stomach lurch.

She didn't want to think about all the children Whitney had conducted his experiments on. The adults had been bad enough, but she knew there had been children involved. The man was still out there, on the loose, condoned and aided by a group of power-hungry men who believed themselves above the law. The men in Ghost-

Walker Team Three were all members of her family. No, they weren't bound by blood, but they'd chosen years ago to band together and make it through life together. Now they were all in jeopardy.

"I can't save them," she said aloud, and then was horrified that she'd spoken without thinking.

She could no longer trust either Mack or Kane. They had embraced their new bodies and minds and they believed they could make a huge difference. They were honorable men and they fought for what they believed. She was no longer part of that circle. No matter how familiar, no matter how much she loved them, she had to remember she wasn't part of what they were doing and if orders came down regarding her — both men would follow those orders.

As if reading her mind, Mack sank into the chair beside hers and reached out to take her hand. "We're here in San Francisco hunting this shipment of weapons and the men who are going to buy them. It's our one chance to get at the Doomsday unit. They happen to be in the same neighborhood you're living in. Whatever that means. However it happened. Someone is threatening you. Let's just call a truce until we remove the threat and I have my terrorists

133

in custody."

"You don't take them into custody, Mack," she pointed out. "You assassinate them."

"I do whatever it takes. And I'll do whatever it takes to keep you alive, Jaimie. Whatever is going on here is not of my making. You wanted out. I was hoping you would get out and make a life for yourself."

He had hoped she'd come back to him and tell him she was missing him every single minute of every single day — that she couldn't breathe without him. That hadn't happened. It didn't look like it was going to happen anytime soon.

"We're a family," Kane added. "We'd never leave you until we knew the threat to you was past. So we'll be moving in here for a long while. We've already gotten permission. The boys are setting up their rooms; we'll be here with you. You'll be safe."

"What does Sergeant Major want in return? He doesn't do anything for free."

"That's for us to worry about," Mack said. "Not you. Let's just enjoy whatever time we have together while we figure all this out. I missed you, Jaimie." There was an ache in his voice. An unexpected lump in his throat. She had no idea. He'd felt shattered. Fractured. And he'd had no idea how much he needed her or depended on her until she was gone.

There was resentment in him. Stubbornness. She'd *left* him. Walked out. Whatever her reasons, however stupid he'd been, she'd left him. For a moment it took all his discipline not to yank her out of the chair and shake her into seeing sense. They were meant for each other. He'd thought — hoped — that when he saw her again, the impact she had on him would lessen, but it was worse than ever. He craved her like some terrible addiction. He wanted the adoration back, that look of absolute love in her eyes. He wanted her soft body streaking fire through his. He wanted the sound of her laughter and her trust. More than anything he wanted that back.

Jaimie pushed both hands through her hair. Living with Mack again. She doubted she could survive it. But what else could she do? She wasn't stupid. Someone had sent GhostWalkers after her and that meant Whitney was probably on to her and she was in danger. If he knew the evidence she'd been compiling against him, he'd never let her live. And she was tracing his connections, getting closer to his supporters. They would be even more dangerous than Whitney. He was obscure. A ghost. But his back-ers had political lives. They were powerful men with lots to lose and they'd never let her expose their crimes to the world.

She'd known when she started researching and documenting that she was entering a dangerous game, but she had always known she had to find a way to protect her family. She loved them and she wasn't going to see them thrown to the wolves. No one was going to set them up to be killed by sending them on a bogus mission. She'd make certain of that.

"Can't you stay in one of the places around here, Mack? I'm used to being on my own and you're bossy."

Kane made a sound in his throat that was cut off when Mack shot him a warning look. "I'm not in the least bit bossy. I know how to keep you alive, and you tend to trust everyone."

She scowled at him. "I do not. Do you see what I'm talking about? I've been in business for two years, Mack. I haven't needed you to tell me who I can work for."

"That doesn't mean you couldn't have benefited from my experience."

A slow smile curved her mouth. "Now you're just teasing."

"I'm glad you remember what teasing is."

She deserved that, she knew. Mack and

Kane were the two people she loved most in the world and she hadn't exactly been hospitable. She'd accused Kane outright of betrayal, and there was still a certainty that he had known the address was wrong. He had been close to the one new man when they'd come into her home, the one they weren't certain of, and it had been Kane who had blocked his weapon, almost before Mack had identified her.

"Okay, fine. But you're getting your own beds. I mean it. I'm not sharing my bed."

"Who wants that tiny little thing?" Mack scoffed. "We'll get manly furniture tomorrow."

The two poking around are leaving, Top. I have the feeling they'll be back, Gideon reported. *But they're going to do a little investigating. Superman has slipped away.*

Did he see you? Mack asked.

Naw. I just became part of the wall. Never moved.

We're going to get some sleep. Thanks, Gideon. Be careful. And don't trust anyone not our own.

Okay, Mom. Gideon laughed softly in his ear.

Mack sighed. Trying to keep them all in line was difficult. "We can turn in. The threat's over."

"Lucky us," Jaimie muttered.

CHAPTER 5

Morning light filtered through the windows when a loud blast shattered the peace of sleep. Kane and Mack leapt to their feet, both reaching for their weapons, or at least both tried to. Kane nearly crashed to the floor, whirling around a little wildly, gun in his fist.

"What the hell?" Kane demanded, wiggling free and crawling across the floor to the window.

Jaimie dragged the blanket over her head with a groan. This was not the start to the day she had anticipated. "It's the doorbell. It's probably Joe."

"Doorbell? That's some kind of fog horn. Are you kidding, Jaimie?" Kane and Mack exchanged one long disgusted look. The noise was louder the second time, more insistent.

"Joe?" Mack shook his head. "Lean out the window, Kane. See if you can't get a clear shot at him."

Alarmed, Jaimie sat up, pulling the blankets to her chin. "You can't shoot him."

"Why not?" Kane asked.

He looked wild enough to really do it, his hair spilling all over the place, his clothes disheveled, his eyes fierce.

"Because I forbid it, that's why." Jaimie tried to be stern, but the two looked as if they might have been drinking all night, disheveled and heavy-lidded, making her want to smile. Sleeping on the couch hadn't been as much fun as Kane thought it might be. There was some satisfaction in that since they'd taken over her house. She'd forgotten how crazy they could get, feeding off each other, until she never knew exactly how far either of them would really go.

The doorbell let out another long blast. "That's it." Mack scowled fiercely. "Shoot him, Kane. I'll take the blame and let her yell at me. It's worth it."

"You got it." Kane, looking like a panther, stalked along the bank of windows to one of the long, tall windows overlooking the street where the front door was.

Jaimie nearly flew across the room, laughing, grabbing at Kane's arm. "Don't you dare. It's ten o'clock, we overslept. It isn't his fault."

140

Mack found the intercom. "Drop dead, buddy," he snarled into the speaker.

Jaimie whirled around, horrified. "Mack, I can't believe you just did that. Get away from there." She turned hastily back to Kane, who was unlocking the window. "Get away from the window." She pushed her hands through her own hair, now as disheveled as Kane's. "You're both completely out of control."

"What's he look like?" Mack demanded. "A skinny little runt, I hope."

"I don't think so," Kane muttered, leaning halfway out the window. "He's a big son of a bitch, Mack. Really big."

Jaimie tugged on his arm. "This is embarrassing me, Kane. Get your head back inside this minute."

"Big? How big?" Mack lifted Jaimie right out of the way, craning his neck to peer out the window, fending Jaimie off with one hand. "Hell, Kane, he's over six foot. Shoot the bastard."

Jaimie bit her lip, laughing, pushing at both of them, trying to pull Kane's arm down. "You're both so insane. Get away from the window. You're going to embarrass me. And if he sees that gun, he's going to call the police and then what are we going to do, smart ones?"

The doorbell boomed a deep, dramatic, and very insistent intrusion. Mack headed toward the speaker. Jaimie put on a burst of speed and beat him to it, although one of Mack's talents was something close to teleportation so he'd obviously let her. She coughed twice, trying to control her voice, trying not to laugh.

"Joe, sorry, my family arrived very late last night and I overslept."

Mack reached around her trying to get to the intercom. She pushed at the solid wall of his chest as she spoke, so she sounded out of breath.

"You need help, Jaimie?" Joe's voice floated out from the speaker a little distorted. Jaimie's brain immediately sought out the reason and made a mental note to correct the problem.

"No, she doesn't need any help, you baboon," Mack answered rudely, stabbing at the talk button around Jaimie.

Fortunately, she cut off his last few words. "All right, that's enough. If you keep playing around, he's going to call the cops. How do you expect to explain the arsenal you brought up here? Go make yourself useful. Make coffee!" Jaimie turned back to the speaker. "Why don't we take today off, Joe? I'll make it up to you later."

"You're sure, Jaimie?" Joe sounded suspicious.

"Absolutely. I'll see you tomorrow. I'm sorry, we stayed up all night talking. I'm a little tired. You understand, don't you? I should have called you."

"If you're certain." Joe didn't sound certain. He sounded worried.

"Make it up to him? Exactly how do you plan to do that?" Mack's snort of disgust was loud. "Did you hear her voice, Kane? Pure syrup. She was dripping with it."

Kane closed the window with unnecessary force. "I heard her." His vivid green eyes pinned her. "We don't know the first thing about this character. He could be a mass murderer. Did you do a background check on him?"

Jaimie threw her hands into the air. "You should take your act onto the road. He's a carpenter helping me, not a serial killer. Stop being crazy and get yourselves coffee. It might make you civilized."

Kane's glinting green gaze met Mack's fathomless black one. Simultaneously they both shrugged powerful shoulders. "I'll call and get someone on it," Kane decided, making a move toward the phone.

"Don't you dare, Kane." Jaimie caught the receiver, slammed it back in its cradle. "I told you, I know Joe."

"How could you know him, Jaimie, really know him?" Kane demanded. "It's our job to look out for you."

"She serves him beer in her bedroom," Mack muttered helpfully.

"Go make coffee, Mack, and stop harping on the beer in the bedroom." Jaimie flung herself into one of her deep, comfortable armchairs. "You two have given me a rip-roaring headache."

Mack was immediately repentant. "We're only teasing, honey. We aren't really going to shoot him." Semi-teasing. They were going to investigate Joe Spagnola so thoroughly they'd know what kind of toothpaste he used in the morning.

The phone rang. Before Jaimie could move, Kane snagged it. "Dr. Fielding's residence." He sounded curt and inhospitable.

Jaimie rolled her eyes, and slid farther down in the chair. Why did she think she had missed them? They were totally impossible. She raked a hand through her thick mass of tangled curls. Even her hair had gone wild and primitive with them around. They thought they were a combination comedy and protection team.

"Your friend Joe," Kane announced, handing her the receiver, his eyes eagle sharp and slightly condemning.

The smile fading from Kane's eyes left Jaimie with a knot in the pit of her stomach. She had remembered all the good things about having Kane and Mack watching out for her and forgotten about this part. She never knew exactly how they were going to react to any given situation, and when it involved a man, they never reacted very well.

She glanced at Mack, who stood by the coffeepot. His hands stilled in midair, his head coming up alertly. His black eyes went ice-cold, a graveyard reflected there. His rugged features went completely expressionless, perfectly still, as if carved from stone.

Great. She'd seen that expression before. Mack wasn't taking this well. She forced a smile into her voice and greeted Joe.

Kane winced at the sweetness in Jaimie's voice and glanced at Mack. The last remnants of his humor drained away. He had known Mack McKinley every year of his life. They had done it all together, watching each other's backs along the way. Mack was the coolest, most easygoing, ice-cold bastard Kane had ever met. Unless Jaimie Fielding was involved. From the first moment Mack had laid eyes on the forlorn little girl, he had been crazy about her. She'd been so intelligent and courageous and Mack had always admired her. Mack was also the most dangerous, lethal human being Kane knew. And no one brought out that side of Mack like Jaimie did.

Jaimie seemed oblivious, laughing into the phone, reassuring Joe she was just fine, that her family joked around a lot. Kane watched Mack, wishing he could read that implacable mask. Mack never once took his eyes from Jaimie's face, obviously assessing her tone, her expression and body language. There was no mistaking that Jaimie had affection for Joe. There was even a flirty note in her voice.

Kane sighed. He had known Mack was in love with Jaimie long before Mack had even realized where his feelings for the girl were heading. They had both loved her for years, but Mack with a fierce, unswerving possessiveness he didn't seem to realize was unnatural. In those days, when they were kids, Mack thought he just wanted to protect her. As she'd gotten older, Mack refused to acknowledge what he felt for her, calling it "need," not "love." Kane suspected Whitney had made that need for her much stronger. Mack didn't look at other women, yet he was stubborn when it came to Jaimie. He was used to her unswerving devotion and when she'd left, he'd been blindsided. Kane had tried to warn him, but even Kane hadn't expected her to really leave.

Mack had always made their decisions, dictated their moves. Falling in love with her hadn't helped matters, especially when he couldn't acknowledge the emotion to himself, let alone to Jaimie. His feelings for her were too intense, too uncontrollable. He didn't handle her very well. Right now his face was as dark as thunder and his eyes had become a turbulent storm.

Kane let out his breath. *Hang up the phone, Jaimie,* Kane entreated silently, giving her a little push. Whitney had made the men more aggressive and certainly more dangerous when it came to their women. He had wanted to ensure there was a strong pairing, but as Kane had found out, he didn't always give the woman a choice in the matter.

Jaimie had always loved Mack, but Kane didn't know if she still did, or if the chemistry between them was genuine or manipulated. And how long could something like that last?

Jaimie's gaze met his and she hung up the phone and flashed a heart-stopping grin. "He thought maybe you two were desperate criminals holding me hostage. See, I told you he was sweet."

Mack dumped the coffee into the filter, a controlled violence in his movements. A muscle jumped in his jaw. "Yeah. Real sweet," he muttered.

His black gaze leapt to Kane's, a clear order in that look. Joe Spagnola was going to be so thoroughly checked out, they would know when he sneezed last. Kane's nod of agreement was nearly imperceptible, but there was satisfaction in the set of Mack's mouth when he poured the water into the pot.

"So, did you say there was only one bathroom in this place?" Kane took matters into his own hands to defuse the situation. He snatched up clean clothes and began edging toward the only walled-in room on the floor.

"Oh, no, you don't." Mack took the bait, hurrying to cut him off. "The shower's mine. You always fall asleep."

"Halt." Jaimie's clear command stopped both of them in their tracks. Looking very haughty, she took a stack of fluffy towels from the linen closet and marched purposefully across the room. "I can't believe your manners. This is my house."

"Hey," Kane protested. "We're honored guests."

"Who told you that lie?" Jaimie asked sweetly. "I'm a lady, in case you hadn't noticed, and ladies go first."

"I'll bet some woman made up that law," Kane groused.

"Haven't you ever heard of women's lib?" Mack asked.

Jaimie stuck her head around the door with a butter-melting-in-her-mouth kind of smile. "Of course I have. You two can cook."

The two men stared at each other. Mack flexed his muscles. Kane cracked his knuckles. They grinned at each other. "So, what does she have in the refrigerator?" Mack asked.

"Well," Kane drawled, "we know she has beer."

Jaimie shook her head as she listened to their combined male laughter. She was smiling again for no apparent reason. Her men were crazy and having them back was so familiar and comforting when she could hear them from a distance. She relaxed, letting the tension drain from her. All the rest of it would come with time, but for now, these few moments, she was going to savor being with them.

She stepped into the shower with its intricately tiled encased space. Both men looked good, both of them physically fit as always. Better than always. Kane had startling coloring with his blond hair, green eyes, and black lashes, brows, and bluish jaw. Even from a sisterly standpoint, Kane was good-looking. There were signs of strain on his face — lines that hadn't been there before. And shadows in his eyes. He smiled, but it wasn't all the way, never quite reaching his eyes.

Jaimie allowed the hot water to run down her face, over her full breasts, soaking the aches from her muscles. Mack. Just looking at him could make her weak. She'd loved him for as long as she could remember. It had taken a great deal of strength to pull away from him, to realize he wasn't compatible with her. She didn't have his adventurous spirit. For a long time she felt inferior because of it, but somewhere along the way, she'd come to learn that people were different. She wasn't wrong or inferior because she had a different makeup.

It hurt more than she'd expected to see him, but on the other hand, she had to face him someday. She'd set up a partnership so when he and Kane retired, they'd have a place to come. She had hoped to be married with five children by that time so she wouldn't crave him, but she could handle this. She had to handle it.

Damn it.

The cold, grim tone made him hesitate. Mack wasn't going to help his cause by getting angry. The last time Jaimie had a gun in her possession, things hadn't ended up going very well.

Jaimie, damn it, don't give me trouble, Mack snapped, shoving the words into Jaimie's mind. *We're in a world of hurt right now. Take the damn gun and use it if you need to. You know how to shoot.*

She didn't argue. She took the gun from Javier and laid it in her lap. She kept her face averted. Javier felt as if he'd slapped her. Tattling wasn't fun.

Jaimie stayed very still, drawing her knees up, trying desperately not to allow images into her mind. This wasn't her life. She had left it all behind. She'd tried to tell Mack what was happening, but the adrenaline rush was too addictive for a man like him to do without. Who could ever compete with that? He didn't care that the experiments had altered them genetically as well as enhanced their psychic abilities.

Their GhostWalker team had brought them all back together. That was what Mack and Kane saw. A chance to be together again, to look out for one another, to use their considerable talents in a positive way

69

■ ■ ■ ■

Mack stared out the window to the streets below. He didn't dare move. He leaned his forehead against the thick glass, desperately trying to shut out the sounds of the water running. Just the thought of Jaimie naked, eyes closed, her face turned up to allow the water to cascade over her breasts, run along her narrow ribs, her flat belly, still lower to the silky triangle of tight curls . . . He just stopped himself from groaning out loud.

Kane, damn him, would know immediately what was wrong. Mack rubbed his pounding temples. It felt like someone was using a pile driver on his head. His entire body burned, throbbed with pain. He hadn't felt this way in his worst teenage years.

He had a sudden vision of Joe Spagnola in that elegant glass shower with Jaimie, his hands moving over her body. Mack's large hand balled into a fist, slammed into the window ledge, instantly dispelling the scene.

Kane whistled softly. "Need a couple of aspirin?"

"The woman makes me crazy," Mack said between clenched teeth. His voice grated.

"The woman has always made you crazy," Kane was compelled to point out.

"Don't laugh about this, Kane. She's living in this . . ." Mack gestured wildly with his hands, swinging around to encompass the huge floor. "Look at this, a fucking warehouse in a not so great part of the city. And . . . *and,*" he added when he saw Kane's mouth twitch, "she's got some six foot Adonis drinking beer in her bedroom."

"Let's be fair, Mack, she probably had him drink it in the living room or maybe the kitchen," Kane replied mildly.

"Just how the hell can you tell the difference? If he's sitting in her living room, he can see the bed, can't he? Don't you think that's going to put a few ideas in the bastard's head?"

"Looking at Jaimie probably put ideas in this guy's head," Kane corrected. He poured two mugs of coffee.

"I think I'll have a private little chat with him. Find out what the hell he wants with her."

"What do you think he wants, you idiot? He's a man, isn't he? She's beautiful, intelligent, going to make a load of money, and she's single. He's no fool."

"You aren't helping, Kane." Mack curled his fingers into fists and hit his thighs. "He's looking to take advantage of her because she's lonely."

"Don't do anything to make her feel sorry for him. You know Jaimie and her underdog syndrome." Kane flashed a small grin. "And she didn't look all that lonely to me, not with beer in her fridge."

"It was a big mistake to give her all this time." Mack accepted the steaming mug of aromatic liquid. "So, all right, Jaimie doesn't like what we do . . ."

"Back up, Mack," Kane cautioned. "It's more than that and you know it. Jaimie can't stomach it. End of discussion. You, better than anyone, know that. You saw her. Don't get any ideas about discussing it with her. She was traumatized. In shock. She can't live this life."

"We can't just dance around the subject." Mack's black eyes gleamed like firestones.

"Isn't that exactly what you said the night she left?" Kane rested a hip against the butcher-block table.

Mack swore softly. He had bungled that so badly. "The whole thing went wrong from the start." He pressed his fingertips to his eyes, remembering that horrible night.

The weather turned bad as they were nearing the shore. They were in dark, skintight clothing, crepe-soled shoes. Nine men, one woman. Rhianna had been chosen for a special assignment in Brazil, leaving Jaimie

153

the only woman on the team. The raft was put over the side and the men took up the oars. No one spoke, their faces like masks in the reflection of the choppy water.

Mack hit the sand first, covered the others as they pulled the raft onto shore. The raft was camouflaged and the group headed stealthily up the beach. Two cars waited for them. No one spoke. At precisely 3:58 the cars split up, one stopping at the top of the block, the other at the other end. The silent team closed in on either side of the fourth building. Rain hammered at them, visibility was poor.

"Sentry," Jaimie hissed softly. "Another across the street, on the roof."

Kane moved around her to take care of the guard in front. A second man split from the group to warily cross the street. The rest waited, crouched in position, until first Kane and then Javier signaled.

They moved like lightning, entering the house from two points, heading for the second floor, third door on the left. Their informant had been positive the two French hostages were still alive in that room.

Jaimie suddenly signaled, her eyes wild with fear. "They're waiting for us, it's a trap, there's at least two dozen of them."

Mack didn't hesitate. "Pull out! Pull out!"

Mack gave the order clearly, quickly, into the radio.

All hell broke loose, machine gun fire erupting from all directions. They were forced up the stairs to the second floor. "Don't touch the doors, none of the doors." Jaimie yelled the warning into her radio, danger emanating in waves from their surroundings.

Mack stayed in the lead with Jaimie behind him, the others, and, finally, Kane bringing up the rear. Screams, blood, dragging their friends — it was an eternity of hell. A hailstorm of bullets followed them everywhere. Jaimie found their escape route with her unerring, uncanny, undefined ability. One door, looking like a closet, not wired, but locked. Jaimie dispatched the lock holding up two fingers.

Mack rolled in going to the left, Jaimie to the right, guns tracking. Two women, both screaming in French. "Hostage! Hostage!" Mack lowered his gun. In the same heartbeat, one of the women raised an Uzi. The other woman continued to plead in French, tears coursing down her face. She was between Jaimie and Mack's assassin.

"Shoot!" Kane's voice roared in Jaimie's ears and then both women went down in a hail of bullets.

It all happened in seconds. Jaimie screamed a horrified protest. Kane pushed her through, trying to keep her away from the second woman's body. Jaimie went to her knees, trying to cradle the dying woman's head in her arms. Bullets spit at them from every direction. Mack yanked her to her feet, dragging her out.

They nearly lost three men, carrying the bodies to the car. Brian, Jacob, and Gideon were all shot to hell. Jaimie had been stark white, her blue eyes two dark, haunting holes. There was blood on her clothes, and all over her hands, as she tried desperately to stem the life force draining from the men she'd grown up with. It had been a nightmare journey home, a fight all the way to keep the three men alive.

Hours later, when they were finally safe, Mack held Jaimie while she was sick, again and again, violent, gut-wrenching spasms. She hadn't spoken, hadn't said a word, rocking back and forth with a blank, horrified stare that had scared the hell out of Mack. He'd tried to shake her out of it, order her out of it.

"It might have been better if we could have proved the other woman was also part of the Doomsday terrorists. Unfortunately the French hostages are both dead. No one knows where their bodies are. We'll never know for sure," Kane said softly.

"I know," Mack insisted firmly. "My gut

knows. It was a trap, a great trap. I was dead. If you hadn't come in, I was dead."

"Maybe she can't forgive us for not knowing if the second woman was innocent, but I know she can't forgive herself for not being able to pull that trigger to save your life. She loves you. She's always loved you. In her eyes, she betrayed you. And when you came down so hard on her, you betrayed her by not understanding, by not seeing." Kane shook his head. "She's wired differently than we are, Mack. All that blood. Seeing the others covered in blood, you know she had to remember finding her mother."

Mack shook his head. "She was such a little child. All eyes. That killer smile. No kid should have to see that."

"I think blood brings it all back, Mack. She can't take it."

Mack swept an unsteady hand through his thick, springy hair. "I see. I understand. Jaimie probably isn't capable of killing another human being either. That's all right with me. It doesn't make me think any less of Jaimie. I can understand her feelings."

"No, you can't," Kane denied. "Neither can I. It doesn't mean we think less of her, it means she's different from us."

Mack rubbed at his temples. Jaimie was different. And maybe he didn't understand,

157

but it didn't matter. He wanted her in his life. She was so good at what they did, yet she couldn't take the blood and gore, freezing, rendering her useless when push came to shove. She'd been a liability and as much as they needed what she could do, he had to accept that she would never be a part of his work. Never be a part of the biggest part of his life. Jaimie was smarter and quicker at figuring things out. Maybe she'd already figured that and had walked away because she couldn't accept it.

Jaimie emerged from the bathroom in faded button-up Levi's, a soft blue sweatshirt, bare feet, and a towel wrapped around her wet hair like a turban, and both immediately ceased their conversation.

"What? No breakfast? There's no room service, you know," she chastised. "I had high hopes that one of you would do the cooking."

She walked beautifully, even in blue jeans. Mack's black gaze was hot as it followed her to the barstool. She'd always been graceful, and now she glided, her feet making no sound on the floor. He loved her hair, a halo of shiny curls. Her hair had always been unruly, messy, like a woman after a man spent a long night making love to her. He took a deep breath and let it out, avoiding Kane's piercing gaze. The man knew him too well.

"We managed to make coffee," Kane pointed out, pouring her a cup, taking pity on Mack.

"What's this 'we' business?" Mack protested. "If you hadn't kept us up, Jaimie, half the night with your incessant chatter, we might be a bit sharper this morning."

She laughed at him, her vivid blue eyes dancing. "You always did wake up crabby, Mack."

"You take a shower first," Kane insisted generously. "I suggest a cold one. It will work wonders."

Behind Jaimie's back, Mack gestured rudely. The two men burst out laughing simultaneously.

"Towels are on the sink," Jaimie provided helpfully. She looked a bit smug, very happy and extremely kissable.

Mack reminded himself to quit staring at her mouth. It wasn't helping to relax his body. "Thank you, honey." Deliberately, his voice was low and silky and caressing. The bastard Joe might be six feet tall, but he had nothing on Mack when it came to knowing what Jaimie liked best. He knew every hidden spot, every secret shadow.

She touched the tip of her tongue to her

lip, eyes going wide and darkening to a royal blue. She suddenly found her coffee interesting. He managed to walk to the bathroom as if all parts of his body were cooperating.

Kane leaned his elbows on the counter across from Jaimie. "That floor is as hard as nails. I was serious about ordering a bed or two. Would you mind?"

Her small white teeth chewed nervously at her lower lip. Kane was grateful Mack was in the shower. This particular look would have him flinging himself right out the window. "How long do you think you'll have to stay?"

Kane shrugged casually. "A couple of weeks, a month. The truth is, little Jaimie, we need a base anyway. Now that Mack knows you've permanently settled here, even when we clear up the trouble, he's going to want to stay."

"I'm not going back to that life, Kane."

"I know that, honey. Mack knows it too. That doesn't mean we aren't family."

A shadow crossed Jaimie's delicate face, darkened her blue eyes. "I guess we can go shopping for furniture today, then, but if you're sleeping in it, you pay for it. We'll need food too. I guess you both expect to eat."

"He's had a rough time of it without you,

Jaimie." Kane poured himself another cup of coffee. "I have too."

Her gaze met his. "I needed time to establish myself, to become my own person." She curled her fingers around the warmth of the mug. "I would have written if I had an address for you."

They both knew she couldn't just write to the military and find them. GhostWalker missions were kept strictly secret, but she knew Sergeant Major Griffen, and could have gone to him to get word to them had she wanted. She hadn't done it.

"We kept track of you," Kane admitted.

"Obviously." Jaimie smiled at one of the many pewter dragons standing on its back legs, claws extended, a fierce expression on its face. "I cried for two straight days when the first one arrived."

"Mack always refers to you as a fire-breathing dragon. That's where he got the idea." He looked at her over the top of his coffee mug. "Mack went a little crazy when you moved again. We had no idea you were in San Francisco."

"I had to find a place for my business and there's work here. I wasn't exactly hiding. In the end, you would have found me."

Kane unexpectedly reached across the counter and flicked her chin. "Don't ever disappear like that again, you hear me, Jaimie?"

She nodded solemnly. "I won't. I have a business now. I'll be easy to find."

"Is this Spaghetti person . . ."

"Spagnola," Jaimie corrected, trying to scowl.

"Whatever. Is he married?"

"Kane, really, does it matter?" When he was silent she shot him an exasperated glare and slid from the barstool. "No, Joe is not married. What difference would it make?"

"Probably the difference between life and death," Kane muttered.

"Excuse me?" Jaimie said. "I didn't hear you."

"It would make Mack feel better," Kane substituted prudently.

"Yeah, right. He'd just think Joe was out for an extramarital affair."

Kane laughed softly. "Most likely you're right about that. He isn't the most easygoing guy where you're concerned."

"That's putting it mildly and you're almost as bad." Jaimie opened the refrigerator and scowled at the contents. "Maybe we should go out for breakfast."

"What do you usually eat for breakfast?" Kane inquired.

She slammed the door with unnecessary

force. "Coffee. I'm usually too busy to eat."

"The Spaghetti guy arrives at ten and you don't have the time to eat?" Kane's eyebrow shot up. "Lazy little thing."

"I am not," Jaimie denied indignantly. "I have all kinds of things to do. I'm usually up by seven. And don't call Joe 'the Spaghetti guy.' Sometimes we have breakfast, lunch, and dinner together, which is why there is meat in my refrigerator, smart one."

Kane groaned. "I suggest you keep good old Joe away from Mack. *Don't* tell Mack you eat with this clown on a regular basis. And try not to say his name in that syrupy voice."

"I don't say his name syrupy."

"Yes, you do. All soft and dreamy. And your voice changes when you talk to him. Mack is going to throw him out on his ass if you keep it up."

"Mack will have to learn some manners." Jaimie flounced across the room to the bed, Kane on her heels. "And Joe might not be so easy to throw out."

Kane straightened slowly from where he was bending to help her make her bed. "Jaimie . . ." he began. "You aren't blind. He's not going to let another man into your life."

"Joe is a friend. And it's not Mack's business anymore, now, is it, Kane?" Jaimie said, sticking her chin out. "He let me go. He doesn't get to just walk back into my life and think things are going to be the same."

"Hey!" Mack emerged from the bathroom, towel-drying his hair, steam escaping all around him. His chest and feet were bare, creating a mood of intimacy. "You two all right? You look like you're arguing."

"Don't you ever wear a shirt?" Jaimie demanded.

He smirked at her. "Bothers you, does it? Kind of takes your breath away?"

Jaimie rolled her eyes. "You probably spent the last fifteen minutes staring at yourself in the mirror." For a moment he actually had taken her breath away and she was certain Kane knew it. He'd been standing close enough to hear her swift indrawn breath and now he was grinning ear to ear. She narrowed her eyes at him. "Don't say a word."

Kane held up his hands in surrender, ruined it by winking, walked around her, slapped Mack on the back, and disappeared into the bathroom.

Mack tossed his towel aside and took a step toward Jaimie. Her head came up, eyes suddenly wary. Mack smiled when she stepped backward. The bed caught the back of her knees and she sat down rather abruptly. The move brought her eye level with the undone top button of Mack's jeans. She blushed for no reason at all, her eyes traveling up his narrow hips, the muscle-cut stomach, to his heavily developed chest.

"This is silly, Mack. Get some clothes on." Her mouth had gone so dry it was difficult to speak normally.

"I have clothes on." He stepped close enough for her to feel his body heat. He pulled the makeshift turban from her head and gently began to rub her hair with the towel.

He was so close Jaimie was forced to close her eyes. It didn't seem to matter, he filled her vision anyway. He smelled of spicy aftershave mingled with his clean, masculine scent. Beneath her long lashes she could glimpse every defined muscle of his chest and arms, the way the hair on his chest grew down in a fine V to disappear into his jeans. His hands were evoking all kinds of sensations Jaimie didn't care to remember.

She stood it as long as she could before clenching her teeth and reaching up to capture his wrists. "I'm perfectly capable of drying my own hair."

His wrists were so thick, Jaimie couldn't get a good grip on him and he merely twisted his arm so that her hands fell free. "I know you can. I've always liked doing it. You have beautiful hair."

His words triggered warm memories of Mack down on one knee, wiping tears from Jaimie's face, brushing back strands of muddy hair, assuring her they could make her hair beautiful again with a quick shampoo. She found herself smiling. "You've always said that, even when I was a little girl."

"It's true, I love your hair." Mack tossed the towel aside and began using his fingers, tunneling through damp strands to pick it dry.

It seemed far worse with his fingers than with the towel, much more intimate. Jaimie could barely breathe, every nerve ending alive, a hot ember coiling, growling in the pit of her stomach, spreading discontent, spreading need. His jean-clad knee brushed against her shoulder. Something deep and feminine, hot and demanding, unleashed inside of her. Without conscious thought, her hand curled around his calf muscle. A connection.

The moment she touched him, she knew it was a mistake. His body was hard and hot and so inviting, and memories flooded in. She had loved him so much, had been so proud that he'd been hers. And he'd thrown her away for his adrenaline rush.

Mack's body went taut, every muscle contracting. The heat licking up his leg was like flames, each running hotter and faster than the last until he was consumed with it. For one moment his fists bunched in her hair, the physical need so great he shook with the craving, but then she let go. He heard her breath hitch.

Abruptly he released her, turned away quickly to move stiffly to the bar. Kane was a blessing and a curse. Mack wanted to be alone with Jaimie, needed to be alone with her, but he didn't dare. His hand was a little bit unsteady when he poured his coffee.

Jaimie sat very still, her heart pounding somewhere between alarm, anticipation, and frustration. There was no mistaking Mack's body's sudden urgent demand and the ensuing struggle to control his desire. For a moment, she had been afraid he was going to toss her on the bed and take her right there. For a moment she had wanted him to. She touched her tongue to her lips and forced herself to take charge.

"Kane and I were discussing going out to eat." Jaimie tested her voice cautiously. Her tone might have been a tiny bit more husky than normal, but she could live with it.

"What do you think?"

Mack smiled, pure male and taunting. "I think you're a little coward, honey, that's what I think."

The way he said "honey" was caressing, almost tender. It was disarming and totally unfair. Jaimie stayed on the bed with space separating them, feeling it was far safer. He still had a predatory gleam in his eye. "We're discussing breakfast: Go out or stay in. Vote."

"I'd rather vote on other things."

"As usual, you're not making a bit of sense. I don't know why I put up with you."

He swung back toward her, a quick movement of power and grace, his black eyes devouring her face. Jaimie's heart lurched wildly. He came across the floor like a stalking jungle cat. She couldn't move, frozen to the spot, reaching behind her for the windowsill for support. Her heart was pounding in her ears. Mack stopped inches from her, his hand grasping her chin firmly. "I know exactly why you put up with me," he drawled softly, his eyes holding hers captive, his thumb stroking across her full bottom lip.

Jaimie jerked her head away, small teeth snapping at his thumb. "I'm glad one of us does." She crossed her arms protectively across her chest, trying to ignore the way her treacherous body remembered his. Her heart remembered the pain of loving him. "Fortunately, Kane is out of the shower and has saved your life." She pushed around him, forcing herself not to run. It took a great deal of control to walk away from him when anger and hurt and love warred with one another.

CHAPTER 6

Kane waved a forkful of biscuits and gravy in Jaimie's direction to emphasize his point. "That little blueberry muffin is not exactly nutritious, Little Miss Nag. And it wouldn't fill up my big toe."

"Chicken-fried steak, biscuits, and all that gravy ought to shoot your cholesterol level right up to the moon." Jaimie was all righteousness. Her vivid blue gaze pinned Mack, who was trying unsuccessfully to become part of the woodwork. "And no one eats four eggs. That's your week's worth in one sitting. We all studied nutrition, remember?"

"You studied it and forced us to eat the most god-awful concoctions known to man," Mack protested.

"I'm allergic to all that nutritious stuff," Kane said soberly. "Absolutely allergic. Remember the brewer's yeast, Mack? Didn't she almost kill me with brewer's yeast?"

"She killed the popcorn," Mack remembered.

"You were smothering the popcorn in butter," Jaimie was indignant. "Someone had to save you. Hardening of the arteries. You two are getting on in years, you know." She smirked at them rather smugly and at the same time took a quick glance around her.

They weren't alone. She saw Brian and Jacob having breakfast in a booth facing them just to her left. At the table nearest the door, Marc drank coffee across from Ethan, who seemed engrossed in a newspaper. She had caught a brief glimpse of Javier, looking like a teenager with his boyish good looks, and Lucas, looking like a model in a business suit, moving through the crowded street as they'd entered the restaurant.

Both Mack and Kane scowled across the table at her fiercely, hoping to intimidate her. "Getting on in what years?" Kane demanded ominously.

Jaimie broke off a small piece of blueberry muffin, unconcerned with their threatening posture — after all, she had all the boys surrounding her and presumably they were there for her protection. "It's a fact of life. Everyone has to come to terms with aging. One should take a few precautions."

"A few precautions sounds like an excellent idea," Kane grumbled. "Pitching you into the ocean might be a good start."

"I thought we might take a walk over the Golden Gate this afternoon," Mack suggested helpfully, in complete agreement.

"You two have a disturbing penchant for violence," she chided. "Perhaps you should see a shrink. I noticed it way back in high school. All those contact sports, football, boxing, fencing, karate." She shook her head mournfully. "Violent."

"We had a little vamp to protect," Kane defended. "We had to be prepared."

"I beg your pardon?" Icicles dripped from her voice. There was a distinctly regal look about her.

"She was never a vamp," Mack disagreed. "But you were a beautiful innocent and every wolf for a hundred miles was stalking you." There was a caressing note in the deep timbre of his voice. "We had to keep a close watch."

Jaimie burst out laughing, the sound turning heads. "You're crazy. The two of you obviously have a far different memory of our past than I do."

The two men exchanged easy grins. "You never did see things you didn't want to." Kane was pleased with himself; it wasn't easy diverting Jaimie when she was off on one of her tangents on nutrition. There was no way she hadn't noticed the rest of the team infiltrating the restaurant to protect her. He knew she loved them all; she'd grown up with them, so she was happy to see them, but she didn't like what they represented — violence, a way of life, the very thing she'd worked so hard to get out of. He wanted her happy, teasing, that carefree laugh and bright eyes to remain for as long as possible.

"Eat your steak, Kane," Jaimie advised.

"Notice how she changes the subject when it gets a little hot?" Mack asked, his black gaze suggesting all sorts of wicked, sinful things.

Her stomach did that slow, familiar roll that Mack had been causing in her for far too long. She didn't see how she was going to be able to let him live in the same house with her, seeing him every day. It wasn't just that she found him sexy as hell; she liked him. She liked his humor and the way he could laugh at life.

"I'm eating, Mack," she said trying to sound prim instead of desperate.

He had a gift of being able to focus just on her and no one or nothing else. He was doing it now, looking at her as if she were the only person in the world. Before, she had believed she was special and he saw no one but her. Now she knew better. She knew that focused stare was an amazing illusion. He saw everything in the restaurant, knew where every single person was seated and what they were wearing. He probably knew what they were eating.

She glanced down at her plate, suddenly not hungry again. She ached for him. Ached for their lost relationship.

He reached across the table and took her hand, his thumb sliding over the sensitive part of her wrist. "I don't think that's called eating."

"Well, stop looking at me that way. There is nothing sexy about eating, and you're looking at me like . . ." She made the mistake of looking up at him, of meeting his eyes, and just trailed off.

He smiled like a Cheshire cat. "Sure there is, the way you eat."

He leaned toward her and brought her hand to his mouth, closing his lips around the tips of her fingers, his teeth gently nipping and scraping. Heat seared through her like a flash. All at once, the booth was far too small, the room too warm.

She jerked her hand away, uncaring that he knew just how he affected her. "You have sex on the brain, Mack. Get your runaway hormones under control." Jaimie said it looking as schoolmarmish as possible.

Kane choked on a mouthful of orange juice, turned slightly red, and looked surreptitiously around. "Jaimie!" He sounded shocked and lowered his voice, nearly whispering. "I can't believe you said 'sex' or 'hormones' in public."

She rolled her eyes. "You didn't blast him for trying to eat my hand in front of everyone." Her gaze swept the restaurant. Several of the men were snickering between bites of food. "Why didn't you just invite them all to sit with us? Maybe we could walk down the street like a solid wall of testosterone."

Kane choked again, spewing food into his napkin. "If I don't want you to say S-E-X, I certainly don't think you should be saying *that*. Sheesh, woman. You've lost all sense of decorum since you've been on your own."

Jaimie laughed. "You're such a prude, Kane. I can say 'prude,' can't I?"

"I'm not a prude," he objected. "It's just that there some things you don't go talking about in public."

Mack burst out laughing. "I tried to tell you she was out of control. We're going to have to take her in hand." He shamelessly leered at her.

"Tell Mack there are things you don't go *doing* in public," she replied hotly.

"I didn't see a thing," Kane defended piously.

Jaimie shrugged her slender shoulders nonchalantly. "Just for that, you two can fight over the check. Come on, I'm finished." She tossed her napkin on the table and stood up.

"Jaimie." Mack groaned. "Have a heart. We're not finished."

"I can't help it if you're slow eaters and fast talkers," she replied sternly.

"You had a blueberry muffin," Kane pointed out. "We had man-sized meals."

" 'Had' is the operative word here. It's indecent and very bad manners to lick your plate." She smiled sweetly. "I'll meet you at the furniture shop." She half turned.

Mack's hand snaked out with the speed of a striking cobra, and shackled her fragile wrist, preventing movement. "We're finished, honey, don't be in such a hurry." His thumb feathered across the sensitive skin of her inner wrist, sending little fingers of flames licking up her arm.

He was looking at her. She could clearly see that, focusing on her the way that always made her feel special, yet he gave an almost imperceptible nod and Brian and Jacob immediately rose and walked to the counter to pay their tab. They exited the restaurant without even glancing her way.

Jaimie felt the punch in the region of her belly. "You know, Mack," she hissed softly between clenched teeth as she twisted her wrist, tried to pull free. "You don't need to flirt with me to do the job. I'm smart enough to know what needs to be done."

Mack tightened his grip, his thumb stilling over the pulse beating so frantically there. He got to his feet slowly, lazily, his arm sliding around her waist, drawing her to his side. "You aren't going anywhere without me." As an afterthought Mack added, "Without us."

Jaimie set her jaw, but stopped struggling. It was useless drawing attention to them. It wouldn't make Mack stop. "I wasn't really going without you. I'm well aware you're worried about someone coming after me. You don't know me anymore, Mack. Don't treat me like the child you used to know."

Mack crowded her body just a little with his own. "I know you better than you know yourself. I know you better than your own mother did."

"That's not hard. Poor Mama didn't know a thing about me except that I was too smart for my own good." Jaimie briefly closed her eyes, thinking of her mother. Unwed pregnant teenager, boyfriend and family deserting her. The doctors, excited about her exceptional year-old child. Stacy Fielding had adored her baby girl, wanted something better than a life of waiting tables, and she'd struggled hard to give her a different life. Jaimie always wished she'd been one of those girls that had been ultrafeminine and giggly, instead of the serious, studious child she'd been. Her mother deserved that.

"You miss her, don't you?" Mack dropped money on the table for the tip while Kane made his way up to the counter to pay the check.

"Of course I miss her. She had such a tragic life."

She turned away from his comfort, that part of her that was still a child mourning her mother's death unable to accept solace from him. Every morning she'd woken up and known she was facing another day without Mack. Now he was there and she felt more alone than ever. There had been Mack and Kane and her mother before Mack had brought her home to his mother and introduced her into his circle of friends. The boys had accepted her because Mack and Kane had. Now either everyone was

178

gone or she'd lost that closeness with them.

After leaving Mack, she had learned to cope on her own. She didn't want Mack coming back into her life with false promises and letting her lean on him. The memories of her childhood, good and bad, came flooding back with him. And the year she'd spent believing he loved her and wanted her for his wife, for the mother of his children. She'd lost her mother in the worst, most horrific way, and he knew she craved stability. But, when she'd gone to him and pleaded with him to give her what she needed, he'd been arrogant and aloof, pointing out her failings as a GhostWalker. Telling her he was committed to the program and wouldn't have time or energy right then for a family.

Her throat closed at the memory. She couldn't think about her mother, and she didn't want to think about that last parting with Mack. They were together now for a short time, not under the best of circumstances, but she was determined to have a good day with them.

Mack slipped his arm around her shoulders in a gesture of comfort and she allowed herself to be led from the restaurant, sandwiched between the two men. Once on the street, he dropped his arm, stepping to the side of her.

"Keep moving, honey," he ordered. "We studied the route from here and we can walk on the same side of the street all the way down. Stay between us. You know the drill."

"You look like overzealous bodyguards," she complained. It seemed natural to have one on either side of her, a leftover habit from childhood.

"We've been guarding your body for as long as I can remember," Mack said with a teasing grin.

They joined the throng moving busily from block to block. Somehow the crowds seemed to part, the two men never once allowing anyone to so much as casually brush against her. She moved forward, aware that Jacob and Ethan were behind her. Her mind just did that — expanded and positioned the people around her.

The weather was cool and a bit misty, the fog gray and gloomy, but already clearing with a promise of a nice afternoon. She enjoyed being able to move through a bustling, crowded street free of pain, taking in the sights and buildings without the mind-numbing information that always crowded into her head. Mack and Kane gave her that freedom. Most of the time she spent locked away from the world. It had taken months to find Joe, a man she could work with without the psychic backlash that was so debilitating with most people. There were a few rare people that had natural shields and she'd worked hard, interviewing nearly three hundred applicants before she'd found him.

Something odd fluttered into her mind, pushed aside the warm happiness, leaving a sudden cold fear. She snuck a long, slow look around her, making certain to stay in step. She kept her same facial expression, her body language the same.

"What is it?" Mack's voice was low.

He'd always been so tuned to her. It was strange. When he appeared to be paying the least attention, he caught everything, the smallest nuance. When he appeared to be wholly focused on her, he was completely aware of his surroundings.

"I don't know," she said, and there was no keeping the uneasiness from her voice.

We go to red. Mack sent out the order without hesitation. "Let's abort, Jaimie."

She flashed him a quick look. "I'm not on a mission. We're buying a bed. I could be picking up a threat to anyone. Someone thinking about going postal. It's faint and I can't identify it yet. It happens all the time. You know that."

"I don't want to take chances with your life," he said.

"I thought you said the two men Javier took down were going to kidnap me," she pointed out. "That doesn't necessarily read that my life was in danger."

They were nearly to the furniture store. She kept moving forward, her gaze on the entrance, but her heart was beating fast now. Mack was protective, but to take them all to the highest risk when she couldn't even sort out a bad feeling was not like him.

"The tranq wasn't a tranq. It was truth serum. They were going to question you, Jaimie, and they'd brought a few instruments with them."

Her mouth went dry. "Torture?" She looked up at him then. And then at Kane's carefully averted face. A muscle ticked in his jaw and his eyelid flickered. "They were going to torture me?"

"Damn it, Jaimie."

Mack shielded her as a group of unruly teenagers on skateboards rushed past. Javier did a series of showy tricks to the whistles and admiration of the kids, shot her a jaunty grin, and kept going, skating through the crowd, laughing at the curses and snarls as people moved out of the way. He scattered everyone behind them, answering the obscene gestures with one of his own.

"He could be crazy, you know," Jaimie said.

"I have no doubt he is."

"I want to buy the beds today, Mack. I don't want to spend today terrified and locked up in a room alone."

He didn't point out she wouldn't be alone. *You see anything?* He sent the call out to them all, his men, his family, moving in and out of the crowd. Gideon up on the rooftops, following their every move, his rifle an extension of him.

Not a thing, boss. The reports came back, all assuring him.

Do we abort, Top? Marc was at the door, ready to go inside.

They were almost on top of the shop. "Let's just order the beds," Jaimie said. "We're already here and I don't have a strong feeling one way or the other right now. Please, Mack."

We'll proceed, but be careful, Marc. You're my eyes.

Mack recognized it was important to her to be as normal as possible. She probably hadn't been out in public in weeks. Joe had done her shopping, or she'd had everything delivered. He knew her routines. She preferred working alone or in the dead of night in empty buildings where the psychic overload didn't sicken her to the point of brain bleeds. He'd seen it happen before. "Let's just get this done fast. You tell me the first sign of uneasiness. We'll get you out, Jaimie. No one's going to get their hands on you."

She had a bad taste in her mouth. She'd brought the storm down on her own head. None of this was Mack's fault and she was actually grateful he was there. She had no doubt she would have had a good chance of getting away before the two men had gotten to her, but she would have lost everything she'd worked for and would have had to run for the rest of her life.

"Would you have come back to me?" Mack asked, guessing her thoughts.

She took a breath. "No." She would never have brought danger to him. He should have known that without making her say it.

She was looking at his face and caught the flash of anger quickly hidden behind his mask. For a moment her stomach shifted, but then he pushed open the door and Kane moved through, his larger body blocking hers. Mack fell into step behind her. She could feel Mack, and she moved in step with him as she followed Kane without hesitation. She'd never be foolish enough to put them in danger. She loved them, whether

Mack understood her or not.

Do your thing, Jaimie, Kane said.

In here? With all these people? It would hurt like hell, opening herself up that way. She glanced at Mack. He obviously hadn't heard Kane's request, which meant he wouldn't condone it. She bit her lip, took a breath, and expanded her mind, realizing Kane didn't want any of the men in jeopardy. Civilians surrounded them. If an enemy was close, they had to know.

At once she was assailed with energy from every direction. Emotions hit hard, a solid punch to her stomach as anger and guilt and happiness and grief poured in from every direction. She pressed her lips together to keep anything from slipping past her throat, but her footsteps faltered. Mack put a hand on her back, but his eyes searched the customers moving around the store.

"You all right?"

She managed a nod as she waited for her brain to accept the overload so she could begin the sorting process. She forced herself to continue forward, although she had to concentrate on each separate step. As far as she could tell, no one in the store had lethal intentions toward anyone. A woman had lost her son in a car accident and another was contemplating suicide. There were two men who were criminals, a shoplifter, a very harassed mother of two. The list went on and on, but she didn't feel anyone threatening her.

She took a breath, let it out, and breathed away the sickness collecting in the pit of her stomach as she closed her mind to the assault. She tasted blood in her mouth and reached in her pocket for a handkerchief. She pressed it to her nose, keeping her back to Mack as she followed Kane onto the floor they were looking for.

We're good.

You certain?

I told you, didn't I? Did you think I'm so desperate to do whatever I want that I'd put one of my brothers in jeopardy? She let the bite in her voice sink in.

Kane turned his head and looked at her, coming to an abrupt stop when he spotted the red staining the cloth. His eyes widened. "Jaimie."

"What have you done?" Mack demanded, whirling her around to face him. He took the cloth from her hand to examine the amount of blood as Kane blocked any view of her body. "We're both with you. You shouldn't be having this much trouble."

"I'm all right. I've always been far more

sensitive than the rest of you. Even with both of you around, there's no way to minimize the effect with this many people."

"Why the hell did you do this to yourself?" Mack's voice was gruff.

She bit her lip as he gently cleaned the last remnants of blood from her face. "I wanted to make certain there was no danger. I don't want the boys hurt, or any innocent bystanders. If these men were willing to torture me to see what information I have on Whitney, they're willing to hurt anyone around me as well."

"I asked her to," Kane admitted, refusing to allow Jaimie to take the brunt of Mack's anger. He knew Mack, knew his fears for Jaimie, the way he suffered every time she was in pain. He was helpless to stop it, and Mack didn't like to be helpless. "I knew you wouldn't ask her."

Mack's eyes went flat and cold. A muscle ticked along his jaw. He kept working on Jaimie's face, his touch tender. "I'll be talking to you about this when we're alone, Kane."

Jaimie's heart lurched. She brought up both hands to his wrist and stopped him — waited until he looked down at her. "Don't be upset, Mack. He was right and you know he was. If it was anyone but me . . ."

"But it is you." He stared down at her for a long moment, and then leaned forward to brush a kiss along her forehead. "And at least you know that."

"I know. Come on, we know we're all safe. Let's buy you both a bed."

There was a moment. A heartbeat she thought he wouldn't let it go, but the grim reaper in his eyes disappeared and he smiled at her.

"Now you're talking sense."

She smiled back. "I usually do. I'm quite a bit smarter than you, you know."

Instead of taking the bait and teasing her like he usually did, he slipped his arm around her shoulders and nodded. "You always have been. I should have listened to you."

Everything inside her stilled as Mack followed Kane down the aisle toward king-sized beds, taking Jaimie with him. A capitulation. He'd said it so casually. *I should have listened to you.* She looked down at her hands as she pretended to be interested in the talk about mattresses. Mack had never apologized. Not in all the time she could remember being around him. Was he beginning to realize the enormity of what Whitney had done to them all? If so, she felt sorry for him. He would lay the blame squarely on his own shoulders. Mack believed in taking responsibility for his own actions.

"What do you think of this?" Mack asked Jaimie, drawing her out of her reverie. He propelled Jaimie across the room toward a king-sized waterbed.

"Oh, no," she was very decisive, backing away from the massive polished frame. "I will not have that monstrosity taking up space in my bedroom. It probably weighs enough to drop through two floors."

"You're crazy, woman. You're living in a former car garage."

"A warehouse. There's a difference," she countered indignantly.

Mack's answering snort was pure disdain. "I saw a couple of oil stains, Jaimie."

"Heavy equipment. Forklifts. If you make one more crack about my beloved little home . . ."

"Little?" His eyebrow shot up.

"You'll be sleeping on the roof with the pigeons, and I'm not kidding you."

"Oil stains, Jaimie."

"One more crack, Mack," she threatened.

He turned his hands palms up in a gesture of surrender. "We'll compromise, I'll give up the water if you'll go with the size."

"King-sized?" She almost squeaked it. "It

would take up all my space. I need wide-open spaces." She glanced at Kane for help, but he was rolling around on a mattress and moaning in a loud, orgasmic manner. She rolled her eyes and heaved a sigh.

"Jaimie," Mack said patiently, "that third floor is probably five thousand square feet. There's plenty of space for anyone. A king-sized bed is appropriate for that kind of space."

"A double bed is perfectly adequate." Jaimie was snippy about it, one hand on her hip. "Twin beds would be even smarter."

"Forget it." Mack was firm. "We'll settle for the double bed. Find one you like and we'll have them deliver. We'll need sheets, blankets, pillows, the whole bit. And not those silly eyelet things you like."

"We need two beds, unless you plan on sleeping on the couch," Jaimie pointed out, pinning him with a steely gaze.

Mack smirked, black eyes running over her with male amusement. "You concerned about the sleeping arrangements, honey?"

Her chin lifted. "You could say that."

"Personally, I thought they were fine."

"You would." Jaimie crossed her arms and tapped her foot. "You take up too much room."

"I wouldn't in a double," he protested.

"I'm not sharing my bed, it's out of the question."

He grinned at her. "Don't trust yourself, huh?"

"That's right, Mack, I'm liable to smother you with a pillow in the middle of the night."

He circled her waist with his arms, drawing her stiff body against his, laughing openly into her upturned face. "You know you're crazy about me, Jaimie, you may as well admit it."

"Crazy's a good word," she agreed, leaning away from him, her blue gaze avoiding his. Her heart was pounding, her pulse racing. "I'm considering kicking you very hard right in the shins. I'm giving you fair warning."

He bent down, his broad shoulders blocking out everything but his teasing grin, his sensuous mouth far too close to hers, his hungry black gaze devouring her face. "So lucky, honey, saved by the sales clerk." He whispered it in her ear, his teeth grazing her earlobe, sending a shiver of excitement coursing through her. Mack released her with obvious reluctance, turning to the salesman, stating exactly what he wanted.

Jaimie put her hands on her hips and glared at Kane. "Get up. You talk about me being improper in public. You're engaging in illegal sex acts with that bed."

"I'm in love. This is the one. I'm keeping her."

"I don't want her in my house. Not with you rolling around like that. Sheesh. I won't be able to go to sleep worried about what you and that bed are doing."

"Yeah, well, I have to worry about what you and Mack are doing and that's just plain wrong for any brother to contemplate. You can live with the bed."

She stuck her nose in the air and gave a little indignant sniff. "I can assure you, you do not have to worry about what's going to happen between Mack and me. Absolutely nothing is going to happen."

"Whoa!" Mack stopped the salesclerk by holding up his hand. "Why does he get this bed? It's a queen. That's favoritism, Jaimie. He gets a queen-sized, I get one too."

She threw her hands into the air in surrender. "Fine. Take up my beloved room and don't feel at all sorry about it."

The two men high-fived each other and did a series of male knuckle-punching motions that made her laugh and shake her head. "I don't think we're all that far from the caveman era," she pointed out.

Jaimie watched Kane and Mack double-team the sales clerk until he capitulated and agreed to have the beds delivered that afternoon. "You get your way in everything, don't you," she demanded as they fell into step to go from the store.

We're bringing her out, Mack sent to his team.

Marc moved into position in front of them and she saw Lucas drop in behind them. Ethan and Jacob were close, she could sense them, but she didn't spot them. In spite of knowing the team was in place, her stomach coiled with tension. She remembered she'd excelled in all the training, but it was nerve-wracking moving through crowds of people knowing you were a target and those protecting you were people you loved.

She stayed in step with Marc, sandwiched between Mack and Kane, unless they were forced single file, which the two men managed to avoid most of the time. Jaimie knew they looked intimidating and they projected aggressive energy around them and in front of them, forcing people to unknowingly step out of the path.

Coming out, Mack sent to his team outside.

Clear, Gideon reported.

They stepped out onto the sidewalk, into the bustling crowd, and began to make their way back toward the wharf district. As she walked between them, Jaimie couldn't stop the small burst of happiness. Each day had been difficult without Mack, but that aside, their presence gave her the freedom to actually be normal for a short period of time. She could eat out, walk down the street, just pretend, for a few moments, that she was like everyone else.

"You don't really mind the beds, do you, Jaimie?" Mack asked.

"No. I'd never expect you to sleep in a twin bed," she admitted. "I was just giving you both a hard time. Although I'm not certain we should let Kane near his bed."

Mack laughed and Jaimie turned her head to get Kane's reaction when the first warning seized her. The second assault hit right on top of the first.

In the crowd, Mack, he just dropped in behind us. Gideon broadcast the warning. *Shooter on the roof. Second building on the left.*

Get him in your sights now, Gideon, Mack commanded. *Ethan, can you get around to us with the car?*

Lucas moved up behind Jaimie, closing the gap so no one could get between them. They pushed through the crowd, heading for the corner where Ethan waited with the car. The sidewalk was lined with parked cars and traffic was nearly at a standstill.

No chance. I can get to you on foot.

Stay with the car. We may need it.

I don't have a clear shot. Get out of there. I'm moving position, Gideon said.

Break to the right now, Jaimie, Mack ordered as he turned into a shop, yanking Jaimie in after him. Kane and Lucas followed. They made no pretense of etiquette, but hurried at a fast pace toward the back of the store. *Ethan, bring the car around the block. We're going out the back.*

I've got him. He's moving, trying to get around to get into position for a shot at the car. Green light? Gideon asked.

Take him out, Mack commanded grimly, as he kept moving through the store toward the back door.

Fuck! We've got another bogey. Another bogey in the field. I think it's Superman.

Gideon rarely swore, and Mack brought Jaimie to an abrupt halt, shielding her with his body. He was not willing to bring her onto the street, although they were going out a door a block away with a building between them and the shooter. Mack didn't know how many they were up against. He wanted numbers and positions. The longer they waited in the store, the more they lost the slim advantage they'd gained.

Shooter down. I think we both nailed him,

Gideon reported. *That bastard Superman and I are in a standoff, Top. I'm looking right down the business end of his rifle.*

Back away. Get off the roof and clear, Gideon, Mack advised. *I'm sending backup.*

No way. This guy's good, boss. If he wanted me dead, I'd be dead. We'd both be down because I'd take the son of a bitch with me and he knows it. Don't provoke him. I think he's watching over Jaimie.

Can you get clear?

If not, and I miss him, hunt him down for me.

Don't get your ass shot off. I'll be royally pissed.

Royally pissed? Not just plain pissed?

Jaimie felt the tension coiled tight in Mack's body. She reached out, knowing they needed the positions of their enemies. She let her mind expand. She felt the violence of a kill, the dark energy spreading like bloodstains through the air, rushing straight at her. Hurrying, she expanded her mind, seeking enemies, tracking her boys, her family, the men guarding her.

There was Gideon on the roof, his energy a mixture of adrenaline, fear, and determination, and she knew she could read him only because he'd pulled the trigger and violence surrounded him like a net. Javier raced through the crowd to come up on their flank as they emerged. Lucas guarded the front door of the shop. Marc sprinted to take up his position to cover them. People were moving around like chess players on a board. She reached even further in an effort to find the hard-core violent energy of intent to do harm.

He's in the crowd, near Javier. Coming around the block to intercept us. She tried to get the message out to them all before the killing energy hit with lethal force. The wave blasted through her head, hit her nervous system, nearly driving her to her knees.

"Damn it, Jaimie." Mack slipped his arm around her to support her. She was bleeding from her nose and another thin trickle leaked down the side of her mouth. "I need you strong."

"Mack." Kane's voice was quiet. Calm. "She told us where he was. Let's go."

They ignored the clerk trying to wave them away from the door marked emergency exit only and pushed their way through. Lucas fell in behind them as they burst out onto the street and into the middle of a crowd. Traffic was backed up and snarling, horns blaring and fingers gesturing obscenely as Ethan kept the Cadillac blocking the lane right off the back door.

Mack and Kane half carried Jaimie as she coughed blood onto the sidewalk. Javier burst through the crowd on his skateboard just as Lucas whirled to face the threat coming up behind him. The skateboarder flashed past Jaimie as Mack simply leaned down and shouldered her, sprinting for the vehicle. Javier kept going and someone in the crowd screamed, hands up in the air as blood sprayed over them. A man stumbled and went down, still clutching his unfired weapon in his hand.

Lucas ran to the downed man. "Call nine-one-one! He's hurt. Does someone have a cell phone?" As a precaution, he pushed the gun away from the limp hand with his elbow, although Javier never missed. His practiced hands went through pockets, Lucas's body hiding the movement. He came up empty just as he knew he would.

Javier was long gone, lost in the crowd, and Ethan stuck his finger out the window, flipping off the angry drivers behind him, and then put his foot on the gas, taking them out of there.

"He was walking toward me," the man covered in blood said. "Then he just coughed and looked at me and fell. You don't think he's got some kind of disease, do you?"

Lucas jumped back away from the body. "I don't know, man. He could have come off a freighter. I'm going to wash my hands."

A siren shrieked in the distance as the circle of people moved back from the slain man. No one had seen what happened, but then, Lucas really hadn't expected any witnesses. No one had thought a thing of the teen with his skateboard, weaving in and out of the crowd. He backed off more, allowing the talk to swirl around him, and then he simply did what GhostWalkers did best: He disappeared.

CHAPTER 7

"Okay, honey, you're scaring the hell out of me. You've got to wake up for me."

Mack's voice penetrated the layer of pain Jaimie seemed to be drowning in. Her lashes fluttered, but she couldn't quite pry her swollen lids open. Every inch of her head hurt, even her teeth. She detested psychic overloads.

She moistened her dry mouth, ignoring the metallic taste of blood. "Go away." Because she wasn't getting up, not even to hear his voice again.

"Thank God, Jaimie." Relief poured into Mack's voice. "I was about to call for help. Open your eyes."

She swallowed a protest. "What part of 'go away' didn't you understand?" She didn't dare move. Not any part of her body. Certainly not her head.

Top, looks like you're about to have company, Gideon reported. *Big son of a bitch.*

Looks like a model. Really good-looking. There's something about the way he moves . . . There was speculation in Gideon's voice.

Mack signaled to Kane as he slipped a gun out and positioned himself in front of Jaimie's bed. Kane slipped across the room, standing to one side of the window to peer down at the street. Ethan disappeared entirely.

"Jaimie's persistent assistant," he said. "Javier is coming up on him."

Watch yourself, Javier, Gideon cautioned. *He knows he's being watched,* Gideon added. *Boss, you're going to think I'm crazy, but I swear he moves like Superman. I think he's the one watching Jaimie. And that shot yesterday? The winds were ferocious. I had a good angle, but he didn't. To make a shot like that, only a handful of people in the world could do that. If it's him, and I think it is, he's good, Mack.*

I don't think you're crazy, Gideon. Javier, don't approach him. Keep moving.

You're taking my fun away.

Kane swore under his breath. "Javier just buzzed by him, doing a few showy tricks. He's got four other kids with him. Jaimie's little friend watched them every step of the way. Never took his eyes off of them. He's not going to be easy, Mack."

Javier, stop playing with fire. That man's the real deal. I need you to get back here in a few when it's safe.

Javier snorted. *I can take him, Top. You give the word.*

You'll stand down.

Waiting for orders as always, came the prompt reply.

Mack snorted. Javier did whatever the hell he wanted to do and then grinned at Mack sheepishly while Mack lectured him. *I need you on the computer telling me everything you can about this guy. I don't want the bullshit cover story. I want his real identity and who sent him.*

Can I come in behind him and use Jaimie's sweet equipment? Javier sounded eager.

Only if you don't mind if she gets mad at you for touching her babies, Mack said.

"At the door, Mack," Kane reported.

On cue the fog horn blared. Mack stabbed his finger on the intercom. "Yes?"

"I want to see her. Jaimie. I want to see her."

"She told you to take the day off." Mack didn't pretend to be oblivious of the man's identity. What was the point?

"Yeah, well, it's me or the cops. I want to see her for myself and if you think I'm bluff-

202

ing, try me."

He saw us getting her into the car somehow, Kane sent telepathically. *He knows she's hurt, probably had a scope on us and saw the blood as we carried her. You'd want to do the same, get a visual checkup. The guy has balls, Mack.*

Yeah, well, he'd better watch that he doesn't get them whacked off. "Come on up, then," Mack invited into the intercom and waved Kane over to the door. "But come up unarmed."

"I don't need weapons," Joe said, his voice utterly calm.

Kane flashed Mack a grin. "You got to hand it to the guy." There was admiration in his voice. "He knows he's walking into the lion's den."

"He won't come without a weapon." Mack made it a statement.

"No, he won't," Kane agreed.

Mack put himself in front of Jaimie, reaching down for a moment to wipe strands of hair from her face. She appeared to be sleeping again. He was terrified of her slipping into unconsciousness and then a coma. Bleeding on the brain often occurred with psychic overload and more than one death had resulted. His heart beat too fast and he was edgy as hell, not the perfect time for her friend to show up.

The man was arrogant enough to take the freight lift, not bothering to try to surprise them by silently creeping up the stairs. He stepped out of the elevator looking down the barrel of both guns without so much as blinking.

"Search him," Mack said to Kane.

Joe shook his head. "Not a good idea to put your hands on me. I've got a dead man's switch and you come near me, or make a move for Jaimie, and we all go up." He smiled and there was amusement in his black eyes as they glittered at Mack. "Just to let you know, I don't bluff."

"I don't guess you do," Mack said without lowering his weapon. "You take out the bogey on the roof?"

"I think your man and I hit him at the same time."

"Nice shot." Mack gave credit where it was due.

"Thanks. I don't miss what I'm aiming at."

"You want to tell me what you want with Jaimie?"

"You're the one standing over her with a gun. She looks in bad shape. You tell me who you are and what you're doing here."

"You can find out about us the hard way,

just like we're doing with you," Mack said. "You think I'm going to hand it to you?"

"This is going to be a damn long day and she could be in real trouble," Joe pointed out.

"She's my family." *My everything.* Mack didn't say it aloud, but he might as well have, with the gruff voice he used.

Those black eyes studied him. "I look out for her. Step aside and let me see to her. I have medical training," Joe added.

He'll have to let go of the switch, Kane pointed out.

True, but he'll be next to Jaimie. If he's an assassin . . .

Joe sighed. "Keep the gun to my head. Let me take a look at her."

Mack stepped aside. "I'll kill you without hesitation if you even look like you're going to harm her."

Joe's eyebrow went up. "Funny, I was thinking the same thing about you." He walked straight across the floor to the bedside, turning his back on Kane without hesitation.

Cocky bastard, Kane observed.

Joe knelt down beside Jaimie, his back to both of them. They knew it had to take courage to do it, but the man ran his hands gently over her face. "Hey, sweetheart, can

205

you open your eyes for me? I need to look into them. I want to hear you talk." He glanced over his shoulder at Mack. "Has she talked? Slurred her words?"

"She told me to go away and let her sleep," Mack admitted, "so she knew what was going on, and no, she didn't slur her words. But she's in pain. She was moaning up until a few minutes ago."

Sweetheart? Who the hell does he think he is, calling Jaimie sweetheart? he demanded of Kane.

Noticed that, did you? Kane shook his head. *Let it go, Mack. He's worried about her. She always was more sensitive than the rest of us to violent energy, and someone died back there.*

She should never have opened herself up. We could have protected her if she hadn't done that.

We don't know how her radar works. Obviously she had no choice if she wanted to find out the enemy's position. Mack, she's in trouble, we both can see it.

"Tell me what you need for her," Mack said. His gun never wavered. His gut told him Joe Spagnola was there to help Jaimie, not hurt her, but it would take one moment to kill her.

"My medical bag is in the lift."

Kane immediately retrieved the small bag, opened it, and went through it carefully. Joe didn't even glance at him, but had placed his fingertips on Jaimie's head and closed his eyes. Marc was an accomplished medic in the field, working with wounds, but he didn't have the ability to work with brain bleeds. Strokes and even death could follow. The moment the fingers locked onto her skull, Jaimie's facial expression turned to a frown, and her body became restless beneath the thin sheet.

"She has leaking blood in several spots, although none appear too bad. No big clots."

"Can you stop it?" Mack asked. *Do you think he's a psychic healer? The real deal?*

I don't know, boss, but he looks like he knows what he's doing, Kane answered.

"I'll try working to seal off the weak areas. Sometimes I can and other times I don't have the strength to tap into the energy I need. It all depends on how severe the problem is. I have some medication in my bag that should help. Do either of you know how to set up an IV?"

"We both can." Nearly every GhostWalker could. All of them had fundamental lifesaving skills.

Kane removed the necessary equipment

and began the preparations while Mack watched Joe closely. The man kept his fingers on Jaimie's skull, and they could feel the pull of energy around him as he seemed to gather and use nearly every bit in the room. For a moment the smell of burned flesh permeated the room and Mack's heart jumped in response, but he held still, the feeling that Joe was working to help Jaimie strong.

She moaned softly and tried to turn her head, her body moving restlessly under the covers. Her legs thrashed and she lifted her hands, trying to push him away, batting feebly, but very persistently.

"Hold her down," Joe ordered. "It hurts like hell. Basically I'm trying to manipulate the energy to do what we'd do in surgery."

Mack holstered his weapon and sat on the other side of the bed, leaning his weight on her slender body while Kane put the catheter into the back of her hand.

"She should have gone to the hospital," Mack said, angry with himself. He didn't trust her being in a hospital. It would be far too easy for an assassin to get to her. Too many doctors, nurses, and orderlies going in and out of her room.

Joe shook his head. "Too risky. She's a target. You couldn't take the chance and you know that."

Jaimie continually moved her head, trying to get his hands off of her. Her moans were becoming cries of distress. Mack leaned close to her and whispered in her ear. "I'm here with you, honey. He's trying to help you."

His voice seemed to soothe her a little. She subsided, her fingers sliding across the sheet to find his leg.

"You know why they want her dead?" Mack asked.

"I have my suspicions. I hope I'm wrong. I originally was assigned to guard her to keep any foreign governments from trying to acquire her. What about you? Do you know?"

"We just arrived last night. We grew up together."

"You must be Mack McKinley. I read her file. She had a very different background. All of you were friends before you ended up on the same team." Joe visibly relaxed, although his fingertips never lifted from Jaimie's skull.

She cried out softly in protest again and began to thrash under him again. Kane gripped her hand to keep her from ripping out the IV. Her lashes fluttered and she tossed her head, trying to get rid of the insistent fingers and the heat they were generating.

"This is hurting her," Mack said. "She wasn't doing this before."

"I'm operating without anesthesia. Did you think it would be easy? She's a Ghost-Walker, she'll be able to handle it."

"She's not like the rest of us," Mack protested. His stomach was in knots and there was a bad taste in his mouth. He felt as if they were torturing her. Jaimie wasn't cut out for what they did, no matter how powerful her gift. If she opened herself in public, too much energy rushed in to overpower her. He had believed that with practice, all of them could protect her. They were anchors and in theory, the energy should rush to them, but something about Jaimie was different. He'd known it since she was a child, that her psychic gifts worked differently than all of theirs, and that hers was stronger.

"What was she doing?"

"Jaimie isn't an anchor. If she uses her abilities, she pays in a big way."

Joe did look at them then, staring from one to the other. "I read that all of you belonged to Team Three and all of you were anchors. She should have been protected."

"It doesn't matter when it comes to

Jaimie." Mack's gaze met Joe's. "Why do you think you were here? They probably told you to record everything you could about her. No one can figure her out. Short of taking her to Whitney's lab and dissecting her, they don't know how her radar ticks or anything else about her. And as for a foreign government kidnapping her, she may have to worry about Whitney wanting to do the same thing. He likes his little experiments."

"Whitney didn't send me," Joe said.

"Sergeant Major Griffen did, Mack," Kane said. "Acting on my request."

There was a long silence, punctuated by Jaimie's distressed moans. Mack kept his face absolutely blank. He didn't know or trust Joe Spagnola all that much and refused to spill his fury over Kane's admission in front of a stranger. Once again, Jaimie had tried to tell him Kane had been involved in the "coincidence" but he'd chosen not to listen or believe her. If it felt like betrayal to him, then how would it seem to Jaimie? And the man she'd spent time with, carefully chosen out of hundreds of applicants, how would it feel to her to know he'd been working undercover to watch her? Most important, when GhostWalkers usually could identify one another just through the psychic energy, how had Joe managed to mislead Jaimie? And did Griffen or those above him know?

His stomach was a mass of hard knots and he couldn't believe the anger roiling in his gut. Kane was his best friend, the man who walked through death with him, waded through blood. Trust was everything, and he had trusted Kane implicitly his entire life. He had allowed Jaimie to walk away from him because he wasn't about to abandon Kane and the others after he'd led them to Whitney.

As if sensing his distress, Jaimie opened her eyes and looked at him. Her eyes were bloodshot, red and not very focused, but relief swept through him at the awareness there.

"Hey there, honey. You've given us all a bad scare."

Her perusal took in Kane and then Joe, who still had the pads of his fingers in firm contact with her head. The heat he generated couldn't fail to tip her off to what he was. That should have made him happy, that she'd think her hero had feet of clay, but instead, he felt sad for her. He wanted to gather her into his arms and hold her tight against him, shelter her from every hurt.

He'd chosen this life for them all, and he'd embraced it. There was a part of him that still did, maybe the biggest part of him. He loved what he did. He had even grown to love the psychic and genetic enhancements. But Jaimie was everything to him. He needed her. He just didn't know how to reconcile the two. He had told her so many things that night. He'd like to forget he'd said them, but two years had gone by and he had plenty of time to remember word for word how he'd told her she'd come crawling back, begging him to take her back, that she couldn't make it without him. He'd been so angry at her — at least he thought he'd been. Over those long two years he realized he'd been angry at himself for ever putting her — any of them — in the dangerous position they were all in. It was his responsibility and he couldn't walk away, not even when he couldn't seem to breathe without Jaimie.

There was knowledge in her eyes and he knew she accepted Kane's betrayal better than he did. Maybe she even understood it. Jaimie seemed able to see things he didn't. She put her hand up and tried to push Joe away.

"Let me, sweetheart," Joe said. "I can explain."

"We both can," Kane added, more, Mack suspected, for his benefit than Jaimie's. "Just let him work on you. You know how danger-ous brain bleeds are."

Jaimie tangled her fingers with Mack's and clung, but she forced herself to stop fight-ing.

"Her name is Jaimie," Mack said. "Not 'sweetheart.' "

Joe glanced at him. "You're looking for a fight, but you're not going to get one from me. I was just —"

"Doing your job," Jaimie cut him off, clos-ing her eyes, not wanting to look at his face. "I hear that a lot. It's such a great excuse, isn't it? Following orders."

She hadn't known Joe was a GhostWalker or that he'd been sent to watch her. At first she'd suspected. He'd been her second choice, but her first choice had taken an-other job. She'd thoroughly investigated Joe and everything checked out. Even that, she knew, could be manipulated so she'd inter-viewed him several times, trying to trip him up with questions. If a story was rehearsed, it was often retold nearly word for word. Joe had been an easy talker.

And she should have recognized another GhostWalker. Or at least someone with psychic abilities. Judging by the heat in her head, he definitely had psychic abilities.

"It's not like that, Jaimie," Joe protested.

"Really? You didn't answer my ad and apply for the job? You didn't have a cover in place — a very good one, I might add. I'm pretty certain you never mentioned you were keeping an eye on me."

"That your place across the street my men uncovered?" Mack asked.

"I couldn't believe your man spotted me. He's one of a very few who ever have."

"He ID'd you walking up to the front door as well." Mack didn't identify Gideon. He didn't know what was going on and protecting his men was instinctual.

Jaimie tried to think through the pain. It mattered little if they gave her explanations. Betrayal had a certain smell to it and that scent had been all over Kane. Why not Joe? That bothered her. She'd become fond of him. They'd spent many hours isolated together, working to turn the warehouse into a home and office. In all that time, how could she not have known what he was?

She felt him lift his fingertips away and the burning sensation eased. She could taste blood in her mouth. The overloads were getting worse, not better. She hadn't said anything to anyone because who could she tell? Who could she trust? She didn't dare go into a hospital. And what could a doctor do for her? Only Whitney might have a chance of helping her, and he was a monster without scruples. She'd probably come out from under the anesthesia and discover he'd given her wings.

"She should be better if I can get this medicine into her IV," Joe said, sitting back. For the first time he looked strained, his handsome face lined with fatigue.

Mack held out his hand. "What is it?"

Kane put the medication in Mack's hand. Mack closed his eyes, blocking out all sights, concentrating on the vial held between his palms. He inhaled deeply, scenting the liquid, looking for trace amounts of poison, sensing whether or not it could bring Jaimie harm. It bothered him that she couldn't read Joe, and that Gideon, who had the eyes of an eagle, hadn't spotted him easily. He wouldn't have known Joe was a Ghost-Walker if he'd passed by him. If Whitney ever realized that both Joe and Gideon weren't recognizable as GhostWalkers to the others, both men would be in danger. Whitney would move heaven and earth to find out why. Mack handed him the vial and watched him put it into Jaimie's IV.

"I'm giving her a painkiller as well," Joe said. "It will make her sleepy. I'd like to stay for a few hours and check on her. She's not entirely out of danger."

Mack knew Javier was on the second floor using Jaimie's equipment to ferret out Joe Spagnola's secrets. He nodded his head. "Thanks."

He still hadn't really looked at Kane. He wasn't certain he could without punching him right in the face. Kane had asked for the sergeant major to put someone on Jaimie without even coming to him about it. To take manpower from one of the teams, and Joe Spagnola was definitely an elite GhostWalker, Griffen would have asked something in return. Mack knew that somehow Jaimie was going to be part of the price tag.

Joe stood up and stretched.

"I'd be careful moving around," Mack said.

Joe's eyebrow shot up. "I spent a good deal of time studying the safety areas of this room from the rooftops and windows. Your sniper doesn't have a shot."

"Not if he's outside," Mack agreed.

Joe hesitated and then went to the refrigerator and pulled out a Corona, shaking his head, clearly uncertain whether or not to believe Mack. "I see someone's been enjoying my beer."

"I thought it was Jaimie's beer," Kane said.

"She doesn't drink," Joe said and took a

long, slow swallow.

Mack frowned. "You seem to know a lot about Jaimie."

"I know she has nightmares. Bad ones."

Mack couldn't think for a moment; the roaring in his head was so loud it drowned out his ability to reason. He got up abruptly and paced across the floor to stare out the window.

"You going to tell your sniper to stand down anytime soon?" Joe asked.

"I was." Mack whirled around to face him. "I changed my mind. How the hell would you know Jaimie has nightmares?"

Joe shrugged. "A couple of weeks ago, she found a murder victim just a few feet from her door. It was pretty messy. A woman knifed just outside her doorway. She'd been stabbed multiple times. Jaimie hadn't been home and coming home to that really messed her up."

Mack kept his back to Joe, his gaze meeting Kane's. "How many times?"

"What do you mean?"

"How many times was the woman stabbed?"

"Sixteen."

Mack drew his breath in through burning lungs. "How old was she?"

Joe lowered the beer, aware of the rising

tension. "The vic was thirty-one. Lisa Carlston. She taught at . . ."

"An elementary school," Mack finished. "Third grade."

There was silence in the room. Mack sank into a chair and put his head in his hands. "Ethan, stand down," he ordered.

"You really did have a gun on me the entire time," Joe said. "I never spotted him."

"Ethan's like that," Kane said.

Joe looked around the room, into the shadows, and he still didn't see the hidden GhostWalker. "You knew I would come."

"If you were sent to kill her, you would have killed her," Mack said. "Anyone who can make the shot you did would have gotten her a long time ago."

"So all this was . . ."

"I don't take chances with Jaimie's life," Mack said.

Joe handed him an opened beer. "What's going on? How did you know the victim was an elementary teacher?"

"With dark hair," Mack said, his voice heavy with a sigh.

"Dark curly hair," Kane added.

"Like Jaimie," Joe said and put down the bottle of beer.

"Like Jaimie," Mack agreed. "Like her mother."

Joe swore. "Who was an elementary school teacher."

Mack nodded. "Jaimie found her just outside the door of their home stabbed sixteen times. It was Jaimie's sixteenth birthday. She came home late from work, and there was her mother lying dead on her doorstep." His voice shook. The memory still had the ability to shake him.

"No wonder she had nightmares," Joe said. "I had been following her, so I was with her when the cops came. She held it together, but when we came up here, she went to pieces. I got her to sleep and I stayed because I was worried. There didn't seem to be a connection and she didn't say anything, not to the cops and not to me. Of course at the time, we didn't know who the dead woman was or anything about her."

Mack exchanged a long look with Kane. "Jaimie would have known the significance of sixteen stab wounds. She's brilliant. Things don't get past her." Yet she hadn't called him. Hadn't turned to him.

"I don't understand," Joe said. "What the hell are we dealing with? I was asked to keep foreign governments off of her. Someone made a try for her a week ago, but he was no foreign government; he was one of ours. At least he appeared to be."

Mack nodded. "One of my boys took a couple of them down the other day. Former Marines. They were both reported dead over three years ago. Neither had been in the GhostWalker program but they'd both seen plenty of combat."

"Same with the one I took out. I did it quietly and Jaimie never knew," Joe said. He sighed. "You thinking what I'm thinking?"

"Black Ops," Mack said. "This is no foreign government after her. It's our own."

Kane leaned forward to look into Joe's face. "Our two were set up for torture and interrogation, not kidnapping. They were going to kill her."

"She's too valuable to kill," Joe said. "She's got too much training. Why would they put out a hit on her, and yet send me to guard her?"

"Because two factions are at work here, that's why," Mack said and stood up, pacing across the room, unable to contain the energy spilling out. Ordinarily he'd be talking it over with Kane. Jaimie had hit on something big and someone wanted her silenced, but now he didn't know who he could trust.

Kane shot him a look as if catching his thoughts, but remained silent. Mack was grateful. He didn't want to brawl in front of

Joe, but the moment Kane said the wrong thing, there were going to be a few punches thrown.

Jaimie moaned softly and Mack immediately crossed to her side and sat on the edge of the bed. "It's all right, honey. I'm here with you."

He knew Ethan wouldn't take his eyes from Joe and he could fully concentrate his attention on Jaimie. She was asleep. And she was weeping. He'd seen it before. Sometimes she even walked in her sleep, going from room to room, trying to find her mother. He'd had years of those nightmares, heartbreaking and far too frequent. The year they'd spent together, the nightmares had lessened.

Mack bent over her, his fingertips gentle as they brushed at her tears. "I'm here, baby, you're not alone."

She opened her eyes then, but there was only anxiety and blankness. He knew she wasn't aware. "I have to find her. She isn't here. I can't find her."

His heart clenched so hard it felt like a heart attack, the pain gripping him until he could barely breathe. "She's safe now, Jaimie. She's where no one can hurt her."

How many times had he murmured those words, trying to soothe her, quiet her mind when she was caught in the throes of a nightmare? It had always been Jaimie and her mother. Stacy had been fifteen when she'd given birth to her daughter. Her parents had thrown her out and she'd lived on the streets with the incredibly intelligent infant. Stacy had done her best for her daughter, working as a waitress and taking classes at night. It couldn't have been easy and Jaimie had adored her mother.

He stretched out beside her, laying his claim in front of Joe. Jaimie was his. She would always be his, no matter how bad he screwed up, no matter how many mistakes he made. He'd find his way back to her, because in the end, Jaimie was his world.

He locked his fingers with hers, feeling a little helpless, as he always did when she was caught in the middle of a nightmare, restless and lost in another world he couldn't travel into. He wasn't a dream-walker like Lucas or Ethan and he didn't know what would happen if one of them entered her nightmare with her. All of them lived with enhanced psychic abilities, but they were all learning to cope with the skills, even after all this time. For him, he knew his abilities were growing. He could move from one place to another in seconds. At first it had been short distances, but now those distances were growing. It seemed that way with all of them, the psychic talents developing stronger over time and with use. Why, then, hadn't Jaimie known Joe was a GhostWalker? Why hadn't she sensed Gideon on the roof? And why was her reaction getting worse when she used her psychic abilities?

Because they were getting stronger. He closed his eyes as he brought her hand to his chest, just over his heart. That was the only explanation. Jaimie's abilities were growing and the price was higher. Her talent was highly unusual. She could feel intent and, if expanded, she could take in an entire structure. Thinking about it, he realized she'd read the energy around her entire building and down the streets. What had she been reading on the street today? How large of an area?

She would be able to find positions on battlefields, know where snipers had positioned themselves, know if an assassin was in the crowd. She was too valuable to want dead, yet someone very high up had ordered her death. Was she close to finding Whitney's supporters? She must have triggered a red flag in her search. That would be like Jaimie. She would go in where others would be terrified. She might not pull a trigger to kill someone, but she wouldn't flinch when uncovering corruption and seeking justice.

"Stop crying, baby," he whispered. "You're killing me. I hate to feel helpless. You know that." He wasn't good at some things. Kane often had been the one wiping Jaimie's tears away when she was a child and other kids tried bullying her. Mack was usually the one that beat the crap out of them. "Wake up, Jaimie. You're here with me." He pressed kisses along her temple. *Come on, honey, you're safe. I've got you.*

He knew the instant she was aware of him lying beside her. He was in her mind, a place where he'd so often taken refuge in the past. He caught that brief flare of happiness, of completeness, and it settled the roiling in his stomach and mind. She hadn't written him off quite as completely as she claimed, and she certainly didn't hate him.

Every day had been endless without her unless he was in the field working. There had been a huge, empty hole nothing — and no one — could fill. He hadn't bothered to try with anyone else. It was all about Jaimie. His other half. She had looked at him with stars in her eyes, allowing him the lead and following wherever he went. She hadn't asked anything of him — until that night she left him. He was ashamed of himself, of his actions. He hadn't wanted to admit to himself, let alone to her, what kind of power she had over him.

Jaimie. Honey. Can you hear me?

There was a small silence. He could hear the low murmur of Kane and Joe talking. He couldn't hear Ethan, but knew he was somewhere off to his right in the shadows, probably clinging to the ceiling like an upside-down spider. He could hear his heart beat.

Yes. There was a sob in her mind.

I should have told you I wanted you to stay. I know it's not what you want to hear right now, but I was a fucking coward. Give me another chance with you. I don't want to go through my life without you. I should have asked you to stay.

This time he counted his heartbeats. He felt her sadness beating at him. Her regret. His heart beat double-time.

I'm not the same person anymore, Mack.

Is there someone else? He braced himself. She was going to kill him. He detested good-looking, over-six-foot Joe Spagnola, who had stayed all night with her to help her through her nightmares when he should have been there holding her.

Of course not. I loved you — love you, Mack. I always have. You don't just get over that. Well, I don't. You were my world. It took a little time to learn to just exist without you.

He knew she was being truthful, not hurtful. She was giving him facts, her tone all Jaimie and a clear reprimand. He wanted to smile, relief flooding him. Satisfaction. There was no one else. Not even Superman. *I'm not going anywhere again, Jaimie.*

She sighed and turned into him, her head finding a niche against his shoulder. *Until the first time Griffen orders you into the field.*

That's work, Jaimie. You aren't going to be upset when I go to work.

How are you ever going to know he isn't sending you out on a suicide mission?

That brought him up short. He trusted Griffen. He knew the sergeant major. The man was a patriot through and through and he always stood for his men. He was tough, but he took the heat from the politicians. Part of the reason Mack had agreed to the program was because they would all report directly to Griffen. He didn't send his team out lightly.

Jaimie, I'm telling you I want you to stay with me. Be with me.

And I don't doubt it for a minute, Mack. She let go of his fingers and he immediately felt bereft. *My head aches and I need to sleep.*

No nightmares, then.

And tell Joe I'm really not happy with him either.

Mack shifted, leaned in to kiss her temple, and rose. "She's not happy with you, Joe." He didn't bother to keep elation from his voice.

"I figured that," Joe said. "I'm going back to my suite. The place is a dump but it's home, unless your men tore it up."

"They left it intact."

Javier, he's on the move, Mack warned. "How long you figure you're staying around?"

"Until Sergeant Major pulls me off the duty. And that isn't going to be until we find the bastard coming at her."

"Sounds personal to me," Mack said.

"You bet it's personal," Joe said, for once shaken out of his usual calm. "She's mine. I've been protecting her for months. I'm not about to turn her over to you or anyone else. So forget asking your sergeant major. I'm going to find the bastard who put that body on her doorstep and whoever is targeting her for assassination. Not on my watch."

Kane and Mack exchanged a long look as Joe crossed the room, checked Jaimie's pulse, smoothed back her hair, and then, without another word, went down the stairs.

Ethan did a slow somersault from where

he'd been clinging like a spider in the rafters and landed in a crouch. "You know, boss, you just might have a rival for Jaimie's affections again. And this time, I don't think he's scared of you."

CHAPTER 8

"You're not cooking for all the boys, Jaimie. You've been ill. You couldn't get out of bed for two days."

Jaimie gave a little dismissive sniff and brushed past Mack. "I *want* to cook dinner for them. Kane already bought the groceries for me. And why does he have that bruise on his jaw?" She glared over her shoulder at Mack.

Mack shrugged. "I think he ran into a door."

"That's what I thought you'd say. You've been glowering at each other since I've been up. Why don't you kiss and make up instead of walking around like a couple of bears with sore teeth? You always make up, and the longer it takes, the more we all have to suffer."

Mack didn't reply, but came up behind her. Close. Very close. So close she could feel the warmth of his breath on the back of her neck.

She threw her elbow back and caught him in the ribs. "I mean it, Mack. Go make up. I hate it when the two of you stomp around and growl at each other. What's wrong with you?"

"I went to Sergeant Major and asked for protection for you," Kane said.

Jaimie whirled around and found herself up against Mack's body. She felt his inhale, whether at the brush of her body against his or at Kane's admission, she didn't know. "That's no surprise."

"It was to me," Mack said. "He didn't discuss it."

"Jaimie's my sister, Mack," Kane said, his tone one of exaggerated patience. "I don't have to discuss it with you. She left. She wasn't going to let it go. I know her, the way she thinks, and she wasn't going to drop her argument against Whitney. She was going to try to find proof for you."

"You knew he was going to watch out for me anyway," Jaimie pointed out, stepping away from Mack.

"From a distance, Jaimie. I wanted someone on you up close, where when you tripped up, they'd be able to send a report to Griffen and he'd contact me. That was the arrangement."

"Why didn't you just tell me?" Mack demanded.

"Because the sergeant major wanted something in return," Jaimie guessed, her eyes locked with Kane's. "He did, didn't he?"

Kane shrugged. "I knew what you'd do, Jaimie, and I wasn't about to let you get your neck chopped off."

"I'm not giving him my data. That's what you promised him, isn't it?"

"That and how you do what you do."

"That's too bad, Kane, because, had you asked me, I would have volunteered the information to you had I known how I do it. But no way in hell will I ever turn over my proof of Whitney's crimes to Sergeant Major Griffen. He's entrenched in the GhostWalker program and probably embroiled up to his medals in Whitney's scum."

"I can hack your computer."

"You don't have the skills to hack me. And neither do Sergeant Major's little experts." She tilted her chin at him, her eyes dark and stormy.

"Maybe, but Javier does."

She smirked at him. "Maybe, but I don't think so."

Kane's jaw tightened. "You anticipated me trading for protection."

All trace of amusement faded from her face. "I know you just as well as you know me. The minute I saw that dead body, I knew it was a warning. I knew I was getting close to Whitney's protectors. Then you showed up here because of a wrong address."

"Wait a minute," Mack said. There was a note in his voice, a strain of underlying anger that had Kane moving back out of harm's way. Quiet. Nasty. That dangerous tone that made Mack who he was. "Are you telling me that Sergeant Major traded information for Jaimie's safety? He actually knew she was in harm's way and made you pay a price to protect her?"

"Mack," Kane said.

Mack's teeth snapped together. "You watch her, Kane. I'll be back later. I think I'll go have a chat with Griffen."

"You'll be court-martialed if you lay a hand on him," Kane said. "You're not going anywhere."

"Because you think you can stop me?"

"You sound like a couple of little kids," Jaimie scolded. "Let's think this through instead of punching someone. Sheesh, Mack. Are you ever going to grow out of that?"

"I'm sublimating."

Jaimie stared at him. She felt heat moving up her neck and throat to her face. His eyes were black and glittering, but filled with more than just teasing lust. Possession maybe. Whatever it was, it was all male and very compelling. Like a starving wolf. "Well, don't." She croaked the words out. It was the best she could do with the sudden dry-mouth syndrome that seemed to afflict her whenever he gave her that hungry stare.

Mack's eyebrow shot up. "You heard her, Kane. She just gave me permission to punch out a superior officer."

"I did not," Jaimie denied.

"You told me not to sublimate."

She sighed. "You're so crazy, Mack. Sit down and quit prowling around while I'm trying to cook."

She glanced out the window at the sky. The sun had set already and fog swirled in, thick and gray, covering the buildings with a veil of mist. "Are the boys out in this weather?"

"A couple of them. They change shifts," Mack said.

"I'm making lasagna. They all love that with French bread and salad. I'll feed everyone and then call the ones on watch in." She sighed. "Maybe I should invite Joe to show him I'm not that angry."

"You should be angry at that Sicilian Don Juan with his stupid tight jeans and cocky grin. You're too forgiving, Jaimie."

Kane coughed, trying to be discreet. *Don't tell her that. You're trying to get her to forgive you for being so dense, Mack. Are you crazy?*

"A Sicilian Don Juan?" Jaimie echoed. "Joe?" She laughed softly. "Is he even Sicilian? I thought that was his cover."

"You bought the entire Sicilian carpenter persona?" Mack rolled his eyes and then flicked Kane a quelling look.

"He's got the muscles," Jaimie pointed out. "You know, hot carpenter bod and all that. And impeccable credentials. I tried to find holes in his story, but it was solid."

"Javier said that. He tried finding out about him. I take it you lifted his prints?"

She nodded. "First thing, but then, if he's in the GhostWalker program, he's hooked up and can be anybody he wants to be." She worked smoothly as she talked, carefully putting thick, flat noodles into boiling water before turning back to her sauce.

Mack crowded her all over again. "You don't need to be looking at his muscles, Jaimie."

"I can hardly help it, now, can I, Mack? His muscles are rather obvious."

"I told you to shoot the son of a bitch

while you had the chance, Kane," Mack complained. "Now I've got to put up with Jaimie ogling him. And no, there's no need to invite him for dinner. I don't want him to see the boys. Not yet."

Jaimie didn't reply for a long time. "If he's a GhostWalker, and you let him work on me the other night, then why wouldn't you trust him?"

"Because I didn't listen to you last time when I should have. I'm going to be a lot more careful this time around. We have to think this bargain Kane made with Griffen over very carefully. If he's capable of bargaining for your safety, he isn't the man I thought he was."

Kane shrugged. "As long as she's safe, Mack. I don't want her anywhere near Whitney. The way the man treats those women is criminal. And I'm not convinced he doesn't have more orphans locked up somewhere, experimenting on them. I'll pay whatever price Griffen wants to keep Jaimie out of Whitney's hands."

She turned around and rested one hip against the counter to study Kane's face. He was handsome in a tough sort of way, even with the lines etched there. "What happened there, Kane? In Whitney's compound. I know you were assigned to guard the place . . ."

"I wish I'd been assigned to guard the place. That's what I thought. That's what we all thought. But it was for something altogether different. Whitney ran tests on all of us and he paired a few of us with some of the women being held there."

She swallowed hard. She'd hacked into Whitney's files and she had several condemning files. Had Kane really been asked to get one of the women pregnant? She couldn't imagine him doing something like that.

"I'm not discussing it, Jaimie, not yet. It's all too raw and I haven't quite figured out what I'm going to do yet."

"Jaimie! Get down here now." Javier's voice came through the intercom. "You're being hacked. Double-time it."

Jaimie threw the spoon back in the sauce and pushed past Mack. She leapt across the room in two long bounds, landing at the top of the stairs in a crouch and then jumping to the landing below. She was comfortable using her enhanced genetic skills. Mack noted her body was fluid like a cat's as she leapt the remaining distances. He didn't use his cat skills; he used his teleportation speed, flashing from spot to spot and landing right with her.

"The alarm should have gone off upstairs. I've been waiting for this," Jaimie said, seating herself beside Javier. Her eyes gleamed with satisfaction. "Did you touch anything?"

"I turned it off just now," Javier admitted. "It scared the hell out of me."

Her fingers raced over the keyboard at an enormous rate of speed. Javier seemed to know exactly what she was doing, his fingers were flying as well. To Mack the screen was nothing but numbers and red lines streaking in various directions.

"He's been nosing around trying to get past my security, so I set up a nice little trap and the idiot fell for it."

"He's good," Javier pointed out, his eyes glued to the data flowing across the screen.

"Yep, but I'm better," Jaimie said. "I knew he was going to make his try soon. I put out bait and he took it. I'm going to find out exactly who he is."

"Will he know you've traced him?" Mack asked.

"He's bouncing all over the place," Javier hissed.

"He doesn't know we're tracking him," Jaimie said. "I just need another minute to get him. He's hacking into the trap I set and if he makes it in before I get him, he'll be gone."

"I take it you made it difficult?"

"You bet. I want to see how skilled he really is. He's moving through the walls fast."

"He's a pro with resources," Javier added. "Only a few in the world are good enough to hack into your system, Jaimie."

Mack marveled at the speed their fingers flew across the keyboard. Their eyes were glued to the screen. It all made sense to them, but to him it was a jumble of code and nothing more. That didn't stop uneasiness from creeping into him. He felt hunted. Watched. Something evil moving in the room.

Twice Jaimie's breath hissed out and once Javier hunched lower over the keys as if that small movement would increase his speed and dexterity.

The tension in the room coiled tighter and tighter, stretching nerves taut. Mack could hear breathing, feel the blood pounding in his veins, the knots forming in the pit of his stomach. He looked around, into every corner, half expecting someone to come jumping out at them. His hand actually crept toward the knife at his belt.

"I'm almost on him," Jaimie hissed. "I've got you, you toad."

Mack's gut reacted with more knots and

somewhere in his brain a warning flash went off. He cleared his throat. "Jaimie, shut it down."

"Are you crazy?"

"Do it, Jaimie," Kane said. "Shut it down."

"Javier, that's an order," Mack snapped and caught Jaimie, jerking her away from the computer. "Pull the plug. Do it now, do it fast."

"Whose side are you on?" Jaimie demanded, twisting around, trying to get back to her chair. Mack kept his arm around her waist, lifting her off the ground to keep her from the keyboard.

Javier shook his head. "I don't think I'm going to shut it down before he's in."

"Unplug the damn thing now."

Kane was already in motion, sprinting for the power strip.

"No!" Jaimie wailed. "You can't do it like that. You'll mess up my programs. He won't find anything. He'll only think he's in. I put all kinds of crap data for him to find. By the time he wades through it . . ." She broke off, horrified, as the screens went black.

"He'll know you're on to him and he'll know you're coming after him. They'll blow this place out from under you to get you, Jaimie. Right now they only know you're after Whitney. His cover was blown a long time ago. Half the world thinks he's dead or a myth and the other half pretends he's dead. He's an embarrassment, but every GhostWalker team knows he's alive. That was the only reason they didn't kill you. What would be the point? But if they think you know who is supporting him, that's an entirely different ball game."

She jerked away from him, throwing a punch at his chest as she stumbled back. "I know exactly what I'm doing. I had him."

"You mean he almost had you."

"He already knows who I am, Mack, or I wouldn't have had a dead body on my doorstep to warn me off or an assassin coming to my door. I'm so close to getting him."

"Why the hell do you think he sent you the dead body, Jaimie? Someone looked you up and studied you, tried to find the perfect thing to scare you with. They killed some poor innocent woman and threw her body on your doorstep to tell you to back the hell off."

Tears shimmered in her furious eyes. "You think I don't know that?" She pointed to the stairs. "Get out, Mack. Take everyone with you. I'm not doing this with you, not ever again. I mean it; get the hell out of my house." She turned her back on him and walked toward the plug.

"Don't even think about it, Jaimie." His voice dropped low in warning.

She whirled back around and this time there were tears tracking down her face. "I can't believe you said that to me. You think I don't know? You think I'm so stupid I don't get what's going on? You want to hurl insults at each other? You think that's the way to get me to listen? If you'd listened to me in the first place, none of this would be happening."

"That isn't true, Jaimie," Kane intervened softly. "It would have happened to someone else. It did. To helpless children. To unsuspecting men and women. To women trapped in his breeding program. To Whitney's own daughter. It would have happened no matter what. Just not to us. And we're good. We've got each other. We know one another inside and out and that gives us the advantage. If he can't separate us and break us apart, we've got power no other Ghost-Walker team has against him. And we have your brains."

Jaimie didn't look at him. She glared at Mack. "You don't have the right to talk to me the way you do. I'm not one of your soldiers following orders. And I'm not your girlfriend."

"Like hell you're not. You want to prove

me wrong so bad you're willing to risk your life. I already believe you, Jaimie, I've seen the proof. You don't need to put yourself in harm's way in order to get me to believe Whitney's a son of a bitch and he's being protected."

"For once in your life why don't you acknowledge I have a brain? I was this close" — she held up her fingers an inch apart — "to getting the identity of the man or men protecting Whitney. We can't take Whitney down without getting them. He'll just run, even if we expose him with proof. He'll be in the wind and we'll never find him."

"And if those protecting him are untouchable? What do you think is going to happen here, Jaimie? They've sent men trained in combat with enough experience to take on some of our best men. They put a sniper up on a roof to take you out."

"I know when they're close." Jaimie tried to bring her voice back under control. The madder she got, the louder her voice, the quieter he became, making her feel like a child being reprimanded by an adult. "I can feel their energy, Mack."

"You couldn't feel Joe, Jaimie, and he's a fucking sniper. He could have been sent to kill you, not protect you. He infiltrated your base and made himself your right-hand man. Suppose his orders change and he's told to kill you?"

Her chin lifted. "Suppose *your* orders change," she hurled back at him.

Instant silence fell. The room charged with anger until they all seemed to choke on it. Abruptly Mack turned on his heel and stalked to the stairs.

Jaimie stood over her computers, tears running down her face, watching him go.

"Jaimie." Javier slipped his arm around her. "You know I had to follow orders, but I should have realized you'd be in trouble. You got it, didn't you? Right before Kane pulled the plug. You saw the location flash. I wasn't looking at the screen at that point, I was trying to disconnect, but I heard you gasp. Give it up."

"We didn't get it," Jaimie said. "Kane unplugged the system before it flashed on the screen. He didn't make it in and I didn't complete the trace."

Javier and Jaimie stared into each other's eyes.

Is she lying? Kane asked.

I can't tell. It's possible that she was upset because you shut down the system and some of her more sensitive programs might be messed up. That false computer was genius.

They couldn't know it was a trap. They had to believe they'd made it into her hard drive. My guess is they were trying to plant a Trojan to collect her data.

Kane sent him a flash of puzzlement.

A spy inside her system, Javier explained. *They want a look at her files.*

"Don't lie about this, Jaimie," Kane warned. "It's too important. We have to know how far they're willing to go to kill you."

"I think they've made it plain, they're serious, Kane," she shot back. "Maybe if I knew who my enemy was, I would be able to fight back. As it is, you and Mack managed to prevent that from happening."

Did you get a look at her files?

They're encrypted and Jaimie's one of the best at encryption. It would take a long time to get past her security and she probably has more than one fail-safe.

If you take her hard drive, can you get the files?

"Yeah, keep talking," Jaimie said. "I'll really trust you knowing you're keeping secrets."

"What the hell do you expect, Jaimie? You don't trust us. You insulted Mack and now you're insulting us with your lies. If you think you have to hide the truth from us, who the hell do you trust? Joe? Mack's right, the man could get orders any minute to cut your throat. As for me, when I received an order that was wrong, I knew it was wrong and I risked my career and life to stop Whitney. And if you don't know me or Mack by now, you deserve everything that's coming." Kane followed Mack up the stairs.

Jaimie switched her gaze to Javier. "Are you going to yell at me too?"

"No. I want a decent dinner tonight." He sat on the edge of the desk and regarded her with cool eyes. "What's going on, babe? Do you really think Mack and Kane would betray you? If they betray you, they'd have to go through all the rest of us. You're my baby sister. The only one I've got. And don't bring up Rhianna, because you know I don't look at her that way and I never will, no matter what she says."

Jaimie pressed her fingertips to her throbbing temples. "All of you like this life, Javier, including Rhianna. You're all anchors. Using psychic energy doesn't bother you. And all the genetic enhancements enable you to be faster and do really cool things. You all like and maybe even need the adrenaline rush, Mack and Kane included. You're serving your country and you're very good at what you do."

"The point?"

"When you love something, Javier, it's difficult to see the downside."

He shrugged. "But not impossible, Jaimie. You don't seem to realize the influence you have on all of us. You're *ours*, Jaimie. You think you're all alone in the world. And I think you somehow got it in your head that when you and Mack broke up, you broke up with the rest of us."

He was shredding her heart with his words. Of course she thought that. What else could she think? Mack was the head of their family. What he said went. Where he led, the others followed. All of them were strong, independent men, but they worked together like a machine and Mack was always — *always* — at the wheel.

"Jaimie?" Javier insisted. "Did you write all of us off?"

She frowned at him, blinking away tears. There was something in his voice, a note of hurt in that soft inquiry, that gave her pause, made her think from their point of view. She hadn't contacted any of them. Not a single one. When she'd left Mack, she believed they'd all side with him and when she split with the leader of the family, that she'd be the one alone.

"I didn't write anyone off. Why do you

think I'm doing this?" She swept her hand toward the computers. "Do you really think it's to prove a point to Mack? That's so like the way he'd think. He's egotistical and arrogant. I want to keep you all safe. I found out that the first GhostWalker team was targeted for murder. Did you know that? They were incarcerated in Whitney's lab and someone was sending them out on assignments and having them killed. Do you understand what that means, Javier? Sergeant Major could send you on a mission and you'd follow orders."

Javier frowned and crossed his arms across his chest, stretching his legs out in front of him as he regarded her with his dark, unblinking eyes. "You sure about this?"

She nodded. "And the second Ghost-Walker team was sent to the Congo. It was a trap. Two of the members were horribly tortured. The report is very detailed and includes some ghastly photographs. I have plenty of proof that it was a conspiracy involving a senator and another female GhostWalker. There are so many incidents, Javier, where GhostWalkers were sent into impossible situations. Fortunately, when they're together as a team, they've managed to escape, but I've pieced together at least four more incidents where I believe the first two teams were targeted for complete elimination."

"What about us?"

She dropped her eyes and shrugged. Casually. Too casually. "I have only one suspect mission."

"Our first. Where everything went to hell and they were waiting for us. It could have been bad intel, Jaimie."

"Yes. But it wasn't. I believe it was deliberate. If I hadn't been there to warn you all, most of you, or all of you, would have been wiped out on a single mission."

"And the fourth team?"

She shook her head. "They're shrouded in mystery. To get to their files, I have to peel layers and layers of protection away. I think they're hunting terrorist cells around the world. I think they assassinate them and melt back into the shadows. If I'm right, Javier, it would be easy for them to be eliminated."

"You think Whitney is doing this? Killing the soldiers he made?"

Jaimie shook her head, grateful someone she cared about was willing to listen to her. "Not Whitney. It doesn't fit his profile." She paced across the room and back, a small frown creasing her forehead. "It isn't him or his supporters. Those helping him know about his experiments with children and they're covering for him. And they sure know about his breeding program, but they don't want him dead. Or us. They believe his soldiers, all of you — me — are the answer for future soldiers." She shook her head. "No, it's someone else. Another group opposing Whitney's work and they don't mind murder to get rid of us."

"So different groups could be after you," Javier said.

She looked at him. "Probably." He kept looking at her, his gaze locking with hers. She sighed. "Okay. Yes. Two different factions. I think Whitney's supporters know about me and want me dead before I have a chance to expose them. The second group I don't believe has a clue I'm coming after them."

"Walk away from it, Jaimie."

"I can't. You're my family. I'm not letting them target you for elimination. I can't go with you, so this is the only way I have of protecting you."

Javier's smile was slow in coming. "That's so you, Jaimie. In your own way you think you can save the world."

"No, just my family. You and Mack and Kane save the world. I just care about saving you right now."

"Do you really believe you can't trust Mack?" His voice was quiet, not at all accusing.

She swallowed hard. What did she think? Kane had set Sergeant Major on her and what none of them seemed to realize was that he'd known she was digging for information. How had he known? "Mack protects all of us, Javier. He'd go up in flames if he saw I was setting myself up as a target in order to draw them away from you."

His breath hissed out. "You fucking tipped them off."

"I didn't have any other way to keep them from going after you. I *know* they were going to kill all of you. I can't prove it, not even to Mack. He wouldn't listen or believe me, Javier. What was I supposed to do? If Mack, who's known me most of my life and knows how intelligent I am, wouldn't listen to me, why should anyone else? I need proof and in the meantime, I had to take their attention from you and put it on me."

"Damn it, Jaimie. You should be kissing Kane's feet for sending someone to look after you."

"He brought Mack here. Mack wants to control every situation and he does insane things in the name of protecting us. Like pulling the plug just when I had the trace."

His eyebrow shot up. "You can bullshit the others, but not me, Jaimie. You saw where the trace originated. I know you did."

She studied his face. She'd never been all that good at poker, but she was brilliant when it came to dancing intrigue. "If it was there, Javier, then you're the only one who knows. Tell me. I can get them. You know I can. This war isn't going to be fought with guns. It's all about the paper trail."

He shook his head. "Not me. I was following orders. Mack said to pull the plug and I was trying to shut it down fast."

"Not looking at the monitor?" There was disbelief in her voice.

"I wish I had so I could tell you what you wanted to know, although I'm with Mack on this, and I think it's too dangerous."

"It's too late, Javier. They already know or they wouldn't be trying to scare me by leaving dead bodies on my doorstep, or sending two goons after me, or putting a sniper on a rooftop. And I'm not about to hide in a little cocoon while my entire family is slaughtered out in the field."

"Talk to Mack about this."

"Mack should have trusted me. He's asking me to give him acceptance and trust, but he refuses to give the same to me. I'm not going to talk about this with him. I trust

Mack with my life, but not with putting my life on the line."

"None of us want you to put your life on the line, not just Mack, Jaimie. We've got you and Rhianna." The name seemed to stick in his throat. He cleared it. "None of us want to give either of you up or put you in harm's way."

"You wanted me running missions with you."

"Because we could protect you. This is suicide and you know it. You put yourself right in front of a gun."

"You all do it every single day. I have the same training, Javier. I'm not a sacrificial lamb. I have a plan."

"What is it?"

"I'm going to expose them to the world. Once their names are splashed over every television network there is, they'll be too busy running to try to hunt any of us down."

Javier stared at her in stunned silence. "That's it? That's your big master plan? They're going to come at you with everything they have."

"Which is why I needed to get that trace."

Javier shook his head. "You're not invincible, Jaimie. You can't take on people that powerful. They have to be in Congress, or the White House itself."

"Someone has to do it. What's the alternative? They can't be above the law. If they are, there's no chance for any of you. Any day now, they could send you into another trap. Someone told the Doomsday unit exactly where you were going to be. They baited a trap and sent us out. It wasn't poor information, it was a deliberate attempt to eliminate all of us. Just like Team Two was sent to the Congo and the rebels were waiting for them."

"Do you have any idea how often assassination looks like a common accident? If we didn't know what you were doing, if Kane hadn't been alarmed and sent someone in to watch you, and you were killed in an accident, none of us would have been the wiser."

"And if you went out into the field and all of you were ambushed, the world wouldn't even be told about it. You never would have existed in the first place. Well, you exist to me, Javier, and I'll be damned if I let them kill you. I'll find them and expose them."

Javier stood up slowly. "You need to find a way to talk to Mack, Jaimie."

She glared at him. "We're so back to the boy's club, aren't we, Javier? He threw me away, not the other way around. We aren't together anymore."

He shrugged, in no way shaken by her anger. "Maybe not, hon, but we're a family and Mack is the head. You and Rhianna are the heart. You've never seen Mack's tough side. He's gentle around you . . ."

She gave a snort of derision.

"He is, Jaimie. He's different. He jokes and laughs and is a completely different man than he is out in the field. Do you think someone like me would follow him if he wasn't? I'm lethal. You know that. Most of us are. Mack has to be strong to lead us all. He has to be reliable. That doesn't mean he can't make a few mistakes. If we're going to get through this, we have to be all together on it. And we have to trust one another."

Even as he said it he very casually, right in front of her, flicked at a switch on the control panel. Her breath caught in her throat. She brushed her hand over her face, realized she was trembling, and put her hands behind her back. "You have the intercom on, don't you?"

"Of course. We're in this together. I'm not holding back information that may save your life. You're just going to have to accept that we're here and we're going to protect you."

She bit down hard on her lower lip and shook her head. "I need to be alone for a little while. I'm not used to being around anyone anymore."

"Where are you going?"

"To the first floor." She looked at him with a mixture of despair and sadness. "I'm not stupid, Javier, and I don't have a death wish. I won't leave."

"I'm not going to say I'm sorry. Keeping you safe is too important."

"I don't expect you to."

She turned away from him. She didn't fit anywhere anymore. Maybe she never had. She'd been so much younger than the others all through school. They were intensely physical and she spent most of her time inside her brain. She'd been devastated when she'd broken up with Mack, worse than devastated. She'd broken apart inside. He hadn't trusted her. He hadn't believed in her. And he hadn't wanted to spend his life with her.

Mack had been her entire world. She'd spent the first year numb — existing — making it through not each day but each hour. She hadn't realized how much she depended on him and how often she'd turned to him for everything in her life. He'd been her other half. She wasn't complete without him. And to know he didn't trust her had been even worse than his rejection of their life together.

Mack had always been the acknowledged leader, but there hadn't been a single member of their makeshift family who hadn't known she had brains. She'd been shocked when he wouldn't give her suspicions any credence. What was she, then? A warm body he could sate himself with? A woman who fed him and kept his house, but should keep her opinions to herself?

"Jaimie," Javier said softly, trying to reason with her.

There was nothing to say, nothing he could say. She went down the stairs to the darkened first floor. She'd had such plans when she first found the building; now they seemed hollow. She had Mack and the others back in her life, but Mack still saw her as a child to protect instead of a partner he could respect. How was she going to be able to face them all? How was she going to stay in the same room with Mack?

She stood in the middle of the room with her hands on her hips feeling lost and alone. The sound of the water lapping at the pier was louder on the first floor. She'd done very little down here, other than to secure the windows and entrances against intruders. This would have been a perfect home for Kane and his chosen wife. Jaimie and

Mack in her fantasy world would have lived on the third floor. The second floor would have a few spare bedrooms for the boys when they dropped by and a work area for the business.

She sank down onto the floor and dropped her head into her hands. Of course she'd been thinking they'd all work together. She hadn't even realized that had been in the back of her head. She'd start a company, make it a success; Mack would see the error of his ways and he'd come back to her. What an idiot she'd been. All the time she'd been sure she'd been so independent, but all along, she'd been weaving a fantasy.

Jaimie sighed. She'd grown up in a mostly male world. They stuck together, thinking alike for the most part. She should have known Javier would switch the intercom on and try to get information out of her. He didn't view his actions as disloyal any more than Kane viewed his actions as betrayal. Everything with her family seemed to be done in the name of protection. She wished Rhianna were there. Rhianna was very different, much more of a tomboy, edgier, but she at least understood Jaimie's point of view.

She pressed her fingertips to her eyes and sat in silence, wishing she was alone again.

CHAPTER 9

Mack stood at the window and stared down into the choppy, white foam–tipped waves as the water lapped at the pier below. Jaimie had left him, all right, but she'd put herself in harm's way because she felt she had to protect them all. He swallowed the lump blocking his throat. That was exactly what Jaimie would do — go after anyone she thought was harming her family. He should have known. Kane had known, but Kane hadn't come to him. Was he really so arrogant and stubborn that he wouldn't listen to the people he cared about most?

He had been so hurt when she left him. He'd been stunned — shocked. Totally caught off guard. And with him, hurt always manifested itself in anger. He'd come home and she was gone. She'd left him with nothing. He hadn't considered that he would ever be without her. That he would go to bed and not be able to sleep. That he would hate his empty house. That he would listen for the sound of her laughter. He hadn't realized how often he turned to her to discuss every topic, how much he relied on her knowledge. Jaimie had been as much a part of him as his breathing. And then she was gone and he hadn't understood why.

Mack pushed a hand through his hair, a little surprised to realize it was unsteady. Stupid pride hadn't allowed him to run after her. That was all it had been. Pride. Ego. Jaimie was supposed to worship him, and he hadn't wanted to believe she could make it on her own without him. He was certain she would come back — only she hadn't. She'd gone her own way and, worse, she hadn't contacted him to let her know where she was. That was painful too, to have to search and go through channels, so everyone had known he'd been frantic, had known he needed to keep a hand on her. That had been humiliating in itself. Sergeant Major had called him in twice and asked him if he could still do his job.

He shook his head. He should have handled things differently. She'd been so traumatized the night of that first interaction with Doomsday. He'd felt so guilty, recognizing that everyone who mattered to him could have been killed. As it was, three had been badly wounded. He had been directly responsible. Jaimie freaking out on him, ranting about conspiracies, hadn't made sense at that time. He was wallowing in guilt, desperate to get medical aid for everyone, including Jaimie. She'd been a mess, her brain bleeding. He'd been certain he was going to lose her too. He'd wanted her quiet.

Mack shook his head, pressing his fingertips to his eyes, unable to even recall exactly what he'd said to her. When she'd fallen silent, he'd been happy, not alarmed. Not warned. And then that quiet question, *"Where are we even going with this relationship, Mack? Home? Family? Children? The whole thing is based on trust."*

He'd heard children. He'd asked her if she was pregnant. Her expression should have been a warning sign, but damn it all, she was bleeding from her mouth and nose. Even her ears. His mind shut down, refusing to let the image back into his head. He was responsible for that too. What the hell had any of it had to do with a botched mission and wounded men?

He turned abruptly. "Kane. You and Javier finish making that lasagna while I go talk to her. She'd be upset if all that went to waste."

"Whoa there, boss man." Kane drew back,

both hands in the air. "I agree you need to talk to her, but I don't cook. And this is everyone's favorite. If I mess it up, one of them is likely to shoot me."

"If she cries because it isn't done, I'll shoot you myself."

Javier grinned at Kane and shrugged his shoulders. "Guess we're cooking. Doesn't this thing have cheese in it?"

"She has all the ingredients right there. I think the two of you can figure it out."

"Why is it you always get the girl, Top?" Javier asked.

"Because you're still wet behind the ears," Mack said.

Kane gingerly picked up a large spoon and stirred the sauce. "It smells good. We probably could shred the noodles and just make spaghetti."

Mack paused at the top of the stairs and glared at them. "You can make lasagna."

Kane winked at Javier. "You got it, boss man."

"She went down to the first floor to be alone, Mack, but don't count on her staying there. She'll be back rigging her computers again. She won't be able to let it go. Hell," Javier said, "I want to go down and work with them and I didn't set off her trap. I'd love to see who these bastards are and how she set the trap for them."

"Thanks, Javier." He waited until Javier looked up at him. "You risked your relationship with her for me. I won't forget it."

"I love her, Mack. We have to protect her. I figure we're all in this together."

Mack nodded and hurried down the stairs. Behind him he heard Kane mutter, "I got a punch in the jaw for being underhanded and I was protecting her too."

Javier's laughter was in Mack's ears as he made the second-floor landing. A single light illuminated the bank of computers and screens. Jaimie stood frowning, bent over, inspecting something intently. He had always loved that particular expression on her face. He knew she was figuring out a problem, just by the little frown lines between her brows. She glanced up at him — of course she'd known he was there — and her expression changed to wariness. He didn't want it to, but that obvious change hurt.

"I've got work to do."

It was a clear dismissal. She'd never really done that before. She'd always been glad to see him and because he knew she was serious, the words cut deep. "We have to work this out, Jaimie."

Her gaze slid away from him. "I know. I'm

just not ready yet. I still feel a little raw from the last time."

"I don't want to fight."

She shrugged, her fingers moving over the keyboard, her gaze fixed on the screen. "We seem to fight whether you want to or not. I'm not going to agree with you on this, Mack. There's no reason to keep going at each other."

Mack crossed the room, knowing she was aware of his every movement, although she didn't look up again. He came right up behind her and peered over her shoulder. It didn't matter. The code racing across the screen meant nothing to him. It should have bothered him, but he was used to Jaimie and took pride in her abilities.

"I'm staying until I know you're safe, so we have to work this out."

She did look up then. "Really? What do you think is going to happen next, Mack? You'll be sent out on a mission. All of you."

He studied her face. "You believe Sergeant Major is involved."

"I know he is."

He tried not to let the instant anger in his gut surface. He was good friends with Griffen and she knew it. Griffen had been instrumental in Mack making the decision to test for the psychic program in the first place. He'd also been the one to keep them all together. Jaimie had never been comfortable around Sergeant Major, but then, she wasn't military. She loved the boys and Rhianna, but stayed away from everyone else.

Her soft laughter was without humor. "You have such a closed mind. I can tell you're already building arguments against anything I have to say, so really, Mack, what's the point?"

"I'm listening," he replied. She always had been astute in an argument. Jaimie caught nuances others didn't. "It isn't easy to hear bad things about friends."

Jaimie caught up a pen and wrote "Whitney" in the middle of a piece of paper. Above his name she drew a line, put a question mark above that, and drew another line and wrote "White House Who?"

"Someone is giving him a great deal of support. We know that or he wouldn't still be in business. He can pull in GhostWalkers, and military personnel. He can land on military bases. We know he's being protected and even warned when anyone gets too close to him. He has supporters, Mack. Big ones with lots of power."

"I'm aware of that."

"When Kane and Brian both came back

from their assignment to Whitney, what did they do? What did they tell you?"

"That there were irregularities. That Whitney was involved in illegal experiments."

"But Kane wouldn't discuss it with you. You're more than his best friend. Brian has looked up to you his entire life, yet he didn't discuss it either."

"No. They wanted to keep me out of it. They were afraid Whitney might target them and didn't want me involved. I arranged a meeting with Sergeant Major Griffen. They reported directly to him. There were two others who came forward as well. A pararescue Team Four GhostWalker by the name of Malichai Fortunes and . . ."

"Antonio Martinez from Team Two, the SEAL GhostWalker team. All of them made their report together to Sergeant Major," Jaimie finished. "But what happened to the chain of command, Mack?"

"You have been digging for information." Mack didn't know whether to admire her or shake her. "Did you see the actual report?"

"It was a closed meeting, Mack, and all of them — and you — trusted Griffen would take it higher and something would be done. The men turned over all their evidence to the sergeant major as they were supposed to. Did you think it strange that

Kane and Brian were sent out on a mission alone not long after, when your team always works together?"

Mack shook his head. "Not always, Jaimie." But his gut was churning again, always a bad sign. "All the teams are assigned to support one another at times." But he *had* thought it strange. The order had raised a red flag in his mind and he'd sent Javier and Gideon as backup. He'd kept that to himself.

"Things didn't go as well as expected."

"They completed their assignment and they made it back."

"And Sergeant Major has sent all of you out on assignments with specific orders on how to run the operation. Brian and Kane were always put in harm's way."

"We all were. That's the name of the game."

A flash of annoyance crossed her face. "That's your problem, Mack. You think this is all some massive chess game. The human lives you're playing with are your family."

"That's such bullshit, Jaimie." Now he was furious. "I keep them alive. I don't take my men blindly into a combat situation. And I don't let anyone else plan my missions, not even Sergeant Major."

"Which is why Kane and Brian are still

alive. Fortunately for Antonio Martinez, the leader of Team Two seems to be just as good at planning and so far has managed to keep him alive. As for Malichai, he's been wounded twice. The missions for the pararescue team are much more sensitive and harder to get to, but often only three men are sent out together and unfortunately they have no way of knowing he's a target. He's going to have a difficult time staying alive."

Mack was silent, turning over her information. His every instinct told him she was right. For all he knew, Jaimie might be able to hack into the Pentagon computers. She had skills that were incredible. She wrote programs and codes that others couldn't seem to compete with, and the military used her programs. She could look at a report, a picture, and see inconsistencies or patterns long before anyone else. If she said someone was targeting those four men — there was no question about it.

"You hacked Sergeant Major. Maybe someone else did."

"He reported everything to Colonel Wilford, Mack. Colonel Wilford consulted with someone other than the next in the chain of command, someone I can't get to yet. That man turned over all the evidence to Whitney. He's running the teams and he believes in the GhostWalkers, but he's fanatical the way Whitney is. The end justifies the means. If they lose a few along the way, too bad as long as the end results are the super-soldier they believe is the wave of the future."

"You believe Griffen is actually trying to kill four GhostWalkers." He made it a statement.

"I don't know exactly what he's doing, but he takes his orders from Colonel Wilford and Wilford takes them from someone who consults with Whitney. What do you think? I've studied Whitney. He's very removed from human feelings. He isn't going to kill his soldiers outright. If they die, they weren't good enough to live. But he's going to keep putting them in harm's way because they're the most expendable. He knows Griffen gave them an order. He told them they weren't to discuss what they saw at Whitney's compound with anyone. And they haven't."

"Kane told me there's a breeding program."

"Because the rumor was already going around. Team Two has a woman from the program married to one of their members. That isn't exactly news."

Mack sagged against the desktop. Had he

trapped them all in a web of intrigue? He wasn't the intrigue type. Point him at a target and he could take it out without hesitation. He was hell on wheels in a fight, but not this kind of deceit. Friends betraying friends. There was a code of honor. A standard. Sergeant Major was the man who directed his team as well as a personal friend. They relied on each other. Nothing worked if there wasn't honor.

Jaimie moved closer to him. He felt the warmth of her body, inhaled the scent that was uniquely Jaimie. Her fragrance brought back a flood of memories. He wrapped his arms around her before he could think too much about it, and pulled her into his body. There had always been something peaceful about Jaimie he had never found anywhere else. His body always wanted action, but with Jaimie, he found a haven, a place of quiet where he could truly relax, where the coiled tension in his body simply let go.

Jaimie. His refuge. His secret sanctuary that always gave him renewed energy and strength. His everything. She'd walked out on him and he'd been so shaken at the realization that she'd been the one to have the hold on him, not the other way around. He had been determined to live without her unless she'd come back to him on her own.

She'd just about killed his ego and pride and everything he believed himself to be. The leader. The untamable. He was not anything he'd believed himself to be.

Jaimie was stiff at first, but he refused to let go, simply holding her, asking nothing at all but comfort. She relaxed into him, her body all soft curves and heat. He missed her so much. He missed this. Simply holding her. Having her next to him. Breathing her in. When she smiled, everything in his life turned to sunlight. She could make him see the world in an entirely different light. One touch of her fingers on his body wiped out every bad place he'd ever experienced. He'd thought she'd always be there. He'd taken her for granted. It had all been so easy when she was with him.

He buried his face against her soft neck, his hands tunneling through the waves and curls of her hair. Turning his head, he kissed the side of her neck, lingering to savor the feeling of her soft skin and the scent of her.

For a moment, Jaimie leaned into him, but as if catching herself, she pulled herself straight, almost rigid, and stepped away from him. Mack looked down at his hands for a moment, working at keeping his mind and body under control. Abruptly, he changed tactics.

"I want you to do a little experiment for me, Jaimie." Mack sank back onto the computer desk. "I want you to find each of the men. All of them. Exact position."

"Why? You know I can."

"But not Gideon or Spagnola. I want to find out why. If there are two of them, there could be more. I need to know. And I don't want the others to know. Don't document it."

"Or tell Sergeant Major?"

Shadows crept into his eyes. "No one."

"Whitney would take them, wouldn't he?" Jaimie guessed.

"I believe he would and if you're right and Griffen is working with him, then he can't know. We'll figure out how they're hiding from you ourselves."

"It has to be their energy, Mack. Nothing chemical or genetic that Whitney did to them. I read energy. I can feel how someone is feeling. For instance, Javier and Kane are upstairs in the kitchen area and they're amused. It's genuine amusement." She shared her first real smile with him since he'd come to talk to her. "I fear for the lasagna."

"They'd better not do any of the things they were suggesting," Mack said.

Jaimie sat on the computer desk beside

him and swung her feet. "I'll bet both Joe and Gideon have similar psychic abilities and something they have naturally protects them from me reading their energy. And if they have a natural protection, someone else will too. Of course, no one will know it because as far as I know, no one else can pinpoint location in the same way I can. That's why Whitney was so interested in getting his hands on my data and why Joe is protecting me."

"Wait a minute." Mack scowled at her. "I thought you said Whitney wanted you dead."

"Not him. Neither does Sergeant Major. Maybe the ones above them do, but they aren't going to let anyone kill me. They want answers. I opened a can of worms when I began searching out Whitney's supporters. They don't want to be exposed. One of them wants me dead."

"I want to try something, Jaimie. Just go along with me," Mack said, hopping off the desk and holding out his hand to her.

She hesitated just one moment and then with reluctance put her hand in his and allowed him to tug her off the desk. Mack chose the center of the room where it was open, away from the windows and the spill of light around her computers.

She sank down onto the floor where he indicated and he settled across from her, sitting, knees touching.

"I want you to do it again, but this time, really concentrate on Kane and Javier. I want to see how much you can read what they're doing. How they're feeling. Anything at all you can pick up."

She frowned at him, but didn't pull away. "I've never gotten anything other than happy or sad energy and a location."

"I know. But I think you've grown stronger. I think you can do a lot more than you're aware."

"But what about the aftermath?" There was fear in her voice.

Mack framed her face with her palm. "I think when we're together I'm stronger. I think our energies merge in some way. Do this for me. If you get in trouble and I can't shield you enough, we'll stop." He wanted her trust. Even if it was just in that moment. He had to feel it again, the same way he'd felt her closeness. She was afraid. She'd just gone through a horrific night and he was asking her to risk another one.

Jaimie took a deep breath and nodded. She closed her eyes and allowed her mind to expand, to encompass the two men above her on the third floor. She always remained

274

aware of her surroundings, and this time she was particularly aware of Mack. His energy surrounded her as it had never done before. It felt masculine and warm, almost hot, like his skin. The feeling was tactile. Her body tingled, grew warm, and the heat spiraled outward to mingle and merge with her own energy as she directed it away from herself.

She encountered Kane first. She knew his exact position, bending over the stove, as if the energy surrounded him and sent back an echo so that she could "see" him. He was stirring something. "He's overcooking the noodles," she murmured, but the humor faded just as quickly. She felt Kane's emotions. His sadness. His guilt. A huge burden that weighed on him. His fears for Jaimie's safety. Kane could barely breathe as he dipped a spoon almost absently into the boiling water.

Jaimie jerked away from him before realizing she wasn't really catching his thoughts and invading his privacy. It was the energy surrounding him she was reading. She took a breath and let it out, reaching further into the room to touch Javier. His energy was strong, but like Kane's, a mixture of emotion. She'd never noticed those strands before, woven tightly together to form around each person. She had never tried separating the various threads to read them more in depth.

"I thought Javier would have a lot of humor in him, Mack," she mused, "but he has a lot of violence and sadness in him."

"Where is he?"

"He's by the window, standing to one side, staying very still. I've never felt anyone so still, but he's coiled for action."

"Is he alarmed?"

"Not yet. But he's watching the wharf. No, the water."

"Can you encompass the water?"

She took a deep breath again and let it out. Usually by now, using so much energy, her head would be hurting, and she'd feel little pinpricks of pain throughout her skull. She only felt Mack's energy. Stronger. Wrapping her up as if in his strong arms. She actually felt safe and secure, instead of spread thin, her energy slowly seeping out until she had nothing left.

The water gave off a cold rush that she felt flashing through her veins. It was almost electric, tiny sparks spreading over her skin, while her body temperature cooled. Instantly she felt the energy around her shift, adjust, blanket her to warm her. She became so aware of Mack she actually felt the air

276

moving in and out of his lungs and each separate beat of his heart. His energy immersed her in him until she felt a part of him.

Mack held his breath. His mind expanded with hers, locked together in some weird way he didn't understand, but she was taking him with her out over the sea, as if the two of them were soaring free above everything. It was beautiful. Mystical. Like another dimension or realm she'd tapped into, yet he knew they were firmly anchored in that room.

The water's energy sparkled like diamonds and he felt the lick of flames along his skin. The cold rush turned hot so that his blood surged and ebbed in time to her heartbeat. He could almost feel her skin brushing along his, inflaming his senses until he felt her very breath.

A boat rose and fell with the waves and inside two men huddled against the biting cold, peering through the fog, cursing their luck of drawing a bad assignment. Neither was happy, both miserable and both a little angry.

Jaimie looked up at him. "They're watching the wharf, not this building, Mack. I think your Doomsday unit is tracking the weapons and found they were off-loaded on this wharf. Javier spotted them. That's what has captured his attention."

"You're sure?"

"I don't feel hostile energy, more like misery. They don't like their assignment. And one is feeling queasy. That will get worse soon. Both are very focused on watching the area, but my guess is, they aren't alone. They'll have sent someone to watch the street."

"Keep going. Spread out to find the others and our team."

Jaimie glanced at his face and then away, as if the way he was looking at her made her shy. Maybe he was looking at her like a wolf might. He felt hungry, edgy, *needy*. She touched her tongue to her bottom lip. "Ethan, Brian, and Jacob are playing cards in a small room just opposite the bank of windows facing the street. They're on the second floor. Ethan is facing the window and he has a clear view of the street. Brian and Jacob are very competitive. Ethan's seen something outside that's caught his attention and doesn't have his mind on the game."

"How do you know that?"

"His energy is directed outside. Brian and Jacob both have their energy surrounding the table and toward each other."

"Can you tell what they're feeling?"

"Brian's moody. It comes across very strong that he has someone he's thinking about. A female. He's not worried about her, exactly, but he misses her."

Mack frowned. "How can you possibly know he's thinking about a woman?" Brian had never mentioned a woman to any of them.

The color crept up her neck. "There's a thread of sex mixed in."

"I want you to be certain."

Jaimie sighed and rubbed her temples. Mack leaned closer to her, then realized he was trying to physically shield her and relaxed and allowed his energy to expand to enfold her. Now he felt her moving against him, mind to mind, sharing her world of energy. It was exhilarating and intimate, more intimate than anything he'd ever experienced with her. As if he was not only buried deep in her body, but also in her mind. Every part of his body recognized hers, as if they were part of each other.

Mack had no idea if Jaimie felt the same heightened pleasure or if it was just him, but her energy was all feminine and swirled through his own, so that the electricity rushing through his body was like flash lightning. He could taste her in his mouth. She filled his lungs. Was that normal? He knew it wasn't, but now that he'd experienced the joining of energies, he knew he would crave the feeling.

"He's definitely thinking of a woman. Ethan is very distracted now. He's moved to the window, and is looking toward the street, down the block where you believe the guns are stored. I'm picking up another energy in the room. Heavy guilt. Secretive, very furtive."

She was frowning, her mind moving further away, yet taking Mack with her, so he could almost see the room, the table and cards, the filmy window and shadows moving along the walls. He couldn't read the energy, but through her, he shared it. As it swirled around them, he began to feel the ravenous hunger, the way it subtly attacked Jaimie, seeping into her open mind and battering at her. Immediately he was able to shift, to block the energy's backlash. She had no filters the way he did, nothing to protect her, yet he could do it, fitting with her, as if they were one person instead of two.

Mack shifted closer to her, trying to feel where the other energy was coming from. He couldn't tell. He felt it, although he never would have if she hadn't caught it; it was further away and subtle. He was a little shocked that she'd picked it up at all.

"The new kid. The one with a chip on his shoulder. He's sitting in a corner, back to the wall. He doesn't want anyone coming up behind him to see what he's doing."

Mack went very still, alarm spreading through him. "What is he doing, Jaimie?" He kept his voice low and easy, not wanting to chance bringing her back to the room with him.

She frowned and rubbed her temple again. He was there immediately, blocking the attacking energy, refusing to allow it into her brain. The flow came from all directions, tracing back on the route she'd used and stabbing at her brain with spikes, but he kept his own energy in place like a wall. The negative energy continued to circle Jaimie. He could feel it looking for a weak spot, an opening, wanting to rush in and strike.

"He's on a computer. I feel the heat. The way he's striking the keyboard, he's upset, but trying to be quiet so Ethan doesn't notice him."

"Do you know who he's writing to?"

"It doesn't work that way. He doesn't want to get caught. That's all I'm picking up."

Brian. I want you to get the kid's computer.

281

Confiscate that laptop and put him under guard until I give you the word to bring him here.

The energy in the room changed abruptly. Became aggressive. Hostile. The surge around Jaimie was shocking, actually battering at her. It was so unexpected, several spikes got through before he could thicken the shield around her. Jaimie gave a soft moan of distress and he almost pulled the plug on the experiment, but as he became more sensitive and aware, it enabled him to keep building the barrier protecting her.

"They have Paul. He's angry and scared. Ethan didn't even turn around, Mack. He's at the window. Do you want me to try to figure out what's got him so upset?"

"If you're up for it," he hedged, wanting her to make the choice.

His body was going crazy on him. He actually felt as if he were inside of her, all that soft heat surrounding him. Every nerve ending seemed to be centered in his groin, until he was full and hard and pulsing. His jeans were far too tight, the pressure of the material against him hurting. Little beads of sweat dotted his forehead and trickled down his chest.

He felt her energy expand like waves, racing out and away from her, stretching further, encompassing the streets and surrounding buildings. Surprisingly, her energy was like the ebb and flow of the sea, strong and rhythmic, and the very feel of it sent currents of electricity snapping through his body, wrapping around his cock like tight fingers.

"I can feel Lucas in a doorway just at the end of the street. He's sitting hunched over, but he's very alert. Whatever Ethan's seen, so has he. There are two others with him on the steps. Both older. One sick." She looked at Mack with a quick frown. "I hope you're not providing booze to drunks."

He didn't reply, simply waiting. Jaimie could go off on a tangent of moral community responsibility. She'd spent a lot of time in the homeless kitchens and shelters volunteering even as a young teen. She and her mother had spent a great deal of time in both places before Stacy had gotten her teaching credentials and a decent job.

Jaimie sighed and went back to scanning the area. "Marc isn't far from Lucas. One, no, two doors down. He's just inside, standing at the window. He's watching Lucas more than the street and he's worried. Very worried. Something's really caught their attention."

Mack felt her push her energy along the

street, sweeping the buildings up and down the street on either side. Her breath caught in her throat. "There. On the pier by a fishing boat. Three fishermen next to them, but those two aren't in the least interested in fishing. They're very interested in the warehouse on the end of the block."

Gideon, you on this? Aloud he said to Jaimie, "Find Gideon."

"You know I can't find him."

"I think you can." His voice grew hoarse with need.

He shifted, trying to ease the pain in his groin. It only grew worse, heat radiating down his thighs and up into his belly. He had to try to ease the building tension, his hand dropping to the front of his jeans, stroking absently.

Jaimie's energy stroked him as well, with heat and fire, causing sparks to arc off his skin. The energy was soft and feminine like her skin, cupping his cock and balls, massaging him. He swore for a moment he could even feel her tongue licking at him. His cock jerked. Pulsed. Spilled droplets. His mouth filled with the taste of her. He wanted to strip off her jeans and bury his face in the fire of her sheath, devour her until she was writhing and screaming beneath him. He couldn't stop the erotic images flooding his brain. His breath came in ragged, harsh gasps.

Jaimie's lashes drifted down. There was a slumberous, sensual look on her face, her full lower lip in a sexy pout. Her breasts rose and fell beneath her thin tank. Her nipples were taut, two tight pebbles beckoning him, and her skin was flushed. Mack found his hand sliding from the front of his jeans to her thigh, where he traced soothing circles. It took several minutes of searching and he could feel her energy expanding, and with it the rushing in his veins continued.

"I think I'm picking Gideon up on the roof across the street, on the building where Ethan and the others are. It's so faint, but his energy is different. Unfamiliar. A completely different pattern, almost camouflaged the way his skin is. He could be lying down, watching the street, very focused. He blends in with other energies around him. He's getting uncomfortable, Mack. I think he feels mine."

"Pull back," Mack ordered. He didn't want her energy, as sexual as it was, as hot and potent, blending with anyone but him.

"Do you want me to try to find Joe?"

He did, but he didn't want Joe feeling her, not like this, not in a heightened state of hunger. Jaimie had opened her thighs so

285

that his slow circles had climbed higher. He could feel heat coming off her in waves. Hunger was sharp and relentless, an endless, brutal erection that seemed to be bursting his skin. His fingers fumbled with the zipper of his jeans, desperate for relief from the swelling, throbbing pain in his cock.

"Yes" — he could barely get the word out — "but pull back the moment you think he senses you." He massaged his thick, bursting erection, his mouth watering for the taste of her, his palms itching for the feel of her soft skin. He had to touch her soon, had to fasten his mouth to the hot, sweet core of her and draw her honey into his mouth, feel her explode as he kissed her as intimately as possible.

Jaimie was faster finding Joe and he told himself it was because she knew where he was staying now, in that room directly across from her building, three stories up. He couldn't really think anymore, not with the roar in his head and the taste of honey in his mouth. He remembered her unique taste. The cream he loved to feed on in the morning, her breathless cries, the way she gave herself to him unashamedly, without reservation.

"He's eating at the table and going over something" — she frowned — "a report, I think. Something in it bothers him. He's restless. He just got up and paced to the window, but he's standing to the side of it so no one can see him. His energy is as low as Gideon's and has that same strange blending quality."

Was there a caressing note in her voice? One of affection? Or was it just his sensitive state? He only knew he felt a vicious punch in his gut and something dangerous moved inside of him, something he didn't much like. He took a steadying breath and let it out. She was doing what he asked, and he'd been the one to let her go. If she found someone else . . . He drew in another breath and looked at his hands. He was shaking. This wasn't normal, not any of it, but his body said differently.

The energy enfolded him, lapped at his skin like a thousand sensual tongues, teasing and dancing so that he could barely think with need. The intensity shook him.

"His energy nearly matches Gideon's, Mack. The threads are woven differently than anyone else's, almost like the waves react differently. I don't know how I'm picking either of them up, and in a combat situation, without knowing what I was looking for, it would be nearly impossible. I had an idea where to look."

He couldn't answer her, his voice was too gruff, his body consumed, burning, so desperate for her he could no longer sort out actual words, but he knew the moment Joe felt her. Something masculine and challenging brushed against her energy. He caught the nape of her neck and jerked her into him. "Break away." His mouth came down on hers. Hungry. Demanding. Giving her no choice.

She was lost in him instantly, just as he knew she would be. Her breath caught, a sound that shook him. He curled his fingers around the nape of her neck and kissed her, over and over, his tongue sliding over the seam of her lips to demand entrance.

There was no thought of her refusal. The need was too strong, too urgent, far too intense. He needed her the way he needed air to breathe. He devoured her mouth, the silken heat and honeyed taste, but it wasn't enough to sate the fire leaping through him, and the feel of her only inflamed him further.

CHAPTER 10

Jaimie's mouth was heaven, the taste and scent of her filling him, the silken heat of her wrapping him up in desire. Mack didn't think he could survive without being skin to skin, without having her soft body wrapped around his. He couldn't breathe with wanting her. His head was a dull roar, his body on fire. He didn't think, couldn't think. There was only his body, edgy with need for her heat and soft skin.

His mouth left hers so he could trail kisses over her chin and nibble his way down the side of her neck to her sensitive earlobe. His teeth nipped and scraped, his tongue swirling along the soft, tempting skin. Her breathless moans nearly drove him crazy. He kissed his way along the slope of creamy skin, one hand sliding her strap from her shoulder and shoving the material from the swell of her soft, enticing breasts. His other hand pulled her into him, his mouth closing over soft flesh. She gasped and arched her body, pressing into him, her soft cry one of pleasure.

Every secret hollow and shadow of her body was memorized, imprinted in his mind forever, but it had never been like this — a terrible, almost brutal hunger that had him skating along the edge of his control. He felt like a man starving, a terrible addiction that pounded through his heart and soul and settled deep into his body, demanding to be sated. Lust was sharp, consuming him. The roar of his blood thundering in his ears. He could *feel* her response to him. The heat rising, the tremors running from breast to belly, arousal teasing along her thighs. It was a heady, erotic phenomenon like nothing he'd ever experienced.

He slid her shirt below her breasts so they spilled out, rising and falling, nipples taut with desire. She looked so beautiful, her breathing ragged, her eyes glazed, her needy moans driving him wild. He slowly lowered her to the floor, watching her all the while, unable to take his eyes from the rise and fall of her breasts as her breathing grew more and more agitated in anticipation.

He slid his hand over her stomach, pushing the drawstring pants out of his way. He wanted to see every inch of her soft feminine curves. He wanted her open to him, give herself to him. Belong to him. As needy and edgy as he felt. Her stomach muscles bunched and her body shuddered as he leaned forward and licked her nipple, all the while holding her gaze to his.

Jaimie cried out softly and arched her back, pushing her breasts toward him, her hands coming up to cradle his head, holding him to her. He couldn't resist the offering and suckled, pulling the soft, tender flesh into his mouth, using tongue and teeth to lave and nip, sending little darts of fire streaking to her most feminine core. Her body shuddered, her hips bucked, and he kept up the assault, feeling every licking flame as if her body were his own.

His hand made the journey up the smooth silk of her thigh. She gasped, the sensation almost more than she could stand, her eyes wide and dazed with pleasure. He had put that look there, whether she wanted to admit she was his or not. He switched his attention to her other breast, eliciting more gasps and shudders, her legs moving restlessly while his palm stroked higher, close to the sizzling heat at the core of her body.

He licked and nuzzled at her nipple, then caught it with the edge of his teeth. Her eyes went dark and wide. Her mouth opened and she moaned his name, the sound moving through him like music. Keeping her gaze locked with his, he slipped his finger into the damp heat of her silken sheath. She nearly came off the floor, her body every bit as sensitive as his. Her muscles clamped down and he felt the ripple spreading through her belly and down her thighs. Her reaction made him ravenous for more.

There was no controlling his desire, his body one brutal ache that was relentless beyond anything he'd ever known. His heart hammering, he kissed his way back to her slightly swollen mouth, devouring her, taking her sweetness and drowning in it. His free hand worked at his jeans, pushing them from his hips, freeing his engorged cock, so that it sprang forward eagerly, thick and hot, pulsing with hunger. The relief was tremendous. He'd never hurt so bad, felt so full, his blood pounding.

"Mack."

Her voice grew needy, broken, as his hand slipped over her mound, cupping her heat, his thumb sliding through soft velvet folds to find hidden treasure. Her entire body shuddered in answer.

He kissed his way down to her breasts, lingering for a moment, suckling, teeth scraping while she cried out and thrashed.

His mouth licked and kissed, sipping her skin down her belly, pausing only to pay attention to her intriguing belly button before moving on. She sucked in her breath as he nuzzled her legs apart, giving him better access to the feast. Again, he could already taste her in his mouth and down his throat, as if he'd already spent hours devouring her.

He was afraid he was going insane, the need to take her so strong there was nothing else in his mind, only the terrible lust rising like a tidal wave, the love swamping him until he shook with it. He lowered his mouth, his tongue stabbing deep. Jaimie's fingernails dug into the floor, her body nearly lifting, heels digging deep for purchase as he began suckling like a starving man. His tongue found her little nub and stroked over and over until she was sobbing with pleasure, her head thrashing and her fists clenching in his hair.

Mack spread her thighs wider. How many nights had he driven himself insane dreaming of the taste of her? Of her open and giving herself to him again and again? There was a part of him that was still hurt and angry that she had left him so devastated, that she had so much power over him — *that she could leave him.* He would never have left her and yet she managed to stay away for two years and still refused to admit or acknowledge that she belonged to him.

He had thought to let her go, to let her find out there was no one else for her, that there never would be, but he never imagined she might find another man. He never imagined her letting anyone touch what belonged exclusively to him.

"Damn you, Jaimie," he growled and lifted her hips toward his face and buried himself in her.

She cried out, a harsh, broken sound, as he swept his tongue over and into her damp, hot core. His tongue pushed deep, seeking her exotic taste. He'd craved this for so long, her wild, exciting flavor. Nothing else could ever satisfy him. Her cries, her shuddering, thrashing body, soft like silk, hot as hell, all for him. He knew exactly where to touch her, an instinct he possessed, had always possessed, but now it was far more acute. Each stroke of his tongue, each stabbing twist, an artist's flick, the lapping of a cat, all brought sensual writhing and soft, sobbing gasps of mindless pleasure.

No one could ever replace Jaimie and the unreserved way she gave herself to him. She arched her body into him and pleaded for more, nearly as insane with arousal as he was. He sank a finger into her as his tongue teased at her clit. He used the edge of his teeth and she came apart, her muscles squeezing, clamping down hard so that his cock pulsed in anticipation.

It wasn't enough for him. "More," he insisted, his voice harsh with lust. "Give me everything, Jaimie, all of you."

His tongue swept deep, licking and sucking, giving her no respite, demanding she go higher, taking her to new heights, driving her up fast and hard. Her body shuddering, she dug her heels into the floor and tried to squirm and thrash out from under him, but he held her firmly, lapping and sucking, devouring the nectar spilling from her body. His. All for him.

Her energy bled into his, surrounding him, connecting them closer so they seemed so wrapped in each other, he wasn't certain where she started and he left off. He already had a taste of what life was like without her and he wasn't willing to ever go there again. He was determined to bind her to him again.

Her stomach muscles bunched beneath his spread fingers and her voice strangled in her throat as her body locked, clamping down like a vise and then flying apart.

"Mack," she sobbed his name, still trying to move out from under him even as her hips pushed into him.

"That's right, honey. Mack. There is no one else for you, only me. Always me." He bent his head a third time to her, feasting, and she orgasmed again, a wild, broken cry escaping her throat.

He knelt up, dragged her to him, lifting her hips as he drove himself deep, drove himself home, her sweet sheath, hot and tight surrounding him. He belonged. She was home to him and always would be. She was everything. His other half. Her body gripped his, clamping down hard, squeezing and massaging. He pulled back and her soft cry of denial was music to him. He positioned her legs over his arms, giving himself more control and more leverage.

"Jaimie, look at me."

He saw her throat convulse. She turned her head, the mass of damp black curls spilling like skeins of silk around her head. Her skin was covered in a fine sheen, her eyes dazed from the continual orgasms he demanded from her — extracted from her.

"Keep looking at me," Mack commanded. "I don't want any mistakes made about who you're with. About who you belong to." He drove deep through the tight, velvet folds, snapping his teeth together as fire streaked through him. She was scorching hot and getting hotter, if that was possible. He lifted her hips as he hammered down, imprinting his body in hers, reclaiming her, making certain she knew that claiming was what he was doing.

He refused to allow her to look away from him. His gaze held hers captive as his hands gripped her hips and his body took possession. A low, broken cry escaped again as he levered himself over her, his rhythm strong and hard, each stroke deep and deliberate, dragging over the sensitized bundle of nerves again and again, gentle and then rough, at once a caress and a harsh demand.

Her breath came in ragged gasps as he increased his pace, rebuilding the tension inside her, coiling her tighter and tighter, pushing her further than she'd ever gone with him before. Her head tossed, but her eyes never left his. She clung as if he was her only anchor, her nails biting into his shoulders like brands, sending him even higher. He drove between her damp thighs with a kind of fury, a rhapsody of torment and pleasure for both of them.

Jaimie couldn't break his hold on her and she knew exactly what he was doing — proving to her that she would never have this, this absolute torturous bliss, with any other man. No one could nearly kill her with pleasure, drive her so insane she couldn't think, only feel, only burn hotter and hotter until she was desperate, afraid she'd burst into flame from the inside out.

The energy binding them together increased the sensitivity of her already passion-inflamed body, but more, she could feel his body, every stroke of his velvet-encased steel shaft slamming home, filling and stretching her, streaking fire through both of them. She felt his lust rising like a tide. She felt his anger as he hammered home the point — *his*. She was his. She would always be his.

She never wanted him to stop, although fear snaked through her, attacking on a visceral level. He would own her again. She'd managed to survive without him the first time, but now their union was even more explosive. There would be no letting another man touch her. It would never happen. The thought sickened her. It was Mack. Only Mack, taking her over, proving to her that she was nothing without him.

He didn't give her time for coherent thought, jerking her legs up over his shoulders as his hips pistoned ferociously, driving him into her again and again. His face was etched into a harsh mask, his sensual lips over bared teeth as his breath hissed out, but his eyes always dominated, demanding she not look away from him. Commanding her in a way that both thrilled and frightened her because she couldn't stop herself from taking what he gave her. She wanted him like this, wild and out of control, forcing her far beyond every comfort zone she'd ever known.

Her greedy body spilled hot nectar around him, clutched and grasped with ever-tightening muscles. Hotter. Always hotter, the inferno in her building until she thought her life would be forfeit. She could hear inarticulate pleading coming from her throat — for what, she wasn't certain. More. To stop. No, never that. She wanted him hammering into her, the sound of their bodies coming together in a ferocious tango. She *had* to have this, have him.

She writhed, tossed her head, bucked her hips in a wild bid to meet his madness, to force his finish, to take him the way he was taking her.

"Now, Jaimie, for me. With me." He hissed the command through clenched teeth, his gaze piercing hers straight to her soul. Taking her. Capturing everything she was, would ever be, into his keeping, including her ability to orgasm.

His heavy shaft stroked over her inflamed,

swollen bud and she exploded; wave after wave of intense sensation surged through her. Her muscles clamped down around his thick, hammering cock in a painfully erotic vise. Her body tightened more and more, until she thought she'd shatter into a million pieces. Her back arched. Her hips bucked, every muscle went stiff. She opened her mouth to scream, but nothing came out. The orgasm tore through her body, shredding every idea she'd ever had of lovemaking. The explosion tore through her womb, rushed through her stomach like a rolling fireball, into her breasts, down her thighs, as wave after wave hit her.

Just as she thought she'd hit the peak and the rolling ecstasy was subsiding, her body gripped his even harder and hot seed splashed deep, triggering another, even more powerful inferno that engulfed her completely, sweeping her body into a frenzy of flames so that she writhed, so that strangled cries emerged. Her heart pounded and her lungs burned. She burned.

She couldn't look away. Couldn't break his hold on her, and she knew beyond a shadow of a doubt that he was proving a point. He gave her what he wanted to give her. Lust, brutal and strong and controlling, such pleasure she might not survive it.

He'd give her his protection. But it was going to be on his terms, not hers.

"Don't you ever fucking leave me again, Jaimie," he whispered hoarsely, his gaze boring into hers. "Do you understand me?"

She had no voice; she might never be able to speak again. She licked dry lips and managed a nod while deep inside, where no one could hear, she was screaming.

Mack searched her face for a long time before he seemed satisfied. He collapsed over the top of her, sprawling on her as he used to do. It was only then that she realized he still had his clothes on. She was completely naked and she hadn't even realized he was nearly fully clothed until she felt his weight blanketing her. The material hurt her sensitive skin and he must have known it because he nipped her chin with his teeth, and then pressed a kiss over the sting before rolling off of her.

Jaimie closed her eyes as she flung one arm across her face. There was no hiding. She couldn't pretend away the breathless cries or her ragged breathing as she fought for air. There was no way to fake her response to him. He knew exactly what he did to her. He lay next to her, one arm wrapped possessively around her waist, just as he had done so many times before while she lay wishing sex — great sex, mind-blowing sex — would be enough to sustain her, but knowing it would never be.

She hoped he'd go to sleep just like the many other times he'd worn himself out again and again until neither could move and then, without saying a word to her, he'd wrap her up in his arms and fall asleep. Now she didn't want to talk, and he was stirring.

She'd always loved him, from the first moment she'd seen him, so big and sure of himself. So completely confident. Just the opposite of her. It had been hero worship all those years ago and Mack had treated her like a puppy, a little girl all eyes and a mop of curly hair with a brain too advanced for her years. He'd seen her through all those awkward times with a casual protection that evolved into something fierce and primitive.

Jaimie had always wanted to belong to him. She had been desperate to belong somewhere — *anywhere* — all her life, and there was Mack. He was everything she didn't have. And it was dangerous to be desperate, to love someone too much. She didn't think that was possible until right at that moment. She lay naked on the floor of her workroom, her heart pounding, head roaring, weeping inside. She wasn't strong enough to resist him, and she never would be.

"I can feel your energy, Jaimie," Mack said softly and turned his head to look at her.

The jolt, the thrill, she got every time he focused on her was pathetic. His eyes seemed to look right into her soul, a silly cliché, but Mack could make her feel like the only woman in the world just by looking at her.

"I know. You're right, my talent is getting stronger. And I'm not screaming in pain. You were able to shield me." She was screaming in pain, he just couldn't hear her. "I guess we're both growing stronger." She didn't get as much control of her voice as she would have liked, but if she was lucky, he would put the tremor down to regaining her breath.

He pushed himself up and looked around for her clothes. His hands were unsteady as he caught up her shirt. "There's something magical that happens when we're together."

It was the last thing she expected him to say. Her breath caught in her throat. Mack didn't say things like that. He didn't have an ounce of the poet in him. He was all warrior, slashing eyes, grim, tough face, sure of himself. She could only nod her head, her throat closing unexpectedly.

"Sit up, baby. We made enough noise down here to bring the cops, let alone all the boys. We need to get you dressed."

She felt the color sweep up her neck. He meant she'd made a lot of noise. She couldn't remember, but she might have begged him not to stop. Loud. Very loud. There might have been a scream or two punctuating the pleading. She wasn't certain she was ready to face him.

"I know I'm not good at talking to you the way you want, Jaimie," he continued, his voice low as he tugged the T-shirt over her head. "I'm not exactly a smooth talker like Lucas, but I mean what I say."

He'd never said anything. Not once. He'd never told her he loved her. He said he wanted her a million times, showed her he wanted her a million ways. Mack was very demanding when it came to sex — generous and demanding. He was always absolutely certain of himself and his power over her. She avoided his gaze as she lifted her arms and allowed him to slide the material over her head.

"Jaimie? Aren't you going to talk to me?" He paused in the act of tugging her shirt over her breasts. "What's wrong?" There was a soft, ominous note in his voice.

Energy separating was rather like coming

down off a huge adrenaline rush. Their bodies tingled and raw nerve endings sparked and jumped. His shaft jerked and pulsed. Her womb clenched and wept.

"I don't know what to say."

"You can look me in the eye and tell me the next time you're thinking of running, you'll talk to me instead."

"I did talk to you."

"Well, you obviously didn't get through." He jerked her shirt down and stood up, casually zipping up his jeans. He'd always been comfortable naked, padding around their apartment without clothes whenever possible, and he looked just as comfortable now even though they'd nearly brought down the place and the men couldn't have failed to hear.

He had to steady her when she stood up, swaying, her body weak. "What did you want me to do, Mack? Hit you over the head with a two-by-four?"

"Yes, damn it, if that's what it takes. You don't walk out on me, Jaimie."

He kept his hand on her arm as she yanked up her soft drawstring pants. She was trembling. His palm slid up and down her bare skin as if to soothe her.

"I'm not the same person I was," she said, but even as she uttered the words, she wondered if she was lying. She fought hard to stand on her own, but the entire time she'd been building a future with the idea that Kane and Mack might need somewhere to go when they retired. They had to retire sometime, didn't they? Did any of them even have a future?

Mack framed her face. "Don't look so sad, Jaimie. We'll make it."

She wanted to believe that, but she'd seen the evidence stacking up against them and it was enormous. The GhostWalkers had enemies in their own camp. "I'm not like you, Mack. You rush in where angels fear to tread. You really do. You think you can save the world." She gestured toward the stairs. "Every single one of us — Javier, Kane, me, Rhianna — all of us were broken and you picked us up and fixed us. You'd charge hell with a bucket of water. Nothing scares you. Nothing at all. You just do it. Whatever is required. You get it done."

"Being without you scares me," he admitted in a low, reluctant voice. He kept his gaze fixed on her averted face. She was so elusive, just out of reach when they'd crawled into each other's souls. How the hell had she slipped away again?

Her head jerked up and she looked at him. He could read her shock, but didn't understand it. Hell. She'd ripped out his soul when she'd left. Her tongue touched her lower lip, drawing his attention to the sweet, sexy curve of it. He couldn't resist and leaned forward to catch the silken bow between his teeth, tugging gently before he kissed her.

Jaimie blinked up at him, that baffled, dreamy look he found utterly sexy on her face. She touched her lips. "I don't understand you, Mack. I asked you about our future and you said we didn't have one. You weren't ready for the old ball and chain."

There was enough raw hurt in her voice to make him wince.

"And when we had sex I could feel your emotions." Now her voice was strained, so low he had to lean into her to hear. "You were angry, but more importantly, you resent wanting to be with me. Resentment is powerful and it overshadows a lot of other things. There's no mistaking it. It's hard to understand our relationship when you're so resentful."

He shrugged. "I've never been one to want to need someone, Jaimie. How hard is that to understand? It's damned hard admitting to myself let alone you that I can't do without you. You're like some fucking addiction I can't get rid of."

She actually hunched, feeling the punch in her stomach. She swallowed the rising lump in her throat, determined to go all the way. If he wanted her to talk before walking out, then she was going to do it. "What about love, Mack? You've never once said you loved me."

He shoved a hand through his hair in a quick, almost angry gesture, his eyes glittering. "What the hell do you want from me? I just told you how I felt. A few minutes ago you were screaming my name and begging me not to stop. What we have together is good. Great. Can't we just leave it at that?"

"Except you want to be rid of me."

He threw his hands into the air. "Of course that's all you heard." He was the one who was always in control. He had discipline in every aspect of his life but one. Jaimie. There was no discipline with her. No restraint. He turned into an animal, a jealous, primitive beast he barely recognized. Was he supposed to be proud of that?

Just looking at her with her silky curls tumbling in disarray around her face, that mouth that was every man's fantasy, he closed his eyes, remembering how he'd taught her to use it for his pleasure. He'd taught her — everything. And Jaimie always gave herself to him without reservation.

He'd been older, her protector. He knew she was smarter, but he could keep up with her intellectually and provide the stimulus she needed for her mind. The rest, well, frankly, he was the dominate one.

He'd always had the upper hand in their relationship. He'd always known he could walk away from her and be just fine. Until she'd left him. He realized how much he actually managed to fool himself. Jaimie's hold on him was impossible to break. He thought he owned her but it was the other way around. Hell, yeah, he resented it. What man wouldn't? No other woman would do for him.

No one had touched her before him. Two long years. He saw the way Spagnola had looked at her. Had Spagnola touched her? He couldn't ask. Didn't want to know. He was afraid of what he might do to the other man. Mack rubbed his pounding temples. What the hell was wrong with him? Hell, yeah, he resented that she could make him this crazy.

Jaimie shook her head. "We're back to exactly the same place we were before I left. You were fine there, Mack, but I wasn't. I don't want to base my entire relationship on sex. You can have sex with anyone. Women fall all over you."

"We don't just have sex, honey; we have spectacular sex. Come on, you have to admit, no one can do what I can to you — with you."

She shrugged. "I don't know that."

He went very still. Inside, something dark and dangerous moved, coiled and ready to strike. Every vestige of amusement was wiped from his face. He looked what he was, lethal and frightening as he stepped very close to her. "We have an understanding, Jaimie." His voice had gone very quiet again. Violence rode him hard. Aggression. All the characteristics that made him great at hunting prey stared out at her through his eyes, and he let it.

"Do we?" She stared right back, not wilting like the Jaimie of old.

He wrapped his hand around the nape of her neck and drew her to him. "Don't fuck with me about this. We're going to make it work."

"Has anyone ever told you that you don't have one romantic bone in your body?"

His gut knotted, hard, brutal twisting lumps of fear. "Is that what you need to be happy with me, Jaimie? Pretty words?"

Jaimie studied his face. His expression was a mask. Unreadable. But he was holding his breath. Actually holding his breath. If she didn't answer him soon, he was going to turn blue.

"I'd like you to say how you feel about me now and then, Mack. A relationship can only work so long built on sex. What happens if we can't have sex? Is it over for us? Do you just move on?"

He scowled at her. "How shallow do you think I am?"

"I'm looking for a partnership."

"You had that."

"Did I? You didn't listen to a word I said, Mack. You've always led and I followed, but not blindly. I went with you because you made sense. When you didn't, when we were walking into something dangerous, I expected you to talk it over with me first, to at least listen to what I had to say." She sat on the edge of the desk, barefoot, inhaling the scent of sex and his skin. She loved the way he smelled. Masculine and edgy, usually combined with sex.

She'd missed him. Missed everything about him. Especially the sex. And yet, their sex together, as great as it had been, had never been close to what he'd just given her. She'd missed that look in his eyes just before he kissed her. He was incredibly strong, but he'd never once hurt her, not even when they were making wild love and he seemed ruthless and out of control. His touch with her was gentle. She loved that about him, his care of her. Was she just wanting too much? Did she need too much?

Mack stepped into her, reaching for her thighs as if he owned her. As if he knew his touch made her weak. He spread her thighs and moved between her legs. Up close. He loomed over the top of her, making her feel small and vulnerable and fragile. She knew she wasn't, but he still made her feel that way. She'd always loved him. Now she couldn't look at him without craving him. She could taste him in her mouth, breathe him in her lungs.

"Mack." She whispered his name. A plea.

"I'm not letting you go, Jaimie. We'll work it out. Whatever you need. I'll figure it out. Just cut me a little slack. I'm never going to get over you walking out on me. You shook me up and I'm still dealing with it."

"Anger."

"Damn right." He curled his fingers around the nape of her neck and pressed his forehead to hers. "Damn right I'm angry." The words hissed out between his teeth. "I think of you with other men. I obsess about it. Your mouth on someone else. Someone else inside of you." He took a breath like a man drowning. "You're part of me. Bone deep, Jaimie. You can't just think you can walk out and it's going to be okay. You could have come back anytime, but you didn't. I thought . . ."

"What?" There were tears in her voice. "That I'd come crawling back, broken?" Alone. Torn apart inside. Unable to sleep or eat or care.

"That you'd see we were meant to be together. That you'd find out you wanted me." There was hurt in his voice. Pain.

That took her breath away. His pain. She could feel it now. Sharp. Terrible. "Of course I wanted you, Mack. We never had a problem with wanting each other. It's the *more* we have trouble with."

Something flickered in the depths of his eyes and her stomach flipped. She caught a glimpse of his anger. Deep. Bone deep. The way he said she was wrapped inside of him. She'd never been afraid of Mack, not even for a small instant. Sometimes the intensity of their lovemaking scared her, but never Mack.

"Work it out with me, Jaimie."

How could she hold her ground with him? He'd always managed to do this to her. He overwhelmed her and she gave in and nothing changed between them. "I'll try, Mack," she whispered, feeling like she was giving him her soul.

He found her mouth and took her. That easily. He tasted of male and sex. A sinful pleasure that streaked like lightning through her veins, sizzling, taking her breath. She knew what he meant when he called her an addiction. That was what he was to her. She craved him, the taste and scent of him, the feel of him. His laughter and his strength. He was everything to her. He always would be.

"What am I to you?" she murmured against his mouth.

Obsession. Addiction.

The words shimmered in her mind. A blanket of resentment. A wealth of possession. She couldn't find love. If he let himself think it, he didn't acknowledge it. If he let himself feel it, he refused to show her. Anger. He was so angry.

Jaimie pushed at his chest. "We'd better go."

Mack stepped back away from her, out of the light and into the shadows where she couldn't see his face. Where she couldn't see his body tremble or his hands shake.

Tiny red dots appeared, clustered over Mack's heart on his bare chest. A second cluster appeared centered between his eyes. Jaimie gasped and froze. Mack stilled, one hand sliding under his shirt at the small of his back as he looked up. Eight grim-faced men stared at him from across the room, guns drawn and aimed.

"You want to tell me what you're doing with our sister?" Ethan demanded. "Because it doesn't look good from where I'm standing."

Mack let his breath out. "That's not funny. I could have shot you."

"Yeah, well, take your hand out from under that shirt really slow Mack," Kane said. "Jaimie, you take a step away from him."

Color swept up Jaimie's neck and into her face. "Are you all crazy? Put your guns away and stop fooling around."

"Poor choice of words, Jaimie," Javier said. "I think there's been enough fooling around. We aren't fooling. No one, not even Mack, is going to mess with our sister and get away with it."

"No one stopped him when we were living together," Jaimie pointed out, jerking her head up, eyes narrowing dangerously. Her riot of curls went flying in all directions. Usually that was enough to get them all under control, but the guns held rock steady.

"We thought his intentions were honorable back then," Marc said.

"We just got you back," Lucas added.

They all nodded in agreement.

Kane indicated for her to move with his gun. "Get away from him, Jaimie. He doesn't get to lead you on and walk away free."

"You aren't going to shoot him," she said firmly, but she didn't sound too sure.

"No, but we're going to beat the hell out of him," Jacob said. "Go on upstairs while we take care of this."

"Go on upstairs, Jaimie," Mack agreed quietly.

"What century are you all living in?" Jaimie demanded. "This isn't funny. It's not like any of you . . ."

"Not with our sister, we don't," Javier snapped. "Get away from him, Jaimie. I mean it. Go upstairs."

"You're serious."

"He doesn't get to touch you unless his intentions are strictly honorable."

"Oh, for heaven's sake." Jaimie stepped in front of Mack. "You've all lost your minds."

Mack put her gently aside. "You can try to beat the crap out of me, boys, but none of you are that good." He flexed his shoulders.

"Put your weapons up right this minute,"

Jaimie demanded. When no one did, she put both hands on her hips, trying to be seen around Mack's large frame. "This is my house and you're being disrespectful."

"He's being disrespectful," Kane said.

"For your information, and it's none of your business, I seduced him, not the other way around. You're pointing your guns at the wrong person."

The men looked at one another.

"Is that true, boss?" Lucas asked.

"It fucking doesn't matter. You all made one hell of a mistake tonight." Mack's voice was ice-cold. "You pulled your weapons with Jaimie in the line of fire. You want a piece of me, come get it, but before you do, holster your weapons, and you can all consider that a fucking order."

His low tone carried throughout the warehouse, a lethal intent none of them could mistake. Silence fell. Guns disappeared.

Jaimie shivered and laid a hand on Mack's arm, looking up at his face. His jaw was set, his eyes frozen, glittering chips. He wasn't joking. There was no humor or amusement. The level of tension in the room went up several notches.

He moved so fast he was nearly a blur, without warning, launching into action. He went vertical, lashing out with powerful legs in a left, right leg kick, dropping the two men closest to him. Lucas and Marc went down hard, the sound sickening, indicating Mack wasn't holding much back.

They'd all seen him like this before, usually over Jaimie, and the remaining men tried to scramble out of harm's way. Mack was already in motion, coming back to the floor and running two steps up the wall and flipping off it, clearing a ten-foot distance, driving Kane, who had been farthest from him, to the floor.

"Mack, back off," Javier yelled, crouching low, hands up to face the threat coming from up above. "Someone's going to get hurt."

Mack was moving across the ceiling like a spider, his speed incredible, dropping into the center of Ethan, Jacob, and Javier, his leg sweeping out in a spin, knocking them all on their butts. Javier stood up slowly, facing him, palm out as if in appeasement, but he was in a good offensive position.

"I'm going to say we deserved that, Mack, but I'm not good at this kind of discipline. Let's go eat and call it good."

"Apologize to Jaimie and we'll call it good," Mack said.

"I don't need . . ." Jaimie trailed off when

Mack shot her a look.

"Mack's right, Jaimie," Kane said, from the floor. "It was a dumb joke. If one of us had stumbled, you could have been hurt."

"Killed," Mack said. "What the hell have I been teaching you all these years?"

"How to kick the crap out of people?" Ethan muttered under his breath.

CHAPTER 11

"What did you say?" Mack demanded.

Ethan shrugged his shoulders. "Nothing, boss. Nothing at all."

The men turned and started up the stairs, some walking a little gingerly. Jaimie started after them, but Mack caught her arm, preventing her from moving.

"Where's Paul?" he asked Kane.

"First floor with Brian." Kane looked closer. "You're still itching for a fight. We thought you'd be all mellow after . . ." He broke off when Mack shot him a look.

"You thought wrong."

Kane sighed. "Brian has Paul under guard and Javier brought his computer as ordered. You want to fill me in?"

There was a small silence. Mack's thumb slid over the inside of Jaimie's wrist, but he didn't look at her, simply brushed soothing strokes back and forth across sensitive skin. She wasn't certain if he was soothing her — or him.

"Jaimie discovered a pattern with a couple of the missions you've been running lately, Kane. The last three you've been asked for by name — you and Brian." He waited for the significance to sink in. When Kane didn't display any reaction Mack continued. "All three missions went south. If I hadn't had a bad feeling and sent backup, you and Brian would have been killed."

"You think Sergeant Major buried the report we gave on Whitney."

"And all the evidence you'd gathered," Mack added.

Kane rolled his shoulders. "I thought we'd been targeted. That's why I stayed away from you and didn't talk about it. We had orders not to. You knew we were sending our reports on Whitney up the chain of command, but Brian and I talked it over after the first mission where we were ambushed and we decided to try to distance ourselves from all of you just to try to keep from dragging you into our mess."

"That was a bullshit decision," Mack said. "That's not how it works."

"For anyone but you? Everyone I care about is on this team, Mack. Same with Brian. We're not about to put any of you in jeopardy."

Mack sighed and threw another glance at Jaimie. "So everyone is protecting everyone else and putting themselves in the line of fire in the name of love. Great thing to do. You're all a bunch of boneheads."

"What would you do?"

"Exactly what we're going to do. Remove the threat. I won't have you or Brian sent out on a suicide mission. If Sergeant Major is protecting Whitney, then we'll take him out." He made the statement coldly, without passion. "He's a dead man if he deliberately put you in harm's way, but we'll do it smart."

Kane half turned.

"Kane." Mack's voice was low but carried a thread of menace, a wealth of command. "Do we have an understanding?"

"Yes, Top."

The tension in the room eased. Beside her, Jaimie felt Mack's body relax a bit, his fingers still stroking her skin. "Is Gideon keeping an eye on our terrorists?"

Kane nodded. "But he's hungry. He said to eat fast and relieve him. I didn't tell him Jaimie didn't make the lasagna." He grinned. "I didn't want to destroy his good mood."

"I made the sauce. You couldn't have messed it up," Jaimie pointed out.

"Don't count on it, little sister. Javier had ideas."

"You didn't let that man touch the sauce, did you?"

"I tried to stop him," Kane said piously. "I did, Jaimie. He whipped out that big knife of his and started cleaning his fingernails. I had to let him do whatever he wanted."

"He wasn't in my kitchen when he was cleaning his fingernails, was he?"

Kane leaned close, lowering his voice. "I don't think sex works for either of you. You should be relaxed and feeling great, not hostile and tense. Maybe you need to have a little talk with me, boss. I could give you a couple of pointers."

Mack snorted. "You're going to give me pointers on sex."

"I'm willing, boss. Just to help you out."

Mack made a suggestion that was anatomically impossible, accompanied by sign language.

Jaimie put her foot on the stairs again. This time it was Kane stopping her. "You forgot your underwear, honey. I think your thong is under the desk there and your bra is on the floor next to the chair."

Jaimie kicked him in the shins. "If we're all going to be childish, I'm joining right in," she snapped and stomped back across the room to sweep her undergarments up.

She couldn't remember how they came off. Mack was good at that, getting her out of her panties and bra. Half the time when she lived with him, at home, she hadn't worn any. He was prone to throwing her up against a wall or on a table, or bending her over a chair. The flashes of memories made her wet and her nipples hard. She could feel his eyes on her, and heat swept through her body. It was impossible not to think about the multiple climaxes he'd given her, when he was looking at her with that smug, male look on his face. Just for good measure she kicked him too as she swept by, her head up, her haughtiest look on her face.

"What was that for?" Mack demanded.

"We really need to talk, boss," Kane said.

The two men followed Jaimie up the stairs. Jaimie hesitated at the top of the stairs and Mack dropped a casual arm around her, sweeping her beneath his shoulder as he walked her to the bathroom. He kept her close, his body between her and the others, wanting to make certain she was comfortable. These men were her family, ones she'd grown up with, but she was younger by several years and at a distinct disadvantage, unlike Rhianna, who was a rough-and-tumble tomboy. Jaimie lived in her brain and often felt separated from everyone.

Mack turned back to the others. They were already digging into the food, good-naturedly shoving at one another and jostling for position around the lasagna and salad. Javier stood to one side, eyeing a small laptop.

Bring him up, Brian, Mack ordered.

The room fell silent as Paul was brought into the room. Mack could almost feel sorry for the kid — almost. His skin was so pale he looked luminous, his freckles standing out. He was twenty-four, but looked fifteen. Like Javier, he had a boyish face. He was crack shot with his rifle and not bad in hand-to-hand. He'd completed all the required training to become a GhostWalker, which meant he had to have earned his tattoo. Mack knew no one would have gone easy on him, not with his looks. Javier had been driven pretty hard until his trainers began to look over their shoulders at night.

The boy looked scared, but he didn't break. He didn't drop his eyes or look away from Mack's intimidating stare. Mack pointed to the spot in front of him. Paul walked reluctantly through the others to stop in front of Mack.

"I'm going to give you a chance to tell me what you were up to, Paul. Then Javier and Jaimie are going to take your laptop apart and get to the truth."

"Permission to speak freely, Top," Paul said.

"By all means."

"If you're going to tear my laptop apart, I'd rather see how good they really are."

A slow, humorless smile added a mean twist to Mack's mouth. "I think he's just challenged you, Javier."

The kid didn't flinch, not even when Javier walked right up to him, nose to nose, dark eyes smoldering.

"Back off, Javier," Mack ordered. "Just get the information I need."

What am I looking for, boss?

You'll know when you find it. He's guilty over something. Could be nothing, could be treason.

"I'm on it, boss," Javier said. He gave Paul another hard stare, turned, and took the laptop down the stairs to Jaimie's workspace.

She emerged from the bathroom looking fresh. She'd changed her clothes. Mack studied her carefully. He knew her every mood and right now, she was very hesitant. He eased the situation immediately.

"I could use your help, honey," he said. "Javier's trying to get information off a computer for me. Would you give him a hand?" *This is important, or I wouldn't ask.*

Her gaze flicked to his face, then to Paul, who stood stiffly at attention. "Of course. No problem." *Javier know what we're looking for?*

He sent her a negative shake of his head mentally. "Paul seems to think he might have something in his computer to keep you out."

Her eyebrow shot up. "Really?" She flashed Paul a quick, almost respectful grin. "There's much more to you than meets the eye, isn't there?"

The boy flushed a bright red and Mack frowned. Jaimie had a way of looking at a man, never realizing the picture she made with her wild hair and sexy mouth, the combination of innocence and temptress. The thing was, she had no idea anyone ever looked at her. She was wrapped up in her mind, processing, analyzing, not ever seeing the way men saw her. If there was such a thing as bedroom eyes, she had them. Everything about her screamed sex, and few men ever realized just how sexy her brain was. How could a man sit and watch her talk, watch the animation on her face as she figured things out that most people had no clue about, and not find her intensely sexy?

You're staring at me.

Sorry, babe, I just got lost in you for a minute. It happens.

Jaimie blushed and shook her head, turning away from him. "I'll be downstairs."

"You might as well eat, Paul," Mack offered. "We've got a decent meal for once." He glanced at the others. "At least I think so."

"We could lie," Ethan said, shoveling more lasagna onto his plate. "But I think you'd figure it out fast enough." He dragged a chair up to the table next to him with the toe of his boot. "Park it, Paul. And grab yourself French bread before these locusts devour everything in sight."

"You'd better save some for Jaimie and Javier," Mack said, already scooping a Jaimie portion onto a plate.

"Javier already ate half of it," Kane said. "We're not saving any for him." He reached to take the French bread from Mack.

Mack slapped his hand and glared. "Touch that and you lose that hand. That's for Jaimie."

Kane withdrew his hand quickly. "You're a little testy, boss."

"I got to go with Kane on this one," Ethan

said, rubbing his sore jaw. "You get in a fight with your woman?"

Mack covered Jaimie's plate carefully and made certain the men could see his intention to harm anyone trying to come near it. "I don't fight with my woman, Ethan," he replied. "There's no percentage in it."

Kane snorted derisively but subsided when Mack turned a cold eye on him. Mack wedged another chair up to the table right across from Paul. He sank into it and took his first bite of the lasagna.

Kane grinned at the look on his face. "You're right, Mack. No one can mess up Jaimie's sauce. The girl can cook."

Mack did justice to the food, all the while keeping a close eye on Paul. The kid had grit. Mack began to think maybe he'd underestimated him. It would be embarrassing since he had Javier as a perfect example of how not to judge a book by its proverbial cover. Javier looked sweet and innocent. Women tended to want to cuddle and protect him. The man was as lethal as one could get. Was Paul the same way?

Had the kid been sitting right in the middle of his team, rubbing shoulders day in and day out, camouflaged in lamb's wool, fooling all of them? He certainly hadn't raised any warnings. Or had he? Mack kept chewing, keeping his face expressionless. He had wondered from the beginning at the orders. He'd argued about the danger of bringing a new man into an experienced team. They knew one another, could communicate telepathically, not have to use radios, but Sergeant Major had been adamant.

"How often do you report to Sergeant Major?" Mack asked casually.

The kid's fingers tightened around his fork, but he sent Mack a puzzled glance. "You talking to me, Top?"

"Do you see anyone else who sends reports to Sergeant Major?"

"I haven't spoken a word to him, Top."

Mack watched the kid put a forkful of lasagna into his mouth and chew as though nothing was wrong, but he'd scored. Paul hadn't lied. But he didn't need to break silence to report.

"Why didn't you volunteer that you had computer skills? It isn't in your jacket."

Ethan nudged him playfully. "You a secret agent, boy? James fuckin' Bond? Bet you have a souped-up car hidden and maybe a cape."

The table erupted in laughter. "That's Batman, dope," Jacob jeered. "Bond gets all the women."

Ethan slapped his forehead and laughed with the others. "I always get that wrong."

The easy camaraderie and teasing that included Paul put him off balance more than Mack's questions.

"You really good at computers?" Lucas asked curiously. "Like hacking into programs, writing them, all that stuff Javier and Jaimie can do?"

Paul nodded slowly. "I have a PhD in computer science, specializing in analysis of algorithms."

"The hell you say," Marc breathed in awe. "That sounds badass. Where'd you go to school?"

Paul looked smug. "Undergraduate work at CalTech, graduating magna cum laude. My PhD came from MIT."

Mack sat back in his chair and regarded Paul steadily. "None of that was in your jacket."

"No, Top."

To his credit, the kid kept a straight face, but he was smirking inside. Mack didn't have to see the smile to know. "Sergeant Major planted you on my team, and he doctored your background."

Paul said nothing, just ate another forkful of lasagna.

Marc slapped a twenty on the table. "I'm

going to back the new guy. If he can pull the wool over our eyes for the last few weeks, then I'm betting Jaimie and Javier can't break into his laptop."

"I'll take that bet," Kane said, laying out his twenty. "Anyone else in?"

Ethan poked Paul with his elbow. "You really got letters at the end of your name, kid?"

"I do," Paul said.

Ethan slammed down the twenty. "Javier hardly went to school. And Jaimie doesn't have any of those letters."

Mack tipped his chair back lazily. "Are you crazy, Ethan? She has three paragraphs' worth of letters behind her name and three or four pages of awards. Javier didn't need to go to a formal school. He worked with the best in the business and got his education hands-on, not to mention both of them are brilliant. You're betting *against* them?"

Brian tossed his money over Ethan's. "Jaimie graduated high school at eleven, you idiot. Jaimie, all the way. I'm in."

"Jaimie did your homework for you," Kane reminded.

"Where did she go to school?" Paul asked.

Mack deliberately smirked. "She received her B.A. summa cum laude from Columbia University." He tipped his chair forward and

332

looked into Paul's eyes. "I believe that's the highest honors there, kid. If I remember my Latin correctly, summa trumps magna any day, am I right?"

Kane grinned. "And don't you think going to an Ivy League university instead of an engineering institute might give you a little more rounded education?"

"Not necessarily." Paul sniffed. "If you want to play around with other things."

"She was only what?" Mack turned his head toward Kane. "Sixteen or seventeen?"

"I don't think she was even that old," Kane replied.

"Where'd she get her PhD?" Paul asked, the smugness fading.

"She got her PhD from Stanford University." Mack tipped back his chair again, balancing on the two back legs. "She specialized in artificial intelligence." His grin was back. "AI sounds a whole lot sexier than 'analysis of algorithms' to me."

"Is that good?" Ethan asked Paul. "Why would you want to be artificially intelligent? You're the real thing, right?" His hand hovered over the twenty he'd thrown out.

Kane slapped his hand. "Back off, moron."

"Don't worry, Ethan," Paul said. "This is all about encryption."

Mack snorted. "And you're feeling really

confident that she doesn't know much about that, right? Not her strong suit?"

Ethan groaned. "He's taunting us, man. That's not good."

Marc rubbed his jaw. "Maybe we should change the bet. We could put a time limit on her. What does it usually take to do something like this? Minutes? Hours?"

"Try weeks or months," Paul said. "Sometimes years, depending on the encryption."

Mack and Kane exchanged a long look, smug amusement mixed with pride in their grins.

Paul scowled. "It will take years. If they can even do it."

Ethan nudged him. "There's two of them and only one of you. We should get odds on this. And maybe we could blindfold Jaimie."

"Just tell us what you're dying to tell us," Paul said.

"She did her dissertation on a revolutionary, AI-based encryption algorithm." Mack delivered the killing argument with quiet satisfaction. "Her AI dissertation is entitled, 'An Experimental Schema-Based Approach to Mememetric Password Generation.' "

"I can't believe this," Paul said and wiped his face with his hand.

"Not so cocky now, are you?" Mack taunted. "Never, ever underestimate my woman." There was a wealth of pride in his voice.

"Are you saying she might be able to do it?"

Paul shrugged. "It's possible. Depending."

"Well." Ethan's hand slid across the table toward the twenties. "I got carried away."

"Oh, no, you don't," Kane said. "You placed a bet, you're in."

"You're so harsh," Ethan complained.

"Who ate all the lasagna?" Marc demanded. "I'm supposed to go relieve Gideon and there's nothing left." He turned his head toward the covered plate. "Unless . . ."

"Don't even think about it," Mack warned. "Anyone touching Jaimie's food loses their hand."

Marc snatched his hand out of harm's way and put it behind his back. "It's cold out there on the roof tonight." He grinned at Mack. "Those two idiots in the boat are freezing their butts off and Gideon says they aren't happy."

"Well, don't get your head shot off making fun of them," Mack cautioned as Marc sauntered out. He shoved his chair back and added to the others, "Let's get this kitchen clean and talk a little shop while we're waiting."

The men picked up their plates. Paul

hesitated and when no one looked at him, he followed suit. As he approached the sink, his gaze touched briefly on the wooden block of knives and slid away.

"Don't," Mack warned wearily. "I'd hate to have to kill someone I like."

Paul blinked. "You don't like me. None of you do."

"Where'd you get a dumb idea like that?" Mack asked.

"I think you all made it obvious you didn't want me on the team."

Mack shrugged. "What's that got to do with liking you?"

Ethan took the dirty plate out of Paul's hands and rinsed it off. "You're a little sensitive, Paul. We've been a team for a couple of years now. We grew up together. Each of us knows how the other thinks. We know what any one of us will do in a given situation. That gives us an edge in combat. It's nothing personal."

"I keep my boys alive, Paul. That's my job. I do what's best for them," Mack said.

"How do you know whether I'm best or not?" For the first time bitterness crept in.

"Well, with the bullshit jacket Sergeant Major provided, of course I don't. That and you were spying on us."

"You don't know that."

"I know. And you're not very good, are you?"

"How would you know?"

"You got caught."

Ethan nudged him with a good-natured smile. "He's got you there, Paul."

"You don't have anything at all on me. I don't have a clue why you suddenly put me under guard and confiscated my laptop."

"You were pretty hostile," Brian pointed out. "Had a lot to hide or what's the big deal?"

"It's my private laptop. I don't want anyone going through it. You must have things on your computer you don't want to share."

Marc feigned puzzlement. "Just my porn, and everyone knows I'm a star in those videos. It's not like the world can't see me."

A snicker, a few hoots, and snorts of derision greeted his claim.

The intercom buzzed. "Jaimie wants one of her drinks, Mack," Javier said. "And I could use some coffee."

Ethan whooped. "They're getting frustrated."

"They're getting serious," Mack corrected. "You should know by now, Ethan, Jaimie only drinks caffeine when she means business. Gideon's coming in. He'll give us

337

the rundown on our favorite terrorists and we can plan out a little surprise."

"I want to be the gun runner this time," Jacob volunteered. "Kane always gets that part."

"He looks mean and you don't," Mack said as he put on the coffee. "In any case, no one can impersonate Madigan, he's too well-known. And he's always in on a deal. There's never been a time that he didn't personally make the exchange. We can't pass anyone off as Madigan. We can get inside, though, and replace the guards. I don't think, once they've determined the guns are being stored there, that they'll wait for Madigan to get out of the hospital. More likely they'll kill everyone and just take them. Saves them money."

Kane sank into an overstuffed chair in the living room before anyone else could grab it, his fingers forming a steeple as he regarded the other men gathering around. He waited pointedly for Paul.

"You including me in this?" Paul asked, his tone edged with belligerence.

"I don't think you're Doomsday," Kane said. "Sheesh, kid. If you're that kind of spy, we'd kill you and be done with it. You aren't exactly going anywhere. And if you're clean, Mack's not going to give you a vacation just because your feelings are hurt." He leaned forward and gestured until Paul moved close. Kane lowered his voice to an overloud whisper. "I'll let you in on a little secret. The boss isn't a particularly sensitive or nice man."

"That isn't exactly a secret," Paul said.

Mack slammed the coffeepot onto the tray with unnecessary force. "But he does have excellent hearing."

The men burst out laughing. Ethan slapped Paul on the back and then beat the kid to the next most comfortable chair.

"Jaimie doesn't have a lot of furniture," Lucas complained. "I see you bought a couple of beds. Did it occur to you that when we're hanging out here we'll need chairs?" He swung a kitchen chair around and straddled it.

"I discourage company every way I can," Mack said.

Lucas looked up at him. "You and Jaimie moving in together, boss?"

Mack stared him down. "What do you think?"

"That I'd better keep my mouth shut," Lucas muttered.

"Good plan." Mack took the chair across from Kane, looking up as Gideon came in. He frowned. "You look tired. You aren't sleeping again."

Gideon shrugged. "I'm fine. Getting headaches again, Mack." He washed his hands at the sink and looked around. "You know, I'm not all that hungry. I might lie down while I brief you. Do you mind?"

You need a medic? Mack demanded with quick concern. *Don't lie to me, Gideon.*

There was a long pause and it took every ounce of self-discipline for Mack to keep from looking at him, and possibly tipping off the others — or Paul — to their private conversation.

"Use Kane's bed," Mack said aloud. "It will be easier for you to talk."

Marc was the only one of them with real healing and medic abilities and right now, he'd gone out on the roof to keep an eye on their company. But there was Spagnola. The man was pararescue and he obviously had skills, psychic healing skills.

I'll be fine, Mack, Gideon assured.

Any bleeding? Mack held his breath.

A nosebleed. Nothing serious.

Around him the men joked good-naturedly with one another, but Mack could only hear the warning alarm going off in his mind. A nosebleed — nothing serious. It was another complication. He needed Gideon, but the man had to be seen by a doctor and immediately.

"We've got two men sitting out in a fishing boat. Neither is very happy. One keeps puking. They're radioing our two on land. Right now they're sniffing around the warehouses, including this one, so I'm fairly sure they aren't certain of the exact location of the guns. But sooner or later, one of the guards is going to go home and someone else will take their place. There's no mistaking a Madigan man. They wear that cute little tattoo on the inside of their arms, trying to be all scary."

"They don't get one of those tattoos without first killing a Madigan enemy," Mack said.

"They like to brag," Kane said.

"And they strut around the docks. A couple of Madigan's men were in the pub down the street and the local fishermen never even looked at them. It takes practice to keep your eyes off someone like that," Lucas said. "Practice and fear. And these fishermen are tough. When I went up to the bar, one of the older fishermen gestured for me to sit with him. He made sure I was facing away from the bar and the two Madigan men. He didn't say anything to warn me off, but he was definitely trying to convey to the newbie in the neighborhood that you don't 'see' those men."

"Gideon, did you ID any of the Doomsday team?"

"Oh, yeah. We got one of the heavy hitters running the show. Armando Shepherd. Believe me, boss, he's not the one in the boat."

"Why do they all call you 'boss' and not 'Top'?" Paul asked.

"He's been our boss a long time," Kane said. "It's a nickname more than a title. But if the brass is around, or we're running a mission, most of the time we call him 'Top.' "

Mack sent them both a quelling look as he got up to pour a large amount of coffee into a container to put it in the refrigerator. He left the rest on the warmer and returned to his chair. "Now that we managed to settle that important issue, did you ID anyone else?"

"Armando always travels with his psycho buddy, Ramon Estes. The two are home-grown, by the way. Grew up in New York City. Both were Marines. Before that they terrorized their neighborhood until things got so hot they joined the service."

Gideon sounded so tired Mack went over to the bed there in the shadows and carefully inspected him for telltale signs of bleeding. *You take anything for the pain?*

Gideon shook his head. *Wanted my head clear to report.*

Mack bit back a curse as he dropped a hand on Gideon's shoulder. "You're taking something now. Kane. We need the medic bag."

A hush immediately fell over the group. They'd grown up together and Gideon was immensely popular with them all. He had a way of bringing calm to any situation. He tended to be quiet, but was one they always counted on, a good man to have at one's back.

"You don't wait next time," Mack said. "And that's an order." There was no pretending it wouldn't happen again; they all dealt with it. And if he was right, and their psychic talents were growing with use, or with whatever else Whitney had done to them to accelerate it, so were the negative side effects. Mack brushed at the lines of fatigue etched into Gideon's face.

"I'm okay, boss. Just need to sleep. Can't seem to these days."

Lucas had mentioned in passing to Mack that Gideon wasn't sleeping. He should have followed up on it. Gideon often prowled the apartment at night when he wasn't on guard duty, and during the day he wasn't taking his usual catnaps.

His heart beat too fast, and there was a bad taste in his mouth. He recognized it as fear. Mack had always controlled every situation through careful planning, and yet now he had no way of ensuring his men were safe. He took every precaution on a mission, but their health, the consequences of their psychic abilities, was beyond his control. It seemed the stronger the gift, the greater the repercussions.

Kane dropped a hand on his shoulder as he placed the medic bag on the bed beside Gideon. "We all made the decision, Mack," he said quietly.

Mack let out his breath. He knew none of them blamed him, and maybe some of them would have done it anyway without his endorsement, but they had been following him since they were kids and he had known they'd follow him this time. Kane's statement didn't let him off the hook, though he appreciated it.

Kane prepared a shot. "I'm going to get you to sleep, Gideon. Just lay it down for a while. No dreaming. Just go out and let your mind and body rest."

Gideon flashed him a wan grin. "Yeah, I'll try to remember about that dreaming thing."

"Maybe I can help," Paul said, his voice a little thin.

There was instant silence. All the men turned to eye him carefully. The scrutiny was thorough.

"What can you do for him, Paul?" Mack asked. "There's nothing in your jacket indicating you're a healer."

The tips of the kid's ears turned crimson. "The bio was tweaked quite a bit."

"Why?"

Paul shook his head, his gaze sliding away from Mack. "It's not what you think. Protection, not to spy."

"Protection for who?"

Paul heaved a sigh. "Me. Sergeant Major assigned me to your unit because he believes you have the best chance of protecting me."

"Tell me the rest."

"I'm not at liberty to do so, Top."

"Damn, do you think this is a game? You pose a threat to even one of my men, do you think I have the least compunction about putting a gun to your head and pulling the trigger?" Mack stalked across the short distance to stand in front of the kid, glaring, staring straight into his eyes. "I hope you can read, because I'm giving you the gospel here, Paul."

"I read you loud and clear, boss," Paul said.

"You haven't earned the right to call me boss," Mack said. "Until I can trust you, you call me Top."

Paul stared straight ahead. "Yes, Top." He barked it out, a marine to a master gunnery sergeant.

"Just what can you do for Gideon?" Kane asked.

"I have some healing talent, sir," Paul said. "I'm able to visualize the brain and skull and see any damage done."

Mack sucked in his breath. "You're a fucking psychic surgeon," he guessed. There was a note of awe and respect in his voice in spite of his anger at Sergeant Major for planting someone on his team with unknown skills. A psychic surgeon was one of the rarest of talents. Mack had never actually met one. It was rumored they existed, but no one he knew had even seen one. Joe Spagnola, like many others, had the rudimentary skills to heal wounds, but none of them could actually operate as a psychic surgeon was reputed to be able to do. "You're the real damn deal."

Paul's gaze shifted around the room, touching on all the faces. "I could be killed if anyone found out."

"Are you crazy? If you're the real thing, you're invaluable."

"Let me help him." Paul took a deep breath.

For the first time Mack realized the kid couldn't stop looking at Gideon and his hands seemed to be weaving a pattern, fingers moving continually as if he was under a compulsion. Mack stepped aside.

Stay close to him, Kane. I've never seen a psychic surgeon in action, but I've heard stories that they're a little insane. The kid's showing some disturbing signs. I'll take Jaimie's drink down to her. We need to find out what exactly is on that computer.

Why wouldn't Sergeant Major want us to know? Any team leader would give their right arm to have him on their team. We argued against taking Paul on for half a day. Why didn't Sergeant Major just tell us and spare the argument?

More importantly, why didn't he want us to use him? Watch him close. If he looks like he's hurting Gideon, kill him. Don't ask questions.

Mack shrugged. "Go ahead, kid, but you be careful of him. He's our eyes and ears. We're crippled without him."

For the first time, real animation came into Paul's face. He hurried over to Gideon and, holding his palms an inch from Gideon's body, began to pass his hands slowly over the entire frame, taking his time, paying special attention to the head and skull. He looked as if he'd gone into a trance.

Freaky, boss. The kid's out there somewhere, Kane said.

You just make certain nothing happens to Gideon.

The other men were moving in close for a better view. Mack pushed his way to the kitchen. He needed answers and they were on the kid's laptop. Jaimie and Javier had to get inside of it.

CHAPTER 12

"Oh, this isn't good," Javier whispered.

Mack froze at the bottom of the stairs. They *needed* to know what Paul was hiding from them. If Javier and Jaimie couldn't figure out how to open the laptop and hopefully clear Paul's name — well, he couldn't have a spy on their team risking the others.

"I've never seen anything like this," Javier admitted.

"Fortunately for us, I have," Jaimie said.

Mack stood for several minutes drinking in the sight of Jaimie absorbed in her work. This was one of those times he loved the most. The complete concentration and focus, the absolute joy of discovery when she found what she was looking for. She made love to him like that. Wholly focused on him. Every magnificent brain cell, every nerve ending, every particle of her being, was given to him. All of her. Body, mind, soul, and heart. He could see that in her work. Jaimie was an all-or-nothing person. And her work, like her love, was her all.

She enjoyed the journey. The harder the challenge, the more she enjoyed the fight along the way. That, she said, was as good or better than the actual discovery. Unfortunately, she didn't always care about how long it took to get her information. And he needed it immediately.

He came up behind her silently, very aware of her head so close to Javier's. She had great affection for Javier, and he shared her love of computers and code. The two of them could spend days or weeks talking a language that gave Mack a headache, but he didn't care, he loved to see her excited and happy.

"Here you go, honey. One iced coffee with whipped cream." He put it on the desk a distance from where she was working but within reach. He dropped a kiss on the top of her head. "I hope you have good news for me. And here's your hot coffee, Javier. Plenty of sugar. Kane said to tell you real men don't use sugar in their coffee."

Javier snorted. "He doesn't know how to stay up all night."

"Are you getting anywhere? Paul seems to think you'll have a bit of a problem. I told him he was crazy and you'd have this thing spilling secrets to you." He gave her a hope-ful smile. "I was telling the truth, wasn't I?"

"We blew past the operating system pass-word," Javier said. "It wasn't that hard. Virtually all laptops made in the last few years contain Firewire ports."

Mack scowled at him. "I'll take back the coffee if you don't speak English."

Javier shrugged and grinned. "One of those 'holes' you can plug cables into along one of the sides of the laptop. If the Firewire port is enabled, and the laptop is using the Windows operating system, you can break into the laptop via the Firewire port."

"So we just needed to connect another computer — running a Linux operating system instead of Windows — to the enabled Firewire port on the laptop," Jaimie ex-plained. "The machine is then tricked into allowing the connected computer to have read and write access to its memory. We then ran a special program on our computer that found the log-in password in the lap-top's memory. Then we logged in using that password."

"And we thoroughly vetted all the pro-grams. He's got quite a few he modified, and he's good. But then we found this." Javier indicated the screen. "He's got him-self what has to be a classified program. We normally wouldn't have a problem breaking into it, but we were expecting a normal-length password, not this."

"I don't understand." He hated those three words. And he often had to use them around Jaimie and her precious computers.

Jaimie flashed her world-class smile. "Well, Mack, here's the thing. Encryption techniques are now so powerful that it's virtually impossible to intercept encrypted files or e-mail messages in transit and decode them. The weak point in security systems is always at the place where some-one accesses an encrypted file or e-mail message. Usually this is a matter of entering a password chosen by the person. And because people aren't very good at choosing secure passwords, it's not too hard to break into their files. It's not so much that they base their passwords on things other people might guess. It's more that their passwords are too short. In fact, if their password is made of letters and numbers and is less than twenty-three characters long, I can run a special program off a supercomputer that will test every possible combination, and be able to find their password within a few hours."

Javier nodded. "And — even though all the security specialists recommend it —

we'll never be able to convince most people to choose random passwords with more than twenty-three characters." He winked at Mack. "Bet your password isn't more than twenty-three characters."

"I lived with Jaimie for a year. Believe me, I can barely remember the damned thing it has so many letters and numbers."

Jaimie smirked at him. "You can always ask me if you ever forget it."

Mack rolled his eyes. "I told you it was useless. She can get into my computer."

Javier grinned at him. "I don't think you're ever going to get away with sending hot e-mails to Internet babes."

"Another approach people have tried is biometrics: using the unique characteristics of a person's biology to allow only that person, or a group of people, to have access to something," Jaimie continued, giving Javier a warning kick beneath the desk. "The most familiar use of biometrics is retinal scanning: You place your eyeball in front of a retinal scanner, it measures various features of a person's retina against a database that stores the retinal info for legitimate people."

Javier put down his coffee. "We're all familiar with retinal scanners as a way of limiting access to sections of buildings. But you can add retinal scanning to a computer as well, as a way of making sure that only you are allowed access to your computer or to certain files. A major drawback is that you have to add this 'retinal scanning' hardware — a special device you press your eyeball up against. You can't just run a program on your computer. In addition, there are horror stories that go along with this technology, like security break-ins being accomplished by cutting out a person's eyeball and holding it up to a retinal scanner . . ." Javier wiggled his eyebrows to look evil.

"Unfortunately" — Jaimie gave a little shudder — "that really does work."

"Can I just bring the kid down here and shove his eye at the computer, or do you need me to really cut it out?" Mack asked, straight-faced.

Jaimie made a face at him. "I don't think we need to do anything quite so drastic. My PhD dissertation introduced a new approach that combines the idea of generating more secure passwords with the idea behind biometrics: coming up with a unique identifier for each person. Here's the idea. Just like a person's retina or fingerprint, everyone's brain is unique. In particular, everyone has memories that no one else has. If we could identify a unique memory for a person, and find a way to express it in the form of a sequence of words — enough words to be secure of — we'd have a password no one could ever break. The program would be a terrific new tool for security without requiring the extra hardware that biometric approaches like retinal scanning does, and without having to remember an impossibly long sequence of random letters and numbers. I call it 'mememetrics' — because, in contrast with biometrics, it's based on unique memories rather than unique biological characteristics."

"How does it work?" Javier asked.

"Here's how it's done. My AI program conducts an interview with a person aimed at ferreting out a memory unique to that person, and expressing it in six words: the password. A password made of six unguessable words is just as secure as a password made of twenty-three random letters and numbers."

"Because there are about 170,000 words in the dictionary," Javier said, grinning with excitement. "Brilliant, Jaimie. I knew there was a reason I fell madly in love with you."

Mack smacked him on the back of the head. "She's in love with me. Keep talking, Jaimie."

Javier ignored him. "If you choose six words at random from the dictionary for a password, a program trying to crack the password would have to search through an impossibly large number of combinations."

Jaimie nodded. "Multiply 170,000 by 170,000 by 170,000 by . . . you get the idea: six 170,000s multiplied together. Our fastest supercomputers would take over three hundred years to search through all the possibilities. So this kind of password is pretty secure."

"You never told me about this, Jaimie," Javier said. "How does the program work?"

"It has about a thousand different 'schemas' representing different kinds of remembered personal experiences: from happy childhood memories, to low-grade traumatic experiences, to fantasies, to love or sexual memories, to memories of accomplishments, on and on."

Mack frowned at her. "I don't want to know the kid's sexual fantasies, Jaimie, just his password. I need a look into that computer."

"You have no patience," Jaimie reprimanded. "The program is looking to find an *uncommon* memory or fact. So, exactly *not* the kind of thing you often are asked for in security questions like, 'your mother's

maiden name,' 'your favorite pet's name' —
that sort of thing. And *not* your sexual
preference, you perverts. A lot of people
besides yourself could acquire those pieces
of information. So the program steers away
from those sorts of things. Instead, it looks
for facts or memories that are unique to
you, and that you have never shared with
anyone else."

Javier shook his head, his mouth open, his
eyes lit with respect. Mack's chest expanded. He loved how intelligent Jaimie
was, that she could do things few others
could do and he had no understanding of.
But he loved to listen. Sometimes, when she
talked, he felt like her accomplishments
were the best in the world. He was more
proud of her than of anything he'd ever
done. He wanted to show her off to the
world — and he wanted to keep her strictly
for himself.

"The program uses a natural language
interface and a unique AI learning algorithm
that almost always allows it to converge on
a unique memory for a person within five
attempts. So it might start off looking for a
low-grade traumatic experience from childhood — something you remember but never
told anyone else about — but then it discov-
ers that you are someone who basically

doesn't recall any unhappy childhood memories. So upon learning that, the program might shift over to looking for mildly happy childhood memories."

"I see you're focusing on 'low-grade' traumatic experiences or 'mildly' happy childhood memories," Javier said, speculation in his voice.

Mack wished he could keep up; this was obviously exciting stuff.

Jaimie nodded. "Because *horribly* traumatic experiences or the *fantastically* happy childhood memories are the kinds you might very well have told others about. We're looking for a memory that doesn't stand out that much, but is still unique, but is something the person can remember as their password, because after all, it's created from one of their own memories."

Mack made a face at her. "I hate to tell you this, honey, because I hate it when you have something to lord over me, but I have no idea how that applies here."

"Well, while Javier doesn't recognize this program, I do. This was my approach I came up with for my PhD dissertation, but then I went on to create a working program. It was classified. I don't know how Paul managed to get hold of a top security program, but he's using it to protect his e-mail messages. Unfortunately for him, I recognize this. It's definitely my program."

"Are you certain?" Mack asked. "How can you tell?"

"Look at the screen." Jaimie pointed it out. "Look what it reads."

Mack stepped close and peered at the laptop.

ENTER YOUR MEMEMETRIC PASSWORD
[ ] [ ] [ ] [ ] [ ] [ ]

"This is my program. There's no doubt. No other program has an access screen like that or refers to 'mememetric' passwords for memory instead of biometric."

"Tell me you left a backdoor," Javier said.

"Of course. Doesn't every programmer? I should be able to go into any computer using my program and get their six-word password. I just have to load this little tool program of mine."

"I'm so in love with you, Jaimie," Javier said. "Sorry, boss, I can't help it, she's a mega badass."

Mack shrugged. "As long as you know you're risking getting yourself shot. Then I'm okay with it."

"Uh-oh." Jaimie took a drink of her coffee, frowning at the laptop. "Very clever, my boy. You found the backdoor and closed it, didn't you, smart one? But you're not dealing with just anyone here. I wrote this mother. It's my brainchild, honey. You're not defeating me. Good try, but I never leave anything to chance. Let's just see how clever you really are." She set her iced coffee down a good distance away and began typing on the keyboard again.

"Talk to me, honey," Mack said. "Not to the machine."

"He found my main backdoor and shut it down, but I've got another, much more subtle. And he didn't find it. No one would unless they knew exactly where to look and what to look for. The first one would have given me his six-word password straight away. Much easier." She hunched closer, her eyes glued to the screen. "But this isn't impossible. What the second backdoor enables me to know is which 'experience schema' the password is based on — and that should narrow down the possibilities."

Mack groaned. "Narrowing things down sounds like it will take some time."

"Of course it will. The kid's good. He managed to get his hands on top-notch protection. It's his bad luck that it's my program."

Javier burst out laughing. "Everyone calls him 'the kid.' He's older than you are, Jaimie."

"Everyone's older than she is," Mack pointed out.

"Ha, ha, ha," Jaimie said, without looking away from the screen. "There you go, boys. 'Low-grade traumatic childhood experience.' I've got him now."

Javier lifted an eyebrow. "How is knowing that going to help us figure out his six-word password, Yoda?"

"Because, little grasshopper, as creator of the program, I know how the program goes from the schema to the six-word password."

"Yeah, well, I don't," Mack said.

"See the six pairs of brackets where you're supposed to type in your six-word password?" Jaimie pointed to the screen. "Here, let me show you." She dragged a notebook across the desk and hastily sketched a picture for them.

LOCATION WHAT HAPPENED WHY TRAUMATIC
[WORD1] [WORD2] [WORD3]
[WORD4] [WORD5] [WORD6]

"My backdoor showed us that his six

words describe a 'low-grade traumatic childhood experience' that he had. As the designer of the program, I happen to know that, together, word one and word two describe the location where that experience occurred, such as 'cellar stairs' or 'front yard.' Word three and word four describe what happened — something like 'pit bull growling' or 'gun fired.' And the final two words are used to describe why it was traumatic, like 'terrified me,' that sort of thing."

"Jaimie," Mack said in his best you're-driving-me-crazy-get-on-with-it voice.

"Okay. Sheesh, Mack, things take time. I'm running a special purpose, 'brute force' program. The two words for the 'location' are drawn from a database of about a million words. The two words for 'what happened' are drawn from another database of about a million words. And the two words for 'why the experience was traumatic' are drawn from a database of about 100,000 words."

"That sounds like it's going to take more time than I think we have."

"Mack, come on," Javier said. "This is a miracle. If Jaimie hadn't written the program in the first place, it would be virtually impossible to even get close. We'd have to try all combinations of six words and that would take centuries."

"Exactly. It may sound like a lot of combinations, babe," Jaimie assured, "but it's small enough that we can 'brute force search' our way through all the possibilities in under two hours. Can you give us two hours?"

She'd called him "babe." She hadn't done that in two years. It had come out easy and natural, with that little intonation of affection she could never quite mask. It had always annoyed him before because she'd begun doing it in retaliation when she objected to his calling her "baby." He liked calling her "baby," not because he thought of her as a baby but because it was a term of endearment his father had used with his mother. It was one of the few memories he had of his father. He supposed it was silly on his part, and he should have stopped when she'd objected, but he'd continued. She'd retaliated and then gone on from there. He hadn't realized how much he'd missed that small exchange between them.

"I can wait a couple of hours. That kid is quite the puzzle," he added, toeing a chair around and straddling it.

"Actually, boss, everyone likes him. He's secretive, really keeps to himself, but he pulls his weight and never once has objected to the ribbing we give him. He sometimes even gives back as good as he gets," Javier said.

"Who, of the men, is Paul closest with?" Mack asked.

"Gideon, but Gideon gets along with everyone," Javier said immediately. "Probably Lucas and Ethan."

"Turns out our Paul is a very valuable commodity," Mack said. He lowered his voice from habit. "We think he's a psychic surgeon."

Javier turned in his seat so fast he nearly fell. "I thought that was a myth."

Jaimie frowned. "How come you didn't know, Mack? That's big. Huge. No one really believes such a thing exists. I can hardly believe someone has that kind of talent. If he does, no one else must know about it or he wouldn't be in your unit."

Mack frowned. "Every unit should have a psychic surgeon going into combat with them. Think of the lives you could save. If you could take the violence, even you, Jaimie, would have an easier time of it if we had a skilled surgeon. Hell, we talked about this for months when we were in the hospital undergoing the psychic evaluation and enhancement. Psychic surgery was the one talent they screened for aggressively."

"There are a few healers, but not an actual surgeon," Jaimie pointed out. "Do you really think they'd put the only one they had in the field, Mack? They'd want to study him and figure out how his talent works, to maybe try to reproduce it."

Mack closed his mouth, teeth snapping together. "I didn't think about that."

"Like Gideon and Joe, Mack," Jaimie said. "I don't think anyone knows about their differences, not even them."

"Or you," Mack said. "We know Whitney wants to know how your talent works."

Javier flashed a grin at Mack. "Makes you think we're just run of the mill, boss."

"Be grateful, Javier."

"What's with Gideon lately? I'm a little worried about him," Javier said, the smile fading from his face.

"I don't know. I think everyone's talent has been growing. Have you noticed your psychic skills getting sharper? Expanding?"

Javier shrugged. "I don't pay much attention. I just do my thing. I've always been accurate. I have good hand-eye coordination and fast reflexes. I attribute everything to that." He rubbed the bridge of his nose and gave a small sigh. "I don't want to think about it, Mack. We went into this together.

I'm in my element." He flashed Jaimie a wan smile. "Sorry, hon, but I am. Mack is. All of us."

"I know. I'm just wired differently."

"There's nothing wrong with that," Javier said. "We like the way you're wired."

The computer made a rude noise and Jaimie lost all interest in the conversation, turning back abruptly to the laptop and hitting a few keys. She broke out in a satisfied smile.

"Here we go, Mack. We're in. His passwords are on the screen." She turned the laptop to face him so he could read easily. "We got it in just over an hour."

LOCATION WHAT HAPPENED WHY TRAUMATIC
[red] [barn] [bee] [stings] [nearly] [died]

"Poor Paul ran into some very unfriendly bees in a red barn when he was a kid," she explained. "He was probably allergic and most likely went to a hospital. Definitely a nasty experience for him, and one he'd remember, but one you'd never find on his resume. Nothing he would have told anyone. And not something you could grill his parents about and extract from them."

"Can you get into whatever he's hiding?"

Javier scanned the documents. "Letters. To Sergeant Major."

Mack swore under his breath. Deep, in the pit of his stomach, where no one could see, he felt sick. Bile rose. He knew what he would have to do. "I knew the kid was spying. What's Sergeant Major into? Why in the hell is he selling us down the river? Go through them carefully, Javier. You too, Jaimie. I don't want you to miss anything. Did Griffen think I wouldn't catch the kid? And he had to know what I'd do if I caught him. Damn him for this."

Jaimie spun around in her chair. "First of all, you wouldn't have caught him if we hadn't been experimenting. And secondly, what do you mean by what you would do if you caught him?"

Mack shook his head, his gaze meeting Javier's.

"No! I mean it, Mack. I helped you get into his laptop. You never would have if it wasn't for me. Don't you dare hurt him."

"He's selling us down the river." She could make him feel like a fucking monster with her quick condemnations. He'd forgotten that. Forgotten how low he felt, how torn by some of the decisions he knew were right to protect his team. "What do you think I should do with him? Turn him over to the sergeant major? Just find me something to vindicate him."

"This is why we can't be together, Mack. You're not God. You can't make decisions like that. No one can."

"I do whatever it takes to protect my team. And you aren't going to use this as some way to get out of our relationship, Jaimie. I'm sorry you don't like reality, but you're the one who pointed out Griffen sent Brian and Kane on more than one suicide mission. Did you think I wouldn't take you seriously and do something about it? He's not going to get away with it. And anyone working for him is working against us."

"Is he just going to disappear? Is that what will happen?"

"Jaimie, damn it, what do you want me to do? Find something that tells me he wasn't sent to spy. For all you know he could be a trained assassin."

"He's too young. He looks like a kid."

Mack spun her chair around so she was staring at Javier. "Take a good look, Jaimie. What the hell does Javier look like to you?"

"It's not the same. Javier isn't an assassin . . ."

"It's exactly the same. He looks like a kid and yes, he was trained exactly as an assassin. So was I. All of us were. Isn't that what you hate most about me?"

She paused, her gaze sliding over him, sadness in its depths. "I don't hate you, Mack. I could never hate you. I just don't understand you." She pushed her hand through her hair and turned away from him, but not before he caught the sheen of tears. "Let me just read the documents, Mack. There's no point in speculating."

Javier sent him a frown and turned his back on him to help Jaimie. Mack paced away from the two of them, his hands balled into tight fists. What the hell was he supposed to do — lie to her? Hell, he liked the kid, but he wouldn't like him so much if Kane was found with his throat cut or Brian "accidentally" slipped in the shower. His job was to protect his men. That meant making hard decisions no one else wanted to make.

Silence fell in the room while the two began tracing through Paul's private mail. Mack stayed way back, in the shadows, a good distance from the light spilling around the banks of computers. Trying to steel himself for the worst possible news wasn't easy. Paul's looks might be similar to Javier's, but his personality wasn't. Javier was edgy, dangerous, a man who took the slightest threat seriously. Paul appeared to be a boy looking for a place to settle. He seemed more like Jaimie, soft inside, wanting a home and family, not geared for combat.

The boy had joined them weeks ago and every member of his team subconsciously watched over the kid. They didn't want him because he appeared to be a weak link and weak links got one killed. Mack frowned thinking about Paul. It wasn't that he panicked. He had the nerves for combat. He was quiet and steady. He just seemed — young. Yet he was older than Jaimie. Was he undercover and very, very good at it? His stomach knotted. At this rate he was going to have one hell of an ulcer.

"Just out of curiosity, Jaimie," Javier said, his voice low and casual, "if we're going to make it an intellectual discussion. If the kid is really an assassin sent to spy and/or kill certain members of our team, what's the best way to handle that situation?"

Jaimie glanced at him. Javier didn't offer opinions on much very often. If he did, the others listened because he was making a worthwhile point. She knew him well enough to know he wasn't being casual.

"Turn him over to the authorities."

"Which authorities would that be, Jaimie? Sergeant Major, who both you and Mack obviously suspect is up to no good? Which, by the way, I suspected on the last mission when Kane and Brian ran into a firestorm. Someone set them up. If Mack hadn't suspected something was wrong, both would be dead."

She bit her lip. "Not Sergeant Major."

"Above him? Go up the chain of command? Colonel Wilford? Wasn't he the one Sergeant Major gave the evidence to?" Javier prompted.

"I don't know. Someone."

"That's the problem, now, isn't it, Jaimie? It's Mack's responsibility and there's no one he can trust if he can't trust Sergeant Major or Colonel Wilford. So tell me what to do here. You're the one with the brains."

"Javier," Mack said quietly. "Leave her alone."

"We're just having an intellectual conversation here, boss," Javier said. "She's smart. Maybe she has ideas we can use when this kind of thing crops up and someone is holding a knife to our throats. What do you think, Jaimie?"

"I said back off," Mack said. "I don't want to have to tell you again."

Jaimie felt a shiver go down her spine. Mack was protecting her again. He'd been protecting her for as long as she could remember, a young child facing school with far older, bullying children. Who knew why he'd made her his project, a little girl with eyes that took up half her face and a mop of unruly curls, but he had. He'd always been there, watching over her, insisting others treat her with respect and stopping anyone from making her feel uncomfortable.

What would she do if someone she knew, such as Sergeant Major, was sending her beloved family members on suicide missions? She was looking for evidence to expose him, but what if he had a plant in place ready to kill them and they had no evidence? Everything in her stilled. Her stomach did a curious flip. She condemned Mack for his very strength — the strength she leaned on.

Mack had to make the hard decisions to keep the rest of them safe and from having to do it. He was the cleanup man and the leader. Every mistake was his. He took the burden on his shoulders and accepted that weight. All the time she'd been thinking he didn't accept her as she was, but in truth, he shielded her from the more difficult aspects of life. She was the one who didn't accept him. She accepted his protection and strength and yet condemned him for it. That was what Javier was trying to tell her.

Mack had to know what Javier was doing, yet he still was willing to stop Javier to keep her from being upset. Was she such a child that she couldn't accept real life? The good with the bad? Reality? Her hands shook as they flew over the keys, her mind searching for answers. What would she have Mack do? She hadn't been able to pull the trigger and she blamed him for putting her in that position, but in reality, she'd chosen to be there. She was angry and ashamed that she hadn't been able to do it. That she wasn't as strong as he was. Mack knew that about her and he didn't care. He accepted that she couldn't be around violence or commit it herself. Was she punishing him for being stronger than her? She just didn't know anymore, but she was beginning to have doubts about her reasoning.

"You know, boss, so far, he hasn't reported anything at all about any of us or what we've done. He's actually painting a rosier picture than he's had it with us. These letters are short and more reassuring, like a kid writing home rather than reporting. Unless he has a code I can't see."

Jaimie shook her head. "I don't see any pattern. I think they're just letters."

"Why would he hide them behind an elaborate security system?" Mack asked, coming up behind Jaimie and dropping his hands on her shoulders. His fingers dug into her sore muscles, massaging the tension from her. His touch was firm, but very gentle, as always. For all his enormous strength, Mack was always gentle. "Why would he be writing Sergeant Major?" Mack asked. "Come on, Jaimie, you're smart. You've read a few. Who is he? What's he saying? Why the sergeant major? You're an analyst. Analyze."

"Well, the tone of the letters is very careful. He's watching what he's saying, not wanting to reveal too much. Is he happy? Sad? Upset that he's where he is? Or upset that he's having to make reports? Some of it is very genuine. He mentions a couple of funny things with Gideon and Ethan, and there's a trace of affection in the way he words it, as if both men mean something to him. I think he's trying to portray that he fits in, that he's comfortable where he is. Like letters a kid might write home from a summer camp to a parent."

Silence descended as all three let that sink in. The clock ticked out a rhythm. A heartbeat. Mack closed his eyes briefly. "Jaimie. Talk to me, honey."

She moistened her lips, glanced at Javier, and then turned. "I think he's Sergeant

Major's son. He never addresses him as anything but 'sir,' but based on these short letters back and forth between them, I'd have to say, the contents, coupled with the fact that he kept them protected rather than deleting them, say they're related, most likely father and son."

Mack slammed both palms flat on the desk, swearing between his teeth. "What the hell is going on here, Jaimie?" She'd always been his sounding board for as long as he could remember, with her quick brain and sharp intelligence. She could see patterns faster than anyone he knew. She could put together puzzles so quickly computers could barely keep up.

Jaimie bit down on her lip. Mack never hesitated asking her opinion. Never. Even if he knew he wouldn't like her answer. He listened to her, respected her. She knew he did. One time he hadn't listened, and she'd left — walked out on him. He'd been upset. His men had been wounded. He'd nearly been killed. They'd walked into a trap. She'd blamed him for leading them there, and yet, she was just as much to blame. They all were. But in the end, they'd let Mack shoulder the responsibility for it, just as they always did. The others let it go, but she hadn't. She'd accused him, and then she'd walked out when he didn't respond.

She dropped her head in her hands, rubbing at her pounding temples. Instantly Mack's fingers were on her scalp, massaging her head, in an effort to ease the ache. "Are you tired, honey? Maybe we should lay this down for a while. You could sleep a few hours and look it over with fresh eyes."

"I'm okay. Let me go through all of these. I'm reading through Sergeant Major's replies as well. I might find something else."

"I have to agree with Jaimie here," Javier said. "It doesn't make a lot of sense, but either he has the best code in the world, or he's simply writing Griffen a few lines a day, in a way that would tell the sergeant major that he was okay. Everyday stuff."

"What about the times Kane and Brian were sent out and I ordered you and Ethan and Gideon to go as backup? He wanted to go the last time."

"I checked for letters during those dates," Javier said, "and nothing changed. He never once mentioned the mission or any of the men. He didn't say he was disappointed for not going. He skipped a day, but that wasn't unusual."

"His skipped days don't necessarily correspond with your missions," Jaimie said. "I thought of that and checked."

"Could something be buried in the letters we're not seeing?" Mack asked.

Javier snorted and Jaimie gave him a quick, flashing smile. Mack threw his hands into the air. "Okay, okay, I'll shut up. It's just that . . ."

Hell. He liked the kid. He thought of Sergeant Major not only as a good friend, but perhaps a favorite uncle. Contemplating killing both men was not pleasant. And if they were father and son — and the kid was innocent — how was he going to kill Sergeant Major and live with the son? Either way, Griffen had to answer for the suicide missions.

"Damn it, Jaimie."

"I'm doing the best I can, Mack." Her voice was soothing. "I know this is upsetting, but don't think about it until the facts are in."

He knew his mouth gaped open. It was the last thing he expected out of her mouth. Condemnation maybe. But quiet support? She knew what was at stake. What the hell had changed her mind? He would never understand women as long as he lived — at least not Jaimie.

He took up his pacing again. He'd just been handed the biggest asset a Ghost-Walker team could have — a psychic surgeon — yet he'd been kept in the dark. Would the boy have come forward in combat if there was an injury? Paul had been antsy the moment Gideon had stepped into the room. His hands had begun a complicated and obsessive-compulsive pattern, as if his entire body was already psychically tuned to the suffering man. What would have happened if he'd been exposed to Jaimie after she used her talent? Why hadn't Sergeant Major, or Paul, revealed his talent so he could be used when he clearly so needed to heal?

Mack rubbed his forehead. He hated mysteries.

CHAPTER 13

It was late into the night before Jaimie and Javier were satisfied they could find nothing more from the letters. If there was a code, it was a brilliant one they couldn't decipher, and Jaimie couldn't accept that Paul or his father would be able to create anything she couldn't at least get a glimmer of. Maybe it was arrogance, but she'd never failed to see a pattern, even a small one, and she couldn't detect one now.

She pushed back her chair and rubbed at her eyes. "I've got the computer analyzing the e-mails, searching for something we may have missed, but I think we've got everything we're going to out of these letters."

Mack wrapped his arm around her waist and pulled her body into his, letting his warmth seep into her shivering body. She hadn't even realized the temperature was dropping in the room. "Are you both still going with the theory that Paul is Sergeant

Major's son?"

Jaimie put her head back against his chest. "I say definitely. If not, Griffen raised him."

"I'm going with Jaimie on this one, boss," Javier agreed. "There was no 'dad' or 'son' or outward sign of affection, but it was in the feel of it. And why the hell keep the letters at all? He's a kid missing his family."

"His last name is Mangan, not Griffen. His mother is Shiobhan Mangan. She's an ambassador's daughter, a very diplomatic family. She's the current Irish ambassador. He's an American citizen and his file says he was raised here with an aunt. His father is Theodore Greystone. Not Griffen."

Mack snapped his fingers, irritated with himself. "Griffen comes from money," he said. "Old money, some blueblood family from the South. I remember seeing a spread in a magazine once and his family had an old plantation dating back years. The name of the plantation was Greystone. I thought at the time that it fit. The columns were all made of huge gray stones and it made an impression on me."

"What are you going to do?" Jaimie asked.

"Don't either of you say anything to him." He turned his head and pressed a kiss against her temple. "Thanks, Jaimie. I hope to God you're right over this. I like the kid."

"You gonna kiss me too, boss?" Javier asked.

"If you want. Right on the lips," Mack offered.

"I'll pass just this once. Wouldn't want Jaimie to get jealous." Javier winked at him, kissed Jaimie's cheek, and sauntered up the stairs as if he hadn't been up half the night.

"You're very fond of that man," Mack said.

"Very," she acknowledged. "And so are you."

"He worries me," Mack admitted. "They all do, but Javier is entirely unpredictable. There's no way of knowing how he'll react to any given situation."

"You saved his life, Mack. A long time ago, on the streets, he could have gone either way. You pulled him into your circle, and he made the decision to follow your lead. He would have been a criminal."

"He didn't have much of a chance."

"He's always been different. You gave him a moral code. He didn't have that until you came along." She turned her head and looked up at him. "When you talk to me, Mack, sometimes you make me crazy, but I want to try again. Read some books on communicating with women, that's my only advice to you, because you suck at it."

A slow smile accompanied the slow burning deep in his groin. She was so beautiful to him. So sexy. She didn't even have to try very hard. "Now's not the time to give me good news, honey, not with all the boys camping out in our bedroom."

"Everything is not about sex."

His eyebrow shot up. "It's not?"

Jaimie laughed and shook her head, turning to cut off his step before he made it to the stairs. She circled his neck with her arms. "I'm sorry. For earlier. For accusing you."

He settled his hands at her waist, his heart squeezing down hard like a vise. "Don't think I won't do it if I have to, Jaimie. That's part of who I am. I won't like it, but if I have to put a gun to his head and pull the trigger to save everyone else, I'd do it. You have to know who and what I am. This time, I want you to know who you're loving."

Her heart jumped at the word. He rarely if ever used the L word, certainly not to her. "I know. If I told you I missed you every hour of every day, what would you say to that?"

"I'd say you couldn't possibly have missed me more than I missed you. You tore out my heart, Jaimie. Don't do it again. I'm not going to be perfect at this. I'd rather you snap me out of it some way. Kick me in the shins. Punch me. Get my attention. But don't walk out on me when I'm being dense."

She touched her tongue to her bottom lip, a sign he recognized as being nervous. Mack kissed her. Hard. Long. With his heart and soul. He never wanted her nervous when she talked to him. She could twist him up inside like no one else could and maybe that did set his teeth on edge, but he'd pay that price if it meant having her. Keeping her. Waking up every morning to her. He wanted to grow old with her. He wanted her there by his side when he died.

The problem with kissing her was it caused other much more intense reactions. His body immediately made urgent demands, hot and hard, and so painfully full he could barely stand the touch of his jeans. Worse, there was no way to stop kissing her once he started. He devoured her mouth, loving the velvet heat and the way she tasted.

His hand slipped beneath her shirt to cup her breasts. "I can barely stand not touching you," he whispered. "I love your skin. The way you taste. Your mouth." He bit on her lower lip, tugged, and then teased with his tongue. "You've got me hurting like hell, baby."

"I do?" She reached down to slide her hand over the thick bulge in his jeans. "How very unfair of me."

He buried his face in the hollow of her shoulder. "I'm so tired, Jaimie. Sometimes I wonder what the hell I'm doing." He whispered the words into her stillness, her peace. Jaimie was his haven, the only refuge he had, and he'd been lost without her. Without her quick wit and ready smile, the devotion in her eyes and her soft, sweet, welcoming body. She seemed magic and she could wipe out every ugly thing in his life. "I need you, Jaimie. Right now, baby."

To make him forget the image of pulling out his gun, putting it to Paul's head, and pulling the trigger. He would have done it himself, never putting it on one of his men to carry the burden. Just the thought that he could have done it sickened him. He wanted to forget what kind of man he was. Not one who would plan the death of a friend or an untried kid on his team. He wanted to lose himself in the magic of her body and just be hers.

Jaimie heard the need, the ache, in his voice. This wasn't about wild, uninhibited sex. This was something altogether different. She framed his face with her hands and looked into his eyes — eyes full of shadows and guilt. She tipped her head and pressed kisses along his mouth and throat, giving herself to him. Offering herself. A gift. She opened his shirt and kissed her way over the heavy muscles, her hands on the front of his jeans, parting the material.

She heard his soft groan as she circled the impressive girth, her fingers stroking caresses over familiar territory. Before she could kneel, he caught the hem of her shirt.

"I have to look at you," he whispered, that hoarse edge stealing into his tone, the one she loved. He yanked her shirt over her head and dropped it on the floor. Catching her around her back, he urged her into him, bending her nearly backward as he unhooked her bra, spilling her breasts into the night air.

He buried his face in the soft, warm mounds, kissing her, breathing her in. He could hear the blood rushing like a drug through his veins. His heart pounded hard. There was no way a man like him, so dark inside, so lost, could find a way out of his own skin. Jaimie with her unreserved generosity could take him into paradise. He turned his head and flicked a taut nipple with his tongue. Of course her body responded. She always responded. She always gave to him no matter what he asked.

"Everything," he whispered and took possession of her breast, driving her up fast as only he knew how to do. The flicks of his tongue, the edge of his teeth. Suckling hard and then gently. Giving attention to both breasts until she was nearly sobbing.

"Let me," she pleaded.

"Are you sure?"

"Let me," she said again.

He lifted his head from her soft enticing body. Her eyes were liquid, her breath coming in ragged gasps, lifting her breasts in time to her rough breathing. Her mouth was exquisite. Sexy. Pure fantasy.

"I want you in my mouth," she said, her voice a sensual plea.

He knew she was doing it for him, but he could believe her when she looked at him like that, as if bringing him pleasure was the most important thing in her world.

"I love the taste and feel of you. I missed you, Mack, missed all that power filling my mouth and throat."

He was going to embarrass himself just listening to her voice, the ache there. The need and desire. Keeping her gaze locked with his, she slowly knelt, sliding his jeans from his hips. His cock was hard, jerking in anticipation, already leaking small droplets. There was nothing sexier than a beautiful woman, bare breasted, hair in disarray, looking at up at a man with a wealth of love and wanton lust in her expression.

His breath caught in his throat at the sight of her, of his Jaimie, so ready to enjoy pleasing him. He had dreamt of this, night after night. Of her eyes. Her mouth. Her soft, feminine curves. He couldn't begin to think of taking another woman. There was only Jaimie, with the pads of her fingers working magic on his cock. Stroking flames over his sensitive skin.

She leaned forward and he watched, mesmerized, as her tongue slid out and she licked him like an ice cream cone. His entire body shuddered in reaction. Her mouth engulfed him, her tongue sliding over the crown and then teasing the underneath. She knew exactly what he needed, every spot. Every stroke. He had been the one to teach her. She'd been so inexperienced then, and she looked just as innocent now, a tempting, beautiful innocent seducing him with her mouth.

He watched her through hooded lids, unable to take his eyes from the sight of her. Loving him. Lavishing attention on him. Giving him the priceless gift of herself. Jaimie didn't just suck his cock to get it over with, she made love to him with her mouth.

She suckled and caressed, alternating rhythm, one moment hard and tight, the next gentle with a dancing tongue, paying attention to his every reaction. She made him believe that she enjoyed giving him pleasure, that at that moment in her life, bringing him absolute pleasure was the most important thing in her world.

He heard his own groan. Felt his already hard cock swell. He didn't want to finish in her mouth, as sexy as that would be; he needed to be inside her body. He needed to feel her soft skin sliding over his, her channel sheathing him, hot and tight. He wanted to be surrounded by her. His hands were on the sides of her face, holding her head back while she took him deep. It was almost more than he could bear to stop, but he forced himself under control.

"Strip, baby, hurry. I want to be inside you. I *have* to be inside of you." His voice had gone so hoarse he barely recognized it. His lungs burned. His hand circled his cock, stroking, keeping the fire high as she shrugged out of her clothes.

Everything in him went to molten heat, converging in his aching, swelling shaft, at the sight of her shedding her clothes, revealing her bare, peach-soft skin. She never questioned him. Never protested. She was whatever he needed. There was no other like her in the world. His Jaimie. He caught the mop of curls and pulled her mouth to his, taking her kiss, feeding on her sweetness, on the spice of her, while his other hand cupped and kneaded her soft breasts. First one, then the other, as he devoured her mouth.

"Are you ready for me, honey?" he asked, his hand sliding low to test her wetness.

"I'm always ready for you," she answered. "I *crave* you."

His heart jumped, and then slammed hard against his chest. "Put your arms around my neck, Jaimie," he instructed. He lifted her in his arms, skin to skin, her breasts pressed tight against his chest. Just the feel of her made his cock ache with need. "Wrap your legs around my waist, sweetheart. Lock your ankles tight."

Because she was so generous, so giving, she opened herself to him without reservation. His eyes burned. His throat felt raw. He could lose himself for a little while in her — forget the ugliness of the places he'd been, the carnage he'd seen. He gripped her hips tightly and slowly, and inch by exquisite inch, sheathed himself inside of her. He could forget the life or death decisions he had to make, the brutality of his life, just live inside her for a short while and know what peace was.

He felt her body open to his, unfolding like a flower. So tight, so hot, so velvet soft. He pushed into that hot, wet channel, felt her surround him, grip him hard, and draw him into his secret paradise. There was nothing like her in the world, no other place he'd rather be. His breath hissed out between his teeth as she settled over him, so tight she was strangling him, setting him on fire. The roaring in his head quieted. The jackhammers ceased. There was only the volcano roiling in his belly and the fire streaking through his veins.

There was only her smile. Her eyes. Her luscious body wrapped around his. There was the way she loved him. All of her. Everything. There was tenderness, something he hadn't known about but she taught him.

She moved then, riding him slowly, her gaze locked with his, her fingers digging into the muscles of his shoulders. She arched her body, her breasts moving with every undulation of her hips. She was beautiful. Sexy. Uninhibited. The fall of her hair, the sheen on her skin, the way their bodies came together, sent his nerve endings into overdrive.

He let her set that lazy, mind-blowing rhythm for as long as he could stand it, let her drive him to the very edge of his control, a slow, sensual ride. She made small circles with her hips every few strokes, sending electrical sparks sizzling through his groin and smoldering in his belly. His cock was on fire, his body no longer his own, but hers. She took him higher and higher, her sheath gripping his cock so tight his teeth clenched as streaks spread through his body driving out everything but bliss. Ecstasy. There was nothing but this ride. Their bodies coming together, the blood roaring in his ears, the feel of her soft skin, the sight of her perfect breasts.

His fingers dug into her hips, signaling to her that he meant business now. That he was taking control. She laughed softly. Her breath warm. Her eyes slumberous. Her body fiery hot. She did this little thing with her muscles that dragged over his sensitized cock, increasing the friction. He drove harder, deeper, letting the fire consume him, burn through him, burn him clean, burying himself again and again in her heat — *his* heat.

He dreamt of her like this. Liquid heat surrounding him. Her soft moans. Her soft pleas begging him to fill her body, to never stop. He didn't think he could live without her. He'd been without her once, and he knew what he'd lost. What a gift she was. He swore the energy between them became more powerful when he took her. Every sensation seemed to intensify when he pounded into her body, sheathing himself again and again.

He felt the shiver moving through her body and knew she was close. Her soft little cries grew breathless. Urgent. He waited. He needed. Everything in him gathered and centered, waiting. He plunged into her wet heat again and again driving her closer to the edge.

"Mack. Please. Oh, God, please."

Satisfaction. Elation. A powerful aphrodisiac. Her need of him. That soft little plea that meant the world to him. He needed that plea almost more than she did.

"Oh, yeah, baby. For me," he whispered, his voice harsher than he intended.

Her entire body shuddered. Vibrated. Rippled with shocking intensity. And then he heard his own hoarse shout as she locked down on him like a vise. He felt the boiling in his balls, the rise of his ejaculation, jet after jet of hot seed, the hot release milked out of him by her strangling grip. Her body contracted over and over, rippling through both of them, tearing up through her womb to her belly and breasts. His body bucked against hers, matched her shudder for shudder. Waves of pleasure shook him as he emptied himself deep in her. He felt absolutely free. Absolutely light, as if she had lifted a huge burden from him.

He held her close, burying his face between her neck and shoulder, feeling the ripples course through her body, feeling the grip and release of her body surrounding his. He loved this moment, when they were joined together, when the blood roared and pulsed exactly where they were joined and their hearts beat there together, in the center of their beings. He felt they shared the same skin. He was no longer Mack McKinley, the brutal man who made life-and-death decisions. He was clean inside. She'd saved him for a little while longer.

He turned his head and took possession of her mouth. He let her legs slowly drop to the floor, all the while kissing her, his mouth fastened to hers, melded there together, taking the very breath from her lungs. He wasn't ready to let her go yet. He kissed his way down her throat, licking at the sheen on her skin, finding the valley between her breasts, tugging and rolling her nipples while her body shuddered in reaction. She moaned low and long in her throat, sending sparks of arousal streaking through him, although he was spent and sated.

Her face was flushed, her mop of unruly curls damp. He framed her face, staring into her eyes. Jaimie. He could barely breathe with the overwhelming way she made him feel. Emotion welled up so strong it shook him.

She smoothed back strands of his hair. "I love you, Mack."

The intensity in her voice shook him. He leaned down and pressed his forehead against hers while his hands shaped her body. He wanted all night — weeks, months, years — with her. Her eyes changed. Went dark. Shadowed. Her body, so soft and pliant, stiffened, and she pulled away. An inch, no more, but it might as well have been a chasm and he wasn't having it.

He bunched her hair in his fist and pulled her head back until she couldn't look away from him. "Tell me."

She hesitated and he tightened his grip, his teeth coming together with a snap. "We're not doing this. Tell me."

"Do you love me, Mack?"

His breath rushed out of his lungs. He should have known — should have been ready. Love. What did that mean? That a man couldn't escape? That he didn't own his own soul? He detested that word. There wasn't a word for what she was to him, what he felt for her. She was part of him, like breathing. She was the rising sun, the stars overhead. The most turbulent storm imaginable. Everything. Was that love? Was that what she was asking?

"I don't know how to give you the words you need, Jaimie. I can only show you. I show you every time I touch you. Can't you feel it? Will that ever be enough for you?" Because God help him if it wasn't. He couldn't lose her again.

Her eyes searched his face inch by slow inch. He held his breath, feeling as if at any moment his world could come crushing down. Her eyes changed. Went soft. Went liquid. Her body moved against his. Her slow smile warmed him, settled the churning in his stomach.

"I feel it." Why hadn't she noticed before? The answer was in the million things he did for her. Jaimie pressed her mouth to his and then trailed kisses along his throat. "Do you have any idea where my clothes are? I seem to lose them whenever I'm around you."

Mack gathered her shirt and bra, handing them to her a bit reluctantly. "I like you naked. We need a little more privacy."

She laughed and snatched up her jeans, heading for the bathroom. "I have to agree with you there."

Mack dressed slowly. He'd never understood the tremendous pull Jaimie had always had on him. Quite frankly, he'd resented it for a long time. Until she left. Now he wanted to get over that spurt of idiocy. Feeling vulnerable and raw was a small price to pay to have her.

She was sunshine and laughter. She was everything good. He wanted to be those things for her. He needed to be there for her just as much as she was for him. He had to figure out what she needed most and provide her with it, because she deserved anything and everything he could give her. If the tremendous emotion he felt for her was love, he hadn't been prepared for the enormity of it and it all belonged to her. He wanted to make her life the best.

Jaimie emerged from the bathroom. She could take the air from his lungs just by her smile. She held out her hand and he wrapped his fingers around hers.

"Come on. I'm tired. I need a bed." She tugged at him.

He followed her up the stairs, although the last thing he wanted to do was to get back to business.

The men sat in a loose circle talking. They turned their heads as Mack and Jaimie entered the third floor together. Paul lost color and he glanced as if for assurance at Javier, who just shrugged. Silence fell on the softly speaking group. Gideon lay asleep in Kane's bed and Mack crossed to him first, bending low to smooth back the few stray strands of hair as a father might a child. Gideon was actually asleep and looked peaceful, the lines of strain etched deep in his face somewhat eased.

Jaimie smiled at Mack, her smile a little sad, and slowly released his hand, the pads of her fingers sliding over the skin of his. He could feel that touch burning right through his body and tingling in the crown of his cock, but then it burned deeper, wrapping around and squeezing his heart. He watched her go into the bedroom area before he reluctantly turned to the others.

Mack walked up behind Paul, and smacked him hard on the back of the head. "That's for being an idiot." He cuffed him a second time and went on through to the kitchen. "You and your old man both are idiots. Consider that taking a hit for the old man."

He poured himself a cup of coffee, added cream just to keep from looking at the kid.

Silence stretched, a razor-sharp edge along the nerves. He sipped at the hot brew and turned slowly, fixing a cutting stare on the boy. Paul looked exhausted, dark circles under his eyes.

Mack seated himself across from the kid, in the chair Ethan had vacated. "You look like hell. I've never seen a psychic surgeon at work. Does it take a lot out of you?"

Paul shrugged. "Depends on how bad the injury. Gideon's been using himself up. His energy is a little different and I suspect what boosts others doesn't always help him. The weave of energy." He frowned, trying to puzzle out how best to explain it. "Energy is usually in waves, surrounding every person and object. Some is very low-level, other times it's a surge of power. All psychics feed on that energy. Sometimes it's good, and sometimes not so good."

"In the way violent energy harms Jaimie," Mack said.

"Exactly. She's more sensitive than the rest of you. I can see it in her color patterns."

"What color patterns?" Mack asked.

Paul waved away the question. "I just see differently. It began at a very early age."

"Is that when your father decided to change your last name? Did he recognize what you were and tried to protect you that many years ago?"

Paul swallowed and looked away, shaking his head.

"What father wouldn't?" Mack said, as if the boy had answered him. "Tell me about Gideon. I've been worried about him. We've all been. What's wrong with him?"

Paul looked relieved to talk about someone other than himself. "I'll try to explain it to you, but I have to sort of give you a starting point. It's more than color I see, it's all about the patterns. When violent energy rushes toward Jaimie, it invades and damages the actual patterns. Everyone with psychic energy has very distinct threads. Some merge together. Your energy and Jaimie's merge, intertwine, and build a stronger base. I've not seen other couples, but I suspect that might happen with committed pairs. I have to study it a bit more."

There was eagerness in Paul's voice, an enthusiasm Mack had never heard before. Jaimie got that same exact tone when she was on to something in her work.

"I joined the GhostWalker program with the hope that I could learn more about what I could do and why I saw people the way I do, but" — Paul shrugged — "it seemed best not to admit to anyone that I was that different."

"So you played down your skills."

Paul nodded.

"What you really mean is, the old man found out his good friend Whitney was doing a lot more to the psychics than anyone had agreed upon and some of them were dying."

Paul's nod was barely perceptible. "Some were in bad shape. And he was taking apart anyone different. I looked at his color pattern and I knew . . ." He shook his head.

"Knew what?" Mack asked softly.

"That he was damaged beyond repair. He's psychic and his pattern was all over the place. I could see it in his brain, the madness. He believes in what he's doing. I knew if he found out what I could do — what I could see — he'd take my brain apart to figure out how it worked. I was the one who exposed what he was doing to . . ." He broke off and looked around the room. "To Sergeant Major."

"And he told you to play down your abilities."

Paul shook his head. "I was already doing that. Whitney's a brilliant man. His weakness is thinking no one else is quite as bright as he is. His ego defeats him every time."

"So he never guessed about you."

"No."

"And the old man decided to put you somewhere safe."

Paul sent Mack a half smile. "You were the safest person he knew."

"Did it occur to either of you I might blow your brains out, thinking you were betraying us? Your old man needs a lot more than a slap upside the head." Mack glared at the boy. "I considered just shooting you and getting it over with. I'm not one for mysteries in my own backyard. Are we clear?"

"Yes, Top."

"That's boss to you," Mack corrected.

The kid hid a smile, his eyes lighting up. "Yes, Top . . . boss."

"You know we're going to talk about the old man and the things you've been keeping from me. I'll want to meet with him."

"Not in his office, Top . . . boss."

Mack's eyebrow shot up. His eyes met Kane's. If their commanding officer was compromised, and Paul seemed to be telling them he was, they were all in trouble. Why hadn't Griffen found a way to reach out to him? He *really* hated mysteries. If someone wanted them dead, just come at them and make the try.

He sat back in his chair. "They sweep his office every day."

Paul kept his eyes fixed on Mack. "Yes, they do."

"Damn it. Why didn't the old man tell me?"

"He said you'd figure it out."

So the old man had expected him to figure it out. How? Without Jaimie experimenting with him they would never have discovered Paul. But maybe they weren't meant to find out about Paul. Griffen had sent Paul to him as part of the team — not as his son. He hadn't revealed the asset that Paul was because he didn't want the boy compromised. Griffen would never have told Mack that Paul was his son. The sergeant major had expected him to figure out that he was compromised. How?

He did what he always did — he found Jaimie. She sat tailor fashion on her bed, listening. *What do you think?* he asked.

The suicide missions. You obviously had a bad feeling the moment the orders came down. What tipped you off?

It was the one thing that didn't make sense, unless Griffen was working with Whitney. But if he wasn't working with Whitney, then the suicide missions didn't make sense at all. He would never set up the men in his own command. Mack pressed his fingers into his throbbing eyes. Griffen should have found a better way to get through to him. He must have subtly warned Mack, enough that he picked up on it, but not in a way that tipped anyone else off.

The boy was looking at Mack as if he was going to save the world — save his father. He stretched his legs out in front of him, feeling old and tired. A few minutes earlier, Jaimie's soft body was wrapped around him, taking him away from reality, but this — blood and death and the planning of it — was his reality. He felt very alone. Weighed down. Sometimes he thought his back might break under the load.

Look at me.

Her voice shimmered in his mind. Soft. Tender. Like that of an angel. Like sex and sin. Like love and devotion. *Everything.* There she was. He lifted his gaze, his eyes meeting hers.

I'll be here for you. Every minute, Mack. You can do this thing better than anyone else. It's a gift.

It's a burden.

A gift. You are extraordinary. You'll find a way out for Griffen, for Paul, for Kane and Brian. You aren't alone. We're with you. I'm with you.

She sent him her slow, sexy smile. The one

that reminded him how her lips felt wrapped around his cock, how it felt to be sliding in and out of that hot, wet world, her gaze locked with his. Just the memory of her soft moans aroused him, made him so hard he could barely move with the aching demand. Other times, like now, just the touch of her mind in his, the feeling that she could be aroused just by the brush of his hand along her breasts, or thighs, settled his mind right along with his gut.

Paul smiled at him. "Your energy and Jaimie's merge and the patterns weave together. It's very strange and really cool."

Sharing himself with Jaimie was far too intimate to have anyone else "reading" their energy. He couldn't explain how he felt to her, let alone to anyone else. And he certainly didn't want his emotions dissected in some psychic experiment. Jaimie was wrapped up tightly inside him, in his heart and soul. If Paul could see that, it left him stripped and naked, vulnerable to the world. Abruptly he pulled out of her mind, shutting down his raw feelings for her.

She blinked. Frowned. Looked down into her hands.

Mack let out his breath and diverted Paul's attention from his own energy. "So tell me about Gideon. What's going on with him? What can I do differently to keep him from overloading? Do you have any ideas to keep all of us from overloading?"

Paul nodded. "I've been working on a few things."

He seemed eager now and Mack realized it must have been hell for a natural healer to keep from doing the very thing he was born to do. He wanted to talk about it with someone who would understand and value his contribution.

"Each pattern of colors is unique to the individual and to their psychic abilities. Most have more than one talent in varying degrees. Some are stronger than others. Whitney manipulated the brain's filters as well as opening up more areas in the brain to be used. Obviously you're dealing with individuals and because everyone is different, each body and brain reacted differently to his enhancements. Unfortunately, that wasn't good enough for him. He also added genetic enhancements."

Mack nodded. "We've all learned to live with what he did." It hadn't been easy. His team had been lucky. He knew not all those experimented on lived through it. And more died during the initial training period.

"Gideon has a different weave to his pattern. It's almost translucent, as if I can see through it. The colors are lighter, less dense. Jaimie has similar threads. The less density means she absorbs more energy as it swarms toward her. The violent energy punches through her weaves leaving holes, some tiny and others a little larger. Your energy strengthens the weave and prevents the tears."

Mack pushed a hand through his hair. Paul was talking about how he saw each person's psychic energy as an indicator of their health. Paul could figure out a lot of the problems with his team members, but they couldn't share his unique talent with anyone else, no matter the need, because it would endanger his life. He'd given Mack a huge leap of faith by offering to help Gideon and exposing his true talent to them. Paul's safety was a huge responsibility. There could never be any accidental reference to his healing of them.

His gaze strayed to Jaimie. She listened but, like the others, said nothing. He knew they were all aware of the enormity of what Paul was handing to them. He sent her a small smile. *See, baby, there's a reason why you're so soft inside.*

Faint color crept up her neck and into her face at the intimate tone he used.

"I think with Gideon, he gathers energy

around him like a shield," Paul continued, jerking Mack's attention back to the boy. "It builds up until he needs to release some of it. His brain can't take the continual battering. The first sign is, of course, a headache."

"We all get those," Mack agreed.

Paul nodded. "Yes, because we're using parts of the brain never really used before. Whitney activated neuro pathways that we've never used as well. Those pathways don't remain static, they grow in strength and branch out. Some of you have probably already begun to feel the effects."

Mack nodded. "Some of the talents are getting stronger, but so are the repercussions."

"We have to find a way to get our bodies and brains used to the new enhancements."

"We've done that already, haven't we?"

Paul shrugged. "But once Whitney opened the floodgates, your psychic abilities will continue to grow. Whatever genetic changes he introduced to your bodies will continue to grow. If he really does have a breeding program and he paired you with someone, that attachment will grow as well. How could it not? Your psychic pattern with Jaimie is so closely woven, I doubt if you could break it. If Whitney managed to pair you along with your already tight connection, you'd have a hell of a time trying to live without each other."

"He's putting a man and a woman together whose skills complement one another, isn't he?" Jaimie guessed. "So they can work together in the field as a fully functioning unit."

"I haven't seen any couples together other than you and Mack," Paul said. "But I suspect so. I've been trying to keep track of observations without leaving a paper trail anyone can find." He looked up at her. "If they were to access my computer."

She smirked. "Piece of cake. Your bad luck that I wrote that program. I take it Whitney doesn't have access to it."

"Very few people do. It's experimental."

"What did you do for Gideon?" she asked.

"I drained off some of the psychic energy and it allowed him to sleep."

Kane stood up. "I'll use his bed and leave Gideon here, if that's okay with you, boss."

Mack nodded. "Okay, kid, I have a message I want to get to your father. Use your impossible-to-hack-into program and tell him I want a meeting. I'll tell you when and where."

Paul nodded.

"Everyone get some sleep. Lucas, relieve

Marc in a couple of hours. We're going to have some major work over the next few days."

CHAPTER 14

"You're certain about this, boss?" Paul asked, chewing on his bottom lip, frown lines forming around his mouth and brow. "This is my father we're talking about. I don't want anything happening to him."

Mack smirked a little. "Don't underestimate your old man, Paul. Long before you ever thought about getting into his game, he was playing everyone. I'm the slow one. He sent me messages and I just wasn't getting them."

He glanced at Jaimie. He couldn't very well blame her, but he'd been distracted. Knowing he was going to have to find her again. Knowing she'd disappeared and he wasn't going to be able to stand not knowing if she was safe, even if she wasn't with him. He should have had his mind on his work, not on Jaimie, but until he had known exactly where she was, he couldn't think clearly.

Jaimie looked up at him and smiled. He'd dragged her in, needing her skills, and for the first time, she hadn't objected. She'd been working to prove to Mack that Griffen was not only betraying him, but trying to kill two members of his team. Maybe she felt guilty, but it was more likely that her soft heart had kicked in as usual and she genuinely wanted to help the man. That was Jaimie.

Mack studied his team gathering around him, ready to be let loose. His men were a different story altogether. They were going to rescue their sergeant major and it had nothing to do with having soft hearts. On his part, Mack was outraged that anyone would try to compromise Sergeant Major or any member of his team. And he liked the challenge, needed it, the adrenaline rush that accompanied outwitting criminal minds. Maybe he had one of his own, as he knew other members of his team certainly did, but they channeled their aggressive natures onto a path for service of country.

"Paul was able to get a message through to his father, and Sergeant Major immediately arranged to fly to San Francisco on the pretense of a meeting with us over Doomsday and the weapons being held in the warehouse. We asked for more intel on

411

the Doomsday unit. He made a big show in his office of barking out orders to get whatever we needed as we were very close to taking down the cell here," Mack explained. "It's a very legitimate reason for his coming. This is a big coup if we pull it off and Griffen has the rep for seeing to details personally."

And he should have remembered that when Sergeant Major had been so vague about backup for Brian and Kane. His head hadn't been in the game at all.

"I just want to make certain that nothing we do tips them off," Paul reiterated.

Mack shook his head. "It won't. Sergeant Major knows what he's doing. He always stays at the Sir Francis Drake Hotel on Union Square, which is perfect for what we need. He has a routine he rarely deviates from, and he'll follow that routine. We know he's being monitored and we're going to have spotters to catch anyone. We also have Jaimie, our trusty ace in the hole. She's setting up shop in his favorite coffeeshop. He'll take his walk and head for coffee and to read the newspaper before his meeting and she'll be waiting to start the back-trace using his cell phone."

"Whoever is watching his every move is going to be more alert because they have to know we're in San Francisco," Kane said. "Especially because he's meeting us."

"Not necessarily, although I think if we can't get the trace and get him off the hook, we'll put more security in place when we actually carry through with a meeting." He held up his hand, signifying to the others to give him complete attention. "This plan is very detailed and involved for a number of reasons. Each piece has to fall into place for it to work. No one take chances. If in doubt, walk away from your assignment and call it in. We'll switch to our other procedures. You cannot be spotted. If they know we're about to take him, my guess is they'll kill him."

Paul sucked in his breath audibly.

Mack shrugged. "If they lose him, he's of no further use and he becomes a liability instantly. They have to kill him. They have strings back to them that can be followed and the last thing they want is for anyone to identify who they are. And God help Colonel Wilford if this leads back to him." His gaze locked with Jaimie's. "You can do this?"

"Oh yeah. If I'm right, I'm already halfway there. I think whoever is threatening Sergeant Major is the one trying to hack into my computer." She leaned over and touched Paul's hand. "I know I can do this, Paul."

He nodded and gave her a brief, nervous smile.

"Whitney's the one trying to hack into your computer," Mack said. "I don't want him to know you're on to him."

Jaimie shook her head. "Not Whitney, Mack. Someone else. Someone who likes what Whitney's doing and has condoned it, but doesn't want his experiments exposed — or himself, particularly himself."

Mack frowned. *Why would Sergeant Major send Brian and Kane on suicide missions and suppress evidence against Whitney?* he asked her telepathically, not wanting anyone else to hear him.

I think whoever this is aided Whitney to begin with and now they're trying to cover their ass. By choosing Kane and Brian, they throw more suspicion onto Whitney, Sergeant Major, and Colonel Wilford. They're distancing themselves even while they protect him. Whitney isn't going to kill one of us, Mack. We're his creations. He'll experiment on us, and if we die during the process, that's just science to him, but he wouldn't throw any of us away.

"Damn it, Jaimie," Mack snapped aloud. "Did you for one moment think this might have been important enough to tell me? Now's a hell of a time."

"I tried to tell you before, when I was doing the back-trace," she replied calmly. "And don't swear at me. I'm not one of your soldiers."

Javier snorted and then sobered, coughing a bit when Mack pinned him with piercing eyes. Ethan helpfully pounded his back.

"This is going to be tight. We have to work it by the numbers. Javier, he knows you're going to slip the earpiece into his pocket, so he'll be looking for you. Don't be too obnoxious and draw attention to yourself. We'll need you moving in and out of the crowd."

"I know what to do," Javier assured. "I won't blow it. Sergeant Major is family."

"I'm talking about not getting killed here. You never think anyone can get to you."

Javier sent him a small grin. "I know what you're saying, Mama, and I'll be careful."

Mack sighed and shoved his fingers through his hair until it was nearly standing up in spikes. "There will be thousands of civilians. Innocents. You all know the rules. We want Sergeant Major out of there. He's our primary, but we cannot risk civilians. Kills have to be clean and quiet if they're necessary."

They nodded.

"Javier, once you're in that coffee shop, you work fast, but if Jaimie's threatened at any time, get her out of there. Don't worry about Sergeant Major or any of us. Get her clear and keep her safe."

Javier threw a quick, taunting grin toward Jaimie. "You got that, little sister? I get to order you around."

Mack leaned close. "Get this, Javier. She doesn't come out of this with one scratch on her. Not one."

Javier threw his hands into the air. "I got it, Top. I'm all over her." He winked at Jaimie and then wiggled his eyebrows suggestively.

That earned him another glare. Javier laughed. "You got it bad, boss man."

"You're going to get it bad in another minute," Mack threatened, but the dire warning lost a lot since the others were laughing at him. He knew when to give it up. "You all know what to do. We've done this a hundred times. Let's bring him home safe. Take your positions."

His team nodded and began to drift away. He caught Jaimie's arm. "Once you're in the coffee shop, Jaimie, you're exposed. You're a sitting duck if they realize what's happening. Position yourself away from the windows."

He was reluctant to let her go. He'd wanted her working with him, but now everything had changed. He knew her energy was unusual, that it worked differently, but until Paul had given him an explanation, he hadn't really understood why working around violence was so difficult for her. Now he knew, not only was it difficult, it was dangerous.

"I'll be fine, Mack," she assured.

His hand slid down her arm to her wrist, his thumb sliding back and forth in a little caress. "Trust Javier. He's cocky, Jaimie, but he's good. Really good. He'll keep you alive for me." He leaned over and pressed his forehead to hers. "Just keep your head down and the ball cap on. Wear glasses and your hair up."

"Nothing will happen to me, Mack," she affirmed. "I have the easy job. Javier has to boost the cell phone. He'll be in the line of fire."

"Javier is safe from the devil," Mack said, although there was an edgy note in his voice.

Jaimie smiled at him. He was like that, worrying about everyone before, during, and after a mission. "Sergeant Major is going to be fine. I was wrong about him, Mack."

"Let's just hope you were."

"No, this makes more sense. He would never have allowed anyone to compromise secret missions, but for the sake of his son, he'd definitely go a long way to protect the boy. Even then, he had to have known whoever this is running him is not against the United States, or he would have put a bullet in his own head. You know he would have. He counted on you — on all of us — to figure it out."

"I was slow," Mack said. "He'll have a few things to say to me about that."

Jaimie slid her laptop into the case. "Hopefully we'll get to hear." With a cheeky grin she opened the door of the van and exited, heading toward the coffee shop.

Mack moved into place, checking that each of his men was in the optimum location to follow Sergeant Major's progress when he arrived and spot anyone tailing him.

Union Square was teeming with life, just as it was every evening. He had deliberately chosen the square because of the natural topography. The square was a giant sloping bowl shape. From the surrounding sidewalks and buildings anyone in the park could be seen. The concert stage and open-aired café provided easy places for his people to move in and out through the crowd to watch for anyone shadowing Sergeant Major.

The sky had already turned a purplish shade of blue, and shadows clung to the high, towering buildings, spilling gloomy silhouettes onto the streets and square below. The colored lights flashed stripes along the buildings and played over the grounds. The temperature dropped as it often did in San Francisco in early evening. The wind picked up a bit, but not enough to discourage the people wandering through the Art in Motion exhibit. People portrayed famous paintings all around the square.

Sergeant Major on the move, boss, Gideon reported from his vantage point on the rooftops.

Watch for Javier. See if you can spot a tail. Mack felt his stomach settle. It had started. A chess match, and he was certain he had all the advantages. He believed in his team. They were good at what they did and this one was personal.

West end, Ethan reported. *Two men. They exited a black Town Car just after Sergeant Major entered the square. They split up. One's in a trench coat and dark glasses. The other is in jeans and a casual tee with a skull and crossbones. Tennis shoes. Dark hair, spiked. Didn't make sense for them to be together.*

I've spotted them, Gideon said. *Skull-boy dropped in behind Sergeant Major. The other is out of my sight. He headed toward the art exhibit.*

Where's Javier? Mack asked.

I have him in sight, Top, Gideon reported. *He's in the middle of a group of kids talking and laughing. Sergeant Major is approaching the group, about a hundred yards out.*

Watch him close. We don't want anyone in the crowd making a move on him. We've got a lot of civilians here, Mack said.

Javier's closing in on the target, Gideon said. *How the hell does he get those kids to accept him so fast? He's moving through the crowd with a group of teens. I can barely tell him apart from the kids.*

He learns the latest tricks on a skateboard, Kane answered. *And he's damn good at them. He loves that shit.*

Here we go, Gideon said. *Look alert. Second bogey coming toward Sergeant Major. He's in a long trench coat, very James Bond with his cool sunglasses and black leather gloves. He's moving through the crowd fast toward Griffen. Javier, he's coming up on your left.*

I can take him, boss, Javier assured, even as he laughed and shoved one of the kids he was walking with.

Your job is to get the earpiece in Sergeant Major's pocket without anyone suspecting you,

Mack pointed out. *Killing him might be a dead giveaway that we're going to take Griffen back. Just a thought, Javier.*

You never let me have any fun, Top, Javier grumbled.

Everyone's in place, boss, Kane said. *So far, Sergeant Major hasn't done anything out of the ordinary. Nothing will have raised a red flag yet. He hasn't deviated at all from his routine so I doubt they're doing anything but keeping an eye on him. It's routine for them as well.*

Javier's making his move, boss, Gideon reported. *He's dropped his skateboard onto the ground and is showing off his tricks. Sergeant Major is still coming up on his left.*

Mack focused his long-distance vision and watched as Javier did a series of tricks to the boisterous appreciation of the other teens. They were clapping, and several tried to emulate him. He wove in and out of the group and then around them. As Sergeant Major walked by without so much as slowing, it was impossible to see if they had even brushed up against each other.

Did you make the drop? Mack hissed between his teeth.

No faith, Top, Javier said as he and another boy competed to see who could catch more air. Another burst of applause drew attention to the teens. *Not even a comment on my tricks. I worked on that one for hours. I really think I'm underappreciated. Now would be a good time to talk about making some more dough, bro.*

Just don't get killed. What else was there to say? No one could do what Javier did with his particular flair.

Mack honestly couldn't tell Javier from the others. He looked as if he belonged with them and had known them for years. He had a jacket like theirs, a backpack, and the usual ball cap, headphones, and glasses. He looked like any other kid showing off.

Sergeant Major reached up, adjusted his glasses, and scratched his head. At once Mack heard his whisper in his ear.

"You know we're under surveillance right now, don't you," Griffen snapped. "I'm trying to keep you from getting killed, Mack. This is insane. And where the hell are you?" As he spoke he covered his mouth, his eyes darting around as if to ferret out anyone watching them.

Mack sat on the edge of the stairs, obscured by a towering bush. "Just follow instructions, Sergeant Major. You've got two shadows. Maybe more. I don't want you to acknowledge anything, or talk to me. Just do what I say."

The sergeant major kept walking briskly through the crowd, out into the park, and slowed his pace as he walked in front of a framed "picture" of artist Frida Kahlo and her artist husband, Diego Rivera. He studied the two people posing. They stayed absolutely still, a replica of the actual painting. He turned to look at another picture and when he looked back, the two people were once again still, but they were in a slightly different pose. He frowned and walked back and forth, studying the frame from every angle, trying to remember exactly how they'd been posed before.

"They're good," Mack acknowledged. "They changed hand poses. Keep moving. Slow, though. We need a chance to spot anyone tailing you. Take your time."

Griffen gave the two performers a small salute and continued on his way, wandering through the live art. He was an imposing man and easy to keep an eye on. Mack knew his shadows would hang back. The man in the trench coat ambled on the outer edges of the exhibit, although he did study the first picture for a long time just to make certain that small tribute the sergeant major had given them hadn't been anything more.

Gideon, Javier said. *Take a good look at the woman standing just by the first painting.*

Average height and weight. Short dark hair. Dressed like everyone else. She blends in. Gray jacket with hood. She's sipping coffee and thumbing through the art info.

I got her.

I got a feeling about her. She got out of the way when my little group came hurtling through there. Smooth. Fast. Clean. Really clean, Gideon. She's a plant. If not with them, then law enforcement. And she blends too well.

Mack smiled. Javier had a gift. If he said the woman had moved too smoothly, she had. He switched to watch the kid in action. The teens had congregated by the corner of the stage and were doing a mixture of tricks and dance moves. As always, Javier was in the middle of them. No one, not even Mack, could catch him looking at Sergeant Major. And most likely, after dropping the earpiece into Griffen's pocket, he'd never so much as glanced at him. That wasn't his job. His job was to spot the enemy.

I've got her, Javier, Gideon reported. *If she moves when he does, I'll let you know. Right now, Bond-boy is keeping fairly close. I'm guessing Skull-boy takes over when he starts his walk to the coffee shop.*

Ethan, seated on one of the benches, glanced at his watch, folded his newspaper,

424

gathered up his briefcase, and began to walk out of the square toward the coffee shop. He passed the woman Javier had pointed out without glancing at her. His cell phone rang and he stopped, a foot from her, and answered, spoke briefly with his back to her.

Send those pictures to Jaimie, Mack said. *Did you get any of Bond-boy?*

A couple, Top, but I'm not certain they'll be good enough, Ethan answered.

Jaimie can do anything with her program, boss, Javier said. *She's a goddess.*

Mack knew she could work magic with her computer, but this was so important. In the end, all of their lives would depend on her skills. They *had* to know who was supporting Whitney and trying to kill Kane and Brian. They had to bring them out of the shadows and into the open where his team could take them down.

She is, Mack said, meaning it. He was lucky to have Jaimie, to know someone with her skills, let alone have her for his partner.

He watched Sergeant Major make the circuit around the live art show, admiring the various pictures. "Okay, do your usual brisk walk out of there. Get back to your usual routine. Head for the coffee shop like you always do. Get in line, order your favorite drink. Don't sit down. I want you to stand in front of those three posters on the back wall and read them. Javier will be right next to you. Put your cell phone in the right pocket of your coat. Once he has your phone, don't move. Take your time drinking your coffee. This is important, Sergeant Major. He'll be sending the data to Jaimie. If they have a trace on that phone, she'll find it and do a back-trace. They can't know there's anything wrong. They have to think you're the one with the phone, not Javier."

"But . . ."

"Keep walking. He'll drop the cell back into your pocket. Paul will call you, a casual conversation, just follow his lead. This will work. They'll record the conversation with Paul and we'll get an address. And don't talk to us, just go about your business, following the instructions. This is what I'm trained for. You're covered all the way."

Sergeant Major moved into the swarm of people on the sidewalk, heading downhill from the square. San Francisco was all hills. One either went up the hill or down it, but there were very few flat areas. It was good exercise and Griffen was big on utilizing the local terrain for his workout, rather than hitting the gym. Still, it was difficult to walk down the street in the open air, surrounded by tall buildings, where at any moment someone could put a bullet in his head.

I'm moving with him along the rooftops, boss, Gideon reported. *I've got an open route. Lucas is running interference for me. Bond-boy is well ahead of him, almost at the coffee shop. Skull-boy is back about two blocks. They're giving him plenty of room. Someone told them the old man has sharp eyes.*

And the woman?

She hasn't moved yet. She's difficult to spot in the crowd.

Mack's gut twisted. *Marc, hang back and watch her. Don't lose her. Stay up high and watch that woman.*

Ten-four, boss.

Sergeant Major just got stopped. A woman appearing to ask directions. She's handed him a map. She came up from his left. He has the piece in his right ear, Gideon reported.

Mack swore under his breath. Such an innocent thing. A tourist? There were several tense moments.

I've got her in my sights, give me the go, Gideon said.

I can go in for a closer look, boss, Javier said.

Not a good idea, Mack replied. *Hold your position. You pass him too many times and they'll notice you.*

Stay where you are, Gideon said. *Sergeant Major is waving me off.*

Keep the fucking gun on her, Mack snapped. *It isn't his call. Just don't pull the trigger.*

She walked back over to two other women and she's pointing away from the coffee shop, Gideon said, and there was relief in his voice. *Sergeant Major is on the move again and the three women are headed away from him. Skull-boy broke off target and acquired the three women.*

Lucas, you'll have to watch Skull-boy, so move into a higher position. I want to know if he talks to the women. Watch cell phones and if they drop something for him to pick up, Mack commanded. He doubted if they would have such a big team on the Sergeant Major, but he had come to meet with the GhostWalker team and they would want to know what he was up to, no matter how much it made sense. *Did we get a picture of them for Jaimie?*

Jaimie's on it, Mack, Kane said. *Skull and Bond are military or at least have been in the past.*

Just like the two who came after Jaimie, Mack said.

Exactly, Kane confirmed. *Look at the way*

428

Bond-boy moves. He's a fighter all the way.

Jaimie, Javier, Sergeant Major is approaching the coffee shop.

Javier made another teenage joke, got his group laughing, and then he glanced at his watch. Muttering, he dropped his board and pushed off with a casual wave and glided right up to the door of the coffee shop. Kicking the board up, he caught it, tucked it beneath his arm, and swaggered into the shop. He shoved the board into the double loop built into his backpack, freeing his hands as he stood in line at the counter to get his coffee, just a kid looking for his caffeine fix.

Jaimie didn't look up. Her setup on the back wall was perfect. It would be impossible to approach her from any direction other than straight on, and no one could see her screen. The one glance he'd given in her direction had assured him anyone coming in wouldn't be able to recognize her. Her signature curly hair was pulled back from her face into a ponytail, giving the illusion that she had straighter hair. Her ball cap was pulled low, shadowing her face. The glasses were wider frames, a thick black that seemed to swallow her face. She chewed gum, staring straight ahead while her fingers flew across the keyboard. Occasionally she lifted the large coffee and took a sip without taking her eyes from her screen.

Sergeant Major entered and moved into line. Javier took his coffee and moved toward the back where the three posters were. He set up in the shadows. *In position, Top. Jaimie's doing her thing and is in a perfect position. Sergeant Major is getting his coffee and bagel as instructed. Bond-boy has entered the building. He blends so well.*

Mack chose not to reprimand Javier's snicker or urge him to take the enemy seriously. Javier would never change. Life seemed a great adventure to him. The more the adrenaline rush, the more he liked it.

Javier waited until Sergeant Major settled into position, sipping his coffee and reading the posters before leaning over to look into the backpack he'd put beneath his table. He "accidentally" brushed up against Griffen's coat, extracting the cell phone.

I've got his cell. Jaimie, you ready?

Yes. Do they have a chip? Or are they working with a mirror program?

Chip. You can back-trace with no problem, Jaimie. Javier dropped the cell back into the Sergeant Major's pocket as he bent to pull his book out of his backpack. *Everything's in place.*

Initiate the call, Mack, Jaimie advised.

430

They'll begin tracing and my program will begin the trace instantly.

"Incoming call, Sergeant Major. Stay on as long as possible," Mack said. "You'll be talking to Paul. Talk about fishing. Tell him you're in a coffee shop and will see him after the meeting. Follow his lead."

Sergeant Major dipped his hand into his pocket as the phone rang, sipping at his coffee, his back to the room.

Oh, yeah, Javier said, *they're recording his call just like you figured, Mack.*

Mack hadn't realized he was so tense. He let his breath out. *Jaimie?*

I'm on it. I already had a good idea where we were going with this, Mack, Jaimie said. *They're bouncing all over the place, but they aren't going to get away. Not this time.*

She was referring to the trace she'd started in her home. He still wasn't comfortable involving Jaimie. Strange, it had been so important that they work together before. He'd wanted her on his team, believing her special skills could keep them all alive. Now he just wanted her safe and happy. It was much more difficult than he'd imagined trusting her safety to someone else, even to Javier, who he knew loved Jaimie.

He could hear Sergeant Major talking to Paul. His voice was a little strained, but he managed a laugh in all the appropriate places. His respect for Paul rose sharply. The boy sounded relaxed and very much a son calling his father, looking forward to seeing him. He led the conversation skillfully, talking about a fictitious woman he'd met a few nights earlier and was hoping to see more of. He asked about his father staying over and maybe going out to the Farallon Islands to whale watch, and seemed genuinely disappointed when his father declined and said he had to get back to Washington. Several times Griffen shifted restlessly, but he didn't break position.

Got it! There was triumph in Jaimie's voice. *Let's get him out.*

Mack signaled to Paul to end the conversation. The boy talked a few more minutes and told his father he would see him after the meeting. Griffen's voice was gruff as he told Paul he loved him. There was a small silence. Mack had the feeling expressing emotion for his son wasn't something the sergeant major did often.

"We'll get him out safely," Mack found himself reassuring Paul.

Paul nodded. "I know, boss." He flashed a small grin. "Are you going to hit him upside the head like you did me?"

Mack grinned back. "I think I'll skip

that part."

Sergeant Major is getting ready to move.

Mack snapped back to attention. "Walk out the door and turn left. Approach the fountain. Take out your cell phone. They can track you anywhere just using the phone. It has to be thoroughly soaked. Accidentally drop it in the fountain when you get jostled. I want you to get wet and have to buy new clothes. There's a men's shop just up the block. You've bought a couple of suits there before."

Paul had told him that whenever Sergeant Major wanted a nice suit, he preferred the exclusive shop and would fly to San Francisco to acquire one. It was easy enough for Paul to go into the shop, identify himself as Griffen's son, and purchase a new suit for him, made to his precise measurements. It was waiting along with socks, shoes, and underwear as well as a coat.

"Remove everything, Sergeant Major. There's a medical kit. There's a tracking device under your skin. Probably on your hip. That's where we found all of ours. You'll need to remove that. We've got a man inside who will sweep you for more and help stitch you up. You'll need to be fast. Once the tracking devices go down, they'll be on to us. Once we take you, they'll send in their troops to try to kill or reacquire you. This will shake them up. You're here on legitimate business so no one will ever know any of this happened once we take them down, but you can stay under their thumb until we remove the threat or come out now. Your call whether we go all the way or not."

"Get me the hell out from under this bastard," Sergeant Major snapped, his hand coming up to cover his mouth as he faked a cough.

Sergeant Major walked outside, looked around, and whipped out his cell phone again, moving toward the sculpted fountain. He frowned at his phone as he walked, going through his address book with his thumb.

Skull-boy gave up on the women. They caught the trolley. He's on his way back, Lucas reported. *I think they were genuine tourists, boss.*

Get back here and get into place. We're going to need precision. Jaimie, as soon as they're out of there, get clear. Get back to the warehouse and barricade yourself in.

No problem, Mack. I've got the easy part. Be safe, all of you.

Javier wandered out of the coffee shop directly behind Bond-boy. The man stopped abruptly in the doorway, making a show of putting on his dark glasses. Javier bumped into his back, planting the homing device easily.

"Hey, dude. Keep moving," Javier said rudely, shoving past and dropping his board on the ground.

Bond-boy flipped him off, already turning his attention to Sergeant Major. Javier gave a small kick-push and took off down the sidewalk.

Sergeant Major pushed the call button to begin dialing a number as he leaned down to look at the bottom of the fountain where the light display played through the water. Something bumped his arm and he whipped his head around to see an elderly man reeling, trying to maintain his balance. He dropped his phone and caught the man.

"I'm sorry, I was pushed," the man said, looking around. No one seemed to be paying any attention. "Your phone . . ."

"It's all right," Sergeant Major assured as he removed his jacket. "It's just a phone." He rolled up his sleeve but even then, when he reached through the water to retrieve the cell phone, his immaculate white shirt was instantly wet.

Bond-boy isn't happy, Gideon reported. *He's moving in on Sergeant Major. I can take him if he gets ugly.*

435

Give him some room, Gideon, Mack advised. *We knew they wouldn't like losing the cell.*

Sergeant Major retrieved the cell, shook the water pouring out of it, and turned it off, cursing under his breath, even as he again reassured the elderly man that it wasn't his fault. He glanced at his watch and set off briskly going up the block toward the men's shop. The man with the dark glasses fell in behind him, mixing with the crowd.

"Nice job," Mack murmured. "Looks like you've got two shadows."

"I spotted one," Sergeant Major snapped. "*Don't* respond."

Griffen cursed again and picked up his pace, his coat over his soaked sleeve. Mack felt bad for him. The man was a legend, reduced to playing a puppet on a string because of his love for his son. He was a man of action, not someone to let others manipulate him. Mack would bet his life he was armed and willing to use his weapons. Sergeant Major entered the men's store, disappearing inside.

I've got him, Ethan said. *He's stripping to the skin. I'm placing everything in a plastic bag. It's safer to get rid of everything, then take it to Jaimie. I don't want them tracing anything back to her. We'll have to rely on the trace. She'll have the cell phone.*

Hurry, Ethan, you're on the clock, Mack advised. *Get that tracking chip out of his hip.*

Scanner picked up a second one. Ethan's voice was grim.

Mack swore. *Can you get it?*

It will be tough. It's deep. Sergeant Major says to cut the damn thing out of him regardless. Ethan let the admiration for the sergeant major show in his voice. "Sir, we have very little time. Can you stitch up your hip while I try digging for this thing?"

"Whatever gets me out of here fast," Theodore Griffen snapped briskly. Ethan shot him full of painkillers and deadened the area before cutting out the first small chip, but still, it hurt like hell. Griffen didn't care. He wanted the vultures off his back and he wanted to retaliate.

Ethan slipped the knife into Griffen's side, trying to ease the chip out. It seemed elusive, embedded deeper than necessary. Griffen never moved, stoically putting in two stitches at his hip while Ethan extracted the second chip.

"Destroy them," Griffen ordered.

"I'm sorry, sir, I can't do that," Ethan said. "You have to follow this through. You have to dress and go out the front door. I'll be right behind you with the chips. If they know the chips are gone, they'll kill you or reacquire you immediately."

Griffen swore again. "Let's do it, then."

Ethan studied him. The sergeant major's face was pale, but they'd cleaned him up fast. He had stitches in his side as well as his hip, but he walked without a limp even in the stiff new shoes. He walked out just ahead of Ethan. Ethan carried the garment bag with Sergeant Major's clothes in it. The two chips were in his pockets, still transmitting.

Boss, the woman is coming right up on Sergeant Major, the one from Union Square, Marc reported. *She's been in and out of shops, but suddenly she's moving fast and I think her intention is to intercept Sergeant Major. She's a pro, the way she moves through the crowd, very hard to spot.*

As Sergeant Major stepped through the doorway, Ethan pushed him to one side and collided with the woman.

"Go now, fast," Mack instructed in Griffen's ear. "Head for the bistro. Go in and all the way to the back and down the stairs. Move it."

Griffen heard the sound of air rushing out of Ethan's lungs, but he didn't turn, moving fast away from the man in the direction

438

of the bistro as Mack had ordered. Behind him there was a commotion.

Ethan's down, Gideon reported. *I've got the shot.*

Take it, Mack commanded.

Gideon squeezed the trigger and the woman with the knife in Ethan's side went down. Blood splattered across the window, but if there was sound, it was drowned out by the traffic on the street. Javier burst through the crowd, wrapped his arm around Ethan, and half carried him back inside and straight through the store to the back entrance.

"Leave the knife in," he advised.

"I'm crashing," Ethan said, his voice calm.

Javier simply turned, bending his knees, lifting his partner over his shoulder, and hauling him out of the store. *Bring up the van. Hurry up. Paul, where the hell are you?*

How bad? Mack asked.

He's out, boss, I can't examine him. I should have killed that bitch again.

Once was enough. The van's in front of you, Javier. Get rid of the tracking devices and dump the clothes. There's a burn barrel just a few blocks up.

Javier carefully laid Ethan across the backseat in front of Paul, who was already looking for a vein. "I've got him," Paul assured. "Get us out of here."

Pack it in, boys, we've got Sergeant Major. Let's go home, Mack said.

CHAPTER 15

"How is he?" Mack demanded, striding into the room, Sergeant Major on his heels. "Paul. Talk to me. Tell me Ethan's alive."

"He's lost a lot of blood. Jaimie's giving him a transfusion, boss," Gideon said. "You've got to let Paul work."

Mack shot a hard glance at Sergeant Major. "You left out a few pertinent facts in Paul's file. In fact, you left out a few facts altogether. The next time you decide you're going to send two of my men on suicide missions, expect a fucking bullet in your head, because that's what you'll get. Are we clear?"

Silence fell instantly. The tension stretched until the room seemed brittle enough to shatter. Sergeant Major carefully removed his jacket and walked across the room to stare down into Ethan's pale face. Paul didn't even look up. His hands covered in blood, he worked fast to repair the body, using mainly healing energy. Griffen watched his son, a look of awe on his face.

"Look at him, Mack. My son. Worth more than I ever was. The things he can do, the miracle that he is. I would have risked everything for him. You want to put a bullet in my head for that, then you do it."

Mack's breath hissed out in the room, a coiled snake winding tighter. He actually pulled his gun and laid it along his thigh, finger on the trigger. "You son of a bitch. *Everyone* in this room matters to me. Your son as well as every other man. These people are *my* family and they're all extraordinary. None of them are expendable, you hear me?"

"You might want to remember who you're talking to," Griffen said.

Mack's eyes blazed fire. He heard the collective gasp go around the room. His team knew him well and they all realized that was the last thing Griffen should have said.

"I don't give a shit about my career, not when you're so willing to sell us all down the river, so if you believe for a minute that threatening me will save you, think again."

Babe. Jaimie's voice was soothing. Loving. *Calm down.*

He looked up to see her stretched out beside Ethan, tubes running between them, her skin pale, Ethan's so white the dark scruff on his face was nearly obscene, and it made him even angrier.

"Mack." Kane moved up beside him, his fingers settling lightly around Mack's wrist. "Let's all calm down. We just pulled his butt out of the fire. You don't need to kill him."

"I'd prefer that you didn't, if I get a vote," Paul agreed, not looking up from Ethan's bloody body.

Mack jerked his arm away from Kane, but holstered his weapon and stalked into the kitchen. He couldn't look at Jaimie again. Ethan had taken a bad hit. He'd been so certain he could get his men out clean. Maybe he was angrier at himself than at Sergeant Major. "Where's Javier?"

Marc handed him a cup of coffee. "Where do you think? He prefers computers to people. He's tracking our wannabe Bond."

"They have the pictures of Griffen's shadows? All three of them? I want that woman's ID," Mack snapped.

Griffen came up behind him. Marc immediately left the area and busied himself watching the bay from the windows.

"I'm sorry, Mack," Griffen said quietly. "I didn't know how to handle it. I realized Whitney was out of his mind when I went to tour one his compounds. I was with

443

Senator Romney and Brigadier General Tommy Chilton and Colonel Wilford. They didn't share my views of the facility at all, at least not Romney and Chilton; Colonel Wilford was quiet, didn't say much at all. As we walked through that hellhole, I felt like I was in an alternate reality. Paul had already filled out the papers and was being processed into the program. I knew his talent was rare and that if Whitney realized what he could do, he'd never leave that compound alive. Romney and Chilton wield a great deal of power. Chilton has the president's ear. I kept my mouth shut and got out of there alive, although I think Whitney was suspicious."

"You should have come to me."

"The day after I visited the compound, I was hit by a car right outside of my hotel. It was no accident. I was out jogging and the car was waiting for me. I think that must have been when they planted the tracking devices in my hip and side." He rubbed the spots as if they ached. "I woke up in Whitney's hospital. Oh, he was very gracious. Romney and the general were solicitous. The colonel was very quiet and upset, but I knew I'd been warned."

"You should have come to me then," Mack repeated and poured a cup of coffee and handed it to Sergeant Major.

"You sound like a broken record. I answer to the colonel. He answers to the brigadier general. He goes to the president. Who else can I go to, Mack?"

"Me. You come to me."

"And what are you going to do?"

Mack's smile was mean. "I'm going to kill the sons of bitches."

"You don't know for certain it's them. *I* don't know," Griffen objected. "Don't you think I thought of that? They have never once communicated with me. I have no proof. Just the damn bugs. I had to utilize the encryption program to communicate with Paul, and anything secure I'm working on can't be done in my office."

"Who set up Kane and Brian? Was it Whitney?"

"The orders for the mission came directly from Colonel Wilford, as most of the missions do, but his orders come from above. The only thing different was he requested them by name. I had my suspicions the moment he requested them. I had turned over all the evidence the men had gathered against Whitney against my better judgment." He looked directly at Mack for the first time and there was shame in his eyes. "Did they make copies?"

"If they did, they didn't inform me."

"I tried warning you, Mack. I said things to make you as uneasy as possible."

"I must have picked up on it without knowing it, but you should have just told me. You could have used Paul's e-mail."

"I couldn't be certain that everyone on your team was clean, not with Paul's life at stake."

"They threatened him?"

"When I woke up in the hospital, Whitney was there with Romney and Chilton and they were all talking, consoling me, telling me I was going to be all right. And they said how easily these things happen and thank God it hadn't been Paul, because no one wants to outlive their child. I took it as a warning."

"Damn it, Sergeant Major, you should have come to me. You trusted me with your son. You should have trusted me to get you out of it."

"You're a loose cannon sometimes, Mack," Griffen said. "No one, not even me, can predict how you'll act in any given situation. You have a reputation for charging hell with a bucket of water."

Mack shook his head and went back over to Ethan, Griffen following. "Maybe, but I'd put the fire out. I always have a plan."

"They'll know your team has me," Griffen pointed out. "That makes all of you sitting ducks. You'll get orders to go to the Congo or worse."

"Not if they're dead. We just need the proof of who the man is pulling the strings. We get in and get out." Mack walked around the bed, inspecting the damage done to Ethan. He put his hand on Ethan's shoulder, his touch gentle, at odds with his commanding tone. "Give me the word, kid," he ordered Paul. "I'm getting a little worried and we all know that makes me cranky."

Paul flexed his fingers and sagged back onto the bed, slumping, his head down. There was a film of sweat on his forehead and his eyes were sunken in. He looked pale. "Get me some water, please."

Marc handed him a glass and the team gathered around him, waiting while he downed the water. "Maybe you should lie down," Marc suggested, one hand on Paul's shoulder to steady him.

Paul shook his head and looked up at his father. "She was trying to kill you. Ethan took that knife for you."

"I know he did," Griffen replied. "Were you able to repair the damage?"

"She went for the liver. It was difficult getting the bleeding stopped." He rubbed his hand over his face, trying to ease the terrible weariness. "He wouldn't have made it if we'd taken him to a regular hospital. They wouldn't have had enough time." His bloodshot eyes met Mack's gaze. "He'll need a lot of rest, boss."

Mack nodded and forced himself to look at Jaimie. Brave Jaimie. His Jaimie. She'd stayed right there while Paul used psychic energy to heal the aftermath of violence — a particularly violent and brutal attack. She hadn't flinched, or shrunk away from giving blood. Even though she knew the energy was going to tear her apart. He bent to brush a kiss over her temple. "Thanks, Jaimie. Thanks for taking care of him. I know what it cost you."

Paul glanced at her over his shoulder. "I'll help you as soon as I can."

"It's just a bad headache," Jaimie assured. "I've had many. And somehow I think you're in worse shape than I am. Did Javier get the information we need? I can . . ." She started to sit up and Mack put a restraining hand on her shoulder at the same time Paul did.

"Rest," Mack ordered. "Javier will get it."

"Boss," Lucas said, "I hate to bring this up now, but we've still got Armando Shepherd and Ramon Estes sniffing around

448

Madigan's warehouse. The signs are pretty clear they're looking to make their move soon."

Sergeant Major nodded. "I brought the latest intel on Doomsday. They're pushing hard for the weapons deal because they're gearing up for something big. The chatter's been increasing steadily."

"Where?" Mack asked.

Griffen shrugged. "It's anyone's guess with them. We have a chance to cripple them."

"How many, Lucas?"

"So far we've only ID'd Shepherd and Estes, but Javier went out last night with a bunch of his new little pot-smoking friends and brought back a couple of photos of the other two. They aren't homeboys."

"Javier on that as well?" Mack asked.

Jaimie frowned. "I can help him, Mack. You have no idea how much work it can be to run all the databases. I have multiple programs he doesn't know about."

"He's been in your workroom for a while now, baby," he said gently. "Believe me, Javier's found your programs. He's a maniac when it comes to computers." He bent down and kissed the tip of her nose. "Like you. Just rest a little longer. Gideon, I know you're tired but I need your eyes out there."

"I'm on it, boss," Gideon said.

"Does anyone in this room remember they're in the military?" Griffen demanded.

"Occasionally," Mack said, "when we get bad intel."

A ripple of laughter hastily suppressed went through the room. Mack squeezed Jaimie's hand and went over to the table, sitting down and gesturing to the others. "All right. Let's see what we've got. What's the latest on Madigan? Is he out of intensive care yet? Has anyone been to see him in the hospital? He's going to get antsy wanting to move those weapons."

Marc tossed several pictures onto the table. "This is Dane Fellows, Madigan's right-hand man. He's reputed to be a high-profile killer, Madigan's enforcer. We took these in the bar just down the street. It wasn't difficult to spot Madigan's people, they walk around like they own the place. The locals ignore them for the most part, although once in a while a fight breaks out between the dockworkers and Madigan's men. Fellows usually controls his people fairly quickly."

"Which means," Mack said, "they want to keep this area out of the spotlight."

"Yeah, that's my take," Kane agreed. "Word is, Madigan has an in down here with someone in the police station. Someone tips them off every time there's been an investigation into his activities." He glanced at Griffen. "If we run this, it's probably best to get in and out without the locals knowing we're running an operation."

"Homeland Security is going to love that," Griffen said. "I do have to answer to them, you know."

"Let Colonel Wilford give you heat after," Mack suggested.

Griffen pressed his lips together tightly, his bushy eyebrows coming together as he frowned. "He's still the person I have to report to, Mack. I don't know for certain if he's dirty. If I knew, don't you think I'd do something about it? I'm not a man to take this kind of thing lying down."

Mack's head went up sharply. He narrowed his eyes and studied Sergeant Major. No, Griffen wasn't the kind of man to put up with being threatened. He'd tried to buy himself time by sending his son to Mack to babysit while he . . . "You've been conducting your own investigation. Did you bring us any more pieces of the puzzle?"

"I don't know if what I've got helps. I followed the general from a meeting. He called someone on his cell phone. He was angry and I heard my name come up twice. He was objecting to whatever was being said. The senator's car followed him and when they pulled to the curb beside him, Chilton stopped his call immediately. The senator offered him a ride and General Chilton not only refused, but he backed away from the car. I've never seen him scared, but he looked scared."

"Why did you follow Chilton?" Mack asked.

Griffen went silent. His fingers drummed on the tabletop. Mack sat back in his seat, tipping the chair. "I see. But you changed your mind."

"Nothing seems so certain anymore, Mack. I'd get out, but that would leave you and the rest of the GhostWalkers hanging out there, more vulnerable than ever."

"Whitney doesn't want us dead," Mack said.

"No. He's proud of his soldiers," Griffen agreed. "But you've got enemies, someone working against all of you, and that someone is powerful. They aren't the ones pulling my strings." He glanced at the bed where Jaimie and Ethan lay side by side, both asleep, and where his son sat, still slumped, head in his hands. "Jaimie opened a can of worms when she started her campaign to gather proof against Whitney. His supporters don't want

452

his experiments coming out into the light."

"They know it's her?"

Griffen shook his head. "I knew. I knew the minute the senator and the general came to me saying someone was hacking into top-secret files. She would never walk away from the rest of you and she was convinced Whitney was doing things he shouldn't have been from the start. She came to me and told me she'd done research and that someone had been murdering GhostWalkers. She was afraid for you all. I thought, at the time, that I'd convinced her Colonel Higgens had been killed and his people rounded up and everyone was safe. Months later, the senator shows up in my office and tells me they have a problem. I knew it was Jaimie."

"Why didn't you tell them who you suspected?"

"By that time, I was already worried about Whitney, and Paul had applied and been accepted into the program. I wanted to do some investigating of my own."

"So when Kane came to you and asked you to provide a guard for Jaimie, you just thought you'd take advantage of that and get something in return."

Griffen shrugged. "I was happy he came to me, Mack. Someone had to keep an eye on her. Joe Spagnola is a good man. I knew him personally and I trusted him. If anyone came after Jaimie, he would protect her."

"And if he found any incriminating evidence against Whitney and his supporters, he could turn it over to you, just as you'd instructed Kane to do." He sat forward, putting both hands onto the table. "You should have brought me in on this, Theo."

"So now I get a 'Theo.' I thought maybe you'd forgotten we were friends."

"I wasn't being friendly."

"I got that."

Mack didn't reply, just continued to stare down the sergeant major. Griffen sighed. "You were my ace in the hole, Master Guns. I didn't want you anywhere near this mess. I sent you Paul because I knew you'd keep him alive."

"And Kane and Brian?" There was a challenge in Mack's voice. "Did you expect me to keep them alive as well?"

Griffen's teeth snapped together impatiently. "Damn right I expected you to keep them alive. And you did."

"We're in the middle of a maze, Sergeant Major. There're only a handful of people we know we can trust. We have to rely on one another." Mack leaned across the table. "Know this. Jaimie is not a pawn. I don't want you to think you can use her as a bargaining chip with these people."

Griffen burst out laughing. "Do you think I'm stupid, Mack? Do you think anyone in this room, anyone who knows you, would make a move against Jaimie and not kill you first? No one wants you for an enemy. Even Whitney wouldn't be that stupid. He's the one who wrote the profile on you. I protected Jaimie. I wanted her data, yes, but only to add to my own. What's she going to do with it? Take it to the newspapers?" He gave a snort of derision.

Silence once again descended. Griffen's eyebrow shot up. "Not to the newspapers. Come on, Mack. Within hours they'd have an entire history of her being in mental institutions. They'd discredit her so fast she wouldn't know what hit her."

"She knew that. But it would still be out there and the evidence would be where everyone could see it. She'd ruin them."

Mack. Joe Spagnola's on the rooftop across from me. He's spotted Shepherd's men and I'm afraid he thinks they're watching Jaimie, Gideon reported.

Mack sighed. "How well do you know Spagnola?"

"He's my best friend's son. A good man. I've known him since he was a kid."

"And you trust him," Mack said.

"Yes."

Mack turned around. "Paul. You feeling better?"

"Not much. I need to lie down for a while."

"How much can you tell about a man by his energy? Can you tell if he lies?"

"It depends on whether or not he believes the lie. In other words, if he believes he's telling the truth, there's no way of knowing differently."

Signal him in, Gideon. Tell him we're running a couple of missions and could use some help.

"I hope you're right about him, Top," Mack said, finally giving his friend a title of friendly respect. "Paul, after you see Spagnola and tell me what you think, I want you to get some sleep. All of you will need to rest up. I'm going to need you, Kane. We'll hash this out and come up with a plan of action."

"Plan of action?" Griffen echoed.

"Let's take the guns," Mack said. "We're GhostWalkers. We get in and get out like the ghosts we are. No one knows we're here. Madigan loses his shipment and Shepherd either is dead or goes home empty-handed. We don't have a lot to lose."

"You have to track them," Griffen said.

Mack shook his head. "We don't have to track the weapons. We've got four of them here. We only need to let one of them get away. We just have to figure out how to put one of those nice little homing chips under his skin."

"I see your point."

"Is Rhianna still out of the country?" Mack asked.

Griffen nodded. "There's no way to use her. She's still on loan to the Mossad, Mack. I can't pull her back. Can we use Jaimie?"

"No way. Don't even think about it. Jaimie doesn't work as a field operative. Rhianna can handle it, but not Jaimie. It was just a thought because we know her. We'll find another solution."

Joe's coming toward the warehouse, Mack. Don't let Javier kill him.

He is over six feet, Mack pointed out.

The sound of Gideon's laughter pushed into his mind, lightening his mood. *There is that, boss. He's a pretty bastard, isn't he?*

Jaimie looked at him.

Gideon's amusement increased. *Well, I could see why he needs to die, then. Six feet, good-looking, and Jaimie looking at him. He's a dead man walking.*

Mack laughed softly. "Joe's at the door. Kane, you want to bring him up? Gideon thinks Javier might do him in and, although I tend to agree with Javier on who needs killing most of the time, we might have need of Joe."

"I read in the reports that many of you have become more aggressive," Griffen said. "I'm beginning to think it's true."

Mack stayed silent. He might trust Sergeant Major with his own life, but he was not going to report that their psychic talents were growing stronger. Or that Gideon and Joe had a different energy that helped make it impossible for other psychics to spot them. Jaimie was amazing with the things she could do — especially that. The Ghost-Walkers, including Paul now, had to stick together and believe in one another. They had no other choice. The deck was stacked against them. In the end, Sergeant Major had spent a lifetime in the Corps. He might feel compelled to report when asked, and Mack wasn't going to put him in the position of choosing between his men and his career.

Coming in, Mack, Kane sent.

"Paul, can you manage to make it over here to the table?" Mack asked.

"No problem, boss." The kid was game and Mack's respect for him grew. Using psychic ability was draining and performing surgery psychically had to drain one's strength even more. Paul hadn't complained once.

Marc and Lucas closed in from either side and helped him as he staggered over to the table. Mack pretended not to notice. The kid deserved his pride remaining intact. Paul dropped into a chair, taking the one just out of the light, probably to keep anyone from noticing a resemblance to his father. The pair had become adept at distancing their relationship publicly.

Joe was wary, looking around, noting each man, his gaze dwelling for a moment on Ethan, the IV, blood, and Jaimie lying asleep, so pale, beside the obviously wounded man. He waited for Kane to move in front of him before crossing into the kitchen area.

"Looks like you've had some trouble," he greeted. His gaze shifted to the sergeant major and back to Jaimie and Ethan.

"You could say that," Mack agreed.

"Is Jaimie all right? And your man?"

"Ethan Myers," Mack provided. "Jaimie's tired. She gave blood. Ethan will be fine." He said it with more confidence than he felt. "Everyone, this is Joe Spagnola." He waved his hand toward the table. "You want to sit down?"

"Maybe over here," Joe said. He stayed clear of the light, away from the window, and where he knew no one had slipped behind him.

Mack sighed. "Joe, if we wanted you dead, it would have happened the first time you came up and we had a gun on you."

Joe winced. He hadn't spotted the man. "Which one of you?"

Mack gestured toward the bed. "There's your man right there. He took a knife for the sergeant major."

"I've got to meet him. He's damn good."

"All my men are good," Mack said. "I thought, since you were hanging around, you might want some action."

"You're talking about the tough guys hanging around."

"They're Doomsday. They're sniffing around the wharf looking for their weapons. They had a deal with an arms dealer named Madigan. He's known far and wide as the Spider. He likes tats, has about a dozen spiderwebs covering his back and torso and down his arms. We think the weapons are in the warehouse at the end of the block. The deal was set and Madigan had a heart attack and is in intensive care at the hospital."

"You taking the guns?" Joe asked.

"We're not taking the chance of them fall-ing into terrorist hands. We'll take the weapons and tag a couple of the suspects. If they lead us to the nest, we can wipe them out for good."

"Any chance of making the deal ourselves and taking them out that way?"

Mack sighed. "Madigan is too well-known, as are his men. We'll have to get the weapons out of there before Shepherd and Estes decide to make their move and try to steal the guns. We think they're getting ready to do just that."

Joe nodded slowly. "I'd say you were right. There's been a lot of activity this evening. I've spotted four."

"Same number here. First we have to remove the weapons and take over the warehouse without tipping them off."

"Should be easy enough," Joe said.

Joe's eyes took on a silver sheen, gleaming bright and hot as if the very thought of finally getting in on the adrenaline-laced ac-tion had changed the chemistry in his blood — or at least the energy surrounding him. Mack was beginning to understand the energy of the psychics was a little different with each one. Joe and Gideon shared something quite different, the layers shield-ing them from others. He glanced at Paul,

461

still slumped with fatigue, his face in the shadows. Paul nodded once, the movement nearly imperceptible, but it was enough for Mack.

"Marc, you and Lucas take Paul back to the room and get him to bed. Make certain he drinks a lot of water. I need you in shape as fast as possible," he added.

"I can handle it tonight," Paul said.

Mack scowled at him. "I wasn't asking. Get your ass back to that room and go to sleep. If he can't sleep, Lucas, knock him out. Take the med kit with you. Are we clear, kid?"

Sergeant Major stirred. Mack shot him a warning look.

"Got it, boss," Paul said.

He stood up, swaying slightly. Lucas and Marc immediately closed in on either side of him. Paul glanced at his father, nodded his head, and went out.

"What the hell happened?" Joe asked. "You've got three down."

"Jaimie gave blood and you know how she is with violent energy," Mack said vaguely. "She'll be fine. Ethan and Paul will both come around."

I've got something, boss. Javier's voice slid into Mack's mind seamlessly. *The woman assassin was Lieutenant Roslyn Kramer,*

462

formerly of the army. *This is her second death. The first time was three years ago in a car accident in Berlin. She's a real ball-breaker, this one. And Mack, her file was flagged. The moment I accessed it, through a thousand walls — and yes, I am the greatest — someone began erasing it and back-tracing at the same time.*

Mack swore. *You're on Jaimie's computer. You'll lead them right back to her.*

Javier snorted. *Give me some credit, Top. I was ready for them. After the first six firewalls and encryptions, I figured they'd be ready for a hacker. I knew the moment I got to the file, alarms would go off somewhere. I had part of it downloaded before the flag went up. The moment the trace started, I bailed.*

Which database? The army?

Nope. Homeland Security has their own supersecret database no one knows about. We're in there, boss. Want your file?

If it's so damned supersecret, how did you know about it?

The amusement faded from Mack's mind as Javier sobered. *Okay, I didn't know about it. Jaimie did. She has amazing programs, Mack, things I've never seen before. I think she may have worked on some of these. Each person has a sort of signature code, and I swear some of these look like hers.*

Mack wasn't certain exactly what Javier was talking about, but he knew Jaimie worked on many programs for the various agencies. She developed self-learning programs that adapted as they were used. He'd heard her talk about her ideas, and loved the sound of her enthusiasm, but in truth, he didn't understand half of what she said. He was proud of her accomplishments even if he'd never fully comprehend them. If she was developing extremely sensitive software for the various agencies, then chances were it was impossible to hack unless she was using her own program to hack it. Which meant that would lead them straight back to her door as well.

As for her databases, she either developed them herself, or she stole them. Jaimie was resourceful, which made her invaluable to Colonel Wilford whenever he wanted information for his teams. Mack knew she still worked for the colonel and because her skills were needed on the computer, they didn't insist she do fieldwork. That and the fact that it was common knowledge that anyone wanting Jaimie was going to have to go through Mack to get her kept her safe.

He rubbed his pounding temples. He was exhausted with trying to keep so many people protected. *Do you have anything on that address for me, Javier?*

Javier didn't ask which address and Mack was grateful. A headache was kicking in hard. Talk flowed around him, Kane had picked up the slack immediately, but Joe was watching his face and Mack knew little escaped those eagle eyes. He kept his face without expression.

It looks like a drop to me, Mack. An apartment building in Virginia.

Who owns the building? Who is the apartment registered to?

That's the thing I find interesting. A man by the name of Earl Thomas Bartlett owns the building. He appears to have no social security number and no driver's license, yet he owns several companies. There's a Lansing International based in Nevada he recently acquired and a company called International Investments. He has an entire list of companies in various states, all international. He owns a Falcon 2000 executive jet that seems to be able to land on any of our military bases in any part of the world, which he acquired from Lansing before he ever took over the company. And Mack . . . Jaimie has a file on him as well.

He shouldn't have been surprised by anything she did, but he was. Jaimie was thorough. When she began digging, she wasn't going to let anything stop her. *What's in the file?*

I have no idea. Jaimie's private files are encrypted. I wouldn't be in the databases except that she gave me a password to use on this particular machine for the various databases she's tapping into.

Javier, how much trouble is she in?

There was another long silence. *Honestly, boss, it's hard to tell with Jaimie. She covers her ass, and I don't think a computer working on her encryption could break it in a hundred years — she's that good. But she's got stuff here I've never seen before. And Mack.* Javier hesitated. *She's not working alone.*

The words were a punch in the gut. Mack cursed under his breath. *Are you certain?*

She's not only backing up her work; she's sending it to someone else.

Damn her. I swear I'm going to wrap my fingers around her throat and strangle her. Mack flexed his fingers and shot Jaimie a glare. Joe watching him be damned. He would shake her until her teeth rattled. Why hadn't she told him?

Boss. If you kill her, do I get all this cool equipment?

I'm not in the mood, Javier. Who is it? Can you get me a name?

Not a chance, Top. Remember that encryp-

tion program Jaimie was telling us about?
Well, she uses it. I can't hack her mail.

Do whatever she did to get into Paul's. You
were there. She talked you right through it.

Not exactly. She knows the code, not me.
She told me what she did, not how she did it.
She has a backdoor into the program, boss,
not me. I could search for . . .

Yeah, I get it. A hundred years.

More like a thousand, boss.

It felt like a betrayal to him. She had been
corresponding with someone else, sharing
her data, her conclusions, her suspicions —
with someone other than him. And she
hadn't told him. Had he really lost her trust
to that extent? The blow was enormous. He
stood up so abruptly his chair nearly fell
over. Kane caught it, shooting him a strange
look, but Mack paced away from them,
wishing them all gone. Needing them to be
gone so he could be alone to reason out the
why of it. Why had Jaimie kept this from
him?

It seemed impossible to separate his emotions, as intense as they were. Jaimie was
his. His world. They'd talked about resolv-
ing their issues. Hell, they'd shared the best
sex he'd ever had in his life. Everything was
right. But this . . . Why hadn't she told him
she wasn't working alone on trying to

expose Whitney and whoever was backing him?

Kane, get them out of here.

What's wrong?

I'll tell you later. After he strangled her.

He stalked across the room, vaguely aware of Kane closing down the meeting with the others, filling them in on the plan to retrieve the weapons. Mack stared down at Jaimie's face. So innocent. So pale. Her midnight black hair, so dark it gleamed bluish black whenever the light hit it, only made her skin look almost a pearl white. Her lashes were thick and long and every bit as dark as her hair. There was even a curl on the ends of them, hardly surprising when her hair was so naturally curly.

He reached down and pushed the coil of tubing from around her arm and gathered her into his arms. She stirred, her lashes fluttering, lifting. Her eyes were so blue, like the deepest sea.

"Mack," she said his name softly, a drowsy, slumberous, oh-so-sexy note.

Her smile was slow, drawing his attention to her mouth. The one he spent far too much time fantasizing over. His stomach did a slow roll in time to her smile. "That's right, baby. It's Mack. I'm putting you to bed and sending everyone home." He bent his head to brush a kiss over her forehead. "You'd better not be giving other men that particular smile."

"I reserve it just for you," she assured.

He carried her across the room to their bed. He was glad they hadn't gotten rid of the twin-sized thing she'd been sleeping in. The bed was tucked along the side wall. Kane would have something to sleep on with Ethan in his bed.

I'm assigning Brian to Sergeant Major. We'll put him in his room. There's no way to trace him there, Kane said.

Sounds good. I'll need Javier and Gideon to go with me to Washington.

I knew you were going to go, Kane said, resignation in his voice.

You might want to see if Joe can communicate telepathically. If so, put him on the roof when we're gone. If not, Lucas would be my next choice.

Anything else?

Don't get anyone killed while I'm gone.

I'll do my best, boss.

CHAPTER 16

"What are you doing?" Jaimie asked, coming up behind Mack. She'd known the moment he'd left her bed.

Light was creeping into the windows. The sun could barely make it through the thick fog drifting in off the ocean, casting gloom over the early-morning light. She'd followed him on bare feet down to her workroom after making a cup of tea, more to give herself time to assess her feelings than for the need of her early-morning cup.

Lying all night in Mack's arms, his body wrapped tightly around hers, with Ethan and Kane lying only a few feet away, had been a kind of hell. He had touched her continually. Her breasts, her ribs, her belly, his hand sliding between her legs, fingers moving inside her. She had the marks of his mouth against her neck and even on her breast, his hands and mouth keeping her aroused and on edge, but he'd never said a

470

word. Never took her over that edge, even quietly beneath the covers. She'd never felt so aroused in her life. Every square inch of her body felt sensitive and needy.

"Trying to hack into your files," Javier answered her without looking up from the screen. "Using your own program of course."

She was glad he hadn't looked up. Her nipples were peaked and hard beneath her thin top and lacy bra. "I see." She wrapped her arms around Mack's neck and leaned against his back, careful to keep her tea from spilling, needing to hide her body and feel his warmth at the same time. "Are you getting anywhere?"

"No." Javier shot her a look of pure malice over his shoulder. "I'm thinking of pulling out a gun and shooting your hard drive."

"Why didn't you just come ask me?"

"Would you have given me your password?" Javier challenged.

"No, and I'm thinking of throwing you out of my house and banning you from ever using my equipment again." Jaimie actually had to work to keep her voice normal. Her tone had gone throaty, almost husky. She didn't look at Mack when he turned his head to glance at her over his shoulder. She couldn't. Afraid he might know. He did know. He arched his back enough to put pressure on her sensitive nipples.

She gasped and straightened, trying to look casual, but that slight brush of her breasts against Mack's back sent arousal sizzling through her veins, from breasts to thighs. She looked down at her hands and found she was trembling. He looked so completely composed while she was a wreck.

She moved away from Mack's solid frame, putting a little distance between them, to perch on the long desktop. Swinging one leg, she sipped at her tea, glaring at Javier, mostly to avoid looking at Mack.

Javier threw his hands in the air, palms out in surrender. "Mack made me do it. Direct order. You know I always obey."

"Lightning is about to strike," she said. She braced herself to look at Mack. It was strange, but she could actually taste him in her mouth. When she drew in air, she felt him in her lungs, as if their energy had knit tightly together and somehow she had left part of herself behind in Mack's body. She kept her gaze squarely in the middle of his chest. "What do you need, Mack?"

There was a silence, forcing her to meet his eyes. *You. Right now. Naked on the floor writhing under me. Screaming. You scream-*

ing for me.

She honestly didn't know if he sent the words into her mind or if she'd answered her own question, but his eyes were predatory. Hungry. He looked as edgy and moody as she felt.

Mack jerked his head and Javier sighed, stood, and then stretched. "If I'm going to be any good to you, I need rest."

Mack nodded his assent. "We leave in a couple of hours. Have your gear ready. You can sleep on the plane."

Jaimie's stomach tightened. She waited until Javier left before she looked at Mack. "You're leaving?" She had to set her teacup aside so he wouldn't see her hand tremble.

He stepped close to her, so close she could feel his body heat. His eyes darkened, glittered at her as if she riled him. "You knew I'd have to go. What did you think? That Griffen can live on the run indefinitely? We don't have a choice here."

"We could do what I was going to do in the first place, Mack — go to the newspapers, put it on the Internet."

"They'll destroy you, Jaimie. Your reputation, everything. You know they will."

His hand dropped to her knee, just rested there, but she was terribly aware of the heat generated by his palm through her thin drawstring pants. "I hate the mysterious 'they.' 'They' rule our lives. What are we going to do? Sit around and wait for them to kill us off one by one?"

His gaze met hers. There was absolute purpose there.

Jaimie's heart jumped. "Mack."

"I need to know everything you've got on Earl Thomas Bartlett, along with every company he's associated with as well as friends and acquaintances. And don't tell me you don't have a file on him, Jaimie."

She didn't want to do this, give him the information he needed, but she knew she would. She'd much rather pretend she had found nothing at all, but instead, she nodded slowly. "He's big, Mack. I know Homeland Security is supposed to have taken over everything, and coordinate with all the various security offices, but you and I both know that's not altogether true. There are splinter groups that protect their superiors by being very compartmentalized. Everything Bartlett is associated with is shrouded in secrecy. I take it Javier gave you his name."

His smile was almost worth it. He looked at her as if she was amazing even as he nodded his head. "Javier found a reference to him on the computer you let him use. How did you find him?" His hand moved, made little circles just above her knee.

Jaimie wasn't certain he even realized how much he disturbed her with his touch, how her body responded even though they were talking about something so important. She took a deep breath to steady herself. "His name kept coming up. There was an obscure newspaper article I read. It should have been on the front page, but ended up buried. I knew the reporter had stumbled onto something big. Bartlett's name is on several small shell companies. Each owns a private jet and seems legitimate. In fact, the companies file taxes and never turn much of a profit, everything very under the radar."

"What kind of companies?" His hand moved up her thigh, those lazy circles getting wider. Closer. More compelling.

Jaimie could have stopped him. All she had to do was put her hand over his. He seemed to be just smoothing the pads of his fingers over her inner thigh absently. Her womb spasmed and she felt her panties go damp. She ached for him.

"Jaimie," he prompted gently.

She forced her mind onto briefing him. "Quite a few of the companies are to do with foreign investments, but what I found the most interesting is the research facilities. Bartlett has ties to Donovan Corporation, built just outside of this city. Whitney is the majority stockholder in that company. Bartlett's name appears on a company in Oregon as well as several tracts of land in Wyoming, Colorado, California, and Nevada. The land in Wyoming is supposedly used as a secret military training facility, as are all of the rest of them. We know the facility in Wyoming was really a research lab for Whitney's experiments, specifically his breeding program, because Kane was stationed there."

Mack's hand moved to the hem of her top and pushed at it. His fingers brushed against bare skin right at her waist. "Bartlett is the name tying all of these places together?"

Butterflies flooded her stomach. She swallowed hard but continued. If he could breathe normally, then so could she. "I believe that there are more secret places supposedly used for military training, but Whitney remains hidden and this fictitious Bartlett is helping him."

"You're talking about the CIA." His voice was soft. Sexy. He leaned into her just a little, bunching her shirt in his fist, raising the material inch by slow inch. He was looking at her body, not at her.

She was having difficulty breathing no

matter how hard she tried to stay cool. "Bartlett's got to be their money man, Mack. And he doesn't exist anywhere."

"But you know who he is." He made it a statement as he bent forward until she could feel his warm breath against her belly.

Jaimie closed her eyes. "You won't believe me if I tell you."

"Why wouldn't I?"

Had his voice shaken? She didn't know. His lips were against her skin as he spoke. She could feel them, velvet soft, moving over her tummy. He moved into her, forcing her body back to give him more room.

"Because he was arrested and charged with murder and espionage and convicted. He was serving out his sentence in a military prison. According to his records, he attempted suicide by hanging himself and lost brain function. At that time he was transferred to a hospital for the insane and is currently residing there." She dared to touch him. To put her hands in his hair, that thick mass of short hair that felt so good moving over her skin.

"He does all this from the hospital with no brain function?" His tongue moved in her belly button. His fist yanked her shirt up over her breasts. He frowned at her. "Why the hell do you always wear a bra?"

"I'm modest."

"Take it off." He stood there, wedged between her thighs, angling her body back over the desktop, his fist holding her cami up. "Take it off for me, Jaimie."

Her fingers trembled. She glanced at the stairway, but she unhooked the front clasp and let the cups part in the middle, spilling her breasts out into the open air. There was relief as the cool air touched her skin. "I thought I was briefing you."

"You are. You were telling me about your suspect losing brain function and still running things from a mental hospital."

She took a slow breath, her breasts heaving. Mack just kept his head close to her body, his mouth pressed against her belly button. She could barely think with the roaring in her head. "I don't think he was ever in prison, Mack. I think someone else was taken to prison, probably this man . . ." She caught his head in her hands. "I'm going to need the computer."

"Then take off your top."

"You want me to brief you topless?"

"Yes." He stepped back slowly, his eyes moving broodingly over her face.

"Will you remember what I tell you?"

"Every damn word," he said, "will be etched into my brain."

"Well, then." Jaimie drew her top over her head and set it aside.

Kane, I need some time down here alone, Mack reached out to his second-in-command.

You got it, boss.

"Your bra," he prompted.

She let the bra straps slide down her arms and she placed the lacy scrap on top of her shirt. She heard his indrawn breath and found herself smiling as she turned to her computer, her fingers flashing across the keyboard to bring up a picture of a young, earnest-looking man with dark hair and scared eyes. "This is Thomas Matherson. He was an aide to Phillip Thornton, who happened to be CEO of Donovan Labs a couple of years ago. Matherson disappeared right after Thornton was arrested. Everyone thought he was involved and that he ran. The rumor is, he was paid off and is living the high life in Costa Rica."

Mack ran his finger down the side of her breast, but his eyes stayed on the screen. "But you think he's in a mental hospital as Phillip Thornton."

"Absolutely I do." Her fingers flew over the keyboard. "There are tons of documents with Bartlett's signature, Mack. There's no picture of him, but his signature is everywhere." She brought up a document and enlarged the signature at the bottom. "Earl Thomas Bartlett" had been signed with a flourish. "Now look at Thornton's signature. Our brain-dead Phillip Thornton." She placed a second signature beside the first.

Mack walked right up to the large screen and studied the two signatures. "You ran them both I take it and there's no mistake?"

"Numerous times, Mack. The signature was really the only consistent thing I had to ID him with, so I ran it against every single person that had a past with Whitney. Thornton worked for him, with him, for years. They went to the same school together. He was implicated in Whitney's supposed murder."

"You think he helped Whitney disappear and that he's assumed a new identity and is now providing Whitney with everything he needs to stay gone?" He turned away from the screen, his gaze moving possessively over her body.

Jaimie faced him, very conscious of the fact that he was fully clothed and she was half naked. There was something very sexy and exciting about having a man look at her the way he was, his gaze hot as it moved over her. "Yes, I absolutely believe he's the man covering Whitney's butt. I think he tipped off Whitney that there was a conspiracy to kill the GhostWalkers. General Ronald McEntire was assigned to the National Reconnaissance Office, building spy satellites. He was a major influence in the Donovan Labs getting government contracts. He went to school with Thornton and Whitney. They were all thick as thieves for a while."

Mack sank into a chair, rubbing his shadowed jaw as he looked at her. "Are you wearing panties, Jaimie?"

"Is that relevant? What exactly are you doing?" Now he was making her nervous.

"Looking at what's mine." He crooked his finger at her. "You've really dug deep, haven't you?"

She took two steps toward him. "I had to. Thornton has been Bartlett for years. Some of the documents have been around for years. He's got a lot of clout, Mack."

Mack pointed to the spot in front of his chair. "How in the world did you find his new identity?"

"He's been in the shadows for so long, getting away with his Bartlett act, simply because the agency covers his ass. He switched identities with his aide. Someone had to have been paid off at the prison to make the switch in the first place, and he had to create a third identity. Which isn't all that hard when you work for the CIA." She took the last few steps until she stood in front of the chair. Her knees felt weak.

"His signature," Mack guessed. "You nailed him through his signature."

"I have Thornton's prints from his records, but even that could have been tampered with. Yeah, I found him through his signature. I assumed he'd be very low profile this time, change his appearance, but Thornton had amassed a fortune. He wasn't going to let that go."

He was just looking at her, his gaze moving hungrily over her face and breasts. "How did he keep his fortune when he was convicted of espionage?"

"Mack, I can't think straight." He was killing her with need.

"Yes, you can." His hands reached out and caught the string at her waist. He tugged her a step closer.

She took a calming breath. "There's a lawyer, a man named Mark Scott. He seems to do a lot of business with these companies. He brokered the deal for three different private jets for three of the corporations. Strange thing is, he works for only a handful of clients, including a Shelton Barstow Reams who also has no driver's license or anything else I can find, but does have two post office boxes and a company in Virginia."

"Are Reams and Thornton the same man?" He played with the string at her waistband.

She shook her head. "No, Reams is another ghost living in the shadows, coming out only to sign documents and put companies in his name. He's like Bartlett. And Mark Scott just happens to be the attorney for both men."

"So this attorney, Mark Scott, really works for the CIA as well."

She shrugged. "I think it's a good bet. That's why I began looking into his client list. Believe me, Mack, it wasn't very long. I found this man." She tried to take a step away from him back to the computer but he held on to the string. "Mack, I need to . . ."

He pulled the string so that the bow slipped open. His hands caught the waistband and widened it so that the pants dropped around her ankles, leaving her standing in a tiny thong. It barely covered the front of her. His hand slid up her bare inner thigh, higher, until he found the junction and the damp material of her thong. "You don't need this, baby. Get rid of it."

She opened her mouth to protest, glancing once more toward the stairs. He pushed the material aside. "Look at me, Jaimie, not the stairs. This is about me. I had to lie in that bed all night, inhaling you, my hands on your body, and I couldn't do a thing. It was torture, so if I torture you a little, you can put up with it."

She hesitated and then hooked her thumbs in the narrow band and pushed the thong from her hips, stepping out of it. "Am I supposed to conduct the briefing completely naked?"

"Yes."

"And keep my mind on it?"

"I'll do my best to occasionally distract you."

Her body felt feminine and sexy, beautiful even, with him staring at her, drinking her in. She turned and walked to the computer, using a little hip action, knowing he was watching the sway of her butt. She bent over the keyboard, turning slightly to give him a bit of her profile, so he could see the swell of her breasts along with her bottom, accepting his implied dare.

Jaimie's overhead screen immediately held a photograph of an older, gray-haired gentleman with glasses. "Meet James Bradley Jefferson the third."

Mack's gaze reluctantly left her body to

study the face on the screen. He waited while Jaimie's fingers flew over the keyboard again. A second photograph appeared beside the first. "This is Phillip Thornton."

The two men were the same height and weight, but their faces seemed different — their noses and jawlines. Thornton wore his hair very short, while Jefferson's was a bit wilder, giving him a rakish look.

"They both favor Armani suits," he said. "Are you telling me that's Phillip Thornton? Or Bartlett? They aren't the same man."

"I ran my handy, dandy program, Mack. It finds bone markers; their faces are structurally the same and it doesn't lie. His nose and chin have been altered, but that's Phillip Thornton. And Earl Thomas Bartlett. And James Bradley Jefferson the third. They're all the same man."

He shook his head. "I don't see it."

"I followed the money, Mack. Thornton's fortune was long gone when they went to find it. He had all his money in offshore accounts. The Feds managed to get his heavily mortgaged home and about thirty thousand dollars. I found fourteen million dollars in one offshore account and a second one holding an additional sixteen, both belonging to Thornton. The money disappeared, just vanished into thin air."

She straightened slowly and turned to face him, conscious of her body and the way his eyes jumped from the screen to her. "It just so happens that around the same time that Thornton's money vanished, James Bradley Jefferson the third suddenly came into being and guess what? He just happened to have the exact amount of money that disappeared from Thornton's account. And one more thing, Mack. Remember those private jets that can land on our military bases? He has one. And his most recent trip was to Oregon, or to be more precise, to a secret training facility."

Mack tapped the arm of his chair with restless fingers. "You really found the son of a bitch, didn't you, Jaimie?"

"Absolutely I did." She sent him a half smile.

"Come here, baby. I think you deserve a reward for all your hard work."

Her heart jumped, began to beat overtime. His voice was dark and sensuous, Mack at his most persuasive. It was always impossible to ignore that voice when he wanted her. That exact tone was one of the reasons she'd left him. She would never have resisted him. He didn't move from the chair, just watched her with hooded eyes.

She stood in front of him. Naked. Without

a stitch. Her body was already betraying her. She could feel the damp nectar moistening her entrance. Every muscle was tight, crying out for him, straining toward him. His gaze drifted over her. Hot. Hungry. Making her mouth water and her body weep.

"You have no idea how beautiful you are, do you?" he asked, and slowly lifted his hand to her breast, stroking a caress almost absently over the creamy swell.

She closed her eyes, savoring his light touch, but she felt it deep, so that her body reacted with a tightening, a cry for his. His fingers tugged at her nipple, sending a wave of heat rushing through her.

"Cup your breasts in your palms. Hold them out to me." His voice lowered another octave, so husky now she could feel the rasp between her legs.

She couldn't help herself, blindly obeying, her hands coming up under the weight of her breasts, holding them for him like an offering.

Mack could barely breathe with wanting her. Anger and arousal intensified his growing desire. His cock was rock hard and the sight of her, offering her breasts to him, her body bare, the moisture gathering on her tiny midnight curls at the junction of her legs, only made him all the harder. She had a lot to answer for, not the least of which was how she made him feel. Looking at her, knowing she had dared to leave him, knowing she'd entrusted her information to someone other than him, made him furious. And right now fury was alive and well, mixing with lust, giving him a need to dominate, to exert control, even to punish her for her betrayal.

She was so beautiful. Her breasts rose and fell, cupped erotically in her own palms. Her nipples were hard pebbles, her skin flushed. She trembled, her stomach tight with arousal, her thighs quivering. He took his time, his movements unhurried when desire coursed through him like a firestorm. His lips settled around her breast, drew the soft flesh into the heat of his mouth, his tongue flicking the taut pebble of her nipple so that a low moan escaped. He caught that little bead in his mouth, suckled strongly, raked with the edge of his teeth, so that she gave another choking, inarticulate cry.

His hand dropped to slide through the moisture gathered in her curls, now slick with welcome. Her body shuddered in response. He lifted his head and when she went to drop her hands he stopped her, shaking his head. "Just stand there waiting for me. Just like that. I love the way you look offering your body to me."

There was that note again, the one she couldn't resist. He didn't take his gaze from hers as he stripped off his clothes and tossed them aside. He was hard, beautiful, his shaft thick and pulsing against his stomach. His heavy erection looked almost as intimidating as the dark promise in his eyes. Her body was shaking now, every nerve ending stretched taut. She'd seen him like this before, and knew what was coming. Mack liked to prolong the anticipation, stretching her out on a tormenting rack of pure pleasure. He'd bring her again and again right to the brink of satisfaction and keep her poised there, never taking her over the edge until she was pleading with him for relief, for anything he wanted. And he always succeeded. His possession was her dark addiction and he knew it and used it whenever he was on edge.

"Get on your hands and knees, Jaimie." His voice was nearly hoarse, yet velvet soft and firm.

She did so, very slowly, watching him the entire time. He just stood, his movements unhurried, his hand absently stroking his erection. Her mouth watered. She touched her tongue to her lips, not taking her eyes from the broad, flared head with the tempt-

489

ing small drops of moisture. She knew his taste intimately. Darkly male. Salty and unique.

He moved around her, dropping one hand onto her hip possessively. The feel of his heat was amazing. He knelt behind her, his fingers flexing at her hips once before gripping her hard. She was unprepared for his entrance. He slammed into her hard, burying himself to the hilt, the velvet steel pushing through the tight folds of her muscles, sending flames racing through her body and scraping over the tight bundle of sensitive nerves until she felt raw and inflamed and so needy she couldn't stop her gasping breath. He hammered into her, over and over, driving her up fast.

Jaimie heard the roar of blood in her head, her pulse thundering. He was rough, but so careful of not hurting her. She loved the way he felt, so thick, invading her over and over, going deep, so deep she swore he was in her stomach. She was so close she pushed back hard, reaching for release. His fingers fisted in her hair and he pulled her head back, suddenly stopping all movement.

Mack leaned forward, his body over her back, his cock a steel spike buried deep in her pulsing body. He put his lips against her ear. "Do you have any idea what it feels like to a man to know the woman who belongs to him doesn't trust him?"

She stiffened. She could feel the anger running through him like a raging river. He pulled back, nearly all the way out, until she gave a protesting sob, following his body with hers. He slammed his body harder into hers. Her womb convulsed. Her body rippled, clutched at his, but he stopped again, leaving her gasping, needing. Mack at his most lethal with her. She recognized danger. His deliberate seduction hadn't been about lying beside her all night needing her body. This was something altogether different.

"Mack, please."

He bit her shoulder. Hard. His tongue swirled over the ache. "Don't Mack me. Who the fuck do you trust with your life when you don't trust me? Joe? Is it Joe, Jaimie? Fucking tell me who it is."

"Not Joe." She tried to move, but his body locked hers beneath him, his fist tight in her curls. She tried to clear her mind. "You pulled the plug on the back-trace. I knew I was stirring up a hornet's nest, but I wanted that last nail in the coffin."

His fingers tightened in her scalp almost, but not quite, to the point of pain. "Those two men who came here to question you would have destroyed your computers and then they would have killed you. They were definitely Black Ops."

"I knew I was taking a chance, Mack, but I had to do it. I had to make certain you were protected." She held perfectly still. His shaft pulsed and jerked in her, sending hot waves spiraling through her body.

"Phillip Thornton might want Kane and Brian dead, because he doesn't want Whitney exposed. And he certainly can't afford for his new identity to come under scrutiny, so getting rid of Kane and Brian is a good idea for him. Getting rid of you is even better. But there is no way Whitney or this Thornton are the ones trying to murder GhostWalkers. They put too much into us. They think of themselves as patriots. Thornton took the heat and disappeared in order to help Whitney arrange his own death. These men believe in the GhostWalker program."

"So he would kill Kane and Brian and me, but not the rest of you?" Jaimie asked.

"We aren't a threat to him." Mack pulled out and slammed home again.

Her tight sheath clamped down around him like a vise. She was so close, but he held her release just out of reach. "Well, I intend to make certain he won't send Kane and Brian on any more suicide missions," Jaimie said. "And I want Whitney stopped."

"Honey." Mack kissed the side of her neck, suckled there for a moment, branding her. "It won't ever matter what proof you have, they'll only discredit you." He knelt back up, still retaining possession of her hair. His voice changed, the anger breaking through. "Stop fucking around and tell me who else you've trusted with this information and why you trusted them, and not me."

Jaimie swallowed the sudden lump in her throat. He looked cool and calm, but she knew him far too well. He was not only angry, he was hurt. Really hurt.

"Mack." She had to work to keep her voice from trembling. He always affected her that way. She'd never been able to stand up to him when he became like this. It was far worse being naked. "Great interrogation technique. This isn't fair."

"You trusted someone else and you didn't tell me. Did you expect me to be happy?"

"I gave you the information I had on Phillip Thornton. Any information I have on Whitney or proof I've collected, I have no problem sharing with you."

"Why, Jaimie?" he asked, his voice quieter than ever.

She couldn't stop herself from pushing back against him, trying desperately to force him to keep moving, but he held her firm, refusing to give her release. She set her teeth. "You stopped the trace."

"Griffen's phone has been bugged for a while. The setup's been in place and they wouldn't suddenly change it. Someone else was trying to get information about you. You, Jaimie. They were coming after you and it wasn't Whitney or Thornton. Whoever is against Thornton and Whitney is also against every GhostWalker." He bent his head until his lips were nearly against hers, his dark eyes boring into hers. "Let me tell you something, baby. Whether you like it or not, you're a GhostWalker."

Jaimie let her breath out in a little hiss. "All right, Mack. I'll concede you might have been right. I've been concentrating on finding out everything I could about Whitney. I might have accidentally stumbled onto these others without knowing it, but if we find out who they are . . ."

She tried to push back, to move her hips in a slow circle, but his fingers gripped her hard and he held her firmly against him until she could feel the very rise and fall of his breath through his thick, hot shaft.

"No. You're in enough trouble with what

you have. They were going to kill you, Jaimie. Thornton ordered a hit on you." He smacked her butt, as if he couldn't stop the spurt of anger rushing through him, sending waves of heat like a flash through her system. "The dead teacher, Jaimie. That was your warning and you knew it at the time. Who else had access to your file? Thornton was telling you to back off Whitney, but you didn't listen so he sent his goon squad. They were going to torture you to find out what you knew and if you'd told anyone else. And then they were going to kill you." He enunciated each word carefully as if she might not be able to understand him.

She could feel hurt radiating off of him in waves. It was crippling, the way the emotion battered at her, swamped her, reached out and claimed her. Betrayal. That was what it felt like to him. She'd already turned him inside out and now this. She didn't want to experience his emotions but somehow, their energies were so knitted together that she did, regardless of her own desires.

Jaimie closed her eyes as her body rippled with need. "I'm well aware they were sent to kill me, Mack. I had to take the chance."

He went absolutely still as comprehension dawned. "You knew they'd kill you." His breath caught in his lungs. "Oh, God,

Jaimie. You knew they were going to kill you."

She nodded slowly, afraid to move now. "Yes. I had to find a way to keep you all safe."

"Damn it, Jaimie. It was suicide." His hands gripped her shoulders and gave her a little shake. "Did you even for one moment think about me?"

"You're all I was thinking of," she defended. "You were out there risking your life, and you didn't even know the danger was from the one sending you out."

Mack's fingers flexed on her hip. For a moment he laid his cheek against her back, breathing deep, his hands caressing her skin. "I don't want to live in a world without you in it, Jaimie." His mouth pressed tightly against her spine. "Never put yourself in jeopardy like that again."

Her heart turned over. The fury was gone from him in an instant. She'd delivered more than a body blow; it had been a knockout punch. She hadn't meant to shake him. Her decision had seemed so intelligent at the time, her way of saving him, the only way she could.

He trailed kisses along her spine. "I don't know what this is between us, Jaimie, but it isn't just sex. You've never been just sex to

496

me. Don't sacrifice yourself, not for me, not for anyone. If I didn't have you, what would be the point?"

Were there tears in his voice — dropping like burning acid along her back? She couldn't tell and when she tried to turn her head to look over her shoulder at him, he began moving again. Her body responded instantly as he drove deep, a sizzling stroke of pleasure that sent rockets going off in her head. She gasped and pushed back into him, merging, one skin, one breath. Her eyes burned. It was always this way, the mindless pleasure coursing through her veins, her every nerve ending alive the moment he moved in her.

He could rule her body and heart so easily, and right then, when he'd been so furious with her, she felt more emotion from him than ever. It felt like love. Every stroke. Each time he thrust into her, driving deep, taking her up, swelling inside her, pulsing with her, while her sheath tightened around him, gripping with hot intent. She heard his groan, knew he was close. He stopped and she nearly cried.

Mack leaned over her body again with infinite slowness, this time pressing against her most sensitive spot, sending her body spasming, the roar of her orgasm tearing through her womb and up to her stomach so that she went into overdrive, shaking, shuddering. She felt the hot splash of his seed deep inside, but instead of his hoarse cry, she felt his mouth at her ear, his lips moving, small, soft brushes against her lobe.

I love you.

Her heart clenched. Her mind stilled. She wasn't certain he'd actually said the words, but she felt them etched into her mind.

Did you hear me?

She knew better than to look at him. She barely inclined her head, wanting to weep with joy. It was so like him to pick this moment when she didn't know whether he was angry, sad, or overwhelmed with physical lust, but emotion rocked his voice and that was enough for her.

Don't ever leave me, Jaimie.

He knelt up, slowly pulled his body from hers to get shakily to his feet. He helped her up and pulled her into his arms, just holding her to him, his face buried against her neck. "You can't ever do something like that again. I want you to stop this, Jaimie." He pulled back to look into her eyes.

She saw so much raw emotion there it shook her. "You have to hear me on this, Mack. Really listen to me, because it's important. My programs and computers are *my* weapons. In my own way, I'm still out there fighting like you are. You risk your life and you wanted me right there with you. I can't do that, but I can do this. Why is risking my life any different than you risking yours?"

He frowned. Opened his mouth. Closed it. "Damn it, Jaimie." His fingers tightened on her shoulders and he pressed his forehead tight against hers. "Just damn it."

"That's what you always say when you know I'm right." She brought her hands up to his chest. "I'm good at what I do, just as you are. I've never asked you to stop, Mack. I wanted you to open your eyes and see what Whitney was. It was too late to undo what he did to us, so okay, we have to live with it, but we don't have to close our eyes to what he is or what he's capable of doing. I promise I'll be careful and I'll keep you informed every single step of the way."

"Who did you send your backup to?"

"Another GhostWalker, a woman good with computers. I ran into her hacking the CIA computer."

"You can't hack their program."

"I can if I wrote it. She couldn't. She was looking for the same thing I was. We've been sharing information" — she held up her hand — "and before you lose your mind,

I'm careful."

"Did it occur to you she might be a plant?"

"She was more worried about me than I was about her," Jaimie said. "I hacked into her computer and found all her files. We established an uneasy truce and I sent her several things she didn't have on Whitney. She doesn't know who I am. I know her identity, though. She's married to a Ghost-Walker. She was an orphan Whitney experimented on. He gave her cancer more than once."

"You have to go, Mack," Kane called over the intercom.

Mack sighed. "Give me a few more minutes, Kane. I'm gathering intel." He began pulling on his clothes. "Get dressed, baby. And don't leave this place while I'm gone. Stick close to the boys." He leaned down to press a kiss to the corner of her mouth. "I'm going to take out Thornton and any threat to Kane, Brian, and Sergeant Major."

"Just be careful," she cautioned.

"My middle name."

Chapter 17

Gideon eased the ache in his leg with the smallest of stretches. "No movement yet, boss, he's still in there sitting by his fireplace with a drink as if he has all the time in the world."

Mack glanced at his watch. The lights in Jefferson's house had been on for hours. He wasn't retiring anytime soon. He seemed to be waiting for someone — or something. There was no way he could possibly know he was a target. The three had slipped from the warehouse unseen and boarded a military flight. Tucked in the trees, they'd already spent enough hours to be getting cramps, waiting for Jefferson to go to bed.

"Well, he doesn't have all the time in the world, Gideon, and you're right, he's waiting for someone."

The tree they'd set up in was enormous. The great sprawling branches were thick, and they dipped and twisted, giving them a tremendous platform to work from. Phillip Thornton's house had been modest, in a quiet neighborhood at the end of a cul-de-sac. As James Bradley Jefferson the third, the man had treated himself to a home he felt he deserved. The long drive led to a two-story brick estate. Tall pillars rose around the wide verandah, a proud Southern home, surrounded by shrubbery and rolling lawns. The property was nestled in thick trees, an old growth of evergreens, one of the few stands left in the area. The terrain lent the estate a natural seclusion.

"Any phone calls?"

"One, boss, from Senator Romney. But he's definitely waiting for someone. He's checked his watch at least three times. The directional mike is working perfectly. If he does have a visitor, we'll be able to hear every word."

"I want it recorded," Mack said. "We need everything we can get on him. And no evidence left behind. Not so much as a scrape on a tree. When we take him down, no matter how natural his death appears, there will be an investigation."

"He the one after Kane and Brian?" Javier asked, bringing his travel mug to his mouth. The hot coffee warmed his insides. There was malice in his voice.

"Jefferson has a hard-on for both of them," Mack said. "Sergeant Major turned his report over to General Chilton and I'm guessing Chilton turned it over to Jefferson. Either way, all the evidence they gathered is now destroyed. And Jefferson sent those killers after Jaimie."

Gideon and Javier exchanged a long, knowing look.

"We know he's working at Langley, we've watched him come and go," Javier said. "I could have taken out the bastard a hundred times already."

Mack shook his head. "It has to be a natural death or an accident no one can dispute. If I can get close enough to him, I can kill him and everyone will think he's had a heart attack."

Again Gideon and Javier exchanged a long look. Mack almost never mentioned his psychic abilities. His was a rare talent. Mack always played things close to his chest and when he'd filled out the forms, he had never revealed his ability to manipulate electrical energy. They'd heard the rumor that one of the GhostWalkers' wives from Team Two could do the same, but they'd never met her and the rumor wasn't confirmed. Mack's talent made him invaluable to the team and the fact that no one, not even

Whitney, knew he had the ability, made him the perfect assassin.

Getting up close to Jefferson was another matter. He'd proved to be very cautious. Years with the agency and working with Whitney had made him wary of everyone. He changed his route at a moment's notice. Few knew his schedule ahead of time. It was impossible to know which car he would be using. When a car was summoned, it was gone over meticulously for bombs. He had to be taken in his home.

Mack watched Jefferson through the bulletproof glass of his study. "He's waiting for a woman."

Gideon turned his head back toward the house, narrowing his eyes. Jefferson used a remote to light a fire in his fireplace. He poured two drinks from a Waterford decanter on the table beside the sofa. He pointed the remote again and music flooded the room.

"Very high-class seduction scene," Javier said. "Where's the caviar?"

"He's setting the scene, all right," Mack said, "but I don't believe he's in love with this woman. Look at him. He's setting a seduction scene, but he's after something else besides sex."

"He's got something in his hand," Gideon

said. "Can you make it out, Mack?"

Mack watched the man put the object in a small, decorative box. Jefferson moved the box twice and then shook his head and took it back out again. He crossed to the floor-to-ceiling bookcase, removed a book, opened it, and thrust the small object into the hollowed-out pages.

"It's got to be a recorder," Gideon said.

"He's an arrogant son of a bitch," Javier observed. "No guards. He doesn't believe anyone would dare retaliate against him. He has to know Sergeant Major's gone off the grid."

Mack's smile held no humor. "Men like Jefferson come to believe they're above the law. He makes his own laws." He looked at Javier. "There has to be a code of honor. We make the same kinds of decisions he makes. We have to make absolutely certain we're doing it for the right reasons. This can't be about power or personal gain, or we're just like him."

"I get what you're saying, Top," Javier said.

"Or the rush, Javier," Mack counseled.

"It's never been about the rush, Mack," Javier said. "It's about running from myself."

Their eyes met — held complete understanding.

"Car's coming up the drive," Gideon reported.

The Escalade had tinted windows. It slid noiselessly up the drive and a woman got out. She was tall and blond, her hair up in a sophisticated twist that made her look especially elegant. She wore a pencil-thin skirt and a silk blouse with matching jacket that should have made her look all business, but she managed to look sexy instead. Diamonds clung to her ears and a single teardrop necklace glittered at her throat.

No one move. No communication. Mack sent the warning, careful to keep his energy low, to keep it from spilling out into the open where the woman might have a chance to feel it. *Get her picture and send it to Jaimie for positive ID.*

The woman stepped away from the car and looked carefully around, her gaze quartering the area, and then turned her attention to the house. She moved with unhurried, fluid steps up the walkway to the door. Jefferson greeted her before she could ring the doorbell. He waved her inside and only then did Mack let out his breath.

"She looks familiar," Gideon said. "Like I've seen her before, but I've never really met a female GhostWalker other than Jaimie."

"And Rhianna," Javier supplied. He glanced down at his phone. "Jaimie's on it, boss."

"Shit," Mack said. "That's Senator Ed Freeman's wife, Violet. I remember seeing her picture in the news right after her husband was shot. I forget the story. How the hell did a GhostWalker hook up with a senator?"

"And what the hell is she doing here?" Javier asked.

"Maybe we'll get lucky and she'll assassinate him for us," Gideon said.

Mack directed their attention to the couple in the house. Violet leaned in to brush a barely there kiss along Jefferson's cheek. "If Jefferson thought he was going to seduce, he's wrong. She's deliberately tempting him, but that kiss was a definite signal to back off."

"Maybe she's wired too," Javier ventured. "It would be pretty funny if they were bugging each other."

"I don't doubt for a minute she's wired," Mack said. "She's exuding confidence and if Jefferson has a brain in his head, he'll be very, very careful."

"Kind of like entertaining a cobra in your home," Javier said and smirked. He knew he looked like the boy next door. "Glad she's one of us."

"Data coming in," Mack said, frowning down at the small phone in his hand. "Never make the mistake of thinking Violet Smythe-Freeman is one of us. She sold out the women in Whitney's compound. Kane warned Jaimie about her. She was raised with those women, one of the orphans Whitney acquired, and they all believed in her."

"She turned on them?" Gideon asked as if disbelieving. "That would be like one of us turning on the others. We were raised together, a family, like those women. That's just . . ." He cast around searching for the right words to express his disgust.

"The word's gone out to all the Ghost-Walker teams that she's a traitor," Mack read on. "She was at the compound to make an alliance with Whitney when everything went to hell. She was going to help suppress evidence on the breeding program if he backed her husband's bid for the vice presidency. She and her husband are the ones who sent Team Two to the Congo and tipped off the rebels where they were going to be."

There was a small silence while they absorbed the treachery of the woman's actions. There were very few GhostWalkers and all of them knew just how difficult one another's lives were. Violet had been raised with Whitney's youngest, earliest victims, yet she appeared not to have any loyalty to them at all.

"I could take her out when she comes out, boss," Gideon reminded.

"She's not the objective," Mack said. "We're here to protect Kane and Brian and to get Jefferson off Sergeant Major."

"I could stop the car down the road," Javier offered.

"Too dangerous. Jefferson's death has to look like a legitimate heart attack. If we take out a GhostWalker, they're going to know someone was in the area."

Gideon swore under his breath. "We have to just let her walk?"

Mack shrugged. "There'll be another time and another place. There always is. Right now, we're here for Jefferson. We know he's after Kane and Brian and he's certainly the one who ordered the hit on Sergeant Major when they lost track of him. We've got to look after our own first."

Violet sank into a chair, accepting the crystal glass Jefferson handed her. "How's the senator?" he asked as he gave the drink to her.

The voices sounded tinny through the recorder. Javier adjusted something Mack couldn't see, frowning as he did so.

Violet, her eyes on Jefferson's face, held the glass under her nose and inhaled.

"We're on the same side, Violet," Jefferson reminded.

"Anyone in my position can't be too careful, and Whitney and I didn't part on the best of terms. He had my husband shot."

"He saved his life. No one else could have done that operation," Jefferson pointed out.

"He wouldn't have needed the operation if Whitney hadn't arranged for an assassination." She put her drink down and leaned forward. "Let's quit playing games, Jefferson. I want Whitney off our backs."

"It isn't going to happen, Violet. You can join the other side and try to wipe out all the GhostWalkers or you can come back to the fold where you belong. Without us, your husband has no career and without Whitney, he's a dead man."

Mack was watching the woman's face closely. Jefferson was a man in extreme danger. He thought he was holding all the cards, but she was weighing whether or not to kill him. She looked cool and composed, but Mack knew exactly what was going on in her mind.

Jefferson appeared confident, but he must have felt death in her silence. He set his drink aside and shook his head. "What good would it do you to kill me, Violet? Whitney would retaliate against you by letting Ed die. This is about him, isn't it? Your husband? You want him alive. Only Whitney can keep him alive."

"As a puppet," she snapped. "We both will have to do his bidding."

"Without Whitney, neither of you would have a decent life. It's time to pay the piper, Violet," Jefferson said. "It isn't like Ed is a viable candidate for the vice presidency. Whitney had to practically replace his brain."

"My husband can still have a political career."

Jefferson sat back in his chair and once again picked up his glass, regarding her over the top of it. "Now we come to the real reason you're here. What exactly do you want and what are you offering?"

"I can find the missing women for Whitney. They escaped. Whitney wants them back. I can get them for him. I have the resources. And I can tap into the women's networks better than anyone else. In return, I want Ed completely well."

"He was brain-dead, Violet."

"Not anymore. Not with this new technology. Get him up and running and put him back in the political arena. I can handle everything else. No one will ever get close enough to know he's not all human."

"You're asking a lot," Jefferson said, and took a sip of his brandy.

"One of the women is pregnant. The father is a GhostWalker. She has extraordinary talents, as does he. Their child alone will be worth what I'm asking. You and your friends back Ed's career and we're back on track. Whitney will have a friend in the White House for life."

Gideon gasped. "That bitch. She'd sell out her own mother."

"Just make certain you've got this all recorded," Mack said.

Jefferson's smile turned malicious. "He's already got friends in the White House."

"He has enemies too. I can find them for you. You know I'll do it too. I keep my promises."

"Do you?" Jefferson asked. "You turned on Whitney before and you have no problems turning on the women who regard you as their sister."

Violet tapped her perfectly manicured nails on the arm of her chair. "Don't judge a woman in love, James. I would do anything for my husband."

"Or for the power. We both know who's

behind the proverbial throne, Violet, so don't play the loving wife to me. You were prepared to sleep with me if that's what it took, but you knew the moment you looked into my mind that wouldn't serve your purpose," Jefferson said shrewdly.

Javier growled deep in his throat. "She really is a cobra."

Violet shrugged her shoulders. "Why should I deny it? I am prepared to pay whatever price Whitney wants from me."

"And if he demands a fail-safe?"

She sucked in her breath, for the first time her composure shaken. She recovered very quickly. "He's put a failsafe program in Ed?"

"Of course he did, my dear, and he's prepared to use it. You not only will deliver the women to us, but you'll find whoever in the White House is going against the Ghost-Walker program and you'll deliver them as well. If we decide to put Ed back into position to use him, believe me, Violet, it will be our decision without coercion."

Even from his position a distance away, Mack could see the woman's eyes glittering with malicious intent as she rose. "I would be very careful of threatening me, Jefferson. You may hold all the cards, but if you push too far, you'll find out just what a woman will really do when you've put a bullet in her husband's head."

Her voice was utterly cold. Deliberately spiteful. Mack swore under his breath. Jefferson would know exactly what she meant and he would take her threat seriously. That would make it doubly difficult to kill him.

"You're getting him back," Jefferson reminded. "A new, improved model, wholly devoted to you. There won't be any chasing skirts, or aides under his desk; he'll live for you."

Mack inhaled sharply. "Whitney paired her with him, but didn't bother pairing Freeman with her. Whitney sold her into service with Freeman to aid his political career."

"He couldn't know the monster he was creating," Gideon said.

"I can't even feel sorry for her," Javier said. "She's willing to give up the other women to a breeding program, knowing what happened to them in that compound."

"She'd kill all of us if it got her husband one step closer to the presidency," Mack said, watching with a small frown. "He's glanced at his watch again. You think he's got more than one visitor coming tonight?"

"Maybe it will be Whitney and we can blow them both to kingdom come." Javier sounded hopeful, eager even.

"You're so bloodthirsty tonight," Mack reprimanded.

Javier shot him a grin. "Must be the company. Bad influence and all."

Violet put down her drink and stood up, drawing their attention back to the scene in the house. "I have to go, Jefferson. You've given me quite a bit to think about."

Jefferson rose with her. "I hope you'll give me your answer soon, Violet. I don't think Ed has long, hanging in limbo. You want him up and running around, you commit to Whitney's program and work for us, not yourself."

She said nothing at all, but walked, head up, out to her waiting car. Jefferson watched the vehicle pull down the long drive before he snapped open his cell phone. "She was here. She's going to come on board, but she'll turn on us the moment she thinks she has an out. She's ambitious. You might think about getting rid of her before she causes any more trouble."

"You getting this, Jaimie?" Mack asked.

"I'm running a trace," she answered. "I think he's talking to Whitney. I've got a voice analysis program and it should give me a match any second. Yep. Whitney."

Jefferson snapped his phone off and went

back into the house after one more long look after his parting guest. He shook his head, disgusted, and slammed his door.

"I'm sorry, Mack, he didn't stay on long enough," Jaimie said.

Mack didn't take his eyes from Jefferson. The man took meticulous care to clean up after his guest. Several times he looked at the clock. They weren't at all surprised when a second car came up the drive.

"He's busy tonight," Mack said, watching the dark car pull up to the house. "What's behind door number two?"

The driver jumped out and opened the door behind his seat. An older man emerged. Mack concentrated on getting as good a picture as possible. There was only a profile available; the man kept his hat low and his head turned away from them. He looked older, and walked with a cane and a bit of a limp. He was a big man. A trench coat covered his very expensive business suit. He went straight up to the house. Jefferson met him at the door and clapped him on the shoulder, his manner familiar.

"We've got company, boss," Gideon hissed. "I think Violet's come back."

Javier touched the knife in his scabbard. "I need to be on the ground to protect the operation, Mack," he said. "If she spots us, we're finished."

"She can't spot you, Javier. I'm giving you a direct order. Do not engage unless she finds us."

Javier sent a cocky grin over his shoulder at Mack. "I'm hearing every word, Top."

"Before you go, tell Jaimie I need everything she's got on that man now. Right now. Tell her to move it."

"It's not like we gave her much to go on," Javier pointed out, but dutifully sent the text. "Oh, yeah, she's not happy with you and said to remind you that she's not a miracle worker."

Mack glared at him. "Tell her I expect results, not a lot of excuses."

"Oh, sure, boss, I'll just send that to Jaimie. We'll feel the volcano blast all the way from San Francisco."

"I gotta agree with Javier on this one, boss. Give her a few minutes."

Mack scowled at them and turned his attention back to the house.

"Going silent, Mack," Javier said. He sent Gideon a quick, sympathetic grin and hastily made his way to the ground.

"Keep an eye on them, Gideon," Mack ordered.

"You got it, boss."

Mack knew Gideon didn't have to use

517

night goggles or any equipment that might tip off a GhostWalker to their presence. He was the most difficult of all of them to spot. Javier was a ghost, a phantom, stalking the night. Violet could walk right up to him and not know he was there. She'd be uneasy, but she wouldn't find him. Even so, Gideon would ensure that Javier was safe at all times if there was any slipup.

He put the headphones on to listen to the conversation taking place in Jefferson's home.

"What'd she want?" the newcomer demanded.

"The same thing her father-in-law wanted. Of course Andrew thinks his son is intact. Whitney says we're nearly ready for the trial run. If we can fool Andrew, we can fool everyone," Jefferson said.

"I'm not entirely easy about this. Andrew's been a good friend for years."

Mack knew Andrew Freeman was Senator Freeman's father. He had gone to school with Whitney and Jefferson when Jefferson was Phillip Thornton.

"Okay," Jaimie's voice whispered in his ear. "You've got Jacob Abrams there. He's been best friends with Senator Freeman's father for forty years or more. Billionaire. A genius. Banker. He and Whitney and Freeman were all part of a club at their university for very smart students. The club is still shrouded in secrecy. I'm working on more data for you. Abrams controls a great deal in the market and some say he's part of the real power in the world, not necessarily the leaders of the countries. He's a very big fish, Mack."

"Thanks, Jaimie." Mack switched back to the conversation in the house.

Jefferson poured a drink for Abrams and handed it to him. "At least he has his son, Jacob. Ed was brain-dead. Anyone else would have pulled the plug on him. Violet and Andrew had given up and were going to tell the world he'd been killed when Whitney made his proposal to try to save him. He didn't do it for Andrew."

"Enhancing psychic ability is one thing, but stimulating a dead brain with whatever the hell he does makes Ed part machine, doesn't it?" Jefferson sighed and sat back in his chair. "Whitney has no fear of trying anything."

"Ed was dead already," Abrams pointed out. "It wasn't as if Peter did anything wrong. I just don't think fooling Andrew into believing Ed's still Ed is ethical."

Jefferson snorted. Coughed. "That's rich coming from you, Jacob."

Mack leaned into his mouthpiece. "You getting this, Jaimie? Is it making any sense to you? How the hell could he stimulate a brain that's dead?"

"I'm getting it. Paul might be able to help."

Mack glanced out over the thick stand of trees. Violet was making her way toward the window, moving from shadow to shadow. *Gideon.*

I see her, boss. Javier's keeping pace with her.

It was impossible for Mack to spot Javier, although he didn't doubt that Gideon knew exactly where the man was. He sent up a silent prayer that Javier understood he was playing ghost with another GhostWalker. They knew little about Violet's abilities.

Jacob Abrams sighed heavily and walked to the window to stare out, swirling the brandy in his glass. "Is she going to give us trouble?"

"She offered to bring in our missing women, including the pregnant one."

Abrams whirled around. "Do you think she can do it?"

"Violet pointed out she can do a lot from her position as a senator's wife for the women's underground. She'll be a saint to them while she's searching. I'd put my money on her. She wants the presidency, Jacob. And she'll do anything to keep Ed alive, even if it's just his body."

"It's a big undertaking," Abrams said, his voice thoughtful. "I'd like to see one baby before we're dead and gone, Phillip, just to see if we accomplished what we set out to do."

"James. Never forget I'm James," Jefferson responded. "In any case, a couple of the GhostWalker couples have babies."

"Yeah, they do, but *we* don't have them." Abrams turned back to face his old friend. "Is Theodore Griffen giving you trouble?"

There was an inflection. A casual note that was anything but casual. Jefferson visibly stiffened. "Why do you ask?"

"Rumors, Jefferson. I heard you sent a team to San Francisco and one of them didn't come back. Whitney doesn't want the girl killed. He said to tell you to leave her alone."

"Did he even pay any attention to the evidence that's been collected against him? If I hadn't persuaded Chilton to let me handle it, the committee might have shut him down. We got lucky."

"You're afraid the trail leads back to you."

"And you, Jacob. Your reputation is on the line as well. A breeding program and experimenting on children, even orphans, will cause a worldwide uproar, and you know it," Jefferson said. "If we have to sacrifice a couple of his precious soldiers to keep the programs intact, then it's a small price to pay."

"Whitney makes a bitter enemy, James," Jacob said. "Find some other way of dealing with this woman. Bring her in. Get her back under control. Hell, put her in Whitney's breeding program. I don't care, but don't kill her. Get your men to pick her up."

Mack waited, but Jefferson didn't confirm to Abrams that he'd sent the two men to kill Jaimie, but they'd failed and hadn't returned. He didn't answer one way or the other. Apparently there were things Jefferson didn't want to share with his old friend. Or maybe he was afraid. Could the tight-knit friends be splintering?

Violet crept toward the house, coming in from the south side. She took out an aerosol can and sprayed into the slight breeze moving out over the sweeping lawn. Bright beams leapt into the air. Mack could see them without the spray and he was fairly certain Javier could as well. The enhancements Whitney had given them evidently weren't part of Violet's arsenal.

She glanced upward, her gaze sweeping

the surrounding trees, looking for cameras, before inspecting the roof. Mack could have told her where every one of them was located. She didn't hurry, but slid under the beams, taking care not to disturb them. Mack was a little surprised that Jefferson had used something so easy to defeat. The beams were crisscrossed, but still a good foot from the ground where someone as limber as Violet could slide beneath them. The woman used her elbows and knees to propel herself forward. She had shed the elegance of her former appearance and wore a black jumpsuit. Her hair was covered with a tight cap and there were no diamonds glittering anywhere on her body.

Mack caught a brief glimpse of a shadow sliding along the lawn, very low, not ten feet from Violet. He held his breath as Javier rolled clear of the beams and into the thick hedge that ran around the house. Violet wasn't as confident, propelling her body forward with painstaking slowness.

Jacob's voice brought Mack's attention back to the house. "Griffen is no danger to us, James. The GhostWalkers are like his kids. He doesn't want to lose them any more than Whitney does. Once you explain to him that we're all on the same side, he'll understand."

"He's arrogant." Dislike was evident in Jefferson's voice.

Jacob laughed harshly. "Now we're getting to the real reason you're upset. You don't like Griffen."

"He rubs me the wrong way."

Violet was at the window now. She reached her arm up and pressed a small object into the frame. Another piece went into her ear.

Jacob helped himself to more brandy. "He rubs you the wrong way because he doesn't like spooks. You're recruiting his men for your dirty work."

"He doesn't have the balls to make this country strong. We need strong leaders," Jefferson said. "Griffen's thinking is linear. Black and white."

"Still, he not only believes in the Ghost-Walker program, but he runs one of the teams," Jacob pointed out.

"He's squeamish. He talked about women's rights for God's sake. Who gives a fuck? Really, Jacob. We're talking about having the greatest soldiers in the world and he wants to spout off about women's rights. We have a chance to make the United States the most powerful country in the world. Imagine if we could send a lone soldier into an enemy camp undetected and he could assassinate their greatest general and no one would be the wiser because the death looks natural. We could change entire governments, put people in office friendly to our country and no one, *no one,* would be the wiser. Whitney is a man of great vision . . ."

"Yet you don't listen when he tells you he has plans for one of his GhostWalkers."

"He has to be protected, even from himself. And Jacob." Jefferson looked up to meet Jacob's eyes over his drink. "So does Andrew. His daughter-in-law is as cold as ice. She can't be trusted. Whitney chose her to be the senator's wife because she had the least ability to be a soldier, but she has no loyalty."

Mack watched Violet's face carefully. There was no change of expression. None. She might have been listening to a bedtime story. She might not have as many psychic talents as the other GhostWalkers, but he doubted if Whitney had sold her to Freeman because of her lack of talent; more likely he recognized her amoral nature. Whitney would have slated her for termination. He couldn't control her through her affinity for others. If she was loyal to Freeman, it was because Whitney had bound them in some way. Mack would never believe the woman had a genuine care for anyone.

"She's loyal to Ed," Jacob pointed out. "And that's good enough for me."

"She's sleeping with Andrew," Jefferson said. "She controls him as totally as she does Ed. He'll do anything she wants. And she wants Whitney to back Ed so Andrew will bring his full weight behind what she wants."

Jacob sucked in his breath. "Are you sure? That can't be true. Andrew loves his son."

"Andrew's a man. Violet was trained to seduce men. It was part of her 'wifely' duties. Sleeping with Andrew keeps him in line. She has his ear, and he feeds her the information she wants, so be very careful of what you tell him. She does whatever it takes to further Ed's career, including fucking anyone he wants her to. Hell, Ed likes to watch. I've got tapes, Jacob. He's just as sick as she is. Whitney programmed her that way and she's very single-minded. She came here prepared to sleep with me to get her way."

"But you didn't."

Jefferson shuddered. "I'd sooner sleep with a snake. She'd smile at you while she cut your balls off, Jacob. Don't ever trust her."

Abrams regarded Jefferson over the rim of his glass. "I don't trust anyone anymore, James. We live in shifting times." He put down his glass. "I'm an old man and need my sleep. Think about what I said about that girl in San Francisco. Leave her to Whitney. And as for Violet, let's see how it goes with Andrew, whether or not he notices anything different about Ed. Whitney swears he's the same, just more malleable. If Ed passes the test with Andrew, Whitney may want to strike a bargain with Violet and bring those women in. Especially the one he knows is pregnant. I think he'd do just about anything, including making a deal with that she-devil, if it meant getting his hands on the pregnant woman."

Mack cursed softly under his breath. He was fairly certain the pregnant woman they were referring to was the woman Kane was searching for.

"You know one of the GhostWalkers who turned in evidence against Whitney was the one who impregnated her. He's searching for her and Griffen is helping him, using all of his sources."

"You have a line to Griffen. Let them search. As soon as they know where she is, we'll know and we can snatch her first," Abrams said. "Use both of them to get what we want. You can always have the bastard killed on a mission later if he gives you any more trouble."

Jefferson didn't bother to mention he'd tried it several times already.

Abrams put down his glass and picked up his coat. "I've seen Ed Freeman, James. I don't think his own father or anyone else will ever be able to tell the difference."

"Can we trust Violet?"

"We don't have to. If she tries to destroy Whitney or any of us, Ed will die. It's that simple. Whitney has a protection built into the program and there is no way Violet is going to let Ed die. She'll ride him all the way to the presidency."

"And we'll control both of them." Satisfaction purred in Jefferson's voice.

"A triumph beyond measure," Abrams agreed.

Violet swiftly pocketed her listening device and rolled under the beams back toward the safety of the groves of trees. Javier had already anticipated her departure and moved before her, sliding into the shadows just parallel to her, escorting her back to where she'd left her car, just to make certain she didn't backtrack and surprise them.

James Bradley Jefferson cleaned up the glasses, carrying them carefully through to his kitchen, where he washed them thoroughly and put them away. The small recorder he'd secreted in the book was removed and taken with him to his bedroom. One by one the lights in the house went out until only a single lamp shone in the bedroom.

Mack waited until the moon moved across the sky and the sounds of the night had resumed a loud chorus. The slightest thing could alert a pro, including the sounds of insects. As he descended he made certain his energy was suppressed, that he moved with the night itself, keeping the natural rhythm.

Gideon's sole job was to protect him, and Mack couldn't imagine a better backup. Gideon never missed. Javier waited by the house. "He's got two cameras in the back. That's our best bet, boss," Javier said. "Both are on five-second sweeps. You should be able to move through the two of them if you watch each lens, and use that weird-ass teleportation thing you've got. No one will ever know you were in the house."

Mack scowled at him. "I told you, it isn't exactly teleportation."

"Whatever. Just do it and watch where you position yourself." Javier glanced at his watch. "Counting down now."

Mack crouched low, leapt over the high back fence — probably the reason there were only two cameras. He landed just to the right of the house and moved with blurring speed, his body looking to the naked eyes like a shadow made of dust, a blur, and then forming from one spot after another until he crossed the open yard to the back door. He couldn't teleport anywhere he wanted, he could only use short bursts of speed, moving his mass small distances, rather than one long one. He'd found a few uses for his particular talent, but not many, and it took a lot out of him.

It wasn't difficult to bypass the alarm on the door. The box was located on the roof and easy enough to access. Mack slipped into Jefferson's house and padded silently through the kitchen, down the hall, to the bedroom. The door was ajar. A fireplace cast a small glow over the room, illuminating the man reading in bed.

Jefferson wore a pair of glasses and lounged with his robe tied loosely over a striped pajama shirt. The covers were pulled up to his waist. Beside his bed was a cigar in an ashtray and a drink. Mack moved with his blurring speed, looking like a dark shadow materializing beside the bed.

Jefferson dropped his book, his hand sliding toward his pillow.

"Don't," Mack said softly as he removed one glove. "I just wanted to give you a chance to realize you've already accomplished what you set out to do."

Jefferson relaxed. "And what would that be?"

"You wanted to create an assassin who could go into an enemy camp undetected, kill the general, and walk out with no one the wiser."

"You're a GhostWalker."

"How else could I have gotten in without detection?" Mack leaned down and laid his palm very gently over Jefferson's heart. He moved without aggression, utterly calm, almost tranquil, so Jefferson was without alarm.

"You overheard my conversation." He winced. Looked up at Mack. "Oh, fuck."

"No," Mack corrected softly. "You're fucked. You shouldn't have been so stupid as to come after us. What did you think would happen?"

Jefferson slumped back on the pillow, his mouth open, his eyes wide and staring, one arm flung out as if toward the phone, reaching for help.

Mack waited until he was certain the man was dead before he pulled on his glove and

531

exited, turning on the alarm and once more moving undetected through the cameras.

CHAPTER 18

The moment Mack made his way up to the second floor, he felt the instant tension and knew something was wrong. His team — Ethan included — was assembled around a table, an obvious makeshift war room. His beeper had gone off in the plane, so he wasn't at all surprised that there was trouble.

Jaimie looked up, her face a little pale and strained, but she leapt up, a smile blocking out the worry. That look alone was worth everything to him. Uncaring that Sergeant Major was watching, or that his team had grins on their faces, he swept her into his arms and kissed her thoroughly. He took his time, feeling her cling to him, the slight trembling in her body.

He framed her face with his hands. "Are you all right?"

Jaimie nodded. "I'm glad you're back. We have a bad situation here, Mack."

"I can see that, honey." He reluctantly let his arms drop, stripping off his jacket. "Sergeant Major, you're cleared. The mission was a success."

Griffen nodded his head just once in understanding. The old, faded eyes smiled at Mack briefly in acknowledgment before he indicated the computer screens above their heads. "You're looking at the reason for World War Three, Mack."

He looked up and studied the two unlikely faces. A small girl of about ten looked back at him, her shiny black hair framing her face. Beside her was a serious young teenager, perhaps seventeen, with razor-straight, gleaming black hair and dark eyes hidden behind black-rimmed glasses. "And they are?"

"Dae-sub Chun is seventeen. A nice young man, far ahead of his age. The girl is a niece of an old friend. Her name is Micha Song. Dae-sub Chun's father is General Kwang-sub Chun. He just happens to be the ambassador to D.P.R.K. Permanent mission to the UN."

Javier lowered his gear to the floor. "That doesn't sound good."

"Democratic People's Republic of Korea," Sergeant Major reiterated.

"No," Javier said. "I'm guessing anything

534

to do with North Korea right now isn't going to be good, not when our countries are posturing at each other."

"It gets worse," Griffen said. "The girl is the sister of one of our agents. Both children have been kidnapped."

"Was the girl's abduction deliberate?" Mack asked. "Is our agent compromised?"

Griffen shook his head. "No, she was with the boy at a museum. She had been visiting General Chun's family. We don't believe she was the target so much as Dae-sub. Educated guesses by Chun leaned toward blackmail at first. It seems one of their leading scientists accidentally stumbled upon a particularly unstable and highly explosive compound. Somehow Doomsday was able to infiltrate the lab and obtain the information. The general was certain he would be contacted very soon with a demand for the formula and compound. We all know the general's wife was killed last year, and that he loved her very much. It nearly broke him. He isn't a young man and now, with his son in grave danger, well, this is a desperate situation any way you look at it."

"Then you've been in touch with General Chun?"

"Yes, very quietly. He can't be seen talking with us, of course."

Mack found a chair and gratefully accepted the cup of coffee Kane pushed into his hands. He'd been up all night and traveling all day and needed rest. But the room was tense, Jaimie looked stressed, and Sergeant Major Griffen was as grim as he'd ever seen him.

"Lay it out for us," Mack said and waved Gideon and Javier into chairs.

"We took the weapons in the warehouse," Kane said. "The mission went like clockwork, boss. When Shepherd and Estes tried to break in, we killed two of their men. We managed to tag both of them with a tracking device. We couldn't have asked for a smoother operation."

Griffen took up the story. "We traced them all the way to China. Beijing to be exact."

Mack sat up straighter. "China? What the hell would Shepherd and Estes want in China?" He sank back. "Never mind. If you want to go to North Korea, you have to go to Beijing, right?"

Kane nodded his head. "They met with Frank Koit and Holeander Armstice, both known members of Doomsday. The four traveled together to North Korea. The next day, these two children were snatched from the museum and their bodyguards were

536

slain. The kidnappers left behind an American assault rifle."

"To implicate the United States," Mack guessed. "Because we aren't in enough trouble already, with both countries pissed off at each other over the nuclear issue."

"Publicly North Korea has warned of military action against the United States," Kane said. "Even if they knew we weren't guilty of kidnapping these children, to save face they'd have to retaliate if it looked to the world as if we were responsible for grabbing them."

"The world would be on their side," Griffen said. "Using children as pawns in a nuclear debate would be despicable."

"And the children would have to die," Mack added. "You know they'd kill them. What other choice would they have? Even if they pretended, the boy was raised by General Kwang-sub Chun. You know he'd spot any inconsistencies. One thing, he won't panic, not if he's anything at all like his old man."

"Privately, North Korea has asked for us to aid them in getting these children out alive."

Mack sighed and rubbed at his temples. "Are you certain the kids are still alive, Top?"

"We have to believe that," Griffen said. "I want your team to go in and bring them out."

Jaimie made a small sound of distress. Mack swung his head to look at her. She was curled up in a chair a few feet away from the table, partially hidden in the shadows, her face averted. "He makes it sound so easy."

"We have to know where they are," Mack said. "Unless our bugs have stopped working."

"Oh, no," Jaimie said, "they're in place. They're relaying the information just fine." She rubbed her hand over her face. "They're transmitting from under the American embassy in Beijing. The *American* embassy, Mack. If the kids are found there, the world is in trouble."

"Shit," Javier commented.

"Thank you for your contribution," Griffen said. "As you can see, Mack, this requires a delicate hand. You have to get in unseen, scoop the kids back without anyone knowing you — or they — were ever there. That means no shots fired. Nothing that could possibly draw attention to this situation."

"With no shots fired? Against a terrorist organization that thrives on as much violence and publicity as possible?" Mack looked at Kane. "When do we leave?"

"I'll provide as much intel as I can from here," Jaimie volunteered.

"You have to go with them," Sergeant Major ordered. "I'm not asking."

There was a shocked silence. The men looked at one another. Mack looked at Jaimie. She squeezed her eyes closed tightly, fists clenching until the knuckles turned white, until her fingernails bit deeply into her palm. "You know I can't go with them, Sergeant Major," she whispered softly, a thousand tears in her voice, her chest aching. "I would if I could, but it's impossible. I nearly got Mack killed on our last mission together."

"She can feed us intel from here," Mack said.

Griffen shook his head. "I don't need her feeding you intel. I need her to do whatever she does to get you all in and out quietly. If there was another way . . . But she's what we have and we have to use her skills."

"I don't work for you anymore." Her voice was stiff. She didn't look at any of them.

"You never stopped. And I'm not asking," Griffen retorted.

Jaimie stood up so fast her chair went over backward. "You're not going to do this to me. Arrest me."

"Don't think I won't. This is what you were trained for and, by God, you're going to do your job."

"Sergeant Major." Mack's voice was low. Ice-cold.

The room went dead silent. Kane moved. The action was subtle, but he put his body between Jaimie and the rest of the room.

Griffen rose, his eyes narrowing. He did a slow sweep of the room with speculative eyes. "Are you threatening me, soldier?"

The tension in the room rose significantly. Mack didn't so much as blink, letting it stretch out almost to a breaking point. "I said nothing to give you that impression — sir."

"I fucking *work* for a living, so don't you ever insult me like that again," Griffen snapped. "And you're supposed to be my friend. Have you forgotten that? We have a situation that could throw our country and all our allies into war. I want the best team I can put together to avoid this situation. All of you are aware of what Jaimie can do. Can any of you? Each of you has talents that are needed, but if we're going to send you in with the best chance of success without detection, you need Jaimie. Mack, you know I wouldn't ask if we didn't need her."

"But you didn't ask," Mack pointed out, his voice neutral. "I believe you ordered her."

A small smile eased the tension on Griffen's face. "I'm used to giving orders. I've been doing it my entire life. I'm sorry about that, Jaimie." He switched his gaze to her pale face. "I wouldn't be asking you if this wasn't a desperate situation, and I think you know that. You have a talent no one else has, or at least that we know of, Jaimie. Maybe it's not something we can put a name to, maybe it's undefined, but you have it, and it saves lives," Griffen said. He made every effort to keep his voice gentle, aware of the men watching him. He wasn't used to choosing his words so carefully and his voice came out a little strained.

Her mouth trembled. "What happens if others are relying on me and I fail them and someone dies? I would never be able to forgive myself." *Like last time.*

No one died last time, honey, Mack said gently.

You almost did.

You saved all of our lives. The entire team would have died in that ambush if it hadn't been for you. You never think about that part of it. We'd all be dead.

"Think of the children, Jaimie," Kane suggested. "You know the kidnappers have to kill them. With you, we have a better chance of going in without detection."

"You and Mack and the boys, you go in and get those kids out yourself." Jaimie was pleading now, clearly a last-ditch effort. She hadn't honestly thought about what would have happened had she not warned the team of the ambush and found them the clearest route possible to escape. Maybe they did need her, but . . .

She swallowed hard, her eyes meeting Mack's in desperation. He crossed to her side, his hand going to the nape of her neck, fingers easing the tension from her.

"If we needed cowboys to go in, guns blazing, we'd have any number of men, but we can't do that, Jaimie," Griffen said. "We have to get in and get out with no sound, like ghosts. The boy is the only son of the ambassador to D.P.R.K. I'm sure I don't have to tell you the international implications."

Jaimie sagged against Mack in defeat, her heart going out to the grieving parents, to the terrified children. She had to go. She knew what it was going to cost, though.

I'll be with you, Jaimie, Mack reminded. *We're getting better at blending our energies. And you're stronger. We can do this.*

I guess we have to, she conceded. "I guess I'm going with you."

Griffen smiled. "With your ability you can walk in and take them back without a fight."

"You and I both know it's impossible to control a situation like this. Most of it is pure luck," Jaimie argued. "And good intel."

"Well, we have you for that," Griffen said. Now that she'd capitulated, he was in a better mood. "General Chun is a fine man, a man any military man would respect. He has a code of honor. But let me tell you all, right now he's afraid, terrified even, and a man like Chun should never have such a look in his eyes. I didn't meet the little girl's parents but you know her brother, you went to the university with him and trained with him before you became GhostWalkers."

Jaimie's teeth bit into her lip again. There had been one recruit from North Korea, and she should have recognized the name. Kim-son Song. He had spoken of his younger sister often. She'd been born many years after him — an unexpected gift, he called her.

It was Mack who actually voiced the question, Mack the field commander, Mack who felt totally responsible for his men. "Does

543

he know?"

"Yes. He's been briefed. He blames himself of course, but we're fairly certain she was just in the wrong place at the wrong time."

Jaimie let out her breath and glanced at Mack's face. He'd gone utterly still, even his black eyes appeared lifeless. Kim-son Song had been in his command, an invaluable asset in Europe and the Eastern Bloc nations. Most important, he was a friend. Jaimie instinctively held out her hand. For a moment, Mack didn't move, and then his eyes touched her face. Empty. Cold. Jaimie shivered under his gaze, a sudden tremor of fear rising. There was something very dangerous buried deep in Mack. Jaimie didn't like the rare occasions she caught glimpses of that lurking monster.

Mack fought back the demons clawing at his gut. Innocent children this time. Who would use children as pawns? Someone had hired Doomsday to do their dirty work, to carry out their idea. Doomsday had no personal agenda other than to make money.

Everything in him rose up to do battle with the abductors, a berserker's cold, deadly rage. He detested terrorists — murderers. There was no excuse to kill the innocent. There was no excuse for using political agendas to murder untrained civilians.

His gaze focused on Jaimie's transparent face. He could easily read the jumble of confused emotions. Fear was among them. Instantly he made himself take a deep, calming breath and relax. He softened the hard angles and planes of his face with a smile as he laced his fingers through hers.

"It's okay, baby; we'll get them back." He sat down, cradled her in his lap, his arms strong and comforting. His Jaimie. She had such a gentle heart, thinking only of the children and their families with compassion. The truth was, he wanted swift, brutal retaliation against the perpetrators. His fingers tangled in the blue black silk of her hair. God, but she overwhelmed him with intense emotion. Love. Whatever one called it.

"Do we know who's behind this? Does General Chun have any ideas?"

"A few. There are a couple of powerful people who believe that if the United States was caught resorting to the kidnapping and murdering of children, the world would make concessions on their nuclear program."

"So he wants prisoners."

Jaimie stiffened. "If we turn those men

545

over to the general, you know what he'll do to them. We can't do that."

"They took his son, Jaimie," Griffen pointed out. "He has a right to question them. We can't do it. We can't let anyone know we were even there."

Her breath hissed out between her teeth. She looked around the room and knew immediately none of the men had the least bit of sympathy for the terrorists.

"What do you want us to do with them, Jaimie?" Javier asked.

"That's enough," Mack intervened.

"No, he has the right to ask," Jaimie said. "Everyone's entitled to their opinion, especially if we're all going in, risking our lives. I'd rather see them dead than tortured, Javier. And imprisoned rather than dead."

"I can arrange their deaths," Javier agreed and turned to Sergeant Major, one eyebrow raised in inquiry.

Griffen shook his head. "As much as we'd like to settle things that way, we can't. We have to pull those kids out of there without a shot fired. No one can know. We'll get them out of China and back into General Chun's hands immediately. You tranquilize whoever you find and walk away. I mean it. Leave them where they lie and get those kids out of there. That's your part of the mission."

"Is that all? You're sending us in without bullets?" Mack asked.

"It has to be this way," Griffen said. "You're ghosts. Get in and get out. We don't have much time. We can't take the chance that they'll move those kids again. It's one of their favorite tactics with hostages, moving them every few days to a new location."

"They won't move them, Sergeant Major," Mack said with a small sigh. "And I think you know that. They're going to kill them and leave the bodies near the gates inside the embassy. God only knows what they'll do to the kids first. You can bet they'll have pictures and arrange for reporters. They're looking for a big splash. The video will be a YouTube hit on the Internet. You know they've got someone ready to record the deaths."

"We have military transport standing by," Griffen said. "You can sleep on the plane. You'll leave in two hours. You'll be infiltrating the U.S. embassy in Beijing. We don't want anyone in the embassy informed at this time other than the captain."

There was a long, shocked silence. "You're not letting the embassy know?" Mack echoed softly. "I don't think so. What the hell are you trying to pull?"

"I told you it was a hot one. What better way to start an international incident? If the children are found there, the United States would be publicly blamed," Griffen snapped. "Who do we trust? You know there would be a leak."

"The Marines guard all of our embassies," Jaimie pointed out. "Security is ultra tight."

"Don't worry, we've planned for that."

"The Marines, rather a Marine, spotted them. A very smart young man. Instead of shooting it out, he quietly reported to his captain. He was able to find the traitor working with them and to uncover the cell underground," Griffen said. "They took the information directly to the secretary general."

"They entered the embassy through a tunnel?" Jaimie found that unbelievable.

"The tunnel had been sealed years earlier. Someone spent a great deal of time and energy reopening it. We knew about the tunnel and also the seven seals that were cleverly worked into the building structure that amplified sounds so we could be monitored."

"Someone on the inside helped," Mack said.

"Three people. One, a young man who will be very quietly court-martialed,"

Griffen continued. "Another works on the grounds. Both contributed a great deal. The work was done on the guard's shift and the groundskeeper kept everyone away from the area with various ingenious ploys. He did it right out in the open in front of embassy officials, guards, personnel, everyone. We also suspect a low-level paper pusher who is a friend of the Marine guard. No one has moved on any of those involved."

"Who knows about this?" Mack asked.

"The secretary general was apprised of the situation immediately by the commanding officer, and of course the young Marine. The secretary general asked specifically for this team and I told him you'd do it."

"He doesn't want the terrorists dealt with?" Mack asked.

"Not by your team. He wants them tranquilized quietly. Once you're out with the kids, the Marines will go in and sweep the tunnel. They'll be turned over to Chun's men."

Jaimie stirred but she didn't say anything.

"You won't object to our defending ourselves if it comes to that, right, sir?" Javier demanded.

"Defend yourself with tranqs," Griffen said. "We've got one chance to do this right. If we don't get those children back, the

United States will be very embarrassed and North Korea will be put in an impossible position."

"They could be dead," Mack said.

"If that's the case, we get them out, kill everyone involved, and lose the bodies. We'll have to deny all knowledge."

Jaimie closed her eyes briefly as she leaned back against Mack's chest, pulling herself in. This had to be done. She could see the reasons clearly, but it still didn't stop her from feeling sick about it. "I take it you have all the intel we'll need."

"The layout, guards, the total security system. We'll have full cooperation once we contact the embassy and let them know you're there. We'll do so at the last possible minute."

Jaimie was already shaking her head. "Too risky, too many people in on it. We can't know who else they've bought. If this was really over some formula the terrorist wanted, that might work, but not this. This is designed to pit the United States against North Korea."

"The guards will be handpicked, assigned a special duty, because the embassy will be receiving a surprise visit from a bigwig dignitary."

"Please God, tell me it isn't General

Chun," Jaimie muttered aloud. "It sounds like something brilliant someone sitting behind a desk would come up with."

"It wouldn't be so unusual," Griffen countered.

"Nothing would put that group on alert like a surprise visit from the kid's father."

"What do you suggest?" Mack asked, his voice strictly neutral.

"A dinner party."

"Excuse me?" Griffen scowled at her.

"A dinner party. I know you've heard of it. Coat, tie, maybe a tail or two. Open the place up. Up the security. Get tons of dogs out sniffing the grounds."

"You're crazy, Jaimie." Kane scowled at her. "That will only add to the nightmare."

Mack shook his head his slowly. "No, wait a minute, Kane. She just might have something."

Jaimie jumped up and paced across the floor with her quick, fluid step. "Excuse me, guys, but this happens to be my area of expertise. You go out, shoot 'em up, bang, bang, but I plan for stealth, silent training if you recall. Trust me on this. If the embassy is putting on a high-profile dinner party — announced, say, now — the security will be upped like you wouldn't believe. They won't be able to kill those children. They'll have to stay tucked in that tunnel waiting until security eases a bit."

Gideon cleared his throat. "Sergeant Major. If there's even a small chance that the terrorists will kill the children, shouldn't the Marines on-site go in and rescue them now? Not wait?"

"Doomsday will kill them. You know they would, Gideon," Mack said. "You've seen the way they operate. At the first sign of trouble, they'll kill the kids and try to fight their way out. The few times an operative has been close to capture, they've blown themselves and everyone around them up."

Gideon nodded. "I knew you'd say that, but I had to ask."

"I think Jaimie's on to something," Mack said. "Doomsday will be pinned down until we get there. They'll keep the kids alive until after the dinner party. They'll need to just for insurance, for bargaining chips. They'll want fresh bodies for the optimum scandal, probably cut their throats on the embassy lawn. Hopefully the captain has kept the corporal from guard duty so he hasn't given them the opportunity and won't before we can get there."

"He has," Griffen said grimly.

Javier pulled his knife from his boot and began sharpening it. Griffen shot him a speculative look.

"You'll have to keep your men in line, Mack," he warned.

"My men know what to do, Top," Mack said.

He caught Javier's eye and shook his head. Javier sighed and put the knife away, having made his point. "Maybe we should make some fresh coffee and give ourselves time to think this through."

"I'll make a fresh pot," Marc volunteered.

Javier snorted. "No way am I drinking his coffee. I'd rather go to this embassy buck naked and armed with only water guns."

Laughter accompanied the shudders that went around the room. Almost as one they stood up and headed for the stairs. Jaimie turned off her computers and followed. Mack waited on the bottom stair for her, reaching for her hand.

He brought her fingers to his mouth. "We'll do this, baby."

"I think we have a good chance. We've got all the right people," Jaimie agreed. "You know if something goes wrong, I probably won't be much of an asset to you."

"You can fire a gun, Jaimie. No one's going to ask you to shoot through a hostage. We're there to save them."

She took a deep breath and let it out.

"Don't worry. Really, Mack. You know me, once I make up my mind to do something, I'm in all the way."

That was true. She was very disciplined and methodical. She'd be a huge asset in planning how to get in and out.

It was Kane who put on a new pot of coffee while the men raided the refrigerator and cupboards, reminding Mack of locusts.

Jaimie and Mack followed Griffen to the comfortable chairs and sank into them. Jaimie leaned toward Sergeant Major. "Put your handpicked embassy Marines at the gate, let them watch all the people going in, but don't tell them about us. Believe me, Sergeant Major, if the guards know someone is meant to slip through, they'll never be as alert and neither will we."

"You have a plan?" Griffen asked.

Mack nodded. "You said the commanding officer was going to take his Marines in and clean up. How exactly?"

Griffen hesitated again.

"I need to know," Mack said.

"We've got a small unit standing by. Special Ops. They'll go in with the commander, take the sleeping terrorists to a waiting unmarked car. It will have tinted windows so no one can see in. The commander will go about his business as if nothing has transpired. The Special Ops team will take the terrorists to the North Korean embassy in Beijing. They'll leave them right outside the gates and General Chun will be notified that they are on the way. He'll have his men waiting. Special Ops will walk away, leaving the car and the keys for the North Koreans to just drive inside their gates."

Mack nodded. "This Special Ops unit. Marines?"

"Of course," Griffen replied.

"Then let's use them to help us get inside. They have to be briefed on what's going on, right?" Mack said. "Put them in the guard's position on the side nearest the tunnel and tell them to stand down when we come over the fence."

Griffen shook his head. "They don't know about the kids. This is need-to-know only."

"But they know someone's going in and tranqing the terrorists. They know the cell is beneath the embassy, right?"

"Yes."

"Put the Special Ops team in uniform and arrange for them to guard the fence near the tunnel entrance. They can know we'll be slipping onto the grounds. Or just one of them. Tell their Top. We can make our way through the roving guards and the dogs both going in and getting out. The danger is at the fence itself, especially coming out with the children. If they know, they can let us slip over the fence with our packages. Once we're clear, the captain can relieve them of their duties and they can get out of uniform and carry out their orders. They can strip down in seconds."

"I hate it when you're right," Griffen said.

Mack laced his fingers through Jaimie's. "I wouldn't mind this one over here admitting I'm right — all the time."

"Not likely," Jaimie said amid the laughter.

"But, damn, she does have a magnificent brain, doesn't she?" Kane nudged Mack.

"Either that, or not one at all," Jaimie interjected sourly. "This is crazy, you all know that, don't you?"

"We were all born crazy," Javier said with a cocky grin.

Griffen nodded his head. "I like it, Mack. At least it should minimize some of the risk to your team getting out. I'll have the secretary general send you everything they have on the tunnels and the workings and security at the embassy."

"This low-level paper pusher," Jaimie said. "By any chance do you have pictures and data on him? If so, I'd like to see it. I'll need everything you've got on all three of the traitors."

"Already sent to you."

"Not from Beijing?" she asked, holding her breath.

"No. The captain didn't know who or what he could trust. He flew in to inform the secretary general."

Jaimie let her breath out and went to her laptop, her fingers flying over the keyboard. The pictures of three men appeared, files flying across the screen, stacking up so fast Mack had no way of reading them. "Corporal David Shanty is our guard and this is his roommate, Corporal Fred Simmons. They entered the Corps in the buddy program. And Mack, this isn't good. Simmons knows what he's doing with computers. The captain was smart to worry that his computer might be compromised. The third man is Chang Lui, a fourth-generation gardener. Father is Chinese, his mother American."

"Just because this kid is good on a computer . . ." Griffen began.

"Trust me on this, Top," Jaimie said. "If they're in it together, Simmons is the one providing intel. His major was in computer science. He knows his stuff."

"What do you want us to do?" Griffen asked with a small sigh.

"Have them announce the dinner party immediately. Tighten security. Put a death grip on that place. As soon as it's locked down, ask the captain to send me everything he has. Use the encrypted program, but before he does, have them check his computer. Tell them they're looking for a hardware keystroke logger. If they've compromised his computer, that's what they'll have used. Tell him to change his password after they've removed the card and then send me everything."

"You're certain his computer is compromised?"

"If he's the captain, everything going on in that embassy is going to go through his office. Simmons is keeping a low profile, but he's working in the office. He'll have had access to the captain's computer at some point. It would only take a couple of minutes to slip a keystroke logger into an unused PCI mini slot. He'd just have to wait for the captain to log on. His log-in information along with everything he types would be recorded. When he's waited long enough to be certain he's gotten everything he needs, all he has to do is wait for the captain to leave the office again and recover the card. He has total access to all the captain's files."

"But the captain would change his password periodically."

"Which is why I think the card will be there. In the meantime, even if they don't find one, have him change his password before he communicates with me, that way we're sure no information will be compromised. If we're going in naked, at least let's make certain no one knows we're coming."

"Done," Griffen said.

"Let's get our gear ready, then," Mack said. "We don't have a lot of time. Anyone have any questions?"

"How are we getting them out of there, Mack?" Gideon asked.

The others, gathered in the kitchen, turned to listen.

"Same way we go in. No one can see us. The idea is that no one ever knows the kids were at the American embassy. We slip in and slip out."

"Through the Marines. During a heavily guarded political dinner."

"Yep," Mack said.

A slow smile spread across Gideon's face. "Just like in the old days when we were training, boss."

"Except this time," Jaimie pointed out, "you'll have a couple of terrified kids who may not understand you're there to help them."

"We don't know what shape they're in,"

Mack added. "Jaimie, you're good with languages. You'll have to do all the reassuring."

"You're just as capable," she corrected.

"Yeah, but you're a girl," he said with a smug grin.

"Paul can monitor everything from DC," Griffen said.

There was a small silence. Paul stood up slowly, a scowl on his face. Mack held his hand up, silencing the boy. "Paul's a valuable member of my team. You're not going to cripple us by breaking up the team now when this is so important."

"You said yourself that Paul couldn't communicate telepathically and would endanger your team," Griffen pointed out.

"That was before I knew him. He's a good soldier and we'll need him and his talents. He's a member of my team, Sergeant Major. You can't pull him without a reason."

For the first time Griffen hesitated. It was clear he didn't want to send his son on what might be a suicide mission, or one where, if they were caught with the children, they might be branded criminals for life — tried and convicted worldwide. Even if they were cleared later, the shadow would forever follow them. And they'd be exposed to the world. Considered a liability.

560

Griffen drew in a deep breath and glanced at his son. Paul looked excruciatingly embarrassed. The other team members were looking anywhere but at him. Griffen forced himself to nod. "Good, then. You must have a plan for communication."

"I always have a plan, Top," Mack said. "But the details of this mission I'll keep to myself. It's the way I always work and it keeps us alive."

Griffen stood up. "I'll leave you to get ready, then. I'll be flying back home. Paul, walk me out."

"You got it, Top," Paul said.

CHAPTER 19

Jaimie crouched on the floor of the van, her heart pounding so hard she was afraid it would burst through her chest. All around her, crammed close like sardines, were men in combat gear, full black from caps to crepe-soled shoes. Her mouth felt like cotton. She was an analyst, not a field operative. Why wouldn't anyone pay attention when she told them?

They had traveled for so many hours, poring over detailed blueprints, talking out every possibility, covering the smallest points, until Jaimie was exhausted and had lost track of time. The clothing was all too familiar; it clung to her like a second skin, as if she belonged. The men trained every day — *every* day in hostage rescue. Each one of them was a marksman. Each spent hours and hours on the range making certain every bullet they fired hit its target. They were all in superb shape. She must have been crazy to do this.

She opened her mouth to make another protest and closed it abruptly. They'd gone over every single detail in the hours of flight. All of them had slept the moment they'd closed their eyes. They'd trained their bodies to rest anywhere they could, under any circumstances. She looked around at the men she regarded as brothers — at the man she loved — and she realized they were born for this work.

She heard the murmur of their voices as if from a distance, the soft ribbing back and forth. Once, Kane leaned over and inspected Paul's pack. She felt the difference in the men even before the van began to slow. The adrenaline rush was unbelievable. For a moment, the chemicals running through her body nearly paralyzed her.

Just breathe through it, Jaimie, Mack's voice slipped into her mind. *You'll do fine.*

She nodded her head, but didn't trust herself to speak. He looked so confident. She couldn't imagine him not succeeding. Failure wasn't in his vocabulary. It was in the way he carried himself, the set of his shoulders. He would have been an extraordinary soldier without his enhancements, and they'd only made him that much better at what he did.

She forced another breath of air through her lungs.

Twenty seconds, Kane intoned.

Although there was an arsenal of weapons available, they all carried tranq guns. She opted for a double-barreled, compressed-air tranq gun loaded with small medicated darts, guaranteed for an instant knockout. She knew the men were just as deadly with or without their firepower. This time, they would be going in and out silently, like wraiths, and they'd leave it to the Special Ops to do cleanup. All that was important was the package.

Ten seconds.

Jaimie wiped the back of her hand across her mouth. The rain was no more than a misty drizzle. It was a night without moon or stars, a night made for some dark, deadly purpose. She shoved the gun around her neck, freeing her hands to go up and over the fence. They had to be in the right sector with the right guards. Once over the fence, they were on their own.

There was a distinct chill in the air despite the closeness of the bodies crammed in the van. She found herself shivering, her teeth wanting to chatter, the overload of adrenaline nearly impossible to handle without action. Mack laid a hand on her arm without saying anything, but his body was warm and comforting next to hers and settled her more.

Five seconds. Kane's voice was like the proverbial tolling of the bell in her head.

From down the street there was the sudden flare-up of automobile headlights, the whine of one vehicle, the purr of another. The honored guests at the ambassador's dinner party were arriving in a steady stream. Sounds of laughter and music drifted on the night breeze. The damp night had not dampened the guests' spirits in the least.

Kane slipped from the van. No interior light glowed. The blackness held intact and he became part of it. He moved in silence, sliding across the grassy shoulder between the road and the high fence. He could hear the sounds of activity just around the slight bend, but he was removed from them. The guard dogs patrolling with their handlers throughout the ten acres had obviously been doubled. Five buildings were connected with circular paths throughout the courtyards. Marine guards were on high alert, and it showed in their patrols. They were in constant communication with one another.

Kane approached the sector where the Special Ops guard was supposed to have been stationed. Gideon slipped out of the van next and worked his way through the short grass and flowers on his belly, his eyes and gun centered on the guard. Jaimie felt the tension instantly. For all of them, this was the most frightening moment. If the Special Ops guard hadn't replaced the regular Marine, the mission could end before it began.

I've got him covered, Gideon sent.

Kane moved into position and let out a low one-two whistle. There was a brief moment of silence. Jaimie's heart nearly exploded it pounded so hard. She was afraid the others might be able to hear it. Then it came, that same soft whistle, a single high-low note they waited for.

Mack put his hand on Jaimie's shoulder and sent Javier out. Kane went up and over the fence, clearing it in one efficient leap. He landed in a crouch, his weapon sweeping the complex.

Clear, Kane whispered in their minds.

Javier didn't hesitate. He went up and over, using the same technique, jumping from a crouch and clearing the fence to land on the other side like a cat. As Kane moved forward into the well-trimmed bushes marking one of the many courtyards, Javier swept the complex with his weapon. *Clear,* he said.

Mack tapped Jaimie's shoulder. She found herself running toward the fence. It loomed in front of her, high and thick. Her breath soared through her lungs. She felt the adrenaline move through her body, felt her muscles like well-oiled machines. She stretched, went up and over, landing silently.

Javier used his weapon to indicate to her to follow Kane. She didn't even glance at the soldier guarding the fence. She'd landed a few feet from him, the ground rising up to meet her feet as if she was a large cat, capable of jumping great distances. He had to wonder how they were doing it, but if he was concerned, he didn't move, didn't look toward them, staring off into the night as if they weren't invading his side of the fence.

She ran toward Kane's position, keeping herself low, reveling in the efficient way her body moved. Elation swept through her. She'd forgotten the sheer joy of using her abilities, having suppressed them for so long. She'd try re-creating the feeling by penetrating corporation's security, but it wasn't the same as life or death. It wasn't the same as working with a team you trusted implicitly. Joy sang in her veins. Every sense was acute, her sense of smell, her eyesight, even tactile feeling. She'd forgotten so much.

Clear. She heard Javier whisper it in her mind.

Mack soared over the fence with ease. His landing was totally silent, an amazing feat for a large, heavily muscled man. Javier moved forward, flanking Jaimie.

Dog coming, Kane whispered in their minds.

He motioned and the three of them went to the ground, lying prone, knowing Mack had done the same. He was out in the open, a few feet from the guard, but glancing back, he'd disappeared entirely. Jaimie knew Gideon was still lying in the grass, covering them with his rifle, but he was impossible to see at the best of times. She'd bet her last dollar that the Special Ops guard had no idea Gideon was even close to him.

The dog reacted restlessly to their scent. Too much large cat DNA. She'd known even before she'd read their files that Whitney had genetically altered all of her family in various ways. With the way all of them could leap distances, it wasn't hard to believe that leopard DNA was used. The dog shied away from the courtyard, not wanting to get too close to the dangerous scent. He pulled on the lead so that the handler sharply reprimanded him.

Kane reached, mind to mind, to calm the

568

dog. It wasn't difficult to penetrate the energy shield around the animal and then push further until he was connected in the brain. The dog settled down and happily walked on through the garden area with his handler.

Jacob Princeton was the last man going in from their team. He could detect a bomb fairly easily, every bit as well as a dog, his enhanced senses enabling him to sniff out the chemicals. He was up and over the fence, moving with Mack to join the others. They moved in single file, careful not to disturb anything, leaving no trace of their passing. They didn't want so much as a blade of grass crushed beneath their feet. They took great care not to snap off any plants as they moved through the garden toward the back wall of the courtyard.

Jaimie didn't look around her to see the other members of the team. In the utter pitch blackness of the grounds, it would have been impossible anyway. There was an eerie feel to moving through the drizzling rain, in the darkness without a sound, almost as if they didn't exist, as if they were the ghosts everyone purported them to be.

A good distance away, Jaimie could see the grounds lit up as the guests poured in. The lights glowed an eerie yellow through the thickening mist and appeared to be far-away UFOs. The mists floated in steadily, here concealing, there revealing broken tails. The fog seemed to have a life of its own, curling around her knees and feet. The ragged bottom edge seemed to rise and lower in unpredictable patterns. The only reference any of the silent stalkers had was their own feet in the wet grass, and the rhythmic call of insects.

Another dog and handler approached, and they all went to ground. Jaimie's heart thundered in her ears. She felt the disturbance of energy as Kane reached out to the animal. She realized just how cohesive the team was. Each had special talents that allowed them to move like ghosts through an enemy line. All of them were superbly trained in combat and rescue, training daily as a rule, for that one single moment when they had to go into action for real.

The dog kept walking calmly with his handler, passing within three feet of Kane's body, but the big German shepherd kept its head averted. Jaimie felt the tap on her shoulder and was up and moving fast again. Not running, but moving in at a steady pace. Twice, guards paced parallel to them. Once, they froze, not daring to breathe as two soldiers did a sweep quite close to them.

Jaimie moved through the immaculate expanse of lawn toward the roped-off area where the newest landscaping was allegedly taking place. She paused now and then to sift through the sounds of the night, reading the information, unconsciously seeking touch with the others. The peculiar brush of wings fluttered in her brain. She went still, crouching in the wet grass, one with the night. *Up ahead,* she warned.

Mack's hand went to her shoulder. *How many?*

Kane dropped back to give her the lead. It was up to her to take them through enemy lines without getting caught.

Two. Jaimie moved forward again toward the mounds of freshly dug soft earth. Rocks were piled everywhere, seemingly at random, but on closer inspection they formed several high walls.

Jaimie crept forward, a slim shadow blending in with the night. One of the guards gave a muffled sneeze. The second guard responded with a low, muttered word of caution. The two men were in the comparative shelter of some boulders. Mack touched her shoulder and she dropped down.

We've got Shepherd and Estes, Mack identified to the team. *Make it count.*

Jacob moved up beside him, as silent as a

wraith. He tugged at his gloves until he had them off and lifted both palms toward the two men and the foundation of the building. *We've got a couple of boomers. They're definitely wired. Possibly the building. I'll have to get closer.*

Mack signaled Javier and Kane forward. Javier practically slid over Jaimie's body as he crawled into position. Mack moved as well, putting himself in a better position to cover his two men. Jaimie aimed the tranq gun and waited, her blood a roar in her ears.

Javier and Kane proceeded forward, moving on the ground, shadows within the shadows until they were in plain sight, but within range. Jaimie's breath caught in her throat when one of the guards — Shepherd — looked right at Kane. Kane didn't move a muscle and the slight breeze sent another finger of misty rain spraying across the excavated area. Shepherd turned his head toward Estes to say something. He never got the chance. Javier and Kane squeezed the triggers, and the darts hit nearly simultaneously right behind the left ear of Shepherd and the right of Estes. The sentries staggered backward, hands to their necks in reflex, and then slid to the ground in a weirdly choreographed ballet.

Jacob, can you deal with the bombs? I don't

want them waking up early and blowing our Marines up.

Jacob crawled forward until he was leaning over one of the downed guards. Kane retrieved the darts and pocketed them. Jacob began to work, his movements deft and carefully controlled. It took him several minutes of precious time to disarm the bombs both men were wearing around their middles like vests.

Clear. Jacob pulled back and tugged on his gloves.

Mack tapped Jaimie to signal her back into lead position. She let her breath out. She couldn't make a mistake. All of their lives depended on her. She should have been quaking, but there was something both undefined and exhilarating to be part of the team again. The men never hesitated, following her without question, believing in her. She'd forgotten what that felt like, the implicit trust of teammates when their lives were in her hands.

Jaimie crawled forward, breathing in the scent of the night, her senses flaring out to check for more sentries. Her energy spread, reached out, seeking more, calling it to her like a magnet. She encountered emptiness. *Clear,* Jaimie hissed in their minds. Certain this time. She was getting a feel for the energy she sent out now, the strength of it, the way it worked. She'd never really known before and, in truth, she'd been afraid to depend on it.

The team members spread out. They were black shadows quartering the ground inch by inch, searching for the entrance to the tunnel. They moved in unison, fitting together easily. Kane and Mack dropped back to Jaimie's position, their bodies close enough to touch hers. It was a protection from the wind and as much comfort and reassurance as they could give her under the circumstances.

Jaimie was into the rhythm, her finely tuned mind and expertly trained body pushing away all nightmares to allow her to concentrate on the job at hand. To her, that meant protecting the team, making certain they were not caught unaware in a dangerous trap. At any moment, they could be discovered by a wandering marine, or worse, the terrorist unit could go on full alert. She was grateful for the thoughtful way Mack and Kane were treating her, but only one small part of her mind registered it. Everything else was listening, tuning in, waiting for the warning rattles all of their lives were depending on.

Here, boss, Javier said. The voice was a

soft blur in her mind, the tone calm and businesslike.

The mists and fog deepened, thickened, swirling around them, enveloping them. The rain was more a haze, but it seeped into their clothes as they moved up to the large boulder. It had to be moved and this would be the most dangerous moment. There would be noise and the added draft the moment they removed the block from the entrance. The tunnel had been completely filled in. Those digging wouldn't have excavated deep under the buildings, just enough to hide a small contingency until they could wreak their havoc. She could hear the blood pumping through her veins, a kind of rhythm with the whisper of drizzling mist. Her pulse drummed in time to the soft beat of drops dripping from the sky.

Mack glanced at her again. This was her moment. She had to know, to be certain. Jaimie sent her energy out, seeking again. It bounced like radar along the narrow tunnel walls and then into a wider opening. She nodded and stood clear as he gripped the boulder. The muscles bunched beneath his shirt. She caught a glimpse of strain on his face. She knew ordinarily it would take more than one man to move that large boulder, but he slid it aside just enough for them to slip through.

Kane went first, moving a few feet into the narrow tunnel, and knelt, his weapon up and ready. They knew the terrorists were wired with bombs to blow. They couldn't afford to make any mistakes. Jaimie shivered in the cold air; adrenaline could keep her only so warm. Jacob and Javier moved back, giving her access to the tunnel. Jaimie had not sensed any hidden alarms, but all of their lives were depending on her built-in radar system. Had some alert terrorist heard them moving the enormous boulder? She crouched in the entrance to the tunnel, narrowing her eyes, peering down the steep stairway as if her vision could pierce the veil of darkness.

From inside she caught the muted sound of music. She started down the tunnel, Mack one step behind her, his pencil flash their only source of light. She knew Mack didn't need it, but she did. Kane moved ahead of them, halting every few feet and waiting for the hand on his shoulder telling him to proceed. Ten feet down, the tunnel curved sharply and Jaimie's warning rattles went off in full force. Mack, so close to her, caught her body language, the sudden tension in her, and he was already hissing the warning before she could. His team flattened against the dirt walls, weapons in hand, waiting for the all-clear. They could not take the chance of all of them being caught in such a small area.

Kane was exposed, lying prone on the dirt floor, his weapon extended as he waited for her to make the call. Mack moved with her as she came up behind Kane, pressing herself against the wall while she sent her energy moving forward. Their footsteps were muffled in the thick carpet of soft dirt. Mack touched her arm, signaling her to halt. She stayed behind Kane and closed her eyes, feeling her way through the tunnel. It was unstable, dirt trickling down the walls continually. Occasionally dirt would fall from the ceiling. Breathing wasn't difficult. Claustrophobia was more of a problem than fear of the terrorists, mainly because the tunnel was so obviously unstable it felt as if it could come down at any moment.

There's an open entrance just ahead. Two men. They're fairly relaxed, at least their energy feels that way. Bored maybe. Annoyed.

Can you feel the children?

Waves of fear coming from beyond those two. Very strong. Someone is terrified. I think the kids are alive and in there, Mack.

She didn't spend a lot of time trying to decipher the fear emanating from down the tunnel, it was more important to make certain she protected her team. Kane stayed in front of her. Mack took the other side of the wall, although there really was little room for both of them. Javier tapped Jaimie's arm and signaled her to let Jacob go next. If the terrorists were wired, he would have to deal with that particular threat.

Mack produced a small mirror and they slid it along the dirt, rounding the corner so they could see. Seated at a cheap table were two more terrorists. Frank Koit and a man he recognized from the many photographs they'd studied on Doomsday, Jarold Carlyle; two of the most wanted men in a number of countries. Their boss, Armstice, was nowhere to be seen. Drinks and a deck of playing cards sat near their hands. Although they were relaxed, slouched in their seats and obviously bored, Koit continually stroked his gun, a Luger 9mm Parabellum. His fingers lingered almost lovingly along the barrel. Kane and Mack exchanged a long look.

Carlyle picked up the deck of cards and shuffled. Mack caught bits and pieces of the conversation. The two men were speaking rapidly in English, but Carlyle had a heavy accent. The words were punctuated with a great deal of laughter. They seemed to find it very amusing that a party was being held while right under the noses of the Americans they were holding hostages. The two terrorists took turns toasting the superpowers and snickering at the Marine guards.

"It won't be long," Koit said. "Another few hours to clear the grounds and get the guards settled down. We want the kids dying in front of the cameras. Blaine will call in the reporters and let us know right when to send them out. I think the little dinner party is only going to add to the condemnation. We should get paid more money."

"You better hope Armstice keeps those kids alive." Carlyle gave a worried glance down the narrowing corridor. "He's a bloodthirsty son of a bitch."

"I went to school with him," Koit said. "I can't tell you how many little old ladies' cats and dogs he sliced up and left on doorsteps — until he graduated to killing the little old ladies." He laughed at his own joke.

Mack watched Koit's long fingers stroking the Luger. He nudged Kane. They'd have to shoot together. Both men were armed. All Koit had to do was lift the gun and fire. His hand was steady as he shot the dart into

Koit's neck. Koit slumped forward onto the table; the hand with the Luger slid in slow motion from his chair to the floor. Mack swore as the gun clattered against the chair frame. He sank into a crouch, the gun in his hand, sweeping the area down the tunnel, every cell alert.

Kane took Carlyle at nearly the same instant. The man simply fell forward, the cards scattering across the table as he went limp. He moved forward while Mack covered him, removing the guns and securing the darts.

Jacob, you're up again, Mack said. *We're running out of time. We've got to stay on schedule.*

Yeah, I'll just yank those bombs right off, Top, Jacob replied.

Mack shot him a look and Jacob sobered, moving forward quickly and silently. Mack and Kane moved up into the narrow opening that led to a crawl space behind the makeshift kitchen. *Jaimie. I need you to tell us what we're facing while Jacob disarms the bombs.*

There's something else here, boss, Jacob said. *I found a switch. A remote. There's another bomb somewhere. Koit's got it right in his front jacket pocket.*

Mack swore. *Come on, Jaimie. There must*

be another guard. And Armstice. Find them.

Jaimie skirted around the two downed terrorists, ignoring the fact that small beads of sweat had formed on Jacob's forehead. She'd taken apart dummy bombs before. It wasn't quite the same thing as working with the real deal.

Concentrate, baby, don't think about what he's doing. And don't think about the children. Just find me those men.

Mack never called her "baby" during a mission. He was always very professional. She glanced at his face. He looked at her with worried eyes. She forced a smile. *I'm fine, Mack. Give me a minute.* So far, Mack's energy had kept the pain at bay, but they were in the lion's den and the violent energy surrounding the terrorists ripped and stabbed at her, the sensation very much like ice picks stabbing into her skull.

She took a deep breath, careful to keep her trembling hands behind her back where Mack's watchful eyes couldn't see. Javier was behind them, but he was facing back the way they'd come, watching their back-trail. Jacob kept his head down, intent on disarming the vest of explosives wrapped around Carlyle. Jaimie sent her energy rushing down the narrow tunnel, into the darkness.

581

As if she'd summoned the devil, energy rushed at her, forceful, ugly, extremely violent and evil. It punched through the shield Mack created around her, tearing at the fabric of her energy, shredding it. With it came fear. Pain. Terror. Rage. Both feminine and masculine and very young. She felt the victims, became entwined with them. She staggered under the assault and would have gone down, but Jacob caught her elbow and steadied her as she sagged against him. She felt him reach out to surround her with his strength and love. He shielded her without reserve, with the love of a brother — a teammate. With confidence in her ability to stand up to the assault.

Top. There was caution in Jacob's warning, but no panic.

His voice and quiet support and loyalty steadied her as nothing else could have. She pushed through the violent energy swarming her and forced her way down the tunnel. *One guard standing about halfway down. He's watching Armstice and the children.* It wasn't her job to figure out how they were going to get the guard before he could warn Armstice, only to report to Mack the position of the enemy and the children. Seconds ticked away. Every moment was dangerous and life threatening.

You can do this, Jaimie. Give me Armstice's exact position. You can find him.

She knew what he was planning then. She moistened her lips. Kane could see through things. He was going to use his eyesight to pierce the dirty blanket at the end of the crumbling tunnel and try to dart Armstice while Mack took out the last guard. She had to give Kane an idea of where to look. He'd only have seconds before his sight shut down on him. It was a terrible risk to use that particular talent and it would leave him without sight for a brief amount of time.

She didn't protest. If Kane was willing to risk his sight and go out of the tunnels blind, then she was courageous enough to push right into Armstice's violent energy no matter what it did to her. She would give Kane the best chance possible. She didn't wait. She rushed the energy, shoving deep, uncaring that it attacked, clawing and pulling her apart. She got a good silhouette of him, as well as a taste of evil that she knew would never quite leave her mind.

She sent the picture to Kane, paying particular attention to the head and neck. Armstice stood over the young male who had positioned his body as best he could between the terrorist and young Mi-cha. Armstice kicked him in the ribs repeatedly and then crouched down, pressing the tip of his blade just under Dae-sub's eye.

Jaimie's stomach churned. She held her energy in place, although it fought her, wanting to curl away from the violence in the surroundings. It seemed forever, but she knew only a couple of seconds passed. Jacob kept his hand on her arm.

Both Kane and Mack squeezed the triggers. The guard hit the ground hard. His gun rolled out of his hand. Armstice slumped forward, falling directly on the teenage boy as he lay on the ground, hands tied behind his back, unable to protect himself from the large body as it toppled over him.

Kane sank to one knee in the soft dirt, covering his eyes. Jaimie immediately took his place, gripping her weapon and following Mack into the lower region, deeper into the bowels of the earth. Dirt fell continuously, sliding with an ominous rumble, just small dusty trickles, but it was distracting and alarming. The walls tapered and crumbled as they neared the end of the corridor. Mack had to walk bent over, but she merely ducked her head a little.

Mack paused to retrieve the dart, pocket it, and then push the terrorist's jacket open. *He's wired, Jacob.*

I expected it, Jacob admitted as he followed them down the narrow tunnel to the fallen terrorist's side.

Mack kept the weapon in his hands and nodded to Jaimie. She caught the edges of the dirty blanket and ripped it down. Mack covered Armstice. *Be careful, Jaimie. Stay back. The kids are probably wired as well. These guys were prepared to take the place down before they were taken into custody.*

Water seeped through the walls and steadily dripped overhead. Everything smelled dank and moldy, mingling with the scent of blood. Mack stepped into the cramped, hollowed-out space. She could barely make out the two hostages, tied together at the far end of the room.

Mack pulled the dart from Armstice's neck. He held up his hand for silence as the girl began weeping. *Tell them to be quiet, Jaimie.*

Jaimie moved up where the young man could see her. His swollen face was a mask of defiance and bruises. He was fighting for breath with the terrorist's weight crushing his chest. She was fairly certain he had broken ribs. There were streaks of blood all over his face from the thin cuts Armstice had made in the boy's skin. His face. His chest. His arms. She let her breath out slowly, her teeth chattering. Her skull felt as if it was exploding, and her stomach lurched. She wouldn't give in to it, not with two tortured children and Kane nearly blind.

"We've come to take you home," she whispered softly in Korean. "You're father is waiting, Dae-sub. And your parents, Mi-cha. But you must be very quiet. Not a sound. We're not out of danger. Can you stay very quiet for me, Mi-cha?"

Mack dragged Armstice's body from the boy, who winced and grunted in pain, but refused to cry out.

Dae-sub studied her face and then Mack's. It took a moment for him to believe. "You cannot move us. There is a bomb." He nodded toward Armstice. "He has one too."

Mack nodded his understanding. "We'll take care of it," he answered in perfect Korean.

Jacob, you finished there?

I'm not a bleeding miracle worker, Top. Jacob shuffled forward, making it impossible for Jaimie to stay in the confined space.

"Tell him to take it off Mi-cha," the boy insisted when Jacob knelt beside him.

"He wants you to get rid of the bomb on Mi-cha," she translated.

Jacob had to step over the boy. "Hold the

light up, Mack," he said.

Jaimie made her way back to Kane. "Jacob has to clear them and then we're out of here. Are your eyes clearing?"

She knew little about the effects of using his enhanced vision. It wasn't the same as using "eagle eyes," as they all called seeing great distances. Kane could see through objects, but only for a short period of time, and then he'd get a blinding flash that nearly knocked his vision out. He couldn't take light. The tunnels were lit with old-fashioned kerosene lamps and not quite as destructive on his eyes.

"Let's start moving back toward Javier," she suggested. "Jacob and Mack will have to bring out the kids."

"You'll have to protect them, Jaimie," Kane said. "I can't do it."

Her mouth went dry, but she nodded. "I will. Can you keep the dogs away while we bring them out?" And she knew she would. Maybe it was that she had a tranq gun instead of a loaded weapon, but she thought it was because they were doing something she believed in. And the men had made her feel as if they believed in her.

"Yes," he replied, his voice grim.

She slipped her arm around him and helped him up. He glanced down at her without really opening his eyes. "I can feel you shaking, Jaimie. How bad is it?"

"Armstice is a pretty sick man, Kane," she admitted. She glanced back. Jacob was handing the little girl to Mack.

She cried out in terror. Dae-sub spoke to her and she went quiet, clinging to Mack's shoulder, but keeping her eyes on Dae-sub.

Fall back now, Jaimie. Get Kane out of here. We're right behind you.

Jaimie urged Kane down the corridor at almost a dead run. He stayed right with her, running blind. She guided him, slowing when they were nearing the bends. He never made a sound and her admiration for him rose even more.

Coming up on you, Javier, she warned. *Don't shoot us. Kane's blind.*

Not entirely, Kane denied. *It's nighttime and it's not quite as bad.*

Hell of a shot, though, Mack said.

Jaimie glanced over her shoulder and her heart nearly stopped. Jacob had the little girl and Mack was carrying Dae-sub out in a fireman's carry. The boy was slippery with blood and his face was twisted in a mask of pain. Mack would not only have to carry him through the patrolling Marines, but get him over the fence.

Javier crouched at the entrance to the tunnel. He moved forward to give them room, his eyes moving restlessly, ceaselessly, trying to pierce the heavy blackness and fog. His ears strained to read the night sounds. He crawled forward to get into a better position to defend the party. *Jaimie, do your thing.*

Her pulse pounded in her throat. Her energy was tattered and her skull pounded. She could taste blood in her mouth, knew it leaked from her nose. She kept her face averted to prevent Mack from seeing her. Once again she sent her energy out.

Two Marines with dogs approaching. They're coming directly toward us. They'll come through that small maple garden any moment.

Javier put his eye to his night scope while Jacob and Mack both put fingers to their lips to keep the children quiet. Right on cue, two Marines with German Shepherds on leashes walked toward them.

Kane reached for the dogs just as they began to show signs of agitation. One of the handlers stopped and looked around.

Jacob, Mack hissed. A clear order.

Jacob concentrated on the man. *Go the other way.*

Sometimes suggestion worked and sometimes it backfired. Jacob practiced often, but there was no telling how someone would react. There were a few resistant, but most reacted as if hypnotized, and strangely, the higher the IQ, the easier it was for Jacob to give them a "push." The Marine and his partner walked off and disappeared into the drizzling rain and fog.

Jacob went first with the girl. He whispered soft assurances to her when she clutched at him, scared of the dark, scared of leaving Dae-sub. Once he was in the garden, Mack moved after him, running lightly with Dae-sub, weaving in and out of the shadows and shrubbery.

You ready, Kane? We've got two more soldiers close, but if we hurry, we can slip through to the fence.

Javier? Kane asked.

Right behind you, Gunny, Javier said. *Once we're near the fence, Gideon will have us and he never misses.*

She guided Kane through the dark grounds, running from shrub to shadow until the fence was looming ahead. Jacob, still holding the little girl, cleared it with ease, dropping to the other side and running to the van with his burden.

Mack shifted his burden and crouched low. He propelled himself up and over, using only his leg muscles. Dae-sub cried out softly when they landed, but Mack clapped a hand over his mouth to muffle the sound.

They lay almost in plain sight.

Jaimie dragged Kane down as the guard's radio crackled and running footsteps could be heard.

I've got him, boss, Gideon said. *Give me the go-ahead.*

The guard reported all was fine. It was the longest minute of Jaimie's life with every second lasting an eternity.

The footsteps stopped and faded away.

Go, go, she urged Kane and they ran for the fence as Mack leapt up, dragging the boy with him and sprinting for the van.

Kane and Jaimie went over the fence together. Javier stood beside the guard, showed him his watch, and whispered, "You have thirty-seven minutes left to do your job. Get them the hell out of our country." He leapt the fence and made his way back to the van.

Javier yanked Gideon inside, the doors slammed shut, and the van was hurtling down the street toward safety where General Chun waited for his son and the kidnapped girl. Jaimie could actually breathe again. The little girl began to cry softly and the young man pulled her into his arms protectively. Jaimie knew none of them looked reassuring in their masks and night combat gear, but it was essential to protect their identities. She touched the young man gently to try to give him confidence in them.

Paul immediately began to work on Daesub and she kept her face averted, waiting her turn, her head pounding, but elation sweeping through her. They'd rescued the children and there was no evidence of their participation in the rescue and no evidence of the hostages on the embassy's grounds. She looked up and smiled at Mack through the trickling blood.

CHAPTER 20

Pleasure burst through Jaimie like champagne bubbles. She felt warm and drowsy, her body coming awake inch by slow inch. She felt Mack's body wrapped tightly around hers, his hands stroking over her skin with familiar knowledge, his mouth nuzzling her breast. She laughed softly, feeling complete. She loved waking up to him — to this. She closed her eyes and let the feeling take her, sweeping through her bloodstream on a tide of pure heat.

"You awake, baby?" Mack whispered against her bare skin, his teeth nibbling gently over the swell of her breast.

Jaimie slid her hands over his back, up to his hair. "Yes. I love waking up to you."

"I've been lying here next to you most of the night thinking about us." He pressed kisses along the valley between her breasts up to her throat. He propped himself up on one elbow, leaning over her, his dark gaze moving broodingly over her face.

Her heart jumped. She'd known this was coming since the rescue of the children. Mack had to go back where he belonged. She'd gotten used to being with him, with the others. The others had left a few days earlier and she and Mack had spent days just worshipping each other's bodies. They rarely left the bed for anything other than food and drink and to watch the ocean under a blanket of stars.

She didn't want to do this. She didn't want to lose him again; it was going to tear out her heart. She made a move to roll out from under him but he moved with his incredible speed and pinned her there. His hand on her shoulder was extremely gentle, yet she felt the steel in him, reminding her of the ease with which he'd carried the teenager through the embassy grounds and then leapt the fence with him.

She'd never forget the sight of Mack moving fast, the boy slung over his back, his face determined. Her heart fluttered. He'd been born a warrior. He'd been born to lead. She didn't want to give him back, but she knew he had to go. He'd averted a nuclear war. She couldn't keep him in her bed, tied to her.

Jaimie took a deep breath and braced

herself, reluctantly meeting his eyes.

"Come back to me, Jaimie. I need you to come back," Mack said softly. He pressed his finger over her mouth when she frowned and took a breath. "Listen to me. I laid here for hours figuring things out. You're part of me and when I don't have you, I can't breathe right, let alone function. You make me whole. You keep me mellow. You're the best person I know. I can talk about anything with you. Most of all, when I'm out there doing what I do, you're the reason I do it. You're the reason I know I'm going to make it back." He brushed his mouth back and forth over hers in small, coaxing caresses. "With you, Jaimie, I've got everything. Without you, there isn't much to life."

"Mack, you said . . ." Jaimie's heart was beating so hard she was afraid he could hear.

"I know what I said, Jaimie. It was bullshit. I want a home. With you. A family. You are my family. You want children, we'll have them. I don't give a damn how many. Maybe a dozen so you don't think about walking out on me again."

She knew her shock showed on her face. She'd been dreading the moment he left, knowing he would be ripping out her heart, but she hadn't expected him to ask her to go with him. "But . . ." Her business. Her warehouse. Everything she'd worked for. Could she give it all up and follow him? To what? He'd be gone more than he'd be with her. But could she live, really live, without him?

"I know what I'm asking, Jaimie. I do. I want to wake up every morning to you. I want to sit in a rocking chair with you when we're old. I want to laugh with you, cry with you. I also know what kind of life I'm offering."

"Do you, Mack?" she asked. Because she'd shared the danger of missions with him and when he went out, she'd know exactly how bad it really was. She'd have to sit at home waiting, scared, alone. Completely alone.

His fingers bunched in her curls. "Of course I do, Jaimie. I took you for granted. I'm not going to pretend I didn't or that it won't happen again. And I'm bossy. I won't pretend I don't know the way I am. I can be jealous and stupid when it comes to you, but no one will ever love you the way I do. I detest that word. It doesn't say half of what I feel for you. Everyone loves ice cream. You're my world. My heart. I know what I'm asking, Jaimie. And I know you've built something here. I'll help you build it again with me."

She opened her mouth twice before anything came out. "I wasn't expecting this, Mack. I'm not prepared."

He leaned in and kissed her, not above bribing her or seducing her if it worked. Her mouth was magic, warm and soft and filled with passion, with fire, with everything Jaimie. His mouth left hers reluctantly. He pressed his forehead against hers. "Come back to me, baby."

"I don't know if I can," she whispered, terrified of losing him, of losing herself. She'd fought hard to be her own person. "People establish patterns and we fell into one that wasn't so good. What makes you think it will be different this time?"

He kissed her chin, the corners of her mouth. His teeth tugged on her lower lip and he brushed kisses there too. "Because I'm different. So are you. I know we're good together. I'm better with you than on my own."

Jaimie sat up, needing to put space between them. She couldn't think when he was holding her, when his body was wrapped so strong and protectively around hers. When she felt their energies connected, as if they shared the same skin with one heart beating between them. Not when he was saying words she'd always dreamt he'd say to her. She slid out of bed and paced a couple of steps away, the only safe way to say what needed saying.

Jaimie looked at his face. The hard angles and planes. His firm mouth and strong jaw. Everything she needed was right there. But he was born for something far more and he loved what he did. Loved it. He wasn't going to stop and he shouldn't. But she didn't fit into that world. Tears clogged her throat, burned together into a lump she couldn't swallow.

She fought to keep her voice even. "You know I can't. I built a business here, Mack. I work for Sergeant Major, but he leaves me alone. If I went back . . ." She trailed off, her voice trembling.

Mack dropped his head in his hands and stayed there for a long moment, bracing himself. He knew, in the end, it would come to this. This was going to hurt bad — very bad. He just hadn't expected such a wrench. She'd sacrificed for him once and he'd thrown it away. He could see her point. He straightened, his eyes meeting hers. "Then I'll quit."

She blinked. Shock registered. She actually took a step backward. "Mack. Don't be crazy. You can't quit." Comprehension dawned. Her trembling mouth firmed.

"They won't let you quit. You know that, but I appreciate the gesture."

"It's no gesture, Jaimie. From the moment I woke up on Whitney's table and realized all of us had not only been psychically enhanced, but genetically altered as well, I knew we had to plan for a future. I've been doing that and the boys have all joined with me. It's a little earlier than I'd planned for, but we can disappear if we need to."

"How?" she demanded. "I thought I was out, and look what happened. They manipulated me from the moment I left our house. Every contract, every person I came into contact with. I'm still working for them. And they sent Joe. It was an elaborate babysitting operation. I'm not even certain what's going to happen now. I doubt they'll leave me completely alone ever, not as long as I'm useful to them."

"They won't," Mack agreed. "But if you're certain that's what you want, we have a plan, and the money to do it."

Shivering, she picked up her robe and wrapped herself in it. "How would you get the money, Mack? It would take a *lot* of money. And we'd always be on the run."

"Not necessarily. We're privy to information others might not have. Javier can invest and play the stock market for us when we know we're about to hit something that will affect the market. It's not exactly kosher, but we've pooled our money. Team Two, the SEAL team, has a fortress in the mountains. They've banded together and have a training center right there. We can do something similar. The boys have been researching places if we want to settle and stay in, but also possible retirement areas we can defend."

Jaimie shook her head. "Mack, you would never be happy in retirement. You know you wouldn't."

"What do I have without you, Jaimie?" He looked up at her. "I'm serious. How many times can I go out and come back to nothing? After a while you lose your incentive."

She turned away from him and looked down at her hands. She was trembling. With fear. She wanted Mack, but did she want him to give up everything he was for her? Was that the price she wanted him to pay because he'd hurt her? She detested that she'd put him in this position. "Mack." Her voice was gentle. Aching. "You'd grow to hate me. You live for this."

"I live for you. I *love* being in Force Recon in the GhostWalker unit. That word you always want me to say to you. I love what I do. The missions. The action. The ability to make a difference in the world. I *love* that, Jaimie. But you're my other half. You're everything. I don't know how else to say it to you. There are no words for the way I feel about you. I hurt you, I know I did. I wanted to be *your* everything, more than love. I didn't want to believe you could walk away from me and I let pride get in the way. I wanted you to come back to me on your own."

His throat closed and he cleared it, pressing his fingers to his stinging eyes. "I could never have walked away from you. I still can't. The thought never once entered my mind. We were supposed to be together always. *Always.* Through everything, no matter how bad it got. It was always going to be us."

"You said there was no future."

"That's what you heard, Jaimie; that's not what I said. You were so upset over the mission. Three of my men — our brothers — men depending on me were hurt. We'd walked into an ambush. It really hit home where I'd led everyone. Most of the boys wouldn't have joined the GhostWalker program if I hadn't encouraged them. I probably could have stopped them all. I was wallowing in self-pity, not throwing you away. I needed you right then. More than anything, I needed you."

He held up his hand before she could reply. "I realize you needed me right then too. In any case, Jaimie, all that matters now is what we decide to do about this. You have to make up your mind how important I am to you. If you decide you're going to be with me, it's forever. You can't have one foot out the door because I'm an idiot and say or do the wrong thing. You've got to hit me over the head and tell me to straighten up." He looked up at her, his dark eyes twin pools of emotion. "Say it, Jaimie. Say you choose me no matter what happens."

He held his breath. Every cell in his body went on alert, much the same way it did on a mission. He was aware of the breath moving in and out of her body, of the way shadows chased across her face and the moonlight bathed the room in silver. Her lips parted.

His heart pounded. *Say it.* A whisper in her mind. A plea when he never pleaded.

"There will never be anyone else, Mack," she said, her eyes going liquid.

He didn't dare move. He didn't know whether thunder cracked outside or whether it was his heart. *Say it.* He was rigid. His jaw set, every muscle locked, his gut coiled tight.

"I choose you forever, Mack. Forever."

He wrapped his arms around her waist, under her silk robe, and dragged her to him, pressing his face against her soft belly. A shudder went through his body. His hands trembled. "That's your word, Jaimie. You're giving me your word."

She cradled his head to her, just holding him, her fingers brushing small caresses through his hair. "Yes. And just so you know, we're not going to run away from them. You just stopped a war before it even got started, Mack. I'm not so selfish that I'm going to try to keep you to myself. We can save our money and keep investing. Maybe I can help with that end. If we find a good place, we can all settle there and put in a first-class training facility like Team Two, but in the meantime, I'm going to be taking a big hit on my business."

"Not necessarily." He pressed kisses along the line from her belly button to the top of the tiny black curls, feeling the bunching of her muscles in response. "The government's been giving you contracts because they know the caliber of the work you do and you have a high security clearance. Just indicate to Sergeant Major that you're willing to come back full-time for analyzing and programming, but only part-time on fieldwork. You'll have to train with us all the time, but we'll only use you when we need your particular skill."

"I don't know, Mack," she hesitated. It was so hard to think when he touched her so possessively, when his breathing changed to that harsh rasp, almost as if he was desperate to taste her. His hands were strong, moving over her body as if she belonged to him and no one else, as if every inch of her was his alone.

She bit her lip, trying to puzzle things out when her brain was slowly turning cloudy. She couldn't say she hadn't been exhilarated rescuing the two children, but not a shot had been fired. Things might have been a lot different if they'd had to use live rounds. As it was, she, like the others — particularly Kane — had spent a couple of days recouping from using psychic talent. "I'd be afraid of endangering all of you."

She tried to ignore the way her nipples beaded beneath the thin silk, the way his hands shoved her robe aside, bunching the material out of the way. She heard his low growl, a sound that rocked her. She looked down at him and saw his face, the stark, raw hunger as he focused completely on her. She realized the intensity of his hunger was the way he showed her what she meant to him. Every touch, every claim and demand he made, he was telling her how much he loved her.

His tongue swirled around her belly button, chased her goose bumps down to the junction between her legs. She shuddered against him, clinging as her legs went weak. His hands shaped her bottom, slid to her hips, and gripped her hard.

"Then we'll practice together until we're so strong nothing can get through the shield I build around you before you ever go out on another mission. You're not ever going to endanger us. Unless it's spontaneous combustion, because right now, Jaimie, I think I might go up in flames." His tongue dipped into her heat, lingered for a moment, and then found her inner thigh.

She jumped when his teeth nipped her. He laughed softly out of sheer joy. "I want to get married immediately." He plunged his tongue into her wet heat.

"What?" The word came out a strangled gasp. She closed her eyes and held on to him for her sanity. He licked at her, long savoring licks as if he could feed from her forever. The sounds he was making vibrated through her body, adding to the waves of pleasure his mouth created.

Mack never stopped devouring her, his

mouth clamped over her wet, slick entrance as he turned his body slightly, enough to give him leverage so he could force her back down on the bed. She spilled onto the comforter, her legs splayed, so he could slide down onto the floor, dragging her hips nearly off the bed, assaulting her with his hungry mouth.

She cried out and he reveled in the sound of her voice, the way he could take her up so fast, the way she always responded to his touch. He lifted his head, his tongue licking at the flavor of her on his lips. "I love the way you taste, Jaimie. I swear I could eat you for breakfast every damn morning."

"Inside me. Right now, Mack. I can't wait." She tugged at his hair to try to force him to blanket her.

"I love to torture you," he whispered, his fingers moving inside her, stretching her, finding that secret erotic button that had her writhing on the bed, her hips bucking, and her feminine muscles squeezing tightly. He watched her eyes widen and glaze, the flush spread over her body. Her stomach rippled and her breasts lifted.

"Again, baby, this time go all the way," he ordered and replaced his fingers with his mouth. His tongue speared her and she bucked against him hard, her breath exploding out of her aching lungs. She heard herself sob as the fire streaked through her. Her body thrashed, but he held her firmly, his tongue teasing and stroking, insisting on his way. That fast she flew apart, an explosion of her senses ripping through her body like a hurricane.

Before she could catch her breath, he pulled her thighs apart and stood over her, his cock in his hand, poised at her pulsing entrance. He waited until her eyes locked with his and then he plunged deep, driving through her tight, sensitive folds. Fiery hot. Velvet tight. His body reacted, the scorching heat rushing through his veins like a drug. Addicting. Real. *His.*

He held her still, open to his invasion as he plunged deep over and over, savoring the grasping, viselike grip of her muscles surrounding him with fire. She made him hot. She made him wild. She made him forget everything ugly in the world. There was only Jaimie with her body and her love surrounding him with such mind-numbing pleasure he sometimes thought he might not survive it.

He could feel flames licking over his skin, surrounding his cock, streaking through his body, down his thighs, up into his belly to settle into a rolling ball of fire. "Damn, baby, you're so fucking tight. So hot." Another low growl rumbled in his chest, a sound so animalistic it shocked even him. Nothing mattered but the fire building.

Her muscles tightened around him, locking down, imprisoning him in a velvet inferno. "Don't. Baby, you've got to stop or I'm never going to hold on." He wanted to be there forever. Live there. Just stay locked inside of her where fire purified them both. Streaks of flames blazed through his cock, teased his thighs, and raced down his legs to his toes.

He plunged deep into that scalding heat and she writhed again. His breath hissed out, a harsh, rough demand. "Stay still, Jaimie."

Pure need rode him now, a thousand demons intent on prolonging the ecstasy. He set his teeth and gripped her legs, jerking them over his arms as he levered over her, thrusting hard over and over while her soft mewling cries accompanied the frantic, harsh rhythm he set. The tension grew and stretched in him. He felt the boiling in his balls, as they drew tighter and tighter. He didn't take his eyes from her face, watching her every inflection, every transparent expression, each nuance. Every time her breath hitched or she arched her body, or thrashed her head, he slammed home, driving deeper, claiming all of her, taking her body for his own.

Her cries crescendoed as the tension wound tighter and tighter and the fire built into an all-consuming blaze. This was the moment, this tightening of her body to the point of pain around his cock, strangling, gripping, drawing thick jets of seed from him so that ecstasy tore through him, taking him soaring. She screamed, the music he'd been waiting for, and he caught her flailing hands, anchoring her as her body rippled and pulsed, milking his.

He collapsed over her, his hair damp, a fine sheen of sweat glistening over his skin while the aftershocks rippled and danced around him, her muscles tightening and releasing, taking the last of his seed from his body.

Mack pressed kisses over her belly and between her breasts and then rolled over and stared at the ceiling so that both of them lay half on and half off the bed. "You know one of the things I missed most?" Besides her sense of humor. Her brain. The way she looked at him as if he was the best man in the world. He turned his head to look at her. "The way you always woke me up in the morning."

He couldn't imagine the feeling her mouth created, that warm, amazing pleasure, the moment of complete awareness; there was only reality or nothing. Fantasy didn't cut it, not when he'd had the real thing. She paid attention to detail. She always had. What turned him on. What made him hard as a rock. What made him lose his mind and thrust helplessly into her silken mouth. Jaimie always made him feel as though she loved every part of him, as though bringing him pleasure was her pleasure.

"I missed it too," she admitted. She touched her fingers against his until he tangled them together. "I love making you happy, Mack. I always have."

He rolled onto his side and propped himself up, pushing damp curls from her face. "I need you to tell me the truth, baby. Can you live with what I do? I swear to you, I'll leave it for you. We'll find something else."

She shook her head. "I know what you need in your life, Mack. I've always been about making you happy. I like keeping your house, and cooking for you. I love waking you up in the morning and meeting every need you have. I've always loved being yours. I needed to know what we have isn't all about sex and I've learned that. We're so hot together, so wild and out of control sometimes, that I needed to know there were feelings involved."

"See, honey." He leaned in to kiss her. "I just don't get that. How could you not have known?"

She smiled at him. "I guess women need the words sometimes, Mack."

His teeth flashed at her. "You're going to be getting words, honey. We've got to get you packed before they call me. You know it will be soon."

"I'm going to work, not just stay home naked waiting for you."

"I know you will. You always have. And you want a baby, we'll have a baby."

"Do you?" Her gaze remained steady on his.

A slow smile warmed her. "If I'd thought about it before, I'd have realized having you tied down with children only helps my cause. Sure. I can handle a few kids."

"That boy, Dae-sub, he was an amazingly stoic teenager. He was tortured."

"He's his father's son. And he protected Mi-cha as best he could. I have to say, honey, I didn't feel too sorry for Armstice thinking about him in the hands of Dae-sub's father."

"Sergeant Major said the Special Ops

team drove them right to the front gate of the Korean embassy, got out, and walked away, and just left the car."

"A guard was waiting. He drove the car onto the embassy grounds and they were all officially taken into custody. The great part was, they had no idea what happened or how they got there. The only one to escape us was Blaine. He was outside the embassy, waiting to call reporters and film the kid's death. If North Korea or China manages to pick him up, all to the good."

She sat up, trying in vain to tame her disheveled curls. "I hope the general can figure out who paid Armstice to kidnap those children."

"Believe me, they'll find out," he said grimly. "And did you read the newspaper report on Jefferson? They gave him a wonderful burial. A heart attack. Very sad. A good man cut down in his prime." He glanced at his watch. "We'd better get moving. We've got a lot of packing to do. I'm not going without you and if they call . . ."

"You've got to go."

"And you'll be coming without all of your fancy equipment."

Jaimie straddled his body, settling over his hips, her knees on either side of his thighs. "Are you absolutely certain we have to go right this minute?"

He reached up to wrap a hand around the nape of her head, slowly pulling her down to him. "I guess we've got a little time." He fastened his mouth to hers and just let himself drown.

ABOUT THE AUTHOR

Christine Feehan lives in the beautiful mountains of Lake County, California. She has always loved hiking, camping, rafting, and being outdoors. She is happily married to a romantic man who often inspires her with his thoughtfulness. Please visit her website at www.christinefeehan.com.

The employees of Thorndike Press hope you have enjoyed this Large Print book. All our Thorndike, Wheeler, and Kennebec Large Print titles are designed for easy reading, and all our books are made to last. Other Thorndike Press Large Print books are available at your library, through selected bookstores, or directly from us.

For information about titles, please call:
   (800) 223-1244

or visit our Web site at:
   http://gale.cengage.com/thorndike

To share your comments, please write:
   Publisher
   Thorndike Press
   295 Kennedy Memorial Drive
   Waterville, ME 04901